Jane Lark

I love writing authentic, passionate and emotional love stories. I began my first novel, a historical, when I was sixteen, but life derailed me a bit when I started suffering with Ankylosing Spondylitis, so I didn't complete a novel until after I was thirty when I put it on my to do before I'm forty list. Now I love getting caught up in the lives and traumas of my characters, and I'm so thrilled to be giving my characters life in others' imaginations, especially when readers tell me they've read the characters just as I've tried to portray them.

www.janelark.co.uk
@JaneLark

D1390592

80003433511

PRAISE FOR JANE LARK

'Jane Lark has an incredible talent to draw the reader in from the first page onwards'

Cosmochicklitan Book Reviews

'Any description that I give you would not only spoil the story but could not give this book a tenth of the justice that it deserves. Wonderful!'

Candy Coated Book Blog

'This book held me captive after the first 2 pages. If I could crawl inside and live in there with the characters I would'

A Reading Nurse Blogspot

'The book swings from truly swoon-worthy, tense and heart wrenching, highly erotic and everything else in between'

BestChickLit.com

'I love Ms. Lark's style—beautifully descriptive, emotional and can I say, just plain delicious reading? This is the kind of mixer upper I've been looking for in romance lately'

Devastating Reads BlogSpot

The Reckless Love of an Heir

JANE LARK

A division of HarperCollins*Publishers*
www.harpercollins.co.uk

Harper*Impulse* an imprint of
HarperCollins*Publishers*
1 London Bridge Street
London SE1 9GF

www.harpercollins.co.uk

A Paperback Original 2016

First published in Great Britain in ebook format by Harper*Impulse* 2016

A catalogue record for this book
is available from the British Library

ISBN: 9780008139858

Set in Minion by Palimpsest Book Production Ltd, Falkirk, Stirlingshire

Printed and bound in Great Britain

Chapter One

The carriage passed between the large stone lions that held the shields engraved with the Barrington coat of arms and entered the Farnborough Estate through the open wrought iron gates. Henry sighed heavily and removed his foot from the opposite seat of his father's carriage. The carriage had been sent to town to collect him, on his request.

Pain shot from his right shoulder down to the elbow that was held bent within a sling. His left hand lifted and braced the shoulder.

The damn thing killed. He would be glad to get out of this carriage. Each rut in the road had jolted his arm.

He'd dislocated the shoulder in a fall from his curricle and sprained his wrist besides acquiring several bruises and the bloody thing made it impossible to dress or shave himself and he was equally unable ride a horse, or drive his curricle.

He'd been told by the surgeon in London that he must wear the sling for a month while his shoulder healed, and so he had chosen to come home; where at least he would have his father's valet and his mother and sisters to look after him.

He picked up his hat from the far seat, using his good hand, and put it on as the carriage passed the gate house then began its journey along the snaking avenue, with its tall horse-chestnut trees either side. The trees were covered in pillars of white spring blossom.

Henry looked towards the distance, between the trees, trying to catch the first glimpse of the house.

Home. He felt a pull from it, a tug at the far end of what had once been a leading rein. The land and property that would one day be his had a place in his chest that inspired pride and affection. Yet, he was equally happy to be away from it. Since he'd resided in London life had opened doors and windows he'd not seen through before. He did not regret moving there at all. It would have been hideous here, once he'd finished at Oxford. The restrictions his father and mother would have set over his life if he'd returned to Farnborough would have been unbearable, he would have become their coddled child again. In London he could do as he wished, without judgement.

There.

He saw the house.

Farnborough was caught in a ray of sunlight that had broken through the clouds, the clouds that had been hovering over the carriage throughout his journey.

The modernised medieval property had a particular charm, and it did tug at his heart, regardless of his lack of regret over leaving it, and the childhood he'd known here, behind.

That small tug became an overwhelming sense of coming home when the carriage passed beneath the archway of the oldest part of the house underneath the ancient portcullis of the original castle. The emotion was spurred by the sound of the horses' hooves and iron rimmed carriage wheels ringing on the cobble and sending metallic echoes bouncing back from the walls of the house around the courtyard.

His sisters came out, surrounded by his father's giant grey deerhounds before the carriage had even drawn to a halt, followed by his mother—there was another pull in his chest. Love. He

2

loved his family, no matter that he had left them behind here. It had been easier to leave them because he'd always known when he needed them, they were here.

The dogs' tails waved in the air like flags of welcome on the castle's walls, as they surrounded the carriage.

A footman moved before the women to open the carriage door. Henry climbed down, gripping the carriage frame with his left hand, trying not to move his right arm, because the thing still hurt like the devil from all the damned jolts it had endured to get here.

The noise of the fountain running at the centre of the court-yard echoed back from the old stone about him; another sound which spoke of home.

Samson, his favourite among his father's dogs, slipped his head beneath Henry's good hand urging Henry for a petting. He stroked behind Samson's ear in an idle gesture, that recalled years and hours spent with his father's dogs.

His mother came forward, her arms lifting to embrace him, as her face expressed her concern over the sling holding his arm.

"Mama," He acknowledged as she wrapped her arms about him.

She held him too tightly, though. He pulled away. "My shoulder." The jar of pain was sharp and twisted nausea through his stomach as well as shooting pain down his arm and across his back. He gritted his teeth, trying not to wince from it.

"Oh, I am sorry. Are you so badly hurt? You have had your father and I worried beyond measure."

"How far did you fall?" Christine his youngest sister asked. She was not the youngest of his siblings, though. He had two sisters but his brothers out numbered them two to one. Fortunately the younger ones were away at School and not here to disturb him. The eldest, Percy, the next to Henry in age was twenty and at University in Oxford. Christine was seventeen.

"Too far," Henry answered her.

"Were you winning the race?"

His good arm settled about Christine's shoulders, in brotherly comradery, as they all turned to walk towards the house, the dogs with them. "Of course. Do you not remember? I always win."

Sarah, who was eighteen, and to have her come out in London in a few weeks, was walking ahead of him. She looked over her shoulder and smiled. "I have sent a groom over to the Forths' to tell Alethea you are home. She wished to know as soon as you arrived so she might call and see you at once."

Henry smiled. God bless Alethea… He would be required to feel guilty within the hour then. Yet they were not officially engaged. It had been an unspoken agreement cooked up almost from their births. A plan formed between his father and his father's friend, Uncle Casper, Lord Forth, who owned a neighbouring estate.

After Henry's birth Lord and Lady Forth had been blessed with a daughter—and probably even while wetting Alethea's head—it had become the perfect plan, to match the two.

The expectation placed upon him had been talked about as far back as he could remember. He'd never disagreed, nor disliked the idea, it was simply that he had not yet gone along with the plot and said the words that would seal the agreement and he had no intention of doing so during this visit home either. His marriage could wait, he was currently very much enjoying his bachelorhood and he was only twenty-three, it was too bloody young to betroth himself.

"I am sure you need to sit down," his mother said. "You must be tired. Is it painful still? It must be. Have you taken laudanum?"

"I took some when I last stopped, but it is not intolerable, you need not fuss." Yet he had come home because he'd known they would fuss and he was in a self-indulgent mood; a mood which appreciated their fussing. It did hurt, and his mother's concern was the best balm—for a spoilt son.

He smiled at his rumination and allowed Christine to take

4

hold of his good hand and pull him over the threshold of the house.

The square hall welcomed him, with its dark, wide, oak staircase, that wrapped itself about the walls, leading, seemingly, forever upward in an angular ascent. He loved the house. It smelled the same—of polished wood, candle wax and his mother's perfume.

Christine tugged his hand and pulled him on, not to his father's stately drawing room in one of the more recently built wings of the house, but to their smaller family drawing room. The dark oak panelling and the window full of Elizabethan lead-lined diamonds, made it seem austere, yet to Henry it induced that final sense of being home more than any other place in the house.

He sat down on an old sofa that his mother had had reupholstered in a gold velvet. The room brought back numerous happy memories of his childhood. This was where they had spent their days when he was young, playing and laughing, and many evenings too when he'd returned from school for the holidays—

"Must your arm remain in the sling always?" Christine asked.

"Always, for a few weeks."

She made a face at him. "You knew what I meant."

"You should see my shoulder and my arm, then you would have cause to make a disgusted face, I am black and every shade of red and yellow." His hip was black too, and half his leg, and elsewhere there were other bruises. He'd truly shaken himself up. He'd lived carelessly his entire life, but his fall had made him realise more than just that he'd nearly broken his arm, he had nearly broken his neck, and the thought of that, that he might not have survived was the thing that had shaken him up. He had been given a second chance at life, he supposed. A chance to consider what he had done with his life. If he had died, he would have left no legacy. He'd spent his years carelessly and recklessly.

"Do you wish for tea and cake? You must be hungry…" His

mother did not await his answer but turned to pull the cord to call for a maid. "And if you need to rest," she said when she turned around, "you are in your old rooms."

It would be as though he had never left home then. He smiled. He'd needed a sanctuary, and comforting, and as he'd known his mother and sisters were here and ready to offer both. "Thank you, Mama."

He had at first moved to London to avoid her mollycoddling, and yet now he'd received a hard dose of fate's medicine he'd realised that at times it had a value. His low spirit craved it.

"Here." Sarah picked up a cushion from another chair, as Samson settled down, laying beside Henry's feet and resting his head on Henry's boot as he'd always done. His tail thumped on the floor as it continued to wave. The other dogs lay down on the hearth rug, their eyes on the returned prodigal son. "Sit back, Henry. Rest against this."

Christine picked up a cushion too. "You may rest your arm on here."

They arranged the cushions about him so he might sit more comfortably. Then Christine fetched a footstool for him.

He was being truly pampered. It had been a very good decision to return.

~

"Mama! Mama!"

Susan looked at her sister as Alethea hurried into the drawing room, waving a letter.

"He's here! At Farnborough! Henry is home!" Alethea turned to the footman. "Please have them prepare the carriage." Then she looked back at their mother. "Mama we must go. If he is in pain…"

"If he is in pain he deserves to be in pain." Susan said quietly towards the book which lay open in her lap. She was sensitive

6

of all wounded animals and concerned for those in need, but she did not care for young irresponsible men.

"Susan." Alethea scowled at her.

She had not intended Alethea to hear.

"How can you be so cruel. It was a terrible accident. He has been injured and you are wishing more harm on him."

Susan closed the book and set it aside. "He was in an accident because he was driving his curricle foolishly. He only has himself to blame and it was only his arm that was injured, he is hardly in a state that requires extreme sympathy." And even if he was worse Susan would not feel in the least sympathetic as he'd brought it upon himself. It was his family who ought to receive sympathy for having such a careless, reckless son who constantly treated their concern with no regard.

"Then do not come to visit him with me. You may stay here if you intend to be irritable and rude to him. I have not seen him for months. I will not have the moment ruined."

Susan did not care. She had no desire to see Henry. In her view he had been a spoilt brat who had grown into a spoilt, insensitive, selfish, careless man. She lifted her eyebrows so they must be arched above the rim of her spectacles, making an I-do-not-care expression at her sister.

"Mama, you will come with me. I cannot go if you do not. Please?"

"I cannot. I am busy. You two will have to settle this argument. Susan will have to accompany you. Your father will be returning in an hour and expect me to be here to receive Mr. Dennison."

Susan sighed and stood up. She was not to escape Henry's odious company then. "I am willing, if you wish me to join you." She was not cruel. She would not deprive her sister of his company when Alethea had waited so long for it. *She* was not selfish.

"He shall not thank me for bringing you when you are in this mood, but at least then I shall see him. Fetch your bonnet and cloak, I wish to go as soon as we may." Having cast her commands Alethea turned to leave the room.

That Alethea was very well matched to her anticipated fiancé was not something Susan would say aloud and yet at the back of her mind it was a thought she kept in constant hiding. She did not wish to malign her sister and yet the comparison screamed at her at times.

Alethea stopped at the door and turned back. "Aunt Jane and Uncle Robert will most likely ask us to dine, Mama, and so I doubt we shall return until late. You do not mind?"

"Of course I do not mind, but then you must take two footmen with you as well as the grooms; I will not have you accosted by highwaymen."

"We are only to drive to Uncle Robert's. It is the neighbouring estate. We will hardly be accosted in the four miles along the highway."

"But it will be near dark and we know there are highway men in the area—"

Susan picked up the gauntlet and tackled her mother's fear. "And no one will know we intend to use that very small stretch of rarely travelled road at that hour. I am sure that highwaymen do not have psychic powers and they would not lay in wait with the potential hope of never seeing a single carriage pass. We will be safe."

Alethea smiled at Susan, with a look in her eyes that said, *thank you*, before she left the room.

Susan's mother shook her head, but her lips twisted in a wry smile. "There is always an answer from you. Your sister should be more grateful."

Susan did not mean to argue but if there was sense and reason to be spoken or a fact to be taken into account, she would say it, that was all.

Susan gave her mother an amused smile, mimicking the humour her mother had spoken with. "I shall go up to my room and fetch my bonnet and cloak." She bobbed a very quick curtsy before turning to leave, to prepare for their arduous journey of a few moments.

"Enjoy your day, dear! Give my regards to Jane and Robert!" Her mother called after her.

She did not mind visiting Farnborough really, she liked her aunt and uncle, and Sarah and Christine, Henry's sisters. And Uncle Robert's huge library, which was three times the size of her father's was a strong persuader.

When she walked down the shallow steps to the hall after collecting her things, Alethea awaited her.

"There you are. Hurry!"

Susan smiled. She was as different to her sister as it was possible to be, both in looks and character, and yet they were close. But it was just the two of them, they did not have a large family like Henry's, or his cousins'. Henry and his cousins had the opportunity to choose the brother or sister who most suited them as their closest confidant, she and Alethea had each other and that was all. Susan was happy for it to be so, though, there was a bond between them that might not exist in a large family.

A footman opened the door. Alethea turned and walked out, at her usual hasty pace.

Alethea was forever in a hurry to experience and enjoy every single moment of life. Susan preferred not to hurry, to dwell on things, to look at them for a length of time and study them in detail, not rush past. She had often stopped Alethea to point out a beautiful view or a wild flower, a butterfly or a bird in a tree. There were so many things that Alethea missed.

Susan smiled at the thought as she stepped off the last stair.

Alethea's nature was not hers, but it was infectious. She did love her sister no matter that they were so different. Alethea's enthusiasm could not be ignored.

Susan quickened her pace and hastened out of the door in pursuit.

Alethea was climbing the step into the carriage, her fingers clasping the hand of a footman.

A second footman stood on the plate at the back of the carriage holding the iron bar and an additional groom sat beside the coachman on the box. Susan's mother had instigated a larger escort for her precious daughters regardless.

Susan took the footman's hand, climbed the step into the carriage and sat beside Alethea.

"Do you think he may have changed?" Alethea asked when the door shut.

The carriage jolted forward into motion and rocked to the side as the footman who had helped them jumped on to the second perch at the rear.

"It has been less than a year." Yet it had been nearly a year.

"I know, but he writes of such larks in town, do you think he will think me dull now?"

"He will not think you dull. No one that we know has ever thought you dull." No one could accuse Alethea of that, she was constantly in motion or conversing.

"But he has the women in London to compare me to and he describes London society as such an improvement on our quiet, country life."

"Yet the moment he is home he has sent for you. He cannot dislike the idea of your company."

Alethea looked at Susan and bit her lip for a moment. It was a very slight gesture but Susan noticed the sign of self-consciousness and uncertainty. It was unlike Alethea.

"He did not." Alethea clarified. "Sarah sent the letter. I asked her to."

Oh. That redeemed him a little in Susan's current ill-judgement, if he had not sent for Alethea to come and play nursemaid. "He will love you still," she reassured. "Merely look at his expression when he sees you and it will show you."

His brown eyes, the rich colour of sweet chestnuts at the

10

moment their green pods split open, had always lit up with the warmth of an appreciative smile whenever he looked at Alethea. Even when they'd been young he'd thrown glinting looks at Alethea and challenged her to a race or the solving of a conundrum or the telling of the best joke.

But then Alethea had always been the pretty and the vibrant one and Henry the handsomest and wildest. They were well matched.

Susan pressed the tip of her finger on to the bridge of her spectacles and slid them a little farther up her nose. Alethea had golden hair and eyes the colour of forget-me-not petals. She was often called a remarkable beauty in Susan's hearing. So why would Henry not admire her no matter how pretty the women were in London.

Susan had mousey-brown hair and eyes that were steel-grey not blue. She had never received the same accolade—people did not use the word beautiful to describe her.

It was fortunate, really, that she was not like her sister in character as much as they were unlike in looks, because if she had Alethea's nature she would be jealous. As it was she was as much in awe of her sister's beauty as others and she thanked heaven that neither jealousy nor vanity were emotions she was afflicted with. She was quite content to be herself, the less amusing, less charming and less attractive sister. Susan could stand in a room and very easily disappear by simply not speaking, which meant that if she did disappear and leave a room, no one noticed her slip away.

"What should I say to him, when I see him?"

"Hello, perhaps…"

"Do not tease me. Tell me. My stomach is all upside down. I wish it had not been so long. Do you think he will look different?"

Alethea's questions and her stream of concerns continued as the carriage gently rocked and creaked, navigating the rutted road leading to the Barrington's estate.

Chapter Two

Alethea clasped the footman's hand and descended from the carriage into the courtyard at Farnborough.

When Alethea had let go Susan held his hand and climbed down.

The air was full of the sound of the splashing water pouring from the fountain.

The front door opened. Davis the Barrington's elderly butler stood there, ready to welcome them.

Alethea immediately said, "I wish to see Lord Henry."

"He is in the family drawing room, Miss Forth, do come in. Shall I introduce you?"

Alethea was already stepping in as he spoke, she had not awaited his invitation. Davis was used to her ways, though. "There's no need, Davis. Sarah sent for me. They are expecting us, and we know where it is of course."

Susan stepped into the hall. Davis bowed to her.

They'd spent many hours here as girls, because their parents were such close friends. The Barringtons were like an extension of Susan's family, she thought of Lord and Lady Barrington as an aunt and uncle, and called them so, and Christine and Sarah were as good as cousins to her. She had known the boys less, though, because they'd spent so many years away from home, at school.

Alethea led the way again, full of energy, excitement and concern for Henry.

The door to the smaller family drawing room, in one of the older parts of the house, stood open. Alethea did not knock but walked straight in. Then exclaimed, "Henry!" and rushed on.

"Sarah sent me word you were home…" Alethea said as Susan followed her into the Barringtons' homely drawing room.

The walls and ceiling were covered in wooden panelling, making the room dark, but it had a sense of being frequently used. The walls were full of past and present tales.

"Oh dear you poor thing," Alethea declared, pulling out a cushion from behind Henry. He sat forward to allow it and looked up at her with a smile of welcome and humour.

He had one arm in a sling, and his feet up on a footstool where Samson rested his head, and his sisters and his mother were seated about him, all sitting forward on their chairs their postures expressing concern, while Henry had been laying back against his bed of cushions looking perfectly content.

There was nothing poor about him, he was busy enjoying every moment of the attention his injury had brought him. A frown pulled at Susan's forehead. She had a natural empathy for wounded things and people, she could never abide to see anything in pain. She was forever rescuing and nursing injured creatures, to the upset of her mother, who was even concerned about her visiting the sick in case she came into contact with some dangerous illness. Yet her father understood. Twice she had spent the night in the stables with him watching over a foal, encouraging it to take a bottle when it had lost its mother.

Henry's pretence annoyed her. He did not deserve pity for his foolishness.

When Alethea set the cushion back down, to Henry's credit, he lifted his feet off the stool and stood to welcome her properly. Samson stirred and rose too. "Alethea." He nodded his head in greeting, but he did not attempt a bow with his injured shoulder so wrapped up. He did however clasp Alethea's hand with his free hand and lift it to kiss the back of her fingers. "It is my extreme pleasure to see you again and perhaps the good in the bad of my accident."

Alethea gave him her flirtatious smile—the smile that made her look her prettiest. A smile Susan had watched practiced before a mirror to achieve its perfection.

Henry's smile lifted in return, becoming something more personal and his eyes filled with the twinkle they only sparkled with when he looked at Alethea. Alethea had had no need to worry. Henry might wander away but something would always bring him back, and when he came back his eyes said he remembered why he liked Alethea.

For as long as Susan could recall whenever the two of them had come together within half an hour they were whispering conspiratorially and laughing at something shared between them and no one else.

Henry passed his smile on to Susan. His eyes lost their glimmer and his smile twisted slightly giving it an edge of sarcasm. None of his looks were practiced. Henry did not deploy guile or artifice. He was naturally full of rakish charm. Only for Alethea that charm shone, for Susan it mocked.

She gave him a closed lip smile and bobbed a scant curtsy. "Good day, Henry." Samson slipped his head beneath her hand, encouraging her to greet him.

Henry nodded. That was all.

While he and Alethea had always had an exclusive friendship, he and Susan had shared an undercurrent of hostility—or perhaps on his part it was indifference.

"Good day, Susan." He still held Alethea's hand. He looked

back at her. "Sit with me." Then he looked at Susan. "Before you sit would you call for a maid? We'll have another cup of tea now you are both here."

She wished to make a face at him for his arrogance but she did not.

"Do not worry, Susan, I shall do it." His mother rose, "I presume you will both stay to dine with us, so I will need to speak with cook anyway." She approached Susan and squeezed her hand gently. "Hello, dear." Then she walked on to call for tea and arrange for them to join the family for dinner.

Alethea sat beside Henry, regaling him with some tale about local society as she undid the ribbons of her bonnet, then took it off and set it down beside her. She stripped off her gloves too, before looking at Susan. "Would you take them for me?"

Without even acknowledging the request Susan moved forward and picked them up then turned and took them out into the hall to find a footman to take care of them. When she did find a man she took off her own bonnet, cloak and gloves.

Alethea had not worn her cloak for fear Henry would be awaiting them in the courtyard and not then be able to observe her figure at its best advantage as she descended from the carriage.

When Susan returned to the room Henry and Alethea were laughing. Susan sat beside Christine, who was also avidly listening to Henry's conversation. But Henry was her brother, and he had been away for a long time.

The other dogs, Goliath, Hercules and Zeus rose from the hearth rug, and came over to her for a pet, their tails wagging their welcome. Samson had returned to his position by Henry's feet. He had always had a penchant for Henry over anyone else. Strange dog.

When they drank their tea Susan spoke with Aunt Jane, as the dogs settled back down by the hearth. But afterwards she decided it was time to remove herself. She was not a member of the Henry Marlow Appreciation Society and as the conversation orientated entirely around him she was neither involved nor interested in it. "May I look at the books in the library, Aunt Jane?"

"Of course, dear."

Susan rose without taking her leave of anyone else, the others were intently absorbed in some droll story Henry was telling about his friends in town. She opened the door and then shut it quietly, wondering whether either Alethea or Henry ever noticed her leave.

She did not care, though, it had always been like that when Alethea and Henry were together. When they'd been young she and Alethea had often played with Henry and Percy, the brother next to Henry in age, when the boys were home from school, and Susan had always trailed behind, forgotten.

In the library, she looked along the spines of the books. She loved Uncle Robert's library. It had been her sanctuary at Farnborough for years. She came here to be alone. When she had been forgotten, and then finally remembered, this was where people found her.

All four walls were lined with books, floor to ceiling.

Her fingers ran over the bound leather and gilded titles, as reverence swept through her heart.

At the end of the row, on the middle shelf, she came across one of her favourite books, *The Native Orchids of the British Isles*. She smiled and lifted it out. It was bound in light brown leather, more than a dozen inches tall and a couple more inches wide, and it smelled wonderful. It smelled of the things which made her feel better, security and comfort.

Security and comfort, then, could be found within aged leather and dust.

She smiled more broadly as she carried it over to Uncle Robert's desk and set it down, then opened it on a random page. Her fingers touched the image, *Platanthera bifolia; the Lesser Butterfly-orchid*. It looked so dainty, and the illustrator had brought it to life beautifully with lighter colours and deeper shading.

Susan had longed, ever since she was a little girl, to make her own book of painted flowers, the desire for such skill as this illustrator was an ache in her chest. This book had been her inspiration. She had sat in the window seat here and stared at every page for hours.

She sat down in the chair before the desk and turned the pages. The longing to paint like this flourished in her chest again as she considered every minor stroke of the brush.

The images were so beautiful.

To be able to create something that beautiful…

~

It was damned awkward trying to eat one handed, especially with Alethea sitting on one side of him. Christine sat in the chair on his other side, Susan and Sarah were seated across the dinner table and his mother and father at either end.

The soup had been the only simple course, for everything else he'd needed to use a bloody knife and fork, and trying to cut something then spear it was not proving successful.

"Here, let me, Henry," Alethea pulled his plate over to cut up his food for the third time. "I do not mind…"

He damned-well minded! It was uncomfortable. He did not like the need to be reliant on her in such a way. He hated the need to be reliant on anyone. Yet he bore it gallantly—even though the pain in his shoulder and the rest of his body cast him into a very ill-mood.

Alethea's lips pouted delicately as she focused on the task.

She'd grown into a very pretty woman. Although he had known prettier in town.

Some of her blond hair had become loose from the knot secured on top of her head. It fell in tiny curls on to the back of her neck. The curls slipped forward as she cut up his food. The back of a woman's neck was one of the places on a woman's

17

body he'd always thought the most appealing—he liked the delicate curve.

When Alethea had finished she looked up and slid his plate back towards him. "There." She sounded as though she spoke to a child, but she said it with a smile. There was no ill-meaning. She was simply being kind.

When Henry's gaze lifted as Alethea focused on her own food, he caught his father's eye. There was a look of expectation. He'd seen Henry admiring Alethea. Henry was perfectly happy to oblige their parents and fulfil their wish—but for God sake not yet.

He looked at his plate and pierced a piece of the mutton with his fork. Then looked across the table, to avoid catching his father's eye again. Susan was speaking with Sarah. He doubted Susan had looked across the table once. Certainly she would not seek to engage him in conversation.

She made him smile, and laugh, in private. She was so different to her sister. Her fingers lifted and pushed her spectacles a little farther up her nose. His smile rose; it was just one of her quirky little habits.

"Where did you go to this afternoon, Susan? You disappeared."

Her grey eyes turned to him. Her eyes were a little magnified by the prescription of her spectacles, but not overly so, and her spectacles did not make her look awkward, merely intelligent and perhaps distinguished—

"Withdrawing to the library is hardly disappearing. I walked out of the drawing room. I did not vanish."

It was a harsh whip from the lash of her quick wit and sharp tongue. Henry laughed. He equally laughed at the thought of her being distinguished, though, she'd never been that—rebellious yes, angry often, and independent always. But distinguished— never. "The library is the answer then. What did you find there? Did you enjoy it?" Of course he was teasing her, it had been one of his favourite pastimes as a boy, mocking her sharp retorts. She was clever, but he was clever too and he liked spurring her.

She had always disliked him and perhaps it was his own fault for teasing her, yet he'd always liked her oddness, it amused him.

She was forever stopping to pick a tiny flower in a field, or point out a butterfly or beetle. Alethea, though, was impatient in nature, and so they had often left her sister and her odd observations behind.

Her lips twisted in the same annoyed look she'd always given him. "I enjoyed it very much, thank you." She looked away from him, at his father, baring the nape of her neck. None of her brown hair had escaped its knot.

It was a very vulnerable curve, it expressed a side of Susan she never showed.

"Uncle Robert, would you mind if I used your book of orchids and copied the paintings in it? I wish to learn how to paint as well as the illustrator and it occurred to me that if I copied the images, it might help me understand how to build that level of detail."

Henry shook his head as his fork lifted another mouthful. He was truly home. Nothing had changed here. His mother and father were the same, Alethea was the same, and Susan was the same—as bookish, dogged and independent as ever.

"You may borrow it of course. Take it home with you if you wish?"

"Thank you. But may I paint here? Alethea will want to visit Henry and I will need to accompany her."

"I am in accordance with whatever arrangement suits you, Susan. I shall be out of the house visiting the farms this week and next, or with Rob the majority of the days, so you may have the freedom of the library."

"Thank you."

Susan's thank you resounded with heart felt pleasure. Over painting bloody orchids… He smiled in the same moment his father looked at him.

"Rob is looking for a new ram. We are going to the market together. You might wish to join us?"

19

"My shoulder is not really up to it." And he had no interest in competing with his cousin. Rob rented a property from his father and all Henry heard every time he came home was Rob has done this or is planning to do that. His cousin had become the son his father had always wanted and every comment was made with an intent to incite Henry into an interest and a desire to compete. It was one competition he'd not been drawn towards, land management… One day, when he inherited the land it would come with the package of such responsibilities but until then he was happy to avoid it. His father managed it all well enough without his help.

Sarah asked Susan something about the book she'd asked to borrow. Susan responded with animation, the pitch of her voice lifting and a light of excitement catching in her eyes.

She *was* an odd woman.

The voice in his head laughed. He'd met a hundred women like Alethea in town, but not a single one like Susan. Perhaps because that type of woman did not go to balls, nor mix with men like him. Clearly Susan would not mix with him by choice; she had withdrawn to the library rather than join in the conversation in the drawing room earlier, even though she had not seen him for almost a year.

She was rebellious—not distinguished. The impression her spectacles gave was a lie. He doubted anyone else would call her rebellious, though, that was the side of her nature she saved solely for him.

Her head turned and her gaze caught on his, as though she'd sensed him watching her. She did not immediately look away. Perhaps she saw the laughter in his eyes because her mouth formed a firm line, expressing annoyance. She looked down at her plate and focused on eating.

A little sound of the humour that he tried to catch in his throat escaped his lips as he turned to Alethea again. He coughed, choking on his silent laughter, then smiled. "Now Susan has decreed you will visit me, so that she may paint orchids, you must visit me often."

Alethea gave him one of her brightest, prettiest smiles. "Susan knows me well enough to be certain I would come. She did not force my hand. You are injured. So she was not being presumptuous if that is what you are hinting at, merely kind enough to understand how much I want to be with you."

Prettily said, and very commendably done. The sisters were close. Whenever he and Susan sparred verbally in Alethea's hearing she would step in to defend her sister. Not that Susan had need of a defender, she was perfectly capable of defending herself.

When he answered Alethea his voice turned sickly sweet for the sake of Susan's hearing it across the table. "Then thank you. I will look forward to your visits."

But he was truly melancholy and feeling selfishly sorry for himself since his accident, and he would, without any jesting, appreciate Alethea's presence; she would jump at his every breath to please him. There was much to be said for being at home when he was ill.

Alethea's bright turquoise eyes, shone with the strength of her happiness. Her moods were as open to a person's view as one of the books in the library which Susan loved, while Susan, the book lover, held all her pages firmly closed.

"So tell me, then, how are we to fill our time while I recover?" The less joyous part of his return was that he was fully prepared to be bored to death as there was so little he was capable of doing.

"I shall call every day if you wish, and we can play cards or chess. Or I can read to you…" Alethea reassured.

Chapter Three

The door to the library opened. Susan looked up. She was sitting at Uncle Robert's desk. Her fingertips tightened their hold on the thin paint brush. "Henry..." *What are you doing here?* The last words did not erupt from her mouth but sounded in the use of his name.

If she had spoken the words it would have been too rude; it was his home. But having let the tone of them slip into the pitch of her voice she sensed herself colouring when he looked at her with a questioning gaze. She had not meant to be rude, she had merely been engrossed in her work, and caught by surprise. She had not seen him yet today, she had come directly to the library.

He was in dishabille, informal, wearing trousers, a shirt and his sling, he had no black neckcloth or waistcoat or morning coat on. It was unseemly really, but she supposed it was due to his injury, and this was his home—if he could not be comfortable here then where?

He hesitated, the door still open in his hand. Samson stood beside him, awaiting Henry's next movement.

Some decision passed across Henry's eyes and he turned and shut the door.

They should not be in a room together with the door shut no

22

matter that they had been raised almost as closely as a brother and sister. Alethea had been treated like his sister too and she was to marry him.

"Sorry," he uttered in a low tone as he crossed the room, with Samson following, "I forgot you were in here."

He was not his normal bold, brash self. He looked from her to the leather sofa which stood side-on to the hearth, facing the tall windows. He had an odd expression. He walked past the desk where she worked, towards the sofa.

When he passed one of the windows, the bright spring sunlight shone through the fine cotton of his shirt outlining his torso in silhouette. He was very lean, yet not thin, muscular, in the way the grooms were in her father's stables. They were the only other men she had seen in their shirts, when they had been birthing the mares.

An odd sensation twisted around in Susan's stomach. "Where is Alethea?"

"Taking the other dogs for a turn about the garden with Christine and Sarah. I told her I wished to sleep."

"Then why are you not upstairs?"

"Because I prefer to sleep in here. It is more comforting. I like the smell. It reminds me of my youth."

"When did you spend any time in this library as a child?" Her retort was swift and sharp, and again her pitch carried a rude note. She could not help herself where Henry was concerned. Heat flared in her cheeks. She never really intended to be rude, he just seemed to prick her ire.

"I spent hours in here, Susan." His voice did not rise to match her boorishness but purely denied her accusation. "They were just not the hours I spent with you and Alethea. Papa used to bring me in here and we would sit together and go through the books all the time. He taught me to appreciate such things and hold the responsibility for—"

"He must be so disappointed." She really could not help herself with Henry.

23

"Why?" He had reached the sofa but before he sat, he turned and looked at her, challenging her for the answer with his gaze as well as the question.

His good hand lifted and rested on his bad arm—as though he was in pain.

She smiled, trying to mimic the mocking smiles he regularly gave her. "Because you are hardly responsible. Only a fool would drive a curricle in a race on the roads, you might have broken your neck not sprained your wrist."

He sat down, looking away from her. Samson sat too. "Believe me, I am well aware. I nearly broke my neck and in the process dislocated my shoulder, not merely twisted my wrist. Now if you'll excuse me, Susan, I am bloody exhausted and in agony, I have just dosed myself up with laudanum and I am in no mood for you to chastise me. Let me rest."

He was much paler than normal.

He lay down without looking at her again and sprawled out flat on the long leather sofa, laying on his back with his bad arm on his chest and one foot on the floor while the other turned so his leg lay bent across the seat, as his foot hung off the edge.

Samson rested his head by Henry's side, as though asking to come up and sleep beside him.

Perhaps that was why Samson was so loyal to him, if Henry had allowed Samson such liberties when he was younger.

His good arm lifted and then lay above his head as he shut his eyes.

"I shan't make any noise," she said, to annoy him.

He opened his eyes a little, his dark eyelashes cloaking his gaze as he looked at her. Samson looked at her too. "I did not doubt it, painting is hardly a noisy activity. Let me sleep if you please, Susan."

She smiled and looked back down at the orchid she was recreating.

There were very fine green lines on each pale cream petal, and that was what she was seeking to capture, only the lines in the book seemed to give the petals depth, and she had not succeeded in mastering that. Perhaps she needed to use more than one shade of green? But the lines then would have to be very, very narrow and far more cautiously done. She needed to develop a steadier hand.

She leant forward and looked closer at the image. The artist had done them so well she could not even see a different shade.

Henry's breathing became deeper and slower.

When she heard him move she looked up. Samson now lay on the floor beside him. Henry's bent leg lifted and his foot settled on the sofa so his knee could rest against the back of the seat. He sighed out. The arm which had lain above his head fell down and hung over the edge of the low sofa so that his hand was placed slackly on Samson's head.

She looked down at her work and carried on adding detail to the petal she was working on.

The slightly different shade of green did add depth, though the variance of colours in her image was very visible to the eye. She leant a little closer to the book and looked at the shape of the petals. There were different shades of cream too. The artist must have mixed the colours with a tiny amount of black to obtain the deeper shade. It would be hard to mix without making the cream too dark.

Henry was quiet. She looked up. He had definitely fallen asleep. The sunshine from the window stretched across his leg and stomach. Perhaps that was why he'd come in here, to sleep in the sunshine.

Susan, mixed a little of the green with more white to make the colour paler still and attempted another narrow line, trying to make the difference in shading less obvious. She used the paler colour on the lower edge of the lines across the petal. It was better than her first attempt, but not good enough.

Rather than progress to the shading of the cream, she began

25

another petal. She would conquer this skill before she sought to learn another.

While she painted she intermittently glanced across the room to check Henry had not woken and was surreptitiously watching her. The sunshine travelled across his lean body as the afternoon progressed. He did not wake.

If she had more natural talent he would have made a perfect model, *Young gentleman in repose.*

She smiled as she looked back at her work. Asleep, she would admit how handsome he was—when his personality was not added into the mix. When he was silent, like this, she could appreciate his company. She studied him as she worked, with the same eye that she studied the flower. The waves in his dark brown hair were a little chaotic but he had a very classical handsomeness, with his long dark eyelashes resting against the pale skin of his cheeks...

She carefully painted another flower head, then looked back, he must have slept for more than hour, perhaps even two, she had not looked at the clock. He had appeared exhausted, though, and he was still paler than normal. The sunshine was rapidly advancing towards his face. It would disturb him if it shone on to his eyes.

A huff of sound left her throat as she set down her brush, while her inner voice complained over the need to leave her painting as she rose and walked across the room to the window, to close the shutters. Of course it would affect the light she had to work by, but he had looked exhausted.

Samson woke and his head lifted, slipping away from Henry's fingers, as he watched her cross the room. She walked over to him, rather than to the window. He did not rise, so she leant to stroke his head. "You foolish, dog," she whispered. "To save your loyalty for such a man." Yet animals were like that, they had no judgement of one's character, if you treated them well, they treated you well.

26

The cuff of the loose shirt sleeve covering Henry's good arm had been caught up when he'd moved his arm from above his head, and it had slipped upwards. She noticed dark and vivid, vicious looking bruises that she had not seen from across the room. His shirt had also fallen open into a wide v at his chest, without a neckcloth to hold the collar closed. She could see the little dent at the base of his throat and the first shape of his chest and a sprinkling of dark hair and more nasty bruises.

Her mouth was suddenly dry, and an odd cramp gently tightened the muscles in her stomach. She had always been pulled to the protection of injured things, the sight of something in pain always caught her hard in the middle with a feeling of sickness. Yet this was Henry. Guilt washed across her thoughts. She had been rude to him. She had not cared about his injuries. She had thought that he'd been exaggerating, yet now she could see he had not been.

Her stomach twisted as she looked at his face, with regret. Samson rose and sat beside her, so that she would stroke his head again.

But it was more than a feeling of nausea over the sight of his injuries. Just as she admired the flowers, or the detail in the wings of a butterfly, she admired Henry's face.

She turned away.

It was definitely not a good thing to look at Henry and feel any sort of liking. She did not want to think him attractive. When he was awake she had no liking for him at all and it was better for things to be like that, he was to be her brother-in-law, and as no one thought her beautiful it was very likely that she would live here in her later life, dependent upon him, as Alethea's spinster sister. Her father's property was entailed so when her father passed away her home would be given to a cousin and she would have no choice but to rely upon Henry's generosity.

He moved behind her.

She stopped and looked back.

His bad arm shifted across his chest moving the sling, as a sound of discomfort escaped his lips. His shirt opened wider, sliding off his bad shoulder. There was a large, much darker, almost entirely black bruise covering his shoulder, with yellow and redness at its edges. He'd said he'd dislocated his shoulder; it must hurt considerably. He had definitely not merely come home to act the invalid, then; he had been seriously injured. The pull of sympathy clasped her.

It annoyed her. She did not wish to feel it for Henry. He did not deserve it. He had done this to himself.

She turned away, went to the window and closed the lower shutters, with Samson watching her. He had not moved away from Henry. The shade half covered Henry to the top of his chest. She walked to the next window and closed the lower shutters over that too so that the shade covered all of him, then turned to go back to her painting.

Henry's body suddenly jolted and a sound of discomfort escaped his throat. "Damn it!" he shouted on a breath, but his eyes did not open. "Bloody hell! The horses! What of the horses!" Another sound of pain escaped his throat as he moved as though to rise.

She walked over, unsure whether to leave him to his nightmare or wake him.

"Fuck! The…" His eyes opened and he sat up.

She turned away but he grasped her wrist.

"Were you staring at me?"

He was breathing heavily, and his blood raced in a fast pace through the vein she could see pulsing beside the little dent next to his clavicle at the base of his throat.

"No. I closed the shutters so the sunlight would not wake you, then you started dreaming and woke up anyway."

He let her wrist go, sighed and then twisted around to sit upright with both feet on the floor, Samson moved out of his way. His good elbow rested on his knee and his hand held his forehead as his bad arm lay in its sling on his thigh.

"Are you unwell?"

He glanced up at her, and gave her a bitter, wry smile, very slightly lifting his poorly arm. "Do I look well?"

"Did you dream of your accident?"

"Yes." It was said with a sigh and a pained look. He gave her a more real smile. "I thought my time had run out."

Heat touched her cheeks as she felt Henry's particular method of charm deployed. It was still enchanting even when it was mocking. He was too handsome when he smiled. She turned away from him to go back to her painting, and avoid the sense of empathy which clawed at her. "It was your own fault, though, and I would guess you have still not learned the lesson and will race again."

"Probably," he answered, clearly not in a mood to go into verbal battle.

She sat down behind the desk and picked up her paint brush.

He stood up and his good arm stretched out, as he yawned. He was standing in the sunlight which shone through the windows above the lower shutters that she'd closed. Again she had the perfect silhouette of his body beneath his shirt.

Embarrassment warmed her skin as she remembered all the bruises on him.

She washed out her brush in the small bowl of water, then wiped it on the rag beside her, before dipping it in the paint to begin another petal. "Must you wear no waistcoat and morning coat? I'd prefer it if you wore more clothes if you are coming in here to sleep while I am working."

He laughed. "Much as I would love to oblige you, as it is bloody agony to put either on, while I am at home I intend to make free of my comfort and abstain. You are lucky I have bothered to put a shirt on so that I am decent at all." He walked across the room. "And it is only because Alethea was coming that I endured that feat." He stopped on the other side of the desk and looked down at her work. "That is a reasonable copy."

She met his gaze. "Reasonable? I am proud of it. It is much better than I thought I could achieve. I have been studying how the illustrator has captured the shades to give the flower its life-like depth. I know I shall never be—"

The ignorant oaf laughed.

Susan's eyebrows lifted. He could be so arrogant!

"Sorry, you are just such a ridiculous anomaly. You amuse me."

"If you are going to ridicule me, leave me in peace?"

"I was not ridiculing you. I was admiring your efforts."

"By laughing at them?"

"Never mind, Susan. I am too tired and in too much pain to fence words with you." He turned away. "Enjoy the rest of your afternoon painting."

"I shall!" she called after him sarcastically, as he walked away. She smiled to herself. She preferred him awake. She felt better with things as normal between them no matter how nice Henry looked when he was asleep, and she refused to be swayed by her sympathy for the rogue, even though she knew he was lucky to be alive—it was his own fault.

She and Alethea dined at Farnborough, and Aunt Jane invited them to stay rather than travel back and forth each day, but Alethea denied the offer because their mother would most likely prefer it if they did not entirely desert her.

Although it was as if they were; they had left home at ten o'clock and would most likely only return in time to retire to bed. The days were not yet long.

Henry remained in dishabille for dinner.

He had a sickly pallor.

Susan watched as Alethea took his plate to cut up his food so that he could eat with one hand. His expression became awkward, and there was no glint in his eyes for her kindness and attention—not even a smile. Perhaps he did not feel at all well?

Yet whether he did or not, it was not Susan's concern.

She looked at Christine who was sitting beside her and opened a conversation. Yet Susan's gaze was repeatedly drawn back to Henry as he spoke to Alethea, and she could not stop noticing the small indent at the base of his throat and the dark hairs visible on his chest due to the v formed by his open shirt as she recalled the bruises his shirt hid.

Chapter Four

Susan walked down the stairs, carrying her bonnet, with her cloak hanging over her forearm. Her bonnet bounced against the skirt of her dress with the pace of her steps as she held it by the ribbons.

Alethea stood in the hall below, already wearing her bonnet, but she was not looking up to chase Susan into hurrying, but looking down at a letter.

"What is it?" Susan called.

"It is from Sarah," Alethea looked up and met Susan's gaze. "We cannot go. She says Henry intends to remain in his rooms and so he said it would be a waste of time for me to come."

"Why?"

"He is feeling too ill, he does not wish to dress, but merely lay abed and rest his shoulder."

"He did look pale yesterday."

"I know. I felt so sorry for him. I would sit by his bed and keep him company but I suppose it is not the thing is it?"

"And if he has taken laudanum he will probably wish to sleep."

"I suppose."

But Susan had been looking forward to going over to Farnborough to continue her painting and the carriage had already been called.

"Mama!" Alethea called across the hall when their mother appeared from the drawing room. "We cannot go. Henry is feeling too unwell."

"But I would like to go to paint, Mama." Susan said as she stepped from the bottom stair. "Do you think I might? I was looking forward to painting again today and Uncle Robert said he did not mind my using the library at all for a whole fortnight."

Her mother smiled. "If you wish to go, Susan, there will be no harm in it I am sure."

Susan looked at Alethea, awaiting an offer to accompany her… There was still Sarah and Christine to visit, and after all Susan had only begun her painting project to accompany Alethea.

Alethea turned away and walked towards the drawing room, with Sarah's letter held tightly in her hand.

Susan looked at her mother. Her mother was very like Alethea in temperament and she always gravitated towards her most exuberant daughter. She turned to Alethea, lifting a comforting arm to offer reassurance. "Alethea. Dear. I am sure he will be well enough to see you again soon."

Susan loved her mother dearly but they had never understood one another particularly. Susan was more like her father in nature.

She turned to their butler. "Dodds, do not send the carriage away, I will be going but will you call for a maid."

Dodds bowed slightly. "Shall I help you with your cloak, Miss." He held out a hand.

She passed it over as her mother's and Alethea's conversation grew more distant.

She put on her bonnet and tied the ribbons, then turned so that he could set her cloak across her shoulders. She secured it herself while Dodds opened the door for her.

"Susan…" Her father entered the hall from a door leading out to the rear of the house and the stables. "Where is Alethea, is she not ready? I would have thought she'd be galloping with excitement to call on Henry."

33

"He is too unwell for callers. I am going so I may continue to paint."

His bushy white, eyebrows lifted, and the ends of his waxed moustache twitched. "Alone?"

"It is only to Uncle Robert's. It is only a couple of miles and I am taking a maid."

His forehead furrowed while he considered the idea.

Susan held her breath.

"And Susan is responsible enough to manage herself, Casper, let her go it will do no harm." Susan looked at her mother who had come back out of the drawing room and stood just before the open door.

Only days before her mother had been afraid of highway men, obviously Susan's responsible nature would frighten them away. Or perhaps it was the *ridiculous anomaly* she presented. She heard the words in Henry's voice.

Her hand lifted and her fingers slid her spectacles farther up her nose.

Her father looked at her. "Very well, you may go."

"Thank you, Papa." She walked over and wrapped her arms about his neck.

His arms came about her, knocking her bonnet loose, so it tumbled off her head and rolled down to hang from the ribbons about her neck.

"Enjoy your day," he said into her ear.

"I shall immensely." They let each other go. "And at the end of the fortnight I shall show you my endeavours. I am quite pleased with myself."

"Bless you." His fingertips touched her cheek.

She turned away, without putting her bonnet back on, and walked out through the open door. Dodds was standing outside, speaking with one of the footmen. She had a sense that he had bestowed a warning for the men escorting her to take greater care as she travelled alone with only a maid to guard her reputation. The maid had already taken her place on the seat beside the coachman.

She smiled at Dodds when he opened the door of the carriage, accepted his hand and climbed up.

Within the carriage she righted her bonnet as Dodds shut the door. Then they were away.

She had not travelled in the carriage alone before.

Her heart pulsed quickly as she stared out of the window watching the passing view around the brim of her bonnet.

The tall remains of the walls of the ruined abbey in Farnborough's grounds peaked above the trees in the distance. The Abbey marked the border of Uncle Robert's land and Henry's cousin's, Rob's, property. She had known Rob since her childhood too, his father was also a friend of her father's.

She had always liked Rob. He was quieter than Henry and he'd never been self-obsessed. She liked Rob's wife too. Caro was also quiet, and friendly, though, she shied away from crowds and strangers. They therefore never attended the local balls but Susan saw them frequently at her parents' and Aunt Jane's dinner parties.

The road followed a wall which surrounded Uncle Robert's estate. The wall stretched for miles, but they were not following it all. It broke at the main gateway and the carriage turned to pass between the open iron gates and the giant lion statues guarding the entrance.

The carriage slowed when the gatekeeper came out of his lodge, but he looked at her father's emblem on the side and waved them on.

The drive to the house from the gate seemed nearly as long as the journey had been from her home. But it was pretty this time of year, with the huge horse chestnut trees covered in white flowers.

Excitement gathered inside her when she neared the house.

Her new project was stimulating, she had never been very

good at idleness, and embroidery and sewing were really not her calling. As the carriage passed beneath the arch into the courtyard, she smiled at herself when her reflection appeared in the glass for a moment. Perhaps she was like Alethea in some ways; she had just admitted she was no good at being idle. Perhaps in her, her mother's and Alethea's enthusiasm and constant hurrying and need for activity, was exposed in a desire for an active mind.

Uncle Robert walked out of the house surrounded by three of the dogs. Not Samson.

He stopped and stood still as the carriage turned and drew to a halt then he came forward and opened the door. "I thought Henry had sent word to say do not come." He looked beyond Susan, clearly seeking Alethea, but then he held out his hand to Susan to aid her descent as the dogs barked their greeting. Once he'd let go of Susan, Uncle Robert silenced them with a lifted hand. They continued to wave their tails.

"He did, but I was ready and I wished to come over and paint anyway. You do not mind?"

"Of course I do not mind, Susan, you know you are welcome. Come I shall escort you in before I go about my business."

The large dogs walked beside them, tails swishing at the air. If Samson had been among them he would have surreptitiously, out of sight of Uncle Robert's discipline, nudged Susan's hip for some particular attention. Perhaps that was another bad habit that Henry had encouraged, and another reason why Samson was so attached to the heir of the family.

She did not see Aunt Jane, Sarah or Christine when they walked through the house. He opened the library door. "There." He stepped back and let her pass. "You'll not be disturbed, Sarah and Christine have returned to their lessons now that the excitement over Henry's return has settled down, and Jane is with Henry, I believe."

Susan looked at him as she undid the ribbons of her bonnet. "Is he suffering very badly?"

"I believe so, but it is what he deserves, and it may yet teach him the lesson he has kept refusing to learn from me. But today I think he is simply feeling sorry for himself. He has refused to dress because it is too painful, he has said he merely wishes to remain in his room so he might rest without the need for a sling. I am sure he will be up and about again in a couple of days and Alethea may call to fuss over him once more." Uncle Robert's pitch seemed to laugh at the idea.

Susan did laugh—at his jocular manner—not at the fact that Alethea would fuss or that Henry was in pain.

As Uncle Robert's eldest son, and his heir, Henry had been spoilt horridly.

Uncle Robert had often admitted it too and mocked himself for the error of it, although perhaps never in Henry's hearing. It was usually when he was speaking with her father. Perhaps she was not meant to have heard…

"Shall I have a maid bring you some tea?"

"Yes, please. Thank you."

"I will have Davis tell Jane you are here, and that you are not to be disturbed."

She was not always sure with Uncle Robert when he was speaking seriously and when he was making fun. His tone of voice always held a lilt which had a measure of amusement and unless he chose to reveal the humour in his words, sometimes it skipped past her. His manner of mocking life, and himself, made him extremely likeable, though. She supposed it was where Henry had inherited his charm from.

"Good day, Susan." He bowed his head in parting then turned away. "Come!" he called at the dogs, rallying them. "Susan shall not want you disturbing her, you may go down to the kitchens."

"Good day, Uncle Robert!" She called as he shut the door.

She took off her bonnet and cloak and set them down on a chair. The maid could take them when she brought the tea.

Her parchment, the box of water paints, her brushes and the

book she'd been using were left where she'd used them on the desk yesterday. She opened the giant book and sought a new orchid to copy. *Ophrys apifera*. It had a petal which looked as though a bee was sitting on the flower. It would be hard to capture correctly and yet she wished to challenge herself, and at least on this there were only three small flowers, others had dozens of flowers on a stem.

Her hand lifted and her fingers pushed her spectacles a little farther up her nose. She bit her top lip as she chose a charcoal to sketch the picture with first.

The room seemed darker today, there was not as much light on the desk. She looked up and realised the shutters were still closed over the windows before the sofa.

When she opened them, her mind's eye saw Henry lying on the sofa, asleep, a patchwork of ghastly colours.

A slight knock tapped the door. "Come!" The maid who had brought the tea entered. "Set it there please. Thank you."

The maid bobbed a curtsy and left with Susan's cloak and bonnet.

Susan poured herself a cup of tea and carried it over to the desk, then concentrated on copying the shape of the orchid correctly.

When the clock in the room chimed once, there was a gentle knock on the door.

Susan jumped. She'd been entirely absorbed in her painting. Her tea cup was still full and the tea within it chilled.

The door opened. "Susan." Aunt Jane stood with the door handle in her hand. "You must come and eat luncheon with us. You cannot hide yourself away in here all day and starve."

Susan straightened up and smiled. "Thank you. I will be there in a moment."

"Very well." Aunt Jane turned away. Susan dipped her brush in the water to clean it, then dabbed it on the rag to dry it. She looked down at her painting, it was slow work today because there were so many tiny details on the bee petals, but she thought she was progressing well, she seemed to be improving.

The family at the table were Aunt Jane, Sarah and Christine.

Uncle Robert was still out undertaking whatever business he was about.

"Is Henry not coming down, Mama," Christine asked as Susan sat down.

"He is not. He is not dressed."

"But we are only family, it would hardly matter if he did not have his shirt on."

Aunt Jane looked apologetically at Susan.

"Susan is like family," Christine declared, disregarding the subtle reprimand.

Guilt pierced Susan's side, she had not come here to prevent Henry having the freedom of his home. "I am sorry. I did not realise. I should not have come—"

"Nonsense. Do not be silly," Aunt Jane chided. "It will do Henry no harm to remain upstairs, and he has been sick most of the morning so I do not think he will attempt luncheon regardless of his state of dress."

Susan's guilt cut deeper. "Has he a fever? Uncle Robert said he was only in too much pain to dress." She had thought Henry in a lazy, sullen mood. Her instinctive sense of empathy, that she had fought yesterday evening, pulled within her.

"It is not a fever; he took too much laudanum without eating and is suffering for it. I think he also took a bottle of his father's brandy to his room last night to help further numb the pain, and of course nor do laudanum and brandy mix. I think now he has had enough of laudanum."

Christine and Sarah laughed.

Laughter gathered in Susan's throat too, but for the first time in her life she felt wholly in charity with Henry. She could no longer deny her instinct to feel sorry for him, and wish to help. He had been in a lot of pain when he'd come to the library yesterday she did not think less of him for seeking to free himself from it.

She would not stay long after luncheon, then if he wished to come down and take tea with his family, shirtless, he might. An image formed un-beckoned in her mind of him lying asleep on the sofa in the library, shirtless, an artwork of bruises.

Once Susan had eaten she returned to the library. She would finish the detail on the flower she was working on and then she would ask Aunt Jane if she might travel home in their carriage.

A maid came into the room at three. "Miss Susan, Lady Barrington sent me to ask if you wished for tea?"

She had worked on and on and forgotten the time. "No, thank you, but is my aunt in the drawing room."

"She is, Miss Susan."

"And has Lord Henry come down?"

"No, miss, he is taking tea in his room."

He must have risen from his bed at least then.

"Susan." Christine walked about the maid, entering the room with a quick stride. "Sarah and I are going to take the dogs out as far as the meadow, would you like to come? It is one of those lovely fresh days, with a breeze to sweep away the fidgets and a pleasant sky without the sun pounding down upon you."

Susan looked out of the window. It was a middling day, with a light grey sky, and she could see the breeze was strong as the clouds whisked across it. It would be refreshing to go for a walk before she returned home. She looked back at Christine. "Thank you, I would love to join you."

Christine smiled. "I am going to fetch my bonnet and a cloak." She looked at the maid. "Will you have someone bring Miss Forth's to the hall?"

The maid curtsied in acknowledgement and left them. Christine looked at Susan. "I shall meet you in the hall, then." Then she was gone too.

Susan tidied up her things and thought of Samson upstairs

with Henry, while the guilt she had felt at luncheon skipped around her, taunting her with a pointed finger of accusation.

She shut her paints away in their box, and closed the book. She would not come back until Henry sent for Alethea.

She had maligned Henry in her thoughts too much. He did deserve some sympathy. Perhaps she could offer to walk Samson, as Henry could not take the dog out. Perhaps she should prize Samson free from his precious idol and give him some fresh air too. Henry would most likely appreciate the gesture, and there was little else her sense of empathy might do to be quietened.

She decided to go up to his sitting room before meeting Sarah and Christine in the hall. She knew where his suite of rooms were. She did not need a servant to show her up. They had still been playmates at the point he'd moved into his current rooms.

She left the library and instead of making her way to the family room walked past it and on to the main hall, where the dark, square, wooden stairs climbed upward about the walls. No one was there, the footman had probably gone to fetch her outdoor things.

Her hand slipped over the waxed wood of the bannister as she hurried up the stairs to Henry's rooms on the second floor.

She remembered his huge bedchamber, and beside that a dressing room and a large sitting room, with a desk and about half a dozen chairs in it. He had been allocated the rooms because he was the eldest, the heir—and the most spoilt.

When she reached the second floor she turned to the right. His rooms were at the end. He'd moved into them one summer when he'd been home from Eton, in his last year there, and he'd made Susan and Alethea go upstairs to look at the space he'd been given solely to show-off.

She walked to the end of the hall and tapped on the door she knew was his sitting room. If he was out of bed and taking tea, he would be in there. If he did not answer she would presume him undressed and still in bed and go away.

"Come!"

Her heart pounded foolishly as she opened the door. She could not see him. But one of the high backed chairs had been turned to face the window and she could see the footstool before it and a tray containing a teapot, cup and saucer, and a small plate of cakes, was on a low table beside it.

"Henry?" she said as she walked across the room. "I—"

"Susan…" His pitch carried incredulity as he stood up before her.

He was not clothed! Who took tea in a sitting room unclothed?

Or rather he was clothed but only in a loose dressing gown that covered one shoulder and was left hanging beneath his bad arm before being held together by a sash at his waist.

He held his damaged arm across his middle. It drew her eyes to his stomach. She had thought him muscular yesterday but today she could see all the lines of the muscle beneath his tarnished skin on the exposed half of his body. He sported a variety of shades of blue, black, dark red, bright red and gruesome yellow, and his shoulder was entirely black as she had guessed yesterday, and the bruising ran not only down his chest but also covered his arm.

"What are you doing here? Being rebellious again? What do you wish for?" His initial tone may have been incredulous, but now his voice mocked her as it always had.

Her gaze lifted to his face. "I thought you were taking tea?"

His eyes laughed at her. "I am taking tea, alone, here, in my private rooms."

"But, who drinks tea, in…"

"In what?"

Embarrassment engulfed her. She had been about to accuse him of being naked, although he was not quite. She looked at Samson, who had risen when Henry had, like Henry's shadow. He had been on the far side of the chair.

"You are truly lucky you did not do yourself more harm," she said without looking at him again.

42

"As I said yesterday, believe me, I know what I risked far more than you. I was there. Why did you come up here?" His pitch now lacked amusement and had instead become dismissing.

"We are taking the other dogs out to the meadow. I came to offer to take Samson too. I thought you had risen."

"I have risen, but only as far as my private sitting room so I did not need to strain my damned arm by putting on clothes." She glanced up when he swore, in response to the un-Henry-like bolshiness in voice, a note that came from pain. "And pray do not look your horror at me for using a bad word. You made the choice to come up here and this is my private room, I will speak as I please."

"I'm sorry. I'll go."

He sat down in the chair, almost deflating. His good hand holding his bad arm.

"It must be very painful." She took two steps farther into the room.

He looked at her with unamused eyes. "It is, thank you for the recognition? Now you ought to go, before Mama catches you here and then tells your Mama and then you will earn yourself a scold and some penalty…"

"We are not children anymore, I am—"

His eyes suddenly looked hard into hers. "No, precisely, Susan. We are not children anymore. You cannot run around doing anything you wish."

"Perhaps you should listen to yourself." Her ire rose and snapped in answer, before she turned away. Because, was that not exactly why he was in this state? He had no right to chastise her for anything she did when he hurtled about the roads racing his curricle with no regard for others. "I will not come back until you send for Alethea," she said, as she walked back across the room. "So you may run about shirtless all over the house without fear!"

A sharp bark of laughter caught on the air behind her, she did not look back.

43

"You know you are as bad as me! Admit it or not! You cast your judgements, and yet you are just as rebellious, in your way."

Rebellious? She turned back. She could not see him. He was in the chair, facing the window, invisible behind it, although she could see Samson, who looked back and forth between her and Henry, his tail swaying. "I am not rebellious."

"No? Then why are you here, disturbing me?"

"I came to offer to take Samson out and also to see how you are. You looked unwell yesterday."

"Rebellious with good intent then; but to my room, Susan? Even Alethea would not have come to my room."

"I would not have walked into your bedroom. I only came to your sitting room!"

There was the low sound of an eruption of amusement in his throat that was not quite a laugh, perhaps more like a growl of frustration, or pain. Even as she was angry with him that sense of empathy had its claws in her.

"Believe me, no other well-bred woman I know would have done this! No matter that it is *only* my sitting room!"

She let a soft sound of amusement escape her throat as she turned away again. The sound deliberately defied her sympathy, she wanted to annoy him for his skill in disturbing her. "Good day, Henry! I hope you feel a little better in the morning!"

"Good day, Susan! Thank you! You may take Samson with you, I am sure he shall appreciate the opportunity of a run in the meadow with the others, and in the meantime, I shall run around downstairs shirtless and terrify all the maids."

She laughed involuntarily. Then she lifted a hand to Samson. "Come along, Samson, would you like a walk?" The dog's tail wagged, in answer, but he looked to Henry for permission.

Henry had many faults, and yet the dog adored him. "Go you foolish, hound," Henry dismissed him with an affectionate pitch.

Susan's smile broadened.

"Samson," she called again. When he came to her side she

petted his ear exactly as she knew Henry did, and walked from the room. She closed the door behind her.

The empathy in her stomach had become a different sort of feeling.

In the last three days she had probably shared as many words with Henry as she would have normally shared with him in a month during his stays at home, and she'd found him funny, as well as annoying, and frustrating.

Susan caught her reflection in a mirror on the landing, she was deep pink and Henry would have seen her embarrassment, and yet he had not teased her for that.

She hurried back downstairs to find Aunt Jane, Christine and Sarah, her heart thumping.

The sight of Henry's bruises and the outlines of the muscle beneath his stained skin hovered in her mind. She had never seen a man shirtless before. But she refused to let herself be unsettled. Christine was right, she was a part of their family, it was not odd for her to see Henry half clothed. He was like a brother or a cousin.

When she walked downstairs, Samson trailing in a disciplined, graceful manner behind her, Christine and Sarah awaited her in the hall.

"Where have you been?" Christine asked, holding out Susan's bonnet.

Susan accepted it. "Collecting Samson from Henry's rooms, so he might join us."

Neither Sarah nor Christine queried her statement, or asked how Samson had been acquired. Yet at the very idea, Susan's fingers trembled as she tied the bow of her bonnet beneath her chin, and the footman had to take over and secure the buttons on her cloak, because her hands shook too much.

I am embarrassed. She had seen Henry in nothing but a dressing gown, with half his torso exposed. She had held her wits together in his room but she'd known the moment he stood up she should not have been there.

"Are you sure you will not stay for dinner? I do not see why you should go home, only because you have come alone," Sarah said as they turned to leave the house, the dogs padding about them.

"No, I need to return home. I told Mama I would be back."

Sarah offered her arm, and Susan wrapped her arm about it, grateful of the gesture as her legs felt wobbly too.

~

When Susan retired for the night, Alethea came to her room in her nightdress. Her bare feet brushed across the floorboards as she walked towards the bed, dispelling the darkness with a single candle that made her shadow dance behind her.

Susan lifted the covers. Alethea set down the candle on a bedside chest and laid down next to Susan. Susan threw the covers back over them both as Alethea turned and blew out the candle. The smell of wax and the burnt wick caught in the air, and the mattress moved as Alethea lay back down in the darkness. The pillow dipped and Alethea's breath touched Susan's cheek.

"Did you see Henry?"

"Yes." She had seen too much of Henry. "I said goodbye to him. He looked in a lot of pain. I actually felt sorry for him, and you know how rare that is."

"He told me he was very badly injured. He said he'd thought in one moment he might die."

"He said that to be dramatic, Alethea, you know he did. You know what he is like. He loves being the centre of attention." Yet Susan had seen the bruising on his body—if he had struck his head as hard? He had not been exaggerating on this occasion. She had said the words, though, because she did not want to think of Henry any differently than she normally would.

Alethea sighed. "I do not think he has any intent to propose

46

when he is here. He still speaks to me as though I am his friend. Do you think he will ever propose?"

"Of course he will."

"He has not been home for nearly a year. He cannot think of me when he is away, and he's said nothing about our engagement. Why do you think he is taking so long to propose? I thought this time…"

"I suppose he loves his curricle racing too much," and he is selfish, arrogant and mean—and funny—and in pain.

Instead of Alethea's usual bright tone, a bitter sigh rang out in the darkness. "I will be an old maid… And then what if he never asks? Perhaps I should consider others."

Alethea had never spoken of others before. "But you love Henry…"

"I do love Henry. Yet I am nearly three and twenty. I cannot wait forever."

"That is not old."

"It is almost upon the shelf, and I wish to leave home and begin my own family."

"I am not going to go tomorrow. I said I would wait until he is well and writes to ask for your company."

"I am not sure he really wishes for my company."

"Of course he does. Every time I look up you two are speaking exclusively and earnestly. Of course he wishes you there."

Alethea sighed again. She really was not sure. "May I sleep here?"

"Yes."

"Thank you." The mattress dented near Susan's shoulder and then Alethea's breath and her hair brushed Susan's cheek a moment before Alethea's lips pressed there, bestowing a kiss. The pillow dipped again as Alethea lay back down. "What did you think of the dress which Maud Bentley wore to church last week?"

The conversation slipped into whispered gossip. They talked about fashions, material they wished for, the assembly which would take place this month in York, until their words were claimed by tiredness.

"Good night," Susan whispered last.

"Sleep well," Alethea whispered back.

Chapter Five

While they were eating breakfast, each time a footman walked in, Alethea looked towards the door, but none of the footmen entered carrying a letter.

Once the pot of chocolate had been emptied for the second time, Alethea looked at their mother and proposed a trip into York to look for the ribbons, material and bonnet dressings she and Susan had spoken of the night before.

Susan's mother agreed and joined them, and indulged herself too. It was a pleasant day, but all the time at the back of Susan's mind there was an image of Henry standing beside the chair in his dressing gown, with half his upper body bared and covered in dark bruising. She was worried about him. She had never felt sorry for him before. She did feel sorry for him now, and the feeling was her constant companion no matter how she sought to distract herself from it. If he was no longer taking laudanum, as Aunt Jane had said, then he would be in considerable pain.

When they ate breakfast the following morning the awaited letter from Farnborough arrived, addressed to Alethea. Once she had read it, she looked at Susan. "Henry says that he is feeling a little better, and that we might visit tomorrow if we wish." Alethea looked at their father. "Aunt Jane and Uncle Robert have also extended an invitation for us to join them as a family for dinner in four days."

"I shall write back, accepting the invitation," their mother said. "Will you go tomorrow?"

"Of course," Alethea answered.

She had not given up on Henry yet, then, and perhaps the invitation for them to dine as a family might be to celebrate a happy occasion and Alethea would not need to give up on Henry.

When the carriage turned into Farnborough's courtyard the next day, Henry walked out from the doorway to greet them, with Samson beside him. He must have been waiting and watching for the carriage.

If he had been awaiting the carriage it implied the sentiment that Alethea had feared lacking was there.

His arm was once more in its sling but he was still not wearing his morning coat, nor his waistcoat, yet a short black, stock, neckcloth held his shirt closed. His good hand idly played with Samson's ear as the carriage drew to a halt.

He stepped forward and opened the carriage door. "Hello, ladies."

Alethea took his offered hand and climbed down. "Hello. How are you, truly?"

"Well enough. I promise. I think the journey here just took it out of me, and I did not give my shoulder time to recover. All that it needs is rest and time."

"And he was consuming too much laudanum to kill the pain combined with brandy. Aunt Jane said it made a sickly cocktail," Susan added as she gripped the side of the carriage and climbed down.

Alethea still held Henry's hand. He had not had chance to turn and help Susan. His gaze caught hold of hers and the hard directness in his brown eyes said—*rebellious, anomaly*—when she did not allow him the time to help her.

She turned towards the house, turning away from the memories in her mind's eye, of Henry lying on the sofa in the library and standing in only his dressing gown covered in mottled, awful, bruising. Hateful empathy. "I will leave you two to gossip and recover from your days of separation. I am going to paint." She did not look back nor await an answer but walked briskly on into the house, seeking the sanctuary of the library. If he intended to propose he would not wish for an audience.

The clock chimed twelve times, and almost immediately afterwards there was a hard knock on the library door.

"Come in!"

Henry opened it, and Samson, his shadow, walked into the room. "I have come to see if you wish to take luncheon with us. You are like a mole buried away in here, Susan."

Rebellious… A mole was far more like the names she expected him to call her.

She rested her brush in the bowl of water and straightened. Her hand lifted so that her fingers could push her spectacles farther up the bridge of her nose.

Henry smiled and walked towards her.

At least on this occasion he'd left the door ajar.

"The other day you called me rebellious, I cannot think of two greater extremes. I cannot imagine a rebellious mole." She picked up the rag and took the brush out of the water to wipe it.

"You have been considering that haven't you? I mean you have been thinking about the word rebellious." His voice mocked, but then he smiled at her. "I said it because you like to hide in corners and pretend compliance when really you will walk away from what is expected of you at every chance and hole up somewhere. You always have. So you see the two are very compatible when they are combined in you."

She had never thought walking away rebellious. She looked back down at her painting. "I will eat luncheon with you, yes."

She expected him to acknowledge her answer and turn away,

51

but instead when he reached the desk he leant over, as Samson nudged at her hip for some Henry-style attention. "Very pretty." The crisp, masculine scent of his cologne hung in the air between them.

His presence and proximity sent discomfort spinning out into her nerves. The awkwardness it engendered pressured her to continue talking. "It is not rebellious to walk away or leave a room, though I admit to having little patience with conversations that do not interest me or—"

"People," he inserted as he straightened up.

She met his gaze, still wiping her brush although it must be clean. "People?"

"Or people who do not interest you." One eyebrow rose, and his implication said, *people like me…*

Warmth touched her cheeks.

She turned away to put her paint brush back into the paint box and tidy up her paints.

He leant over once more. "This is actually rather good."

She glanced at him. "Thank you for such exuberant praise."

His lips split into a smile. "There, see, you are a secret hellion. You taunt me horrendously."

She made an intolerant, impatient face and shook her head at him. "I am painting orchids, not racing curricles. I am hardly a hellion. You are speaking of yourself." She closed her paints.

"I have never bothered hiding my nature. But you… You and I have more in common than you think. I would gamble high odds on the fact that Uncle Casper despairs of you as much as my father despairs of me. You do not behave in the ways expected of a woman. The only reason you do not race curricles is that a woman is not given one to be able to race, if you were a man you would race—"

"I am not like you. I would not race. Because there is a vast chasm of difference between us, I think of others not just myself. I would not race because I would not wish to harm another traveller on the road."

He huffed at her, dismissing her argument. It riled her more. "And I do not behave in unacceptable ways—"

"You are not sitting in the drawing room, sewing and talking with the others."

"I like doing different things to the others, that is all."

She turned to walk past him.

"Rebellious." He leant near her and taunted.

She could not win the argument. Her hand lifted instinctively and swiped out at him as her frustration became anger. She struck his poorly arm. "Oh, Henry!" She regretted it immediately as he winced with pain.

"Bloody hell!" He covered his arm and pulled away. Then said more calmly, "You damned hellion." Even in pain he was mocking her.

"I am sorry."

He smiled and shook his head. "I do not think I am."

She did not understand the jest. "Stop teasing me, Henry!"

He laughed. "It is quite inspiring to see you in a temper."

Her hand lifted once more. He stepped back with his good hand still protecting his injured arm. "Did I say you might be a match to a man with verbal fencing? I might be persuaded to include physical fencing. Please, no more violence, Miss Forth. You will have people think my bruises were delivered by your hand, and God forbid my friends heard such a rumour."

He stepped forward again and looked down at her work and at the book to compare it. "You are certainly capturing it. It is a charming flower… Which is something I cannot say for the painter."

He straightened again then, and threw her another smile.

She stuck her tongue out at him as she would have done as a child. He was infuriating, it was no wonder she'd lost her temper and struck him.

His eyes opened wider and his smile lifted, expressing mocked shock, and then suddenly the smile seemed to illuminate the brown in his eyes.

When her tongue slipped back into her mouth, the glint in his eyes became a glow with a greater depth, making his brown eyes as rich in colour as polished mahogany.

Awkwardness pricked. She looked down at her painting. She could not walk away at this moment. "I hope you are feeling better."

"I am feeling better than I was the day you came to my room, thank you." His voice held a dry note that sought to highlight again how inappropriate her behaviour had been in daring to go to his sitting room.

Rebellious. She heard the word in his voice, as it had been said a moment ago when he'd leant to her ear. Perhaps she was a little.

Susan looked up. He was very close, she could see every detail of his eyelashes and every shade within his brown eyes. "You could have said do not come in, you know?" The scent of his expensive London cologne enveloped her.

"I thought it was the footman come to take away the tea-tray."

"You knew it was me when I entered."

"And perhaps then it was more amusing to not yell at you and make you go away." His voice had lost its mocking edge and dropped into a low pitch. "…The lesson was better taught by leaving you to discover what your rebellious nature had led you into."

"Sayeth Lord Henry Marlow, the prodigal son, he who has just been thrown from his curricle in a race and nearly broken his neck and admitted he has probably learned no lessons at all." Her voice had dropped in pitch too.

His eyes seemed full of questions as he looked at her. Then his gaze travelled across her face, studying her as he'd studied her painting. When his gaze came back to hers, he said, "Quite." Then he turned away and began walking back across the room, with Samson in his wake.

"I truly am sorry that you were so badly hurt, Henry!" Susan called after him, her awkwardness and her empathy for his pain, pushing her into more words. "But I do not think that anything I do compares!" She had not known what to say, but she had needed to say something to turn whatever had just happened back into something tangible that she could understand.

He turned and walked a couple of steps backwards, with his free hand cradling his poorly arm. "*I am truly sorry…*Your voice rings with guilt, Susan, as it did yesterday when you saw my bruises. Did you think I had been acting out my pain, and wearing a sling for my pleasure? You… The rescuer of every wounded thing, wild or tame…"

"No." Her instinctive denial cut through the air, and stopped him moving.

He smiled in that hideous mocking way, that said, *I know I am right.*

Oh be honest with him, he would be honest with her. "I thought you deserved to be injured. You are the reckless one. It is you who needed to be taught a lesson. But I would not have wished your life endangered. I came to your room yesterday as much to apologise for the meanness of my thoughts as to fetch Samson."

The rogue looked up at the ceiling and laughed for an instant before looking back at her. The amusement had brightened his eyes. "Think as meanly as you wish, Susan, it will not do me any greater harm than I have done myself. I dare say, on this occasion, I may have finally learned the lesson you wished me taught." He turned away once more.

"Where are we eating?" She called before he left the room.

"In the formal dining room, Papa is home."

When they ate, she had intended to sit beside Sarah, but Alethea drew Susan's attention, and so she could not then walk around the table to sit with Christine and Sarah. She ended up taking a seat on the opposite side of Henry to her sister.

Alethea spoke to Aunt Jane as Henry silently fought to eat his food one handed.

Susan swallowed, she wished to make conversation, to stop herself from suffering with the awkwardness that hung over her. "How are your bruises today, are they improving?" she said lamely.

"Turning from almost black to a lighter purple, but perhaps I have a new one since you struck me."

She looked at him. "Sorry."

He smiled. "If we are on the grounds of apologies, then I owe you one too. I am sorry I did not tell you to go away the other day. I should have done. I did not mean my teasing to discompose you earlier, but I can see it has done because every time you look at me you turn a greater shade of pink."

Oh, she wished to smack him again.

"You are forgiven for striking me, if I am forgiven," he concluded.

"You are forgiven only if you agree never to mention that I went to your room again."

A half laugh rumbled from his chest.

Alethea turned and said something to him. But before he turned to reply, he said to Susan, "Are we friends again then?"

"Henry! Alethea asked for your opinion." his father interrupted before Susan could answer. There must have been some greater conversation about the table they had lost track of. Henry turned away.

Once they had finished eating, Susan rose to return to the library. Every one else stood at the same time. She would have walked on ahead but Henry touched her arm.

"Wait a moment. I have not yet secured your agreement on our pact."

He had not forgotten his desire for a truce, then.

Alethea walked on with Aunt Jane, and his father walked with Christine and Sarah.

"May we call ourselves friends? I do not think we have really been friends for years. I would like to think of you as my friend, Susan."

She hated the way he said her name, his enunciation made her stomach twist about with a strange sensation.

He held out his left, good, hand, which was gloveless. She accepted the gesture.

She wore no glove either. The warmth and the softness of his skin surprised her as his hand surrounded hers. Yet he had not held her hand in the way he held Alethea's hand, he held Susan's in a firm gesture, his whole hand gripping her whole hand, not merely pressing her fingers.

The queasy feeling in her stomach tumbled over. She had never held a man's naked hand, except for her father's.

He shook her hand a single time, firmly, and then let her go. "May I escort you to the library? I wouldn't mind another look at your painting, we might even persuade Alethea to stop by…" His good arm had lifted as he spoke. He was offering it to her…

She looked at his forearm, before glancing up and then laying her fingers on his arm self-consciously.

Her fingers closed about the sinuous muscle of his arm through his thin shirt. The cotton was so fine she could feel the hairs on his skin.

The strange sensation in her tummy coiled up like an adder waiting to strike.

"So how many flowers have you attempted so far?"

Susan swallowed before answering. Her throat had dried. "I am only on my second."

"And how many are in the book? I seem to recall about fifty. You will be here for a year."

She smiled at him. "Or two."

This was Henry at his most persuasive, he could turn this side of himself on and off so easily. She had always found his charm annoying before, but then it had never been solely directed at her.

Now it was directed at her…

It felt complimentary, and he was surely doing it to make her feel at ease with him again, which was kind. Although it must be embarrassing for him if she was blushing at every moment.

His charm was working, though, she did feel more at ease.

For the second time in her life, she felt wholly in charity with him.

Perhaps he would not make such a bad brother-in-law.

Chapter Six

An odd atmosphere arrived in the carriage with the Forths, Henry could sense it even as he looked down into the hall. Uncle Casper's shoulders were stiff and Aunt Julie's manner was much more restrained than normal; she far too calmly kissed his mother's cheek.

Henry walked down the last flight of stairs to the hall as Alethea entered.

She was wearing a light bright blue again so that the material of her evening dress extenuated the colour of her eyes. Susan entered behind her sister, wrapped up in a large paisley shawl, but he could see the hem of her dress. It was a pale, dove grey.

He'd dressed fully for dinner, as the Forths were officially invited guests rather than arriving simply as callers, and so he had his grey waistcoat and black evening coat on over his shirt. His arm was still strung up in a sling, though. Yet it had been less painful to dress, and it was not agony to be clothed now the swelling had declined to some extent.

What remained of the pain, as long he did not make any sudden movements, was a dull constant ache in his shoulder, a soreness in his wrist and stiffness in both. The rest of him was healing quite nicely.

Papa's valet, who had been shaving Henry since he'd come home, was now urging Henry to exercise his bad arm, but Henry had refused to attempt it for another week at least; he did not wish to send it into agony again.

"Uncle Casper." Henry bowed in a swift informal movement. Even though there was no relationship via bloodlines he'd always felt as though Lord and Lady Froth were his uncle and aunt—and Alethea like another of his cousins—and truly that was the level of his affection for her.

He swallowed trying to moisten his dry mouth suddenly, as Uncle Casper's lips lifted in a stiff smile. Definitely there was an unusual atmosphere.

Henry glanced at Alethea as his father came to welcome Uncle Casper more heartily.

He liked her considerably. She was amusing company, funny and entertaining, and she was polite and genteel; she would make the perfect countess when he inherited his father's title. She was good with people, confident and jolly. He knew full well she would manage a house admirably. She had all the qualities of a wife.

But he was not ready to marry. He was too young. Yet he could feel the nets being set about him.

Four times this week she had hinted at the fact she was not going to wait forever for him to ask and Uncle Casper's gaze stated that nor did he wish Alethea to have to keep waiting. They were becoming impatient with him.

Well let them. He would not be forced. His father may call such an attitude careless. Henry would call it wise.

"Good evening, Henry. I trust you are feeling better?"

Henry turned to face Aunt Julie. "I am, thank you."

She gave him a look which seemed anxious, before touching his shoulders and lifting to her toes to better reach to kiss his cheek. On a normal evening, in the past, her arms would have wrapped around his neck and her exclamation would have been, "*my darling boy!*" before she pressed a kiss on his cheek. She had no sons, so Aunt Julie had treated him as though he was her son since his birth. But perhaps her calmness was out of awareness for his injuries.

"It is good to see you again," he said, before kissing her cheek in return.

A very abnormal half-hearted smile stirred her lips.

They had hoped he would announce his and Alethea's engagement tonight. That was it. They had received the invitation to dine and misconstrued its meaning.

Damn it, Alethea must have been waiting for him to ask all bloody week and now she had told them he'd said nothing.

"You are looking very well despite your accident."

"Thank you, Aunt."

She was definitely restrained—unhappy with him.

He looked at Alethea. She smiled at him, but even her smile was not quite so full.

There had been a conversation about him in the carriage, he'd lay a bet on it. One that had berated his lack of a proposal. But he would not be bloody pushed into it. He would propose when he was ready to be settled, not before.

Yet he was not immune to a sense of guilt.

He turned to face her, as she came to him, holding out her hands. He took hold of them, then kissed the back of them in turn, before leaning forward and kissing her cheek. "Hello, you look very beautiful," he whispered towards her ear before he straightened.

She blushed, and smiled more naturally. "Hello."

He smiled too, looking into her very blue eyes, then let her hands slip from his and turned to greet Susan.

He did not normally greet her in anyway, they were too close for formal greetings, and they had no other reason to greet each other with any special welcome. But tonight… He had welcomed her parents having not seen them for months and it would seem odd after that not to say a particular good evening to Susan too.

"Susan." She blushed, not deeply, but there were very definite roses blooming in her cheeks. She had been blushing every time she saw him since their long conversation in the library, or rather since her visit to his room.

She did not offer her hand. He took it from where it hovered by her waist anyway, and kissed the back of her fingers. Her hand trembled and her grey eyes looked directly into his for a moment before she looked at his fingers holding hers.

She *was* a funny anomaly.

He let her go, then turned his attention back to Alethea, and offered his arm.

His family and the Forths turned towards the drawing room.

"We shall have a glass of wine before we go through to dinner, Casper, Julie."

Henry wondered if his father had picked up upon the atmosphere and read it correctly too. If so then Henry would be in for a lecture after they had left.

"You are fully dressed…" Alethea whispered.

"I could hardly dine with your parents in my shirt."

"They would not have minded."

"I would have felt a fool, and I think I might have made them feel foolish too." Sarah had taken charge of Susan and was walking with her. Christine walked beside Aunt Julie, with Henry's mother, while his father spoke with Uncle Casper. "Were they expecting me to announce our engagement tonight?" He'd learned as young as his boarding school years that it was always better to be direct when dealing with an awkward situation, otherwise awkward situations festered.

She blushed a deep crimson, much darker than the colour Susan had been turning for the last couple of days. *Yes*, then.

"Yes. I am sorry—"

"You have no need to be sorry. But I am not going to propose to you while I am home. I'm not ready to settle yet, I am young,

Alethea, it is too soon, and I will not apologise for it." He'd slowed his pace, so that the others walked on ahead, then he stopped and faced her. "I am sorry if that distresses you. I know you will make a good wife but I will not commit until I know I would make a good husband and I think that will be when I am older."

She looked into his eyes—searching for answers—perhaps to understand his feelings. What were hers? Did she think more of him than he thought of her? That thought was a little petrifying.

"But I am getting older too, Henry," she said quietly. "It is different for a woman. If I wait much longer I shall become too old to be considered. What if you change your mind then? Then I will not have another chance."

They had always known there was this obligation upon them and neither of them had expressed any disagreement, and yet this was the first time they had spoken about their marriage openly.

"When will you ask me? I will not wait for you for years. I wish to be married and settled."

There, his speaking openly had led her to do so too. This was the sentiment she had been hinting at ever since he'd returned— that she would not continue to wait.

"I cannot say, or rather I will not, I suppose, because I do not know; someday in the future. You will have to choose whether or not you wait."

Uncertainty shone in the blackness at the heart of her eyes. "I do not know if I can wait." Her hand slipped off his arm and she walked ahead.

Touché. He laughed internally, and followed.

When Henry entered the formal drawing room his father was already offering Alethea a glass of wine. The footman poured it as his father turned and asked Susan if she would like a glass.

Susan had removed her shawl. The dove grey colour of her dress suited both her hair and her eyes, and oddly her light grey eyes seemed more striking than Alethea's blue as she looked at his father and accepted the glass he had taken from the footman to give to her.

Henry walked forwards as the footman poured another glass.

When Henry took the glass, his father's gaze caught Henry's and his eyebrows lifted.

His father had picked up upon the atmosphere too and deciphered it. Henry was in for a hard debate when the Forths had gone. His father would be of the same opinion as Alethea. *Why are you waiting?*

Wonderful. It had been on his initiation that the two families had come together. This meal had been his suggestion, and now he would not be able to bloody digest it. Perhaps he should have spelled his perspective out more clearly when he had written to Alethea from London. Yet it was nonsense for them to grasp at this gesture with such silly hope. In undertaking one rare act of thoughtfulness, which his father had been remarkably pleased by, he had knocked open a hornets' nest.

Lord, though, he hoped his father had not thought the same. Had that been why he'd been so happy with the idea? Damn. This was not meant to be an enactment of the prodigal son parable. He had not intended the fatted calf to be slaughtered and a toast raised to the fact he had returned home and would remain forever. The intent had only been to see his aunt and uncle before he returned to London.

He sipped from his glass. Alethea had turned her back on him and walked across the room to speak with Sarah.

Wonderful!

Yet to be fair, if she fell out with him and married someone else, he would not grieve over it. His heart was not involved; it would not be broken. It would make no difference to him, other than that when the time came for him to take a wife he would have to look for one.

He looked at the back of her head. Her blonde hair was

64

beautifully and perfectly styled, and then there was the curve of her narrow neck. She bowed her head a little as she spoke to Sarah and it presented the area of skin just above the neckline of her dress. He sighed. His heart may not care but other parts of him would very willingly become involved in a relationship with her.

He breathed in, what were her sentiments? Was it merely compliance with their families' wishes or did she have some greater affection for him? Perhaps at some point he should ask her that, and that too should become open between them.

"Henry. You are quiet and brooding, neither of which are terms I would use to describe you. Is your arm hurting?"

He turned to face Susan.

It was uncharacteristic for her to approach him and speak to him voluntarily.

Those pale grey eyes were intensely grey tonight, thanks to her dress, which exaggerated the colour just as Alethea's dress made her eyes bluer. But Susan's spectacles also seemed to make her grey eyes shine with a vibrancy that had more depth than Alethea's blue eyes ever did.

Susan had recklessness within her, she might deny it as many times as she wished, but she did, and a dash of rebellion that her sister never displayed.

Alethea may have just told him she was willing to marry someone else if he did not hurry up and place a ring on her finger, but that had not been rebellion, she had merely hoped to gee him up.

"My arm always hurts since I fell from my curricle," he answered.

"I am sorry."

He smiled, bless her, she did look genuinely sorry for him, too. Since their truce she had become far more tolerant of him, and he might keep teasing her over her rebellious nature but it was no more than a pale shadow compared to his, while her caring side... She out won him a thousand to one on her ability to care for things.

"I am not complaining, I am only stating a fact, not asking for your pity."

She started to smile but her teeth pressed into her lip, to prevent it.

He leant a little forward and said near her ear, in a quieter conspiratorial voice. "You have no need to be sorry for me remember, I did it to myself."

She laughed suddenly, only for a moment, but then she smiled fully. God, had she ever smiled at him before? If she had perhaps he had not seen it up close, but the vibrancy in her smile was quite striking. Alethea had always been the bright, exuberant one. But there was exuberance in Susan, too, it was simply hidden.

"How long before you may take off the sling?"

"Another week or so."

"You will be well enough to attend the assembly in York then. Alethea will be pleased. You will go?" The last was half question half statement.

Alethea will be pleased...

Of course there was another way to glean the level of Alethea's attachment to him, he could ask her sister. They were close, they must share confidences. "I am not so sure she will be pleased, she may prefer to use the occasion to flirt with others and throw me off. We have just fallen out because I believe your family had an expectation that I would have proposed prior to this evening, and I have just assured Alethea that she should not expect it during my current stay or indeed in the months following."

The brightness in Susan's expression extinguished. "Why?"

"Why will I not propose? Because I am not ready. Is it not better for me to wait until I am happy to settle? I am too young. I like my life in town."

"You are so self-centered."

Her words struck him, and spurred him into biting back. "And

66

you are always direct." He swallowed back his temper. "Will she be very hurt do you think?" That was not really the question he was asking.

"Of course she will. She will be cut by it. How can she not be?"

Cut in what way? Cut through the heart? "I have not told her I will never propose merely that she should not expect it yet."

"Then that is even crueller. She is not young and you wish to keep her dangling on a line of hope, like a caught fish you are trying to tire."

Susan was far too quick. "It is not like that. I am not doing it deliberately to vex Alethea or delay—"

"Merely thinking of yourself."

Damn her. "I am being wise. I am thinking of us both. I do not wish her to be unhappy with me, and I would be unhappy if I married her now. Would that not make her unhappy?"

"You are as self-centered as ever, Henry."

"And you judge me as poorly as always, Susan."

"Because you have always been arrogant and only interested in the things which benefit you. You were spoiled as a child, Uncle Robert freely admits it, and you have grown up idle and irresponsible."

Oh Lord. *Idle and irresponsible.*

He laughed internally. "And there was I thinking we had shaken hands upon a truce." He could not defend himself, her accusations were true. He drew an income from his father's estate and lived in town amusing himself with his friends, and women.

It was doubly amusing, though, that considering all the years he'd known Susan, he did not really know her. That also served to prove her point—he was self-centered. He smiled more broadly. "You are probably right, I was and am. But regardless that does not make it right for me to rush into marriage with Alethea, no matter my motives or lack of them."

She huffed out a sigh. "And you are probably right." It sounded as though she was cross that she was forced to agree with him and she looked at the others across his shoulder as though she had had enough of the conversation.

"What is the level of Alethea's attachment to me?"

Her eyes turned back to stare into his. "You should ask Alethea."

"I know, but I believe it might set the vipers upon me. At the current time, it is better to ask you."

"What is the level of your attachment?"

Touché again. "I think I ought to only tell Alethea that."

"Well there you are then."

"Dinner is ready, my Lord!" Davis stated to the room in general.

As Susan stood beside Henry, he offered his arm to her. As she'd done the other day, when he'd only worn his shirt, she did not merely lay her fingers on his arm but held it with a gentle grip that did things to his body he ought not to feel stir when this was potentially his future sister-in-law.

He sat between Aunt Julie and Alethea at the table. The latter turned her head away from him throughout the meal, avoiding conversation, and also left a footman to cut up his food.

Instead of speaking to him Alethea talked animatedly to Susan and Sarah, the conversation flowing across the table. They spoke of the assembly Susan had mentioned earlier. It was to be held in a couple of weeks' time. He would probably be well enough to return to town before the assembly occurred, and yet it was to be Sarah's first, apparently, so he really ought to stay and show his support and dance with her, as her eldest brother.

Self-centered… The accusation pricked.

He would stay. He did not wish Susan to have further grounds for that charge against him. He could act out some part of the story of the prodigal son: returned to become the responsible heir.

When they had finished eating his mother rose and led the

68

other women from the room. It left him in the company of his father and Uncle Casper. When the doors closed Henry's muscles stiffened instinctively. It jarred his damned shoulder. But he sensed a need to defend himself.

Davis poured each of them a glass of port while Henry awaited the onslaught.

It did not come, neither man mentioned Alethea, or their hopes that he would propose to her, instead they asked about his life in town.

Once they had finished their port and conversation, they joined the women in the formal drawing room. When Henry walked in, it was Susan who caught his eye first. She was not sitting with the others but was on the far side of the room searching through the music in the chest there, presumably because she intended to play the pianoforte.

She was being different from the others again. But she very rarely sat and joined in conversation.

As she leant over searching through the sheets of music her bottom was beautifully outlined within the thin muslin material of her dress and layered petticoats. He'd never thought about her figure before, Susan was the sort of woman whose personality absorbed attention too much for any thought beyond it... but now he looked... and thought... She had a very handsome figure.

He looked away. Alethea was sitting with Christine who would be excluded from the assembly in York as she was the youngest and not yet out, as it were. But she was gathering information about it as though that information were precious jewels to be held up to the candlelight and admired with reverence.

He smiled at the thought, it was charming to see Sarah and Christine growing up. There, see, he was not entirely self-centered.

He sat beside Aunt Julie, as Susan took a seat at the pianoforte and raised the lid.

She played the instrument extremely well. He could not ever remember hearing her play before. She also sang beautifully, her voice had an enchanting lilt that was very individual, and as she played she shut her eyes and let the music take her somewhere out of the room. She was rebelling again, in her own quiet way, no longer hiding in a corner, or the library, but hiding herself within the music.

If she felt confident enough to simply be whoever she was when she hid away, he wondered how she would act.

Alethea rose and crossed the room, to collect a cup of tea from Sarah. Henry stood.

Now was his moment. He ought to rectify the situation between them.

He crossed the room as Sarah poured out Alethea's tea.

As Alethea accepted the cup he leant to her ear and said quietly, "Will you walk outside with me? The night is reasonably warm." Hopefully she would not misconstrue the invitation after their earlier talk.

She looked at him with eyes that judged him with condemnation.

His lips twisted in a half-smile, probably in a mocking expression—he'd always been thick skinned—he'd never really been touched by others' ill-opinion. He came from a large family and had attended a boys boarding school, such things made a person less vulnerable. "I think we need to continue our earlier conversation and I would rather not do so in here."

"Oh, very well." Her answer was impatient but forbearing. "Lead on."

He'd always known Alethea had a rigid strength of character, it would be a valuable quality for a countess. In London life, there was a need to be stalwart and to cling to one's morals. Although where people set their bar on morals varied, and he knew his bar was far beneath Alethea's—but that too was a positive. He preferred it that way about.

He lifted a hand, encouraging her to walk before him, towards the French doors which led out on to the terrace. If they stood within sight of the windows there would be no issue with propriety.

A footman opened the door for them to pass through.

Alethea crossed the stone paving, the china cup wobbling on the saucer she held. When she reached the balustrade she set the saucer and cup down on the stone top and looked out over the formal gardens which were etched in bright moonlight. All this would be his one day, and therefore hers too, between them they would care for it and cherish it as his parents did now.

"Sulking does not become you…" he said quietly.

She turned and glared at him. "I am not sulking. I am angry."

"Why?"

"Because I cannot keep waiting! My life revolves about your whims, whether or not you care to come home, and then when you do come I am left to hover waiting to see if you will ask… It is like this is a game to you!"

Self-centered! The accusation shouted in his head in Susan's tone. "I do not treat you as part of a game. This is about my feelings that is all." But damn it, he wanted to know what hers were. "What do you feel for me? Am I breaking your heart by asking you to wait, then?"

She glared at him, her emotion striking him through her eyes. "Is that what you wish for, for me to be here pining for you while you lead a jolly life in town? Susan constantly complains that I see too much good in you. I always thought you better. You are proving her right!"

Susan… He should tell her to mind her own business. "Susan has always had very little tolerance for me; we both know it. Do not let her opinion sway yours. What if all I ask is for another year?" Of freedom, to live life as a bachelor and get the reckless-ness out of his blood. "At the end of that year then I will propose and we will settle here."

"I am three and twenty next month and in a year I shall be four and twenty, perhaps I do not wish to wait a year…"

He breathed in. The net was closing in on him. He could not run from it forever, he'd always known that, and yet he did not feel ready to settle, he felt a trap closing about him. But what she said was true, three and twenty was late for a woman to marry. He sighed out. "Why not come to town then this summer and spend time with me there? I still wish to wait a year, but then we may become better acquainted and you shall not feel so excluded." There, he was not entirely selfish or irresponsible, he could think of her happiness too.

She stared at him, with her lips slightly parted. Her eyes caught the moonlight and shone silver. He had an urge to lean and kiss her but it was hardly in the manner of the moment and he would guess they were being watched.

"Very well," she answered. Her lips pursed for a moment before she then added, "When should I come?"

"I intend to stay here as long as the assembly and then return to town. You may come anytime you wish. I shall write to you when I am there, and you may let me know when it is convenient for you to come in the company of your father and mother."

"I should not have asked you that, should I? You do not own London. Of course I may go there whenever I wish, and when I am there I may dance with whomever I wish. I might allow any man who desires it to court me. You may wait a year, Henry. But I may decide not to." She turned away leaving her cup of tea on the balustrade undrunk, and went back inside.

He smiled. Then laughed.

She had not answered his question, but he did not think her heart involved. He thought her feelings the same as his. There was attraction between them; but the rest was only common-sense; they suited one another and it was what their parents hoped for.

Chapter Seven

"What did Henry speak to you about outside?" their father asked Alethea as soon as the carriage door closed.

A tension had lingered throughout the evening because they had all assumed that Henry had intended to propose before tonight, and he had not.

Susan's father had grumbled about, *that boy,* during their journey here, and now it seemed that he would continue the same theme of conversation on the way home.

"He asked me to wait a year, and then he said he will propose."

"Indeed." Their father grunted.

"It is the most direct he has been, is it not?" Susan tried to encourage a sense of hope.

"It is, and we agreed I might go to town for the season. He suggested it. May we go, Papa?"

Their father nodded. "Well that is at least something." His hand lifted and his fingers twisted the end of his curled moustache, as his fingers always did when he was mulling over some thought.

"The season is only weeks away," Susan's mother responded. "We will need to prepare. We shall have to open up the town house, and have a ball. You must have a presentation there to gather introductions."

Neither Alethea nor Susan had been brought out into London society; it had seemed unnecessary because Alethea had an agreement with Henry, and Susan had never requested to go and hunt for a husband. But if her family were to go to London then she supposed she must go, and therefore also face introductions.

When Susan and Alethea were alone later, lying in bed beside one another, whispering through the darkness, Alethea told Susan more of the conversation she'd shared with Henry. "You were right, though, it is the most direct he has been with me, and yet I feel as though he is manipulating me, I told him I would not play his game anymore. He said it is all to do with his feelings."

"I have always said he is selfish."

"I know, and I told him you have now convinced me of it."

"What did he say?"

"That you have always had very little tolerance for him and I should not allow your opinion to sway mine. But it is not your opinion that is changing mine, it is him."

Henry must lose his charm in the moments when he said no.

"I have told him that I will go to town, but if another man courts me I will let him. I have not promised to wait a year."

Susan smiled into the darkness. "Was he suitably sent into a terror at the thought of losing you?"

"I am not sure he even cares. He asked me if I loved him, but he did not say he loved me."

"What is the level of Alethea's attachment to me?" He had asked Susan that too. "Did you say you loved him?"

"No. That would have been utter folly when he is dangling me like this."

"Do you love him?"

"I do not know. I admire him greatly, he is very handsome, and I like his manner but I am not sure how deep being in love feels... I am not sure if I would even know. How do people know?"

Susan had no answer.

~

Once the library door had closed, Henry's father asked, "What did you say to Alethea outside?"

When the girls and his mother had retired, his father had asked Henry to sit with him in the library. Henry had known immediately what would come next—a berating.

He was too old for this. "Is it any of your business, Papa?"

"I am hoping that it might be. Would you like a glass of brandy?"

"Yes." If he must endure this.

His father turned to pour it. Henry leant back against a leather chair, gripping its top with his good hand, beside his hip.

"So what did you say? When is this proposal coming? It was clear to me tonight that Casper had expected it too." His father turned holding two full glasses. "I think he is becoming as impatient with you as I am. Is Alethea?"

He walked over to where Henry leant on the chair and held out a glass.

"Thank you."

"Well?" His father looked him in the eyes, and his eyebrows lifted, in the way he had of challenging while smiling. His father was so hard to read at times.

His eyebrows remained lifted, waiting for Henry to speak.

Henry was not inclined to, yet his father kept waiting. Henry had borne numerous interviews such as this over his years both at Eton, and then Oxford. He had regularly been in trouble as a boy, and then as a young man. His father's way had never been to shout but merely to unnerve Henry, to make him feel guilty and accept the responsibility for his actions—it usually worked

75

well enough. Until he had returned to Eton or Oxford and then the interview and the guilt had slipped from Henry's mind.

Self-centered.

He refused to feel guilty now. "Alethea is ready to marry. I am not. I have asked her to wait another year. She told me she may or may not wait. But she is to come to town for the season where she will consider my request and other men."

His father laughed, then smiled and shook his head. "She is a good woman for you, Henry. It is not that we wish to force you, it is just that she is—"

"Eminently suitable and conveniently close. I know. And charming, and sweet, and pretty—"

"And that was not what I was saying."

Henry sipped his brandy.

"If she is not your choice, Henry, she is not. It is only—"

"That it would be such a perfect union, to join our families, when Uncle Casper has no son. I know."

His father smiled again. "As you say, for all those reasons, and yet I do not wish either of you unhappy." His father drank some of his brandy.

"We shall suit. We do. It is merely that I do not wish to marry *anyone* yet. You did not marry Mama until you were much older, you cannot expect me to hurry into the shackles."

"You should not think of marriage as shackles if you wish to marry. I was desperate for your mother to marry me when I was younger than you. It did not happen and then I was even more desperate for her to accept me when I met her again." His father sipped his brandy, then gave Henry another direct, enquiring look, which could be either anger or humour. "What do you feel for Alethea?"

Bloody hell. "That is the question I asked of her outside, what does she feel for me?"

"What did she say?"

"She did not answer."

76

"As you have not answered me."

"I will answer you. I care for Alethea. I am attracted to her. I am not sure if that is what you would define as love."

His father sighed. "If it was love you would know." He looked down at his glass and then sipped more of the brandy.

Henry drank the rest of his, then set his empty glass aside, on a table. "I do not believe it is love. But we ramble along well together, you know we do, and I think she feels as much for me as I feel for her. Perhaps while she is in town it will become love. You should not give up on your dream yet, but it shall not be fulfilled this year."

His father drank the last of his brandy. Then picked up Henry's empty glass. "Would you like another, and a game of back-gammon, as I am unlikely to have your company for much longer?"

"Yes, thank you." Henry turned and went over to the table to set up the game.

"It has been nice to have you home, and a novelty to have you at home and not to be angered by you on a daily basis." His father was speaking as he poured the brandy. "When do you take off the sling? When will you leave?"

He told his father what he had told Susan.

"And then…"

"I shall accompany you, Mama and Sarah to the assembly in York. I know that will please Sarah. Then I shall return to town."

"To sow more oats in furrows I disapprove of."

"You may hardly talk I am constantly told about your former reputation, even though I would rather not know it."

"I did not entertain myself in brothels and consort with whores."

"No, you entertained yourself in ballrooms and bedchambers, and consorted with adulteresses and cuckolded a couple of hundred men in society, I think that worse." Henry placed the counters on the board with his good hand. Then looked at his father.

77

His father's eyebrows lifted again.

Henry laughed. "They are not facts I wish to know about my father, but in town they are facts that everyone wishes to tell me."

His father set their refreshed glasses down on the table beside the board. "You know if Alethea discovered how you live… or even if Casper, or God forbid Julie—"

"Papa, I live as all young men live before they are wed. You cannot expect better of me than you did of yourself."

His father huffed out a breath as he sat. "Except that I regret that I lived that way. It brought me no happiness, as your mother will tell you. Given a chance to turn back time she and I would have married when we were young and I would have accepted the responsibility of supporting my father. I shall always consider my wild years, years that I lost or threw away."

"Well I am in my wild years, and I consider them precious. I am not you, and I am not throwing them away."

Chapter Eight

The carriage drew to a halt before the Palladian frontage of the assembly rooms in Blake Street. A footman opened the carriage door. Henry climbed out first, and stood beneath the giant portico, then offered his hand to Sarah to help her descend. It felt very freeing to have his right arm back, and yet the muscle had wasted a little, and his shoulder was still stiff and sore.

"Nervous?" he whispered when her foot touched the pavement.

"Excited," she answered, with a broad smile.

He smiled too. He'd not imagined that accompanying Sarah to her first dance would move him at all, but he had been moved. He was proud of his oldest sister.

She had walked downstairs into the hall with the brightest smile, looking full grown, and beautiful. She had their mother's unusual emerald green eyes and dark brown hair, and with it styled in such a grown up manner… She had become a woman, and somehow he had missed it until this evening.

He offered his arm to Sarah as his parents descended. "Allow me to be the one who walks you in."

She smiled at him again.

Emotion clutched tight in his chest. He was the eldest; one day he would be the head of their family like his cousin John, the Duke of Pembroke, was of his. He'd never considered the idea before. Yet his father was healthy, he hoped it would be years before he must take on the earldom. He would rather his father alive and *he* the heir, who had the time and the money to live a care free life.

They walked into the large assembly rooms. He'd never attended before. It was a long, rectangular room, surrounded with pilasters of beige marble and full of people, music and conversation. Henry could see no one he knew. It was not London.

There was a country dance in progress. He leant towards his sister. "As we cannot join this dance let me take you to find the refreshments."

People bowed and curtsied as they walked past. Of course amongst these people they stood out because of their father's title.

Pride burned with a roaring flame in his chest. It must be the first time Sarah had experienced such recognition and it would be the first time she would dance outside their home, or a member of their family's home. When the season began she would come to London and dance too. His sister, all grown up, and there was Christine to follow her.

A different sensation clasped in his chest, one that was more brutal and aggressively masculine. A need to protect her. He knew too much of London. Too much of what occurred outside the ballrooms. When she came to London he would need to watch her. There would be rakes and scoundrels all about her; men like him and his father.

The thought stabbed him with embarrassment. From that perspective perhaps he could appreciate his father's view. He would not care for Sarah to know anything of his life in town.

"Wine?" he offered when they neared the refreshment table. When she nodded, he picked up a glass and handed it to her.

"Thank you, Henry."

Their mother and father approached. "Mama?" He picked up another glass for her.

Several people in the room stared at them yet others came forward, and then the introductions began. "This is my eldest daughter, Sarah… This is my son, Lord Henry…"

The people Henry was introduced to were mostly the merchants and businessmen of York, though there were a small number of untitled relations of aristocratic families. Of course the businessmen and merchants benefited from his father's patronage and so they were very keen to be introduced to his heir and compliment Sarah. Sarah would have been complimented even if she looked hideous because these men and their wives were merely scraping to gain the interest of an earl.

Henry was glad when the current dance came to its end so he and Sarah could escape all the bowing. His intent, then, was to dance all night and avoid anymore fuss.

He smiled at Sarah, conspiratorially, and lifted his good arm. "Shall we?"

"Yes please."

Sarah's fingers lay on top of the fabric of his evening coat. He escorted her on to the floor.

It was another country dance, they stood and faced one another. Her cheeks had turned pink. She was holding the attention of many people in this room, and as many women as men. He presumed the women jealous of his sister's wealth and beauty. She would have a dowry that would be sought after as much as herself. Yes, he would need to protect her in town.

He winked at her, to make her relax.

She smiled, and then the music and the dancing began.

They smiled at each other every time they came together in the set, and he whispered some quip about their companions. She was laughing each time they parted.

When the dance ended they returned to their parents to take a few sips of wine. Sarah was breathing heavily yet the colour in her cheeks was now from exercise and enjoyment.

The music for the next country dance began.

"Sarah." He claimed her once more. She could have no suitors here. This was only about pleasure, and showing herself off, and so he would not hinder her chances by monopolizing her time.

"I have not seen Alethea," Sarah commented as they walked out on to the floor.

Henry had not even been looking for her, though he'd promised her two dances when he did see her.

Their communication since the Forths' had joined his family for dinner had become irregular and colder. She was still angry with him and she had not visited to pamper her injured beloved since then. When she had visited his home it was with a claim that she had come to call on his mother and sisters, or to accompany Susan, so Susan might paint her flowers.

Though on every occasion Alethea had been immaculately dressed and positioned herself so she might turn a shoulder to him, in a way which ensured he had the best view of her figure, and her slender neck.

Yes, he was attracted to her. But if she continued her sulking and played such silly games, he would lose patience with her. He'd never been amused by coy, calculating women. That was why he'd always preferred the simple association of a whore. There were no games there.

Sarah smiled at him throughout the dance, her inhibitions slipping away. She felt secure with him, comfortable and confident. It was more evidence that she needed his involvement with her introductions in town. Of course the men in their aunt's family would be there too, the Pembrokes, a pride of dukes, and all their sons were his friends.

The only husband of the former Duke of Pembroke's daughters who was not a duke was Henry's Uncle Edward, his father's brother.

"They have arrived!" Sarah exclaimed as she passed him in a shoulder to shoulder turn.

"Who?" He looked at her with a sense of teasing. He knew who, but her excitement was amusing.

"The Forths!" Her gaze came back from looking across the room to catch his eye, as they spun around and then turned the other way. "Oh, Henry, stop it." She laughed, as she saw he had been mocking her.

She glanced back across her shoulder. "Alethea is beautiful. She is the prettiest woman here…"

It was a very feminine, leading, comment, supposed to draw him into gushing sentiments. Sarah really had grown up. But he was not in the mood to play along.

He looked across the room.

Yes, indeed, they had arrived, and Alethea was in very good looks, quite stunning really. He would lay a heavy bet a lot of care had been taken in her appearance tonight to ensure that he noted what he might miss out upon if he did not hurry up and stop dithering.

He looked away smiling. It was duly noted.

When the dance finished he led Sarah back to their parents, who had been joined by the Forths. He bowed to his aunt, and then to Alethea. He did not see Susan, perhaps she had decided not to come, he'd never seen her dance, so perhaps this was not her idea of fun.

"I believe we agreed on this dance and the next." He offered Alethea his recovering arm.

"You are without your sling." Her fingers rested on his arm.

He led her away from the others. Perhaps she did still care about his well-being. He smiled. "I have been without my sling for three days. If you had called within those day you would have known."

"How is your arm?" She looked at it, and therefore he looked too, at her fingers which lay gently atop his black coat sleeve.

He glanced back up and met her gaze. "It is strong enough to dance the two dances I promised you." Although his shoulder was already aching like the devil, but it had healed, and exercise would increase its strength which was what it needed now.

They danced a very lively country dance, which left them both breathing hard, but there was something rather charming about watching Alethea with her colour up and her bosom heaving.

The next dance was a waltz. They had waltzed before, several times, at family gatherings, since he'd been eighteen. His family had a habit of pairing up as couples for an entire evening when they danced, and so he and Alethea had often been paired for waltz after waltz.

He smiled at her as he lifted his arm to form the hold. A waltz would be a harder strain on his shoulder. She held his hand, at last smiling brightly, as she usually did. He set his other hand at her back while she lay hers on his good shoulder.

He spun her into a turn immediately. The easiness he'd always felt with her swept over him. They had shared some sort of bond since childhood, even if that bond was not yet love. "Am I forgiven my reluctance to hurry? A year is not long and you may enjoy a season of courtship in London. It is not such an awful proposition, and I would rather we spent this year as friends if not betrothed."

Her smile held and her eyes sent him a mischievous look. "You are forgiven. But I expect you to be attentive when I come to London, and I will not deter the advances of other men. So you will have to be very attentive if you wish to keep me to yourself."

He laughed. "Very well I shall be attentive. I shall have Sarah to escort anyway so it will be no hardship, Alethea."

Her smile fell and her gaze left his eyes and passed across his shoulder, to look about the room while he turned her. "That is a poor answer, Henry. I expect you to wish to be attentive. You should desire it, and look forward to it, not think it will not be a hardship."

"I do wish it. Did I not invite you?"

84

She looked back at him, with one of her pretty pouts.

She was genuinely vexed with him.

"I am sorry. I wish you there very much, and I shall be attentive because I feel as though we ought to become closer before we make any decision that is final." He turned her steadily as he continued talking. "You did not answer my question the other night, and I assume from that your heart is not deeply involved. Do you not think that it should be?"

"I cannot allow it to be when you are so indifferent to me as to make me wait, and to live miles away from me in town."

"Precisely, and so this year I shall amend that. Let us see if we can find finer feelings within us. I think you attractive. You are very beautiful, and we have always been friends. Your company amuses me. With more time I am sure my emotions will grow and I shall work hard to ignite greater emotions within you."

She gave him the brightest of her smiles. "You shall have to work very hard then, and pay me a great deal of attention."

"I shall and I will. I promise. I shall even come home, here, regularly throughout the year, to see you."

"I shall be spoilt, then."

"Indeed. I shall spoil you. From the moment you come to London for the season." Without speaking the words which actually committed him, he had become committed regardless. But it was for the best. He could not put her off forever and he was willing to go ahead with the match, he had no objection to Alethea. Perhaps his responsibilities were catching up with him whether he willed it or not.

When the dance came to its conclusion he brought her hand to his lips and kissed the back of her fingers. She gave him another broad smile, which lit up her eyes. Her beauty caught him with a firm strike in the stomach. Yes, he had feelings for her, it ought not to be too much of a step for them to become finer.

Their parents still stood together, in conversation, and there was a young man with them. The young man looked directly at Alethea as they neared, and his gaze made it very obvious that he found her attractive too.

"Miss Forth." The young man stepped forward. Alethea's fingers slipped off Henry's arm and instead she offered her hand to the other gentleman. He bowed low over it, then straightened up. "May I have the honour of this dance?"

"Of course, Mr Graham."

Annoyance rattled up Henry's spine, and yet what had he thought Alethea had been doing while he'd been leading a merry dissipated life in town—sitting quietly at home—no of course she had not. She had been attending assemblies and meeting local, perfectly eligible, men.

She looked back at Henry. "Lord Marlow, this is Mr Graham, Mr Graham, Lord Henry Marlow." The introduction completed to a minimum, providing Henry with no information about his rival, Alethea then let Mr Graham lead her away, leaving Henry with their parents.

He turned to his aunt. "Where is Susan? Did she not come?"

"She was dancing, Henry. I'm not sure where she is now. Oh, she is in another set, there, look." He glanced back, following the direction of his aunt's pointed finger.

Susan stood opposite a gentleman who was dressed in the uniform of the local militia and she was smiling brightly. She laughed then, at something the man had said.

She was wearing a deep blue muslin and her hair was dressed with great skill, two ringlets had been crafted to fall either side of her face. When the dance began the ringlets bobbed and swayed with her movements as she skipped through the steps.

He had never seen her dancing, at least not that he could recall.

She smiled as she danced, and her colour was high. Even with the distance between them he could see that her eyes glittered as she held the gentleman's gaze through the lens of her spectacles.

She obviously did enjoy dancing.

She glowed when she danced.

The other night he had wondered what she would be like if she let down her guard—*like this*.

He was at a disadvantage here. Clearly Alethea and Susan were well known and popular in this local society he'd paid little attention to. But of course Alethea and Susan had been out for years. Perhaps that had been an error on his part. He'd not thought these people important. And when he was the earl…

Self-centered. Perhaps Susan had had a stronger point than he'd thought.

"Henry, may I introduce…" His father brought another couple towards him.

Whether he liked it or not this was as much his debut in society here as it was Sarah's.

"Hello…" He shook the hands of the men who approached, while the dancing continued; with the tune of the fiddle and pipe jigging in the air, as the feet of six dozen couples beat out the steps on the parquet floor.

When the dance ended, Alethea and Susan returned, on the arms of their partners. Henry was then introduced to Captain Morgan, Susan's companion. The man bowed to Henry then turned to ask Alethea to dance. Henry sensed that Mr Graham might also swap to the other sister. Henry held out his hand and pre-empted the man's chance. "May I have this dance, Susan?"

Her eyes spun to look at him with… shock.

They had never danced before, but he did not think he made such an awful option.

"I… Yes, of course." Colour flooded into her cheeks. She had truly not expected him to ask.

He supposed the only reason he had never considered dancing with her was because they had never been at a ball together—only at family gatherings when everyone retained their partners. Who had she danced with then? No one. It was why he had never seen her dance.

Damn it. Had she watched them dancing and felt left out?

Self-centered. Her accusation had hovered in his thoughts since it had been made, but tonight it was growing in its intensity.

She did not lay her hand on his arm but gripped his arm when they walked across the room.

The notes of a waltz began.

When he turned to face her, her pale grey eyes looked into his as he raised her hand and formed the hold. Her hair did look very pretty. She was pretty—simply in a different way to her sister. Alethea had a beauty that punched a man in the gut, Susan had qualities which whispered instead. "I have not seen you dance before."

"You have not attended an assembly or a local ball before."

"No." Her fingers clasped about his right hand, as his left hand settled on her back.

Holding her made him aware that she was a little thinner than her sister, her waist was narrower, it lacked the curve of Alethea's.

Her hand rested on his good shoulder. "How are your arm and your shoulder? They must be tiring. Do not dance too much. Your arm was only released from the sling three days ago."

"My shoulder is weak still, so you must therefore forgive me if my hold is limp by the end of the dance, and we end up being the most maligned couple."

She laughed, yet it was not as she had laughed with Captain Morgan. The laughter she saved for him was a polite response.

"Why have you never danced during family occasions?"

"Perhaps because no one ever asked me."

Was that said to make him feel guilty? No. Because she would expect him to dance with Alethea. "Were you hiding in corners there, so no one saw you sitting the dances out? You are not hiding here…"

The dance began and he turned her sharply, she moved beautifully, she was in fact lighter on her feet than Alethea, and yet her fingers held his hand and held his shoulder gently in a way no other woman he'd danced with had.

"I have no need to hide here, here I am asked to dance. There I refuse to play the wallflower and sit and watch."

"So you let your rebellious side free and go elsewhere. I presume to the library."

She laughed more genuinely. "Or the music room."

"I would favour the music room. A good pounding of a pianoforte can do wonders for the soul."

"You can play?"

"I keep it quiet. I am rebellious too, remember. I dread being asked to perform for others. I play for myself."

She smiled at him. "I would like to hear you."

"You would like to hear me so you might mock me. Which is precisely why I do not play for others. I do not care to know your opinion of my skill, or lack of it. The only ears I wish to please with my playing are my own."

"I would still like to hear you, because I would like to hear what you play for yourself. I think it would reveal some secrets of your character."

"So you can study me as you do the images of orchids in that book. No thank you. I'd rather not become your specimen." When they grew older, in their later years, he had always imagined that Susan would share his and Alethea's home, if she did not marry. He had never before thought that she would. But this evening…

She was more vibrant, more engaging… more beautiful. Her eyes spoke to him with lively enjoyment and emotion, as they turned.

"I think you make a rather good specimen to study. You have made Alethea smile again tonight. What did you say?"

"We have been discussing her going to London for the season and I have promised to be attentive and adoring."

89

"She told us you had suggested us coming to London. Mama intends to host a ball for us." Susan sounded as pleased by the idea as Alethea.

"I had never imagined you as a woman who would like a season in London, with all its fuss and parties, and balls."

"Why not, because I love to paint and enjoy studying your father's books? I can like dancing, art and books."

He laughed, because obviously it had been a bizarre assumption. "Yes."

She made a scolding face at him.

Yet, she was right, why should either thing mean she would not enjoy dancing. He'd called her rebellious, he'd sensed a trapped energy within her, dancing would quite obviously be one way for her to express that. "I apologise."

"I suppose it is no different from believing you deserved your injuries and refusing to feel sorry for you. I apologise too."

He smiled broadly at her. *Touché.* She was very sharp. "Yet you know when I gave up using my sling and Alethea did not, and so I know that you cared. So you have nothing to apologise for."

Her eyebrows, which were plucked into pretty narrow lines lifted above the brass wire frames of her spectacles. "Alethea did not know?"

He shook his head slightly. "She commented tonight on the lack of my sling."

"Oh. She was probably simply still too vexed with you. You pushed away her sympathy when you asked her to wait a year."

He laughed again. If Susan had talked this openly and honestly with the Captain he could understand the man's enjoyment of Susan's company, a soldier would appreciate a woman without airs.

"Your eyes are very unusual. Has anyone told you that?" It suddenly struck him. They were very bright when they looked at him so directly, full of joy. The grey was extremely pale, and in the light from the hundred or more candles burning in the chandeliers above them, her eyes had the quality of quick-silver.

Colour filled her cheeks. "Unusual…"

She was shocked. It was in her eyes once more.

"No… No one has said so. In what way?"

He'd never known a woman challenge a compliment before, and her voice expressed doubt, as though she expected him to say something awful in answer.

He smiled, broadly. He'd not even really known why he'd said it; it was just the way she had looked at him for a moment and her deep blue dress made the pale grey such a contrast, and against her dark eyelashes… He'd never looked into her eyes so closely before, that was all. "They are a very light grey. It was a compliment."

"To call my eyes grey is not a compliment."

"They are pretty, Susan."

She seemed to have no answer then, but coloured up once more and looked beyond his shoulder.

His gaze fell to the little flicker of her pulse in her neck. He had embarrassed her.

"When do you return to town?" she asked as they continued turning, typical Susan, not sulking and waiting for him to resolve the discomfort he'd created, but storming in to smash the ice away herself.

"Tomorrow."

She looked back at him—into his eyes. "Alethea will miss you."

"It is only a few weeks until the season, and then she will come to London, and she has chosen to avoid me for the last few days in any case."

"Not because she has not wished to see you, she is still a fully signed up member of the Henry Marlow Appreciation Society."

He stumbled in the turn and his arm lowered a little as the pain in his shoulder jarred. "The what?"

"The Henry Marlow Appreciation Society," she said it with a smile that teased him. "The group of people who are so thoroughly charmed by you they let you get away with anything you wish."

"We are back to the charge of me being self-centered then."

Her smile agreed and continued to mock him.

"Well I have promised your sister I shall court her in London so you may watch me laying on the charm to her in spades and breaking every notion you have created about me. I shall establish a new society, the Alethea Forth Appreciation Society and prove to you I can be selfless when I wish."

She laughed at him, in a carefree way, that he'd never heard before. Dancing changed her. It broke her out of her shell and what he'd known was within her shone out. When they had been in each other's' company as children she'd rarely laughed, she had more frequently simply disappeared, or squatted down to study some insect crawling through the grass.

When the waltz ended her hand slipped free from his, and lifted from his shoulder, his lingered at her back. "Shall we dance the next?"

"I did not know you were so keen a dancer?"

"I am keener to avoid the numerous introductions people wish my father to make."

"You coward."

"How many of these people do you know?"

"More than half," Susan replied as they followed others, crossing the room to form a set for a country dance. Susan glanced about her and smiled at a number of their companions.

"How often do you come to these?"

"Nearly every month." A frown line formed between her eyebrows when he stepped away to face her.

They stood looking at one another in silence, while others joined the line of their set. Then the dance began. It was a dance that was stepped more than skipped, Henry was glad that it was not so energetic; the pain in his shoulder was rising from an ache to bloody agony, consequently he did not lift it so high when they joined hands and made the first turn.

"Your shoulder is hurting…" she whispered.

"It is bearable."

"Why did you ask how regularly we come here?"

"For no particular reason."

"Did you think Alethea sits at home while you entertain yourself in town?"

She was mocking him once more—for his self-centered nature. He smiled as the dance separated them. No, he had not imagined Alethea sitting at home, he'd simply, carelessly, never thought about what she might be doing at all. He would think of it now.

When the dance came to its conclusion he offered his left arm to Susan, not his right, his shoulder ached too damn much.

Everyone turned to leave the floor, then, and the music did not progress.

She looked at him as she held his arm. Her touch twisted something in his stomach and something below it, that his future sister-in-law really ought not to stir.

"You ought not to dance anymore, even if it means facing introductions."

He'd known that, but it pleased him that she was concerned.

When he looked about the room everyone was walking from the floor towards the open doors at the end of the ballroom. "Where are they going?"

"To supper, that was the supper dance."

Oh, that meant he was obliged to join her for supper, but they could sit with Alethea. "Do you think Alethea will have saved us seats?"

There was another smile for him, of the ilk she had shared with Captain Morgan. "I am sure she will have, if only to ensure you may watch her flirt with her last dance partner."

"I am to appreciate Captain Morgan's company then." The

man had retained Alethea's hand for a second dance, as Henry had retained Susan's. "But that will carry little weight if it is meant to prod my jealousy, he danced with you first, so you must be his preference."

She had been looking forward; her head turned, her gaze spinning to him. Her eyes said she did not think herself capable of being anyone's preference.

That was just foolish.

"Alethea was already engaged to dance, I am her sister. He asked me for exactly the same reason you did, to be polite."

That was not why he had asked her.

"Susan!" Alethea called across the room. Alethea had saved two seats at her table.

Susan lifted her hand from Henry's arm.

~

"Susan…" Her mother tapped on the open door of Susan's bedchamber. Susan was sitting on the window seat, reading. She looked up as her mother came in.

"Henry has called to say his farewell."

The book she held dropped against her knees. "He will not wish to see me."

"He has agreed to stay to luncheon, and you must come down it would seem rude if you did not."

And one day you will have to play supplicant and never anger him because he will be keeping you out of charity, as the spinster sister of his wife.

Susan put the ribbon between the pages of her book to mark her place, then set the book aside and stood up.

"Henry was in very high spirits last evening," her mother commented as Susan slipped on her shoes, "and he does seem earnest regarding his affection for Alethea."

Susan crossed the room.

She had enjoyed dancing with him last night. He was a good dancer, even with a weak arm, and he had been pleasant company, he'd made her laugh, and taken her teasing with a solid chin. Then during supper he'd spoken to her as much as Alethea and Captain Morgan. She had discovered likable qualities in Henry during his visit this time.

And he did seem to be earnest in his attentions towards Alethea. Yet… Why did that thought make something heavy tumble through her, it should not make her feel melancholy.

She smiled at her mother, trying to hide the heavy feeling which had settled in her chest.

When they walked into the drawing room, Henry stood up, "Susan," and he actually walked across the room to take her hand and kiss it gently. He did not use his right hand, though.

"Is your shoulder still sore from dancing too much?"

He smiled slightly, and his eyes glittered. "It is yes."

"You are not driving yourself, I—"

"No. Have no fear. I am travelling in my father's carriage."

"You must not race your curricle until your shoulder is fully healed."

"I thought you did not like me to race it at all…"

"Henry…" Alethea clasped his upper arm. He winced as he let go of Susan's hand. Susan's gaze passed to her sister.

"Shall we go through to luncheon?" Alethea encouraged.

Susan stepped aside, so they might walk on ahead and then she walked behind them with her father, who had an expression of proud approval in his eyes, and she presumed the same emotion moved his lips, as the tips of his waxed moustache quivered.

Susan's fingers wrapped about her father's arm as she smiled too. It seemed there was hope for Alethea's happiness and perhaps Henry was growing up.

Alethea talked constantly to Henry as they sat beside each other at the table, yet their father continually broke into Alethea's and Henry's *tête-à-tête* to ask a question of Henry and a number of times Henry looked at Susan and brought her into the conversation with a comment. That was something he would not have done before, their relationship had changed during his visit home this time. They had learned to understand each other, not simply tolerate one another.

Each time he spoke to Susan it made her smile. He was making an effort to be kind to her—denying his natural leaning towards selfishness. Yet it was not selfishness really, merely that he had always been carelessly self-centered, never taking the time to look beyond his own interests and desires.

When he left he said goodbye to Susan's father first, shaking his hand, then her mother hugged him firmly and he kissed her mother's cheek. Next he took both of Alethea's hands and leant and kissed her cheek. The colour in Alethea's cheeks lifted to a pale pink.

Then Henry turned to Susan. "Goodbye." He held out his hand, waiting for hers to be placed within it. It was not a gesture that was common between them. When she set her hand in his he bowed over it. Even the way he touched people had a particular charm, it captured all her senses. But then of course, even though he had put his gloves back on, she was without gloves, and so the sensations were stronger.

"Goodbye." Her response came out on a breath, with a powerless sound.

"We shall dance and spar again in London, I am sure," he whispered with a smile.

She smiled too as he let go of her hand.

He turned to Alethea again. "Will you walk outside with me?"

She took his right arm, and the two of them walked out of the door, to the carriage.

"Let us leave them to have a moment's privacy." Susan's father stated turning away to return to his study and his business.

"Come along." Susan's mother wrapped an arm about Susan's. "Shall we walk outside in the rear garden and discover what new flowers have begun to bud."

Susan pulled her arm free. "I left my shawl in the drawing room. I'll need it. I'll just fetch it." She hurried away, in a manner that was more like her mother's and Alethea's.

But within the drawing room Susan did not go to the sofa to collect her shawl, but walked to the window. It was as though she felt the pull of empathy, and yet it could not be empathy, he was healed. Her fingers lifted and touched the glass as she looked at the carriage in the driveway. Henry was holding both of Alethea's hands and speaking with an earnest expression, while Alethea looked at him her eyes wide, expressing her happiness.

He leant then and kissed her lips, just for an instant.

Was that their first kiss? If it was then perhaps Alethea would speak of it later, but Susan would not admit she'd watched, she should not be watching.

They held hands for a few moments more, then Henry climbed into the carriage. Alethea remained on the drive watching and waving as it drew away.

Susan imagined Henry waving his goodbye from within.

He'd said during luncheon, when she had asked about Samson, that Uncle Robert had told him Samson's habit was to lay in the hall for weeks after Henry had left, hoping for his return. The poor dog may have months to wait.

She would see Henry again in six weeks, at the ball their mother was organising in London. Six weeks seemed a long time away too.

Chapter Nine

Susan looked out of the window at the grand houses lining the street. She had been to her parents' home in London before, but this year was different. This year they were to take part in the season.

"I told Henry we are arriving today. I said in my letter I wished him to call upon us. I hope he calls..."

Henry had written to Alethea weekly since returning to town. He had changed his ways and begun acting with some responsibility, and thought for Alethea. His intent and commitment to pursue their engagement had become clear.

But Susan was looking forward to seeing him too. Alethea had shared stories from his letters and Susan had not been able to forget the amusing Henry whom she'd danced and talked with when he'd come home last. She had been officially charmed and would now shamefully even admit herself to be a member of the Henry Marlow Appreciation Society.

She smiled to herself as she continued to look out of the window.

There was one small issue, though, she was not certain if it was really his dancing and conversation that had charmed her, or if, in fact, seeing his injuries when he had been half naked had swayed her, and watching him sleep in his shirt and trousers within a room with the door shut. He had looked so vulnerable then. The sense of empathy she'd known in that moment still hovered inside her. She could not forget how he'd looked when he'd been suffering.

The carriage rocked and creaked as it rolled over the cobbles, and from outside there were the noises of the horses, other carriages and people.

When they arrived before their town house, her father climbed out first and then lifted a hand to help her mother out, then Alethea, and then with a smile he held his hand out to help Susan. She smiled at him. The tips of his waxed moustache lifted higher. Excitement skipped through Susan's senses as her heart pumped hard in her chest, she was looking forward to the balls, but she was looking forward to visiting museums and galleries too. Alethea had promised to accompany her on some explorations. They had not been to town for two years.

Henry arrived at the house at four. Two hours after they had arrived. Susan leaned over the bannister and looked down as Alethea hurried down the stairs into the hall. He'd come with his cousin, Harry, who was an officer in the army. Harry was dressed in his scarlet regimentals. Henry was in black and grey.

Henry gripped Alethea's hands and then kissed each one.

Susan walked downstairs more sedately than her sister. Her mother and father were in the hall too.

Harry had stepped forward to take one of Alethea's hands and was bowing over it. Henry looked up. His gaze immediately caught on Susan's and clung to it as she walked down.

She smiled.

He smiled in return and the emotion lit up his eyes.

Yes, she had joined the Henry Marlow Appreciation Society. Yet there was no need for him to know it.

When Harry let go of Alethea's hand, Susan looked at him. He looked very smart in his uniform. She had not seen him since he'd become an officer. But he was the son of Uncle Robert's brother, her like-an-uncle Uncle Edward. Like Henry, Harry had been brought up so close to them it had felt as though he was their cousin. "Hello, Harry, I have not seen you for an age." As she stepped off the bottom stair and held her hands out towards him. Harry came forward.

She sensed Henry still watching her but she did not turn to look.

Harry kissed the backs of her fingers. His lips were warm and her hands cold.

Susan remembered the kiss Henry had given Alethea when they'd last seen each other, and wondered how warm a man's lips would feel against hers.

Harry smiled heartily at her, he had always been an easy, jovial companion, if perhaps a little wild, very much like Henry, except less self-centered. "How are you, Susan?"

"Very well thank you, and you? How do you like the life of a soldier?"

"It is nothing but revelry."

"You are entirely suited to it then."

She glanced at Henry. He was still watching her. "Hello, Henry." Her voice was cheery but dismissive, cooled by a sudden awkward feeling. The memory of her feeling of empathy was no longer within her, instead it was as though her insides had been hollowed out. Henry was no longer ill, he was healthy and virile and smiling at her in a way he'd never done before. It bore a resemblance to the way he smiled at Alethea.

Harry let her hands slip free from his. She bobbed the slightest of curtsies in Henry's direction, avoiding moving closer and offering her hand. She could not bear for him to touch her at that moment; the hollow feeling had made her stomach queasy in a disconcerting way. If he touched her, she might vomit.

"Shall we go into the drawing room and take tea," her mother invited.

"Susan," Harry offered his arm.

She took it willingly and gripped it gently. They walked ahead of the others. "Have you been wicked of late or has becoming a soldier dulled you?"

He laughed. "Not at all, I am still very capable of wickedness, but I suppose nothing has livened you up either. I would wager you still have your head buried in books most of the day, and I suppose you have not come to London for the entertainments but to discover what might be learned. Well I have a sennight's leave so I shall offer myself up as an escort if you wish, to ensure you are pleased with your visit to town. What about the new Victoria and Albert Museum, have you been there? Or would you care to go?"

She looked at him. "I have not been and I'd love to go, Harry, thank you."

"We should go as a four." Henry said behind them.

Susan glanced back at Alethea, museums and galleries were not her favourite places and yet she had promised to accompany Susan.

Alethea smiled at Susan, then looked at Henry. "That is a wonderful idea."

Of course his presence would mean that Alethea need not look at the artefacts or the art work but focus on charming Henry.

Susan sent Henry a quick smile, then looked at Harry again as they walked on. He began educating her on what she should expect of her visit to town.

Perhaps the balls would be more fun than she had expected, with Harry to play escort, and he had numerous cousins on his mother's side whom she knew to various degrees, and so she might even have enough partners to keep her dancing.

When they sat in the drawing room, drinking tea, Alethea talked with Henry and occasionally threw a teasing comment at Harry. But mostly their conversations remained separate, except that every time Susan looked at Alethea and Henry, Henry always happened to be watching her and caught her looking. On occasions his lips quirked up at the corner, yet at other times he merely looked back at Alethea.

"We should leave." Henry stated after almost an hour, and rose. "I would not wish to outstay our welcome."

"You are welcome to stay for as long as you wish," Alethea answered standing too.

Henry gave her a warm, charming smile. "I must go, though, Harry and I are due to meet others at our club."

He arranged to take Alethea out driving in his curricle the following day, and then Harry suggested that the day after should be for their excursion to the Victoria and Albert Museum.

"Yes, let's," Susan gripped Harry's hand as it lay on the sofa beside hers, his hand turned over beneath hers and squeezed her fingers for a moment.

"But that will be the morning after Mama's ball and I shall be too tired to do the outing justice," Alethea complained.

Susan's head turned to look at her sister, but instead her gaze caught on Henry. He was looking at hers and Harry's joined hands. He looked up. She slipped her hand free of Harry's.

"Then the next day," Harry said.

"Yes, if you wish," Alethea agreed.

Susan turned sideways on the sofa to face Harry, so she would not be inclined to look at Henry. "I shall look forward to it more than the ball."

"I thought you might like the idea, book-head."

She smiled as Harry stood, and then she stood too.

Alethea wrapped her arms about Henry's neck and kissed his cheek. It was a forward gesture but they were to be engaged. Henry pressed a kiss on Alethea's cheek in return.

Susan looked at Harry.

He held her hand and bowed over it. "Thank you for your pleasant company and conversation, Susan."

"I might say the same." She gave him a bright smile.

102

"May I claim the first dance at your mother's ball?"

"Oh, do. Then I will know I shall not be left to stand awkwardly at the edge of the room at least for the first dance. I know no one in town but you, your family and father's and mother's friends."

"Then I promise I will ensure you are not left to stand awkwardly at the edge of the room for the entire night, as you know the Pembroke family are a horde and I know many people in town. I shall shower you with introductions."

"Thank you." She wished to embrace him. It was a long time since she had seen Harry, and she had forgotten how nice he could be. His mother and father did not live near hers, and so she had not seen Harry's family as much as Uncle Robert's and Aunt Jane's.

"Susan." Henry stood beside her, he'd come across the room to take his leave of her.

Harry turned to Alethea as Henry took Susan's hand. How could his grip be so firm and yet so poignantly gentle? He bowed and lifted the back of her fingers to his lips. "It is a pleasure seeing you again. May I have the second dance tomorrow evening, before Harry introduces you to half of London? I am to dance the first and the supper dance with Alethea."

Susan bobbed a very slight curtsy. "Why thank you, my Lord, I graciously accept."

A smile broke his lips apart then he laughed uncertainly. "I shall look forward to it, Susan." He let her hand go and bowed again, then turned to Harry. "Come on."

They strode from the room, talking to each other in low voices, the aura of virile energy surrounding them left the room too. Susan felt drawn to follow them out, the empathy she'd known for Henry before had become a magnetic pull. Instead she looked at Alethea.

"He came, just as he promised." She smiled.

Yes, it seemed Henry had turned over a new leaf in his behaviour towards Alethea at least.

Susan and Alethea sat down once more, and began discussing the preparations for the ball.

An odd sensation sent Susan's heartbeat skipping into a faster rhythm. Her spirits had never been so keen for the date of a ball to come, but she refused to heed the words inside her that attributed it to Henry's offer to dance with her again. She would not accept that she had become that far absorbed into the Henry Marlow Appreciation Society. It was not, it was because she would be able to dance in her parents' grand ballroom.

~

Henry flicked the straps and set his horses off into a trot. Harry leaned back against the seat of Henry's racing curricle, and lay an arm along the seatback behind Henry.

Harry had been at Henry's father's house, with his parents, when Henry had called there before calling on the Forths. When Henry had said where he was going next, Harry had invited himself along, declaring that he'd not seen Lord Forth's girls for an age. Of course that was not surprising because they had not come to London, but remained in Yorkshire as Alethea had been relying on a promise from *him*.

Henry flicked the straps again and lifted the horses' pace into a canter along a clear stretch of the street. He could not get an image of Susan out of his head, it had been the moment she'd come downstairs. He'd looked up and caught her gaze. He'd forgotten just how striking her eyes were when she wore a darker blue than Alethea. The sight had struck him in the middle of his chest, not just in his gut and his groin. Damn. It was a strange feeling.

The image of her gripping Harry's hand as they'd talked cut through his thoughts. He glanced at his cousin, as he returned the horses to a trot when they neared a crossroads. "Do you like Susan?"

"Of course, they are pleasant girls."

"No I mean do you *like* Susan? Is there an attraction there?"

Harry's arm slipped free from the back of the seat and he sat forward, resting his elbows on his thighs as he stared at Henry. "If you are asking me, am I considering matrimony as you are? Then the answer is a firm bloody, no. Of course not. What would I want with a wife? I am more than happy as I am. I would much rather be me, than you. I was merely being friendly towards Susan because I like her, nothing more. Why? You are not her brother-in-law yet?"

Henry looked at the road as they turned into a busier street. "It was only that you seemed overly attentive."

"I was flirting. Women love a chance to flirt. It is harmless and fun. I flirt with every woman. You know that of me…"

Yes, he did. But watching Harry flirt with Susan had been annoying, he'd never been annoyed by Harry's flirting before.

"Will you be at Madam's tonight? I've not seen you there since I came to town…"

Henry glanced over. Harry and several of his cousins consorted with the same women, at the same brothels. They had done so for years. Henry could not even remember which of them had introduced him to that set, but he'd been involved in it since he'd attended university in Oxford. "No. I have not been going. I am no longer interested." There, the statement was made. It was the first time he'd spoken it aloud and declared his budding responsibility to his friends.

"Why?" Harry asked, abruptness and doubt catching in his voice.

Henry glanced across at him. "Is it not obvious? Alethea is in town. I am courting her. I cannot consort with whores at the same time."

"Ha." Harry exclaimed. "Most men would."

Well then, obviously Henry was not as bad as his father thought. He was not most men. He smiled. "Well, I will not. I have discovered a conscience."

Harry laughed loudly, and heartily.

Henry did not.

His period in Yorkshire had educated him. If he was serious about marrying Alethea he could not continue to be reckless, careless and selfish, as Susan had charged, and keep Alethea waiting. She had other options and she would follow them. He had moved on to the next era in his life; a sensible era, during which he would court and marry Alethea, settle himself down in Yorkshire and become a responsible husband and son. He had accepted his future.

~

There was a commotion outside. Susan looked out of the window. Henry had arrived.

"He is here." Alethea stood.

Alethea had been full of nervous excitement all morning. It was the first time she had been officially courted by Henry. Susan smiled, denying the burning in her chest which hinted at jealousy. The emotion had prodded her with its vindictive, whispered taunts all night.

When Alethea left the room, Susan looked out of the window. She could see Henry's curricle. Was that the one he'd fallen from, or another, a new one?

After a short while Alethea and Henry appeared from the house and walked towards the carriage. He'd brought a groom with him to hold the horses, and presumably to play silent chaperon.

Alethea hadn't said where Henry was taking her, presumably to Hyde Park.

Henry held Alethea's hand solicitously as she climbed up on to the high, open, sporting carriage, then he smiled before he turned to walk around to the driver's seat.

He patted one horse on the rump as he passed it, then brushed a hand along the other's cheek as he walked around the animals' heads. On the driver's side, he gripped the handles of the carriage and climbed up, energetically. His shoulder looked fully healed.

When Henry picked up the reins, his groom let go of the horses and then ran to the back of the carriage, gripped a bar and jumped up to stand on a footplate as Henry pulled away.

Alethea was talking and gesturing with her hands. Henry looked at her and nodded.

A sharp, cruel pain pierced through Susan's chest.

It was not fair. The words slipped through her head. But they were wrong. Henry was Alethea's. He had always been Alethea's. Her spirits may have suddenly decided to favour him too, but nothing could change no matter what she felt, she had no right to feel jealous.

Chapter Ten

Henry arrived at the Forths' ball with his parents. Society would realise tonight that there were plans for the two families to be joined.

He handed his hat to a footman then followed his father and mother towards the receiving line. The ballroom beyond it was not overly full, his family had arrived early, as he was to open the dancing with Alethea.

He bowed over Aunt Julie's hand. "Good evening."

"It is a pleasure to have you here, Henry."

The Forths' had held a ball each year, even though Susan and Alethea had never come to town with them for the season before. Henry had never attended those balls, he'd mostly avoided his family's social circles and spent his time with Harry and his friends in bawdy houses and clubs.

"Uncle Casper." Henry bowed slightly to Lord Forth. Then he reached Alethea.

She smiled very brightly, with the flirtatious smile she saved for him. "Hello."

When he took her hand she lowered into a deep formal curtsy. Their drive in Hyde Park had been enjoyable, she had a zest for life and an easy humour. There was no doubt that if they wed they'd suit. "Alethea." He bowed and kissed the back of her fingers. "I shall see you in a while, for the first dance."

He received another bright, flirtatious smile. Then he moved on.

Good Lord.

The sight of Susan struck him in the chest with a hard thump. Her hair had been styled again and it was magnificently done, it had been lifted from the back of her neck and dressed high on her head, yet a single coil had been trained to fall over her left shoulder. His fingers itched to touch it, and to touch the pale skin of her nape. But most strikingly… "You are not wearing your spectacles…"

"You need not say it as though it is a miracle. I have not regained my eyesight, Alethea merely persuaded me to leave them off; she said it ruined the look of my hair."

"Can you see without them?"

She smiled at him, a very honest natural smile. "I can see you very clearly now, but if you decide to nod at me from across the room later, do not expect me to respond, you will be nothing but a blur."

He smiled at her jesting, as he took hold of her hand. She lowered into a formal curtsy as Alethea had done. "I have already told you your eyes are pretty whether you have your spectacles on or not, but I agree with Alethea, with your hair, so, you look far better leaving them off. You have been hiding your beauty, Susan."

She pulled her hand free from his before he had the chance to consider kissing it, and coloured up. He smiled again and walked on, as she looked at the next guest who'd lined up to be introduced.

The girls would know everyone in London by the end of the night. But that was the purpose of hosting a ball to introduce your daughters. It was a method by which they might then dance with all of the men who came to such events without fearing that they had not already met.

Henry followed his father into the ballroom. They walked over to where his uncle and aunt stood. Harry's parents. Henry did not see Harry, though, but it was as rare for Harry to attend such events as it had been for Henry a year ago, and yet he had promised to dance with Susan.

"Is Harry still planning to attend, Edward?"

"He is, yet he is arriving independently because God forbid that he should be seen with us."

Henry smiled. He liked his uncle Edward. "Ellen." He bowed to his aunt.

She nodded at him. "You look very handsome, Henry, and you are such a rare sight at balls you will have half the young women fainting."

He gave her a wry look and shook his head. They knew that he was promised to Alethea.

He looked at his cousins, Helen and Jennifer. The two girls were inseparable.

They'd been brought out into society together even though there was a year between them, because Helen had waited until she may share the event with Jennifer.

"Hello, Henry." Helen curtsied. He bowed and kissed her hand.

"Henry." Jennifer performed her curtsy.

They had the sort of closeness which meant they would finish each other's sentences. Any one who did not know would think them twins. He smiled. The man who married one must like the other or they would not be married at all.

"Harry is here, Papa," Helen said.

Henry looked across his shoulder. Harry was at the end of the receiving line bowing over Susan's hand as he lifted it to his lips. She smiled broadly at him when he straightened and he hung on to her fingers for a moment and flashed her a smile after she'd said something. Then he moved on. Three of Harry's cousins from Aunt Ellen's sisters followed him; William Wiltshire, who had the courtesy title of Marquis, as heir to his father's dukedom, Gregory Stewart who was the heir to an earldom, like Henry, and Frederick Rush another who already held the courtesy title of Marquis.

All of them were men who Henry and Harry socialised with constantly in the clubs and brothels. In fact, it was probably where they had come from.

One by one they progressed along the receiving line. The Forths were very close friends of William's parents too. They had known both sides of Harry's family for years. Henry supposed that was why his friends had all crept out of the crevices of London society to see the girls.

Henry wondered if they knew of his particular interest. He had never mentioned it but Harry might have. They each bowed over Alethea's hand, and then bowed over Susan's. Something sharp gripped in Henry's gut when Susan laughed. He hated seeing her laugh for others, when she had kept that part of herself from him for years—which was a selfish, foolish thought. But Harry had been correct the other day, Henry had no right to care what Susan did.

Henry sighed and looked away.

Yet if Susan and Alethea knew the true nature of the men who kissed their hands… But if they did they would know his history too, and that was not a good thought.

When his father had said he regretted his past, Henry had mocked the idea. He was learning to understand the sentiment and mock his own bloody-minded ignorance.

He looked back at Jennifer and Helen. "If you will excuse me, I shall join Harry."

Before he made it across the room, though, the orchestra began to play the tune of a waltz. His aim then became a need to collect Alethea.

William had completed his greetings and left the receiving line, but he turned back too and when Henry reached the girls

William was taking Susan's hand. He must have volunteered himself for the first dance with her.

"The first dance was mine, Susan!" Harry had returned too. "You cannot renege on me. Fair is fair, I shall not let you play so fast and loose."

Susan smiled. Alethea stepped about them leaving the others to argue over Susan's hand.

Alethea's turquoise blue eyes shone in the light thrown by the giant chandelier above them as the music swelled and filled the room. Henry took her hand and led her out into the middle of the floor, then held her as he ought for the dance, and began to turn her.

He looked about to ensure they were not likely to collide with anyone else dancing.

Harry had reclaimed his place as Susan's partner and was walking her out on to the floor. She had that light in her eyes that only seemed to shine in a ballroom. When Harry formed the hold of the waltz, Susan had her back turned to Henry. The way her hair was dressed, so high, it showed off her neck to perfection. Her neck was a little longer than Alethea's and while the single coil of hair curled like a serpent about one side, the other was bare and *waiting to be kissed...*

Henry swallowed back the thought, but whoever had dressed her hair had done so deliberately to place an emphasis on the extreme femininity of her nape, and because she was a little thinner than Alethea the fragility of that spot was accentuated without any aid.

"I am so excited. I cannot wait..." Alethea said. Henry ceased day-dreaming and turned his attention back to Alethea. Yet—he could not stop thinking about Susan, and seeing her in his head. He stared into Alethea's very pretty eyes, yet it was Susan's eyes that appeared in his mind.

He bowed over Alethea's hand when the dance ended, and was about to walk her back to Uncle Casper and Aunt Julie, when a man who was older than him, who Henry did not know by name, came to escort her for the next dance. A jolt struck through Henry at the thought of a stranger dancing with Alethea, and yet numerous strangers had danced with her at the assembly in York. Or rather, people who had been strangers to him.

"Lord Stourton," Alethea acknowledged.

He left Alethea to the stranger, as she had obviously been introduced, and looked for Susan. He had promised Susan the second dance.

Harry had walked her back to her parents and was conversing with them.

Henry walked over there. At the same moment he saw William approach her. Damn.

"This is my dance I believe, Susan," Henry said when he reached her, his gaze on her profile. She had turned to face William. She smiled at William then turned to Henry.

He waited for the moment when she would try to renege on him. She looked very different without her spectacles, less dignified but somehow more... more... *touchable*.

She smiled. "It is."

Those eyes were as striking as the image he'd held in his mind while dancing with Alethea—he had not imagined their exceptional quality.

It was a country dance. He wished it was another waltz, he had not forgotten their dance in York. She was very good at dancing the waltz.

She accepted his arm, and held it gently, as she always did, in the way only she did. He wondered if she knew that most women merely lay their hand on a gentleman's arm. "William." Henry bowed his head towards his friend. William smiled wryly. Henry then threw a smile at Harry. Harry sent him a conspiratorial smile back, he had enjoyed his waltz with Susan too.

Henry led her to join a set which made an eight. He could

113

have joined the set Alethea and her partner stood within. He had not.

"You are looking very well," he said when Susan let go of his arm.

"Because I am not wearing spectacles." She smiled. The charm of her ballroom smile struck him in the gut—and the chest. Why was she so different in a ballroom?

"When you let a maid style your hair it looks…" What? Prettier? Every woman's hair was prettier when it was styled for an evening affair. More grown up… *More tempting*… He longed to touch her nape, to clasp his fingers about that delicate curve, but not only that, it made him wish to pull her lips to his. "I like your hair like that." Was the only thought he let escape his mouth.

"Thank you." She gave him a little mocking curtsy.

He breathed in, he should not be thinking such things, Susan was Alethea's sister. He was supposed to be establishing more responsible behaviour—and it had been Susan spurring him that had encouraged his change of heart.

Yet it was only instinct—it was simply the attraction that a woman's body wove about a man. Nothing more. It was what he must learn to overcome if he was to become a married man.

He took his position opposite Susan, awaiting the commencement of the dance, and thought of Susan leaning over her orchid paintings, focused on the task, and then playing the pianoforte, lost in the music, and now… When the dance began she smiled at him gleefully, enthusiastic and excited. He smiled too and threw himself into the dance and lost himself in watching her. Susan was a rare woman. There were not many who had such variety to their nature. He would think of her as she thought of the flowers. As something to appreciate with the mind of an artist.

When the dance came to its end, William approached them before they had reached her parents. "Is it my turn at last? Am I free to dance with you without stepping on anymore toes, Susan?"

She smiled at him. "You may claim me, William."

Her fingers let go of Henry's arm and when she walked away she threw one of her ballroom smiles across her shoulder.

The lack of her grip left a strange sensation.

He turned around and looked about, not really sure what to do. A sense of bereavement caught at him. It was bizarre, yet he felt deserted, empty now Susan had gone.

He swallowed back the odd feeling in his throat. He did not care to dance the next. Fred, another of his friends and Harry's cousins, stood near by. Henry walked across the room, collected a glass of champagne from the tray of a passing footman and joined his friend.

While they talked he watched both Susan and Alethea dancing. Alethea was always bright and jolly, there was nothing surprising in her manner, or the smiles she gave to her partners. But Susan… She expressed a depth of vibrancy when she danced that was entirely abnormal for her nature. She had hidden her true self for years, either that or he had been blind.

Harry joined Henry and Fred as the dancing continued. "Susan is in fine spirits tonight," Harry said, smiling at Henry. "I did not know she could dance so well, nor smile so brightly. The girl is a charm. I do not remember her so when we were children."

"She was not so," Henry replied. "She has hidden in corners ever since I have known her."

"She is not hiding anymore," William jested as he joined them too, having relinquished Susan to another partner.

They all looked at her then, watching her take her position in a new set.

Alethea was the eldest and the one they'd all deemed prettiest for years, the one they'd all hovered near when the girls were with them, while Susan had backed away and eventually left the room.

"She's a good waltzer," Harry added with a laugh.

"I should dance with her too then. If we are to spend the night

115

extolling Susan's charms then I ought to experience them," Fred quipped, mocking them all. "If I am to waste an evening at this ball I might as well appreciate the scenery."

"You must," Harry answered.

Discomfort twisted within Henry's stomach. They had had conversations over preferences like this when discussing whores, it was uncomfortable to hear them discuss Susan.

Henry felt as though he owned both the Forth girls, his instinct was to be as protective over them as he would be over Sarah when she made her debut.

Self-centered Susan had accused. He was, but now his selfishness absorbed Alethea and her. Yet, careless... He did not feel careless anymore.

When the supper dance came he claimed Alethea again, this time for a country dance. He enjoyed the dance immensely, he could find no fault with her at all, she fit well within London's society, she would make a very good countess.

When he led her into dine she spoke of her other dancing partners, all excitement, but he sensed that her jubilant descriptions were designed to spur his jealousy and probably a hastier proposal. She need not waste her breath, he'd not bend on his desire to wait a year.

Susan had danced with Harry again, so they came to join Henry and Alethea, and therefore so did Fred, Greg and William.

They made up a jolly, flirtatious table. Alethea glowed in the company of so many young gentlemen all vying for attention. Susan however became more silent, and spoke mostly to Harry who sat beside her.

Henry had a feeling that if she had a choice she would have taken the opportunity to hide.

"How is your flower painting progressing, Susan?" Henry asked from across the table. "Did you master that book?"

She looked across at him and blushed. She was not easy in company still, no matter that she enjoyed dancing. "My skill has improved. I am much better than I was. But I have not copied them all yet."

"What flowers? What book?" Fred asked leaning more towards her.

Susan began an explanation of her desire to be able to paint images with more detail. Now she had a subject she was comfortable with she conversed more easily, but Alethea then seemed out of sorts.

Henry looked at her and began a private conversation about things they might do together while she was in town. She had always loved to be the centre of attention; perhaps that was why Susan had grown up the shier of the two.

After they had eaten, when the dancing began, Henry stood to the side and watched the girls. They danced four dances without sitting down, he left his friends and walked about the edge of the ballroom, to reach Uncle Casper. Aunt Julie and his parents, who had spent most of the night together. He could not dance with Alethea again, but he could dance with Susan once more.

"Hello, Son, how is your night progressing?" His father gripped his shoulder.

"Good," Henry answered looking across the room as Susan skipped down the centre of a set with a partner he did not know.

"I saw you taking supper with Alethea…"

"Yes."

"She seems very happy…"

"Yes."

"She looks very pleased that you encouraged her to come for the season…"

"Yes."

The dance came to its end.

"Excuse me, Papa." He left his father and crossed the room to meet Susan, before another man might ask her.

"May I have your hand as a partner for the next?" he said

117

when she looked towards him. She stood about three feet away. The notes of a waltz began.

"Yes," she answered, before looking at another gentleman and smiling an apology, as though she had expected him to ask for her hand. The man walked away as Henry stepped forward.

Henry held out his hand. She accepted it, and he lifted it into position, preparing to dance as her other hand rested on his shoulder. His hand settled at her back, his thumb running along the upper curve of her spine, and he looked into those silver eyes. He'd always felt some level of attraction for Alethea… but for Susan… *there was a sudden desperate hunger.*

Because he had never looked at her properly until this spring. The excuse swept through him. But he ought not to feel anything like that for his future sister-in-law, he ought to feel what he had always felt—nothing.

He turned Susan into a spin, without saying a word, and yet he would swear there were words in her eyes, and probably words in his. They were not the words of an artist's description. He'd never speak them.

Neither of them spoke through the entire dance, yet her gaze held his, looking into his eyes as though she sought an answer, while he stared at her with a sense of awe.

When the dance came to an end he breathed in and stepped out of a dream, breaking whatever spell had surrounded them.

"Will you take me back to my father, I think I will sit out the next, I am exhausted, and I would like a glass of something." Her hands slipped from his shoulder and his hold as she stepped back, away from him.

He moved beside her, his hand lifting to hover behind her back when they began walking. "What would you prefer, lemonade or punch? I will fetch you a glass."

"I'd rather lemonade, but Alethea would welcome punch, I'm sure."

"Yes." He brought his arm forward, offering her his forearm

as they walked from the floor. She gripped it gently. Her touch did things to his innards that it really ought not do.

He bowed to her slightly before he left her with their parents, then turned away and breathed deeply, trying to draw some sense into his head.

When he returned, Alethea was with her parents too, and so he and Alethea sat out the next dance together, talking.

He had invited Alethea to town to court her, not to develop an attraction for her sister. This emotion was the height of recklessness. When he was trying so hard to be responsible.

~

Alethea set her candle down beside Susan's bed and slipped between the sheets, lying down beside Susan and she rested her head on Susan's pillow, so they lay facing one another. "Who was the best dance partner that you had?"

Susan took a breath, *Henry*, she could think of nothing but his eyes as they'd looked into hers while they'd waltzed. "Harry," she answered as Alethea turned to blow out the candle.

The scent of the burnt wick carried on the air when the room dropped into darkness.

"Mine was Henry, which is good I suppose…" Alethea said as the mattress moved when she lay back down.

"He is a good dancer," Susan confirmed.

"I saw he waltzed with you too."

"Yes." Susan was glad of the darkness.

"He is being more thoughtful. He is being generous."

"Yes."

"And kind to you…" The words were whispered into the dark.

"Yes."

"I like him more than ever and I believe he is really trying, but I will not let him think he has won me. I wish him to be on his guard and trying hard to win me. He owes me that."

119

"Yes."

"We are well suited. We laugh all the time. Yet I enjoyed the company of every man I danced with tonight, and it only proved to me how many men there are to be met in London, and I might laugh with any number of them."

"Yes…"

Chapter Eleven

Susan's hands trembled a little when she tied the ribbons of her bonnet, in her room, as she prepared to go down to the hall to meet Henry and Harry for their excursion to the Victoria and Albert Museum. She had thought of nothing else but Henry in the hours since their last waltz. Her mind was full of him, and it was more than appreciation. She was not a fool.

She ought not to be thinking of him at all. He was Alethea's beau.

Yet she had become fixated upon the memory of that waltz, upon the detail she had seen in his eyes as they'd stared at one another; upon the sensation of his thumb caressing her back as his hand had braced her, and his hand gently but securely holding hers.

She had no idea how to greet him today. Her tongue might not form a single word. She had become a flustered fool.

She sighed out her breath. The only thing to do was walk downstairs and behave as though nothing had changed.

But everything had changed.

She'd been entirely charmed by Henry, *and I cannot be, he's Alethea's.*

She stared at herself in the mirror. "Stop thinking of him!" But he would not be ordered from her mind.

A gentle tap struck the door of her bedchamber. "Miss!"

"Yes!" Susan called.

The door handle turned and the door opened. "Lord Henry and Captain Marlow are downstairs, miss." Yes, she knew. She had heard Henry's curricle draw up, and Alethea call down the stairs.

"Thank you. Let them know I will be down directly."

The maid left and Susan looked at herself in the mirror once more. However she was to face Henry, the time had come.

She picked up her cloak and slipped it over her arm to carry it down as she left the room. When she reached the stairs she could hear Alethea below, speaking with Henry and Harry.

Susan's heartbeat raced as she walked down the stairs to the reception hall. Alethea stood facing Harry.

Henry looked up as Susan walked down from the last landing, and his gaze struck hers. It was as though he'd slapped her it struck her so firmly. She had not imagined the look in his eyes while they had danced, he was not merely looking at her, his gaze said something else. But it was not the glitter that she had always seen in his eyes when he looked at Alethea.

He smiled. She smiled, and then he looked away, at Alethea.

Did he know how she felt? She hoped he did not.

"You have taken your time," Alethea accused.

"Sorry I was absorbed in my book. I had forgotten the hour." *Liar*. She had been counting down the minutes since Henry had said goodnight to them after the ball.

When she stepped from the bottom stair, Harry came forward. "Good day, Susan, I hope you are looking forward to our outing as much as I?"

"Very much." She smiled, only looking at him, and trying to think only of him. But she had not felt the same emotions she had for Henry when she'd danced with Harry, or anyone else.

"Let me take your cloak." He took it from her arm, her fingers trembled when she pushed her spectacles farther up her nose, before turning so Harry might set her cloak on her shoulders. Then she turned to let Harry tie the cords for her. Her gaze caught Henry watching, as his arm lifted out towards Alethea.

Today would be torture.

"Susan." Henry bowed his head slightly.

"Henry." She bowed her head too.

That minimal level of communication between her and Henry became the theme of the day. She shared only odd words with him, with a stilted politeness, while about those words Henry chatted amiably with Alethea, and Susan with Harry, and Harry with them all.

If Harry or Alethea noticed Henry's and Susan's awkwardness, they said nothing, but it was the way Henry and Susan had spoken to each other throughout their childhood, so perhaps it did not seem strange.

Harry was excellent company, though, and a handsome companion, and he laughed liberally and smiled constantly, jesting about and exclaiming over the displays. He made Susan laugh frequently as she tried her hardest not to look at Henry, even though she sensed him looking at her often.

"Look at this," Harry pointed at a sculpted stone frieze in the exhibition hall they were exploring. She turned to look but as she did her gaze struck Henry's. The deep brown quality of his eyes shot a bullet through her heart. He looked away as she turned to face Harry again.

Harry's eyes were a pale blue, like Aunt Ellen's, but the colour of his brown hair and his looks were Uncle Edward's. All of the Marlows were handsome to the point there was an edge that struck a person. If you walked past any of them in the street you would look back to make sure you had not imagined them.

He smiled at her, "You have very pretty eyes, Susan. I will admit. I do not remember noticing before. Have you been hiding your beauty from us all and blossoming in secret, tucked away in your Yorkshire retreat?"

A blush warmed her skin. She had no idea what to say. She had never thought herself pretty but now Henry and Harry had told her that she was.

When they returned to the house, Susan's mother offered Henry and Harry tea but they declined.

Relief gripped at Susan when they said their goodbyes, and then she retired to her room, desperate to pull herself together and stop herself from thinking of Henry.

~

Damn. Damn!

Emotion swayed through Henry. It was not just attraction, nor affection, it was something more intense.

Susan had glanced at him numerous times, then looked away, and yet in those moments it was clear to him that whatever he felt—she felt it too.

It was absurd. Ridiculous. He had known her for years. He'd spent all his life carelessly disregarding her. Yet now... Now he'd discovered he cared for something. He cared about her.

He flicked the reins of his horses. Harry sat beside him, speaking of the evening he had planned and the things he wished to do before he returned to his regiment. Henry could not focus on a word.

Susan. Why Susan?

They had never even been particularly friendly until this year. *Why Susan?*

He had spent the afternoon with Alethea, the woman he was supposed to be courting, looking at her sister, only hoping that at any moment Susan might look at him—and when she did...

Damn. He'd wanted to kiss Susan even as Alethea's fingers had lain on his arm.

He had always known that he had a reckless nature, a wicked streak. He had never foreseen such folly as this, though.

For the next week, when he called upon Alethea, to fulfil the promise he'd made to her, it was with a darker intent. He longed to see Susan, to spend time alone with her and explore what the hell it was that had possessed him. Yet clearly she had no desire to know. She had taken to rebellion and run. Hiding from whatever it was—and him…

Even when he brought others with him, in the hope of flushing her out of her hiding places, his plan did not work. Yet maybe that was for the best, and this would pass.

Chapter Twelve

When the day of Sarah's debut ball arrived, Susan let the maid dress her slowly, without urgency. Every moment she could delay, she wished to delay. She had spent all day considering feigning a headache, but Alethea knew her too well she would have known it was feigned.

Susan breathed deeply as the maid dressed her hair. In her head she heard Henry telling her how pretty her hair had looked at the last ball.

She had not seen him for a week. He had called here daily, to visit Alethea, but on every occasion Susan had found a reason to escape the drawing room before he entered, even though he'd frequently arrived with William or another of Harry's cousins. She'd presumed Henry had brought the others to entertain her, but she did not need Henry interfering with her life.

Yet if he and Alethea married, when her father passed away, Henry might order her life as he wished. That thought had become unbearable.

She could not live with them. Not now. Not when she had feelings for Henry that she should not have.

When she faced herself in the mirror, she faced a woman she did not know.

She'd known for years that her future would be spinsterhood—a life dependent on her father and then Henry. Nausea spun through her stomach. Her future had to change.

She had to consider marriage. She had to find a husband. She could not live with Henry and Alethea.

The door was knocked, and then opened. Alethea swept in, looking beautiful as she always did. She had chosen to wear a pale almost luminous grey. It made her eyes shimmer and the colour a dozen times more striking.

Susan was wearing a lime green. It was a very unusual colour for her, and yet her mother had persuaded her to take it. But it would make her stand out in the ballroom and she did not wish to draw people's attention. She should not have let her mother persuade her to buy it.

"Oh." Alethea stopped and stared at her, "my goodness. You look… wonderful. I have never seen you look so well. Who would have thought that such a vibrant colour would suit you, but with your brown hair and pale eyes… You look magnificent."

"Thank you." Although she was not sure she wished to look magnificent. She would rather be obscure. Yet, if she must find herself a husband…

"But take your spectacles off. You cannot wear them with your hair dressed, they make the whole thing look silly."

Alethea reached out and took Susan's spectacles off, as the maid stepped back and bobbed a curtsy. Alethea handed Susan's spectacles to the maid, then gripped Susan's hand and pulled her into motion.

They walked downstairs together.

Two footmen stood in the hall, awaiting them with their shawls. Susan turned as the man draped hers across her shoulders. She shivered, but not because she was cold. The evening was quite warm.

When they sat in the carriage, travelling the short distance to Uncle Robert's town house, she shut her eyes, as if by doing so she could hide from all that might come.

How would she choose a husband? How might she find someone who would like the things that she liked? Someone whom she might talk to. Someone who would make her feel comfortable.

The thought of marriage terrified her more than seeing Henry. Her heartbeat quickened the closer she came to his home. Rain joined in the rhythm of her heart, hammering upon the roof of the carriage.

They stopped at the end of a queue of carriages when they neared the house, and then the carriage crept along, as those before theirs deposited guests at the door.

The rain continued its drum beat on the carriage roof.

Nausea turned Susan's stomach over. She pulled her shawl a little tighter about her, then her fingers played with its fringe while they awaited their turn.

When the carriage pulled up outside the house in Bloomsbury Square, her heartbeat leapt into a rhythm of panic. She could not do this, she wished to turn about and run—to scream at the horses and tell them to take her away.

Once her mother and Alethea had alighted, she took her father's hand. Her mother and Alethea ran up the steps and into the house under the cover of an umbrella as Susan stepped down on to the pavement. A footman came forward to offer the protection of an umbrella. The rain pattered on that as her father took it from the footman's hand, still holding Susan's hand too. He walked with her, leading her up the steps to the front door which was swiftly opened to let them in out of the rain.

Her heart beat so hard she could hear the rhythm in her ears.

When she walked into the hall she was greeted with the sight of Henry holding Alethea's hand and pressing it against his lips.

Susan longed to turn away, but Sarah had already caught her eye, so she could not. "Susan!" she called across the hall.

It was a bizarre scene. Guests milled about everywhere in the hall, stripping off dampened outdoor clothing, while the footmen

128

took the umbrellas back outside to walk the next guests in. Susan's father helped remove her shawl and handed it to a footman.

Susan walked forward, desperately not looking at Henry and Alethea, but looking at Sarah. The notion of a receiving line had obviously been thwarted by the sudden rain.

Sarah clasped Susan's hands excitedly. The rain had perhaps made this more of an adventure. "I am so glad you are here. You look beautiful, I have not seen you without your spectacles before, and your hair…"

Susan made a tutting sound. "Pa, you cannot make a fuss over me. Look at you, you look magnificent. Congratulations, you must be so excited. Are you all prepared?"

"The rain has turned everything into a shambles, but Papa said he shall tell the orchestra to begin the dancing soon, and then things shall settle when the flow of guests slows."

"Well you must enjoy your evening, and not allow the rain to dampen your spirits."

Sarah smiled.

Susan bobbed a quick, shallow curtsy towards Aunt Jane and then moved on into the ballroom, having successfully avoided a single word with Henry.

She swallowed against a dry throat as she walked across the quiet ballroom alone. There were only a small number of people, and they were gathered in groups about the edges of the room. But she recognised Uncle Edward and Aunt Ellen, and Helen and Jennifer through her clouded vision. Her heart pulsed quickly as she joined them. "Good evening."

"Hello, Susan, dear," Aunt Ellen started. "I take it you are not alone?" It was said with jest.

"Mama and Papa, and Alethea, are in the hall still drying off and greeting others."

Aunt Ellen smiled. "I think the rain has caught everyone out. We were here for dinner, and so we were fortunate enough not to earn ourselves a soaking."

"Here we are, lemonade for you Jennifer, and Helen…" Susan turned. The Duchess of Pembroke held out glasses towards her sisters-in-law.

Susan smiled. "Katherine."

"Hello."

"Mama, your champagne," John, the Duke of Pembroke held out a glass to his mother.

Susan smiled at him too. "Hello."

He smiled in return. "Susan. Would you like me to return to the refreshment table for you?"

"No, I am not thirsty, but thank you." He was much older than her, yet she had known John, Henry's eldest cousin, since she'd been an infant in the nursery. He had a very officious manner at times, and there were too many years between them for her to have ever called him a friend, yet she had seen the man he was within his home when he shut the world outside and she was not cowed by his title. He and Katherine had a close bond and their children were charming.

The orchestra began to play the notes of a waltz. Susan turned. Her mother and father were some of the first people to enter the room, drawn in by the introduction to a dance. Alethea followed, she was speaking with another of Henry's cousins, Mary, Aunt Ellen's and uncle Edward's eldest daughter, who was already married too.

"Drew and Mary have arrived, I was not sure they would be here, they always leave it so late to come to events," Aunt Ellen said, as though she had genuinely not expected them to come.

"They prefer to be by themselves at home, Mama, that is all, and it is easy enough to travel up to town in a day."

Aunt Ellen looked at John and shook her head. Mary and Drew owned a property on the edge of John's estate.

"Katherine, shall we join Henry and Sarah?" John held out a hand to his wife.

Susan looked across the room. Henry stood in the middle of

the floor holding Sarah's hand, he bowed to her before he formed the frame of a waltz. There was a slight, dull, applause which rippled around the room when they began dancing, as the gloved hands of the numerous friends, family and acquaintances within the room clapped.

John and Katherine began to dance too, then Aunt Ellen and Uncle Edward, and Susan saw her parents join others on the floor as the number of couples swelled. She recognised many of them as friends of her parents, and others as people she had been introduced to for the first time at her parents' ball.

"Susan, shall we dance?"

She turned to face Peter, the son of another of her parents' friends. She had known Peter since childhood too. His parents, Lord and Lady Sparks, were also dancing.

Susan had not seen Peter for a couple of years, though. He was a little shorter than Henry, but only a little, yet he was entirely different in appearance. He had blonde hair and turquoise blue eyes. He looked at her expectantly and lifted his hand higher. "Will you dance with me, then?"

She nodded. "Yes, thank you, Peter." She was more than glad to move away from the wall and let the music flow through her.

She held his offered hand.

When they began to dance, he said, "Susan, you are all grown up, and very beautiful. I did not even recognise you. William told me who you were when I asked. Will you let me claim the supper dance too?"

She nodded. A strange sensation was clogging up her throat. Henry had passed behind them, his gaze fully focused on Sarah. He had not looked at her, yet the sight of his hand on Sarah's back had reminded her of the sensation of his hand at her back and his thumb brushing against the curve of her spine. Having Peter's hand there did not feel the same, and his eyes were too blue, when they ought to be brown.

Yet if she was to find a husband she must give herself a wide choice; it was a man's manner that was important, not his looks or his height.

After she had danced with Peter, she danced with William, and then Fred, and Greg, and all of Harry's cousins who had come. Although Harry was not there to dance with her, he had returned to his regiment.

She was then introduced to their friends and acquired an expanding group of dance partners, who clustered about her, as gentlemen normally clustered about Alethea. Yet Henry did not approach her.

When the supper dance began it was one after midnight, and her feet were sore from dancing. She was ready for a rest but there was one more dance. She accepted Peter's offered arm for the country dance with a smile, and skipped through it, enjoying it regardless of her aching feet.

After the dance he walked her through to the dining room to collect a plate of food for their supper. Then they found a spot amongst his friends. She was the only woman and at moments it was intimidating to be amongst such a group of vibrant men, as they debated with each other in loud voices and laughed. But she refused her sense of reservation—she had known most of them from childhood—and if she was to find a husband…

She also refused to look about the room for Henry, or even Alethea, as she assumed they would be together. He had not come near her and she did not wish to be near him. It would do her no good.

When the supper break was over, and the music began again, she walked back into the ballroom on the arm of one of Peter's friends, for the next dance. She could not help but look at Henry, though, as they passed him. He was sitting at a table beside Alethea, and Sarah too, and her dance partner who Susan did not know, and John and Katherine, and Mary and Drew sat with them. Couples.

Henry glanced at her, as though he sensed her watching.

132

She looked away.

Her heart pulsed in a steady beat while she danced the next country dance, as she fought not to recall the instant of communication she had shared with Henry before the dance began.

How could he invade her thoughts and senses so easily, and fully? Others did not.

"Susan."

She turned and faced Henry. The dance had only just drawn to its end; they had barely stopped moving. Heat flared in her skin.

Her breath stuck in her throat when he caught hold of her hand, taking it from beside her, even though she had not offered it.

There was a frown of determination marking his brow, and his lips were pursed with intent. "I would ask you to allow me to dance the next with you but I would guess your feet are aching, and so instead I shall ask, would you care to sit the next dance out beside me?"

"What of Alethea?" she asked as her previous partner turned away.

"She has a partner. She will be dancing."

"Henry—"

"Do not deny me, you have spent a week avoiding me, you cannot do so forever."

Avoiding him… He'd known…

"Susan." His voice urged her to agree.

She nodded. She ought to feel pleased, jubilant, instead tears gathered at the back of her throat and pressed behind her eyes as they fought to be free. But she could not walk from the floor beside him crying. She blinked and swallowed.

Henry led her away from those forming sets for the next dance. "You have been playing your rebellious hiding games again. I'm tired of it." His voice was low and gruff.

She did not answer.

Did he know how deeply she felt?

He did not stop walking when they approached the edge of the ballroom but walked about others, drawing her onwards, and then out into the hall.

"Henry…" She pulled against the hand that held hers. No one was in the hall, but this was wrong. They should surely not leave the ballroom.

His grip on her hand refused to let her stop him.

"What will people say? Take me back."

"If they say anything I shall tell them you felt faint and needed a moment to rest."

"I have never felt faint in my life—"

"There is a first time for everything."

Her breathing fractured as he opened the door to a room she had never entered before. It was a study, not a large room, and clearly not a room for guests, which is why she would never have been invited into it before.

The sound of her heartbeat filled her ears.

"We need to talk," he said, when he pulled her in. He let go of her hand then shut the door.

He was right they must talk, to dispel the thick, humid, air flowing between them, she could barely breathe, and yet what was to be said? Not the truth, she could not tell him the truth. So there was nothing to be said. How could she speak? *He is Alethea's!*

He stood still before her, his eyes seeming to say all the words her lips had not. Then he stepped forward.

"Susan. I swear to God you are the most beautiful woman in that room this evening." His hands lifted and embraced either side of her face, then he brought her forward as he leant down. His lips pressed on to hers as her fingers clasped about his wrists holding on to stop herself from falling. Perhaps she would faint.

His lips were warm and soft and they pressed over hers again and again. It was not a quick gentle meeting of lips, as he'd kissed

134

Alethea outside the house at home. He kissed Susan's lips and then the skin beside her lips, and the skin across her cheek. "Susan," he breathed her name against her temple, then wrapped his arms about her.

She lay her head against his shoulder, and wrapped her arms about his middle allowing this to happen for a moment, allowing herself to live out everything that she felt and had dreamt of.

His fingers touched beneath her chin and lifted her face again, and his lips were once more on hers.

He feels what I do. The words cried out within her. She had not imagined the connection that had pulled at her. It was real and mutual.

She opened her mouth to take a breath, with her eyes shut as her fingers closed, gripping the material of his evening coat at his shoulder and sleeve.

His tongue dipped into her mouth reaching to touch hers. *Oh.*

Her mouth opened wider as his hand came to the back of her neck, with great gentleness as though not to disturb her hair, while his other hand rested at her waist. She pressed against him as his tongue slid into her mouth, then withdrew and slipped in again.

Pleasant, pleasurable sensations skimmed through her nerves and danced in her blood as she clung to his coat, and his tongue wove a caress around hers. Was this what love felt like?

But she could not fall in love.

They should not be kissing. *He is Alethea's!*

Yet nothing within her wished to stop.

He sighed out a breath into her mouth, then broke the kiss and rested his forehead against hers. He breathed heavily as his finger moved gently at the back of her neck stroking her skin.

She was breathing heavily too.

He'd brought her here to talk, but he'd not spoken bar saying her name, and telling her she was beautiful.

135

If she said anything it ought to be to tell him to stop.

This was wrong.

She continued to say nothing. She did not want their moment together to end.

"We should go back. The dance will have ended. We will be missed."

She nodded—dazed and shocked by the submission and intensity of her response.

He held her arm gently and led her back out into the hall, silent. They had kissed, they had not spoken. And what they should have spoken of was why they should not have kissed.

"Henry…" She stopped beside the stairs and turned to face him.

"Not tonight. Not now, Susan. We will talk tomorrow."

Had he dragged her out here only to kiss her? A million questions began spinning in her head as two women walked out from the ballroom.

She glanced across her shoulder. She did not know them, and if Henry did, he did not talk to them.

Now she had words to speak, she had no time to say them.

She looked into his brown eyes, there was a depth in them she had never seen before.

"Tomorrow, Susan. Take my arm."

Her fingers wrapped about his forearm, and she held on as he began to walk back into the ballroom. What if someone had noticed them leave? What if Alethea had seen? Where would she say she had been? What would she say they had done?

"Shall I take you to Uncle Casper and Aunt Julie?"

"Yes," the word was spoken on an out breath. Every muscle seemed to tremble as she held his arm and walked back into the ballroom. What if he were asked where they had been and said something different from her?

He led her towards the corner of the room where her parents stood, yet… it was not only her parents there but his, and as she

136

neared them Alethea reached them on the arm of the Earl of Stourton.

"Forgive me. Excuse me. I need the retiring room…" She let go of Henry's arm and turned away, not waiting for his acknowledgement.

When she walked across the ballroom back towards the hall, she felt as though everyone must know what had happened between her and Henry—what she had allowed to happen. She felt as though there were lines of bold black ink all across her face, telling people that she was a heartless, cruel, disloyal cheat…

She wove a path through the crowd at the edge of the floor, turning from side to side as couples moved to join the next dance. Then in the hall, her heart racing, and breaths hurried, she walked quickly to the stairs and climbed them as fast as she was able, terrified that someone, Henry, or Alethea, might have followed her.

When she reached the busy retiring room, she dropped down into a seat before a mirror on a dressing table. The maids fussed over other women in the room pinning up their fallen hair and mending torn hems.

Susan sat and stared at herself. She should look different. There should be some sign… But there was none. Except perhaps her lips were a little redder and fuller. Her fingertips touched them.

She had kissed Henry.

She had not imagined it.

It was reckless. Madness…

Why had he done it?

Why had she? She wished to scream at herself. There was no justification for her behaviour.

Rebellious. He had called her that weeks ago… She had never believed what he'd said until tonight. She was cruel. Wicked. A horrible person. She should go home to Yorkshire—banish herself.

Tears pressed at the back of her eyes, and gathered again as a lump in her throat, she swallowed them away, then used a little powder on her face to bring down her colour before adding some rouge on her lips and cheeks, if her redness looked false it would at least hide the guilt cutting her in half.

When she walked back into the ballroom she forced her lips into a smile as she walked towards her parents—and his parents. Alethea was dancing. Susan's gaze instinctively searched for Henry as she sat down in a chair near her mother.

He was dancing with his sister, Sarah.

I have kissed him. The words repeated within her head a dozen times.

"Here," Her father held out a glass of punch for her.

She looked up. "Thank you."

"You look unwell…"

"I am well, Papa, it is only that it is getting late and I am tired."

"Then we will not wait until the breakfast refreshments but leave soon."

"I would not wish to drag Alethea away…" She could not speak Alethea's name without her heart screaming her shame and guilt—

"She has had three quarters of the night to enjoy herself, the loss of an hour or two of dancing will not harm her, and there will be two dozen more balls to attend before we return home."

"Thank you, Papa."

Why did Henry kiss me?

When Susan lay in bed later and shut her eyes she saw Henry's eyes looking into hers with a depth she'd never known in anyone else's. She felt the pressure of his lips, and her lips pressing back and opening then their tongues dancing. She did not sleep.

She was tired when she rose the next morning at eleven. Alethea was still in bed, as was their mother, but their father had risen and gone out riding, he would probably not return until much later, he'd probably then go to his club to meet friends.

Susan ate breakfast alone, but she merely nibbled on dry toast, her stomach was too busy dancing waltzes to eat, as she thought of Henry.

At eleven thirty, a bouquet of roses arrived for Alethea, with a card. The footman brought them to Susan as Alethea had not yet woken. The handwriting on the address declared the flowers as from Henry. "Put them in a vase in the hall for now, then take them up to Miss Alethea's room once she's woken."

"And there is this for you, ma'am." He held out a letter. She looked at the words written across the front, Miss Susan Forth. It was written in Henry's hand.

"Thank you." She took it.

When the footman left her alone, she rose from the table and went into the hall, then climbed the stairs to her room, her heart racing wildly.

As soon as she closed the door of her bedchamber she leant back against the wood and broke the seal. Henry hadn't used a crest, but if Alethea had seen the letter she would have known his writing. Why had he written?

Dear Susan,

I wish to see you today. Will you escape the house? Say you are shopping for books so Alethea will not want to join you. I will wait in Bond Street outside Faulder's bookstore, at No. 42, from one o'clock until two, if we meet there people will assume it was only chance. But please come without Alethea, so we may talk.

H

H… Henry.

What had he said on Alethea's card? Susan wished to run downstairs and open it, but that would break every rule of everything that was right. She had already done enough wrong.

She should not meet him.

But her heart longed to see his face, to hear him speak—to understand…

He must know that she would have seen the flowers. Why would he send Alethea flowers and ask to meet *her*? Because he was reckless, careless and self-centered, and…

Then the answer was certainly no. She should not go to Bond Street. She could not lie to her sister or her mother. She could not continue this deceit.

Oh. Why did the thought cause so much pain in her chest?

A part of her hated Henry again.

Chapter Thirteen

Henry had taken off his gloves, out of agitation. He slapped them into the palm of his other hand, ran them across his fingers and then repeated the motion. He was standing on the corner, so he might easily see along the street in either direction, and on to the other road that he expected Susan to walk along.

It was two.

He'd been standing waiting here for an hour like a fool. If Susan came now it would no longer appear an accidental meeting.

Although only a few people must have noticed how long he'd been here, as the human traffic continuously moved from shop to shop.

But she was not coming. It was two.

Damn her!

Henry turned and walked away from Bond Street.

His fingers lifted and removed his hat, then his other hand lifted and his fingers ran through his hair. They shook a little. He put his hat back on, his hand still clasping his gloves, and walked on, quickly, anger and agitation burning in his blood— and doubt, and guilt, and confusion and… Lord… So many things.

He'd not been able to find a single word to explain or express his emotions last night, and so his body had resorted to actions, responses he knew well, responses that could speak a thousand words, and yet… even those responses had not explained a thing. He'd never kissed a woman like Susan before.

His heart beat on in a steady hard rhythm with the pace of his strides. Madness. Insanity. Something had touched his mind and overtaken him.

She had worn lime green. She had been visible at every moment within that room. Shining. Her spirit, normally so measured, had been… Lord, how to describe Susan in a ball-room? Animated yet genuine. It was so absorbing. He had been envious of his friends who'd sat with her while she'd eaten supper and of every man who'd had the opportunity to touch her when she'd danced.

Even when he'd danced with Sarah, his awareness had been drawn to Susan.

He'd tried to act responsibly. To remember why Susan was in London. To fulfil his duty at the ball and focus on Sarah and Alethea—but recklessness was in his blood. He'd thought himself beginning to reform, but clearly he had not reformed at all. He had been right in what he'd said to Alethea. He was too young to marry her. Incapable of loyalty.

Yet to be disloyal with her sister. What the hell had come over him? *Susan.*

She had come over him. It was nothing to do with a general desire for a woman. It was just Susan.

He'd not slept. Restlessness had kept him turning in his bed, he could not cease thinking of her. Of her lips against his. Of the curve of her neck. Of how her hair had been styled. Of the fit of that dress.

Dash it all, and he was certain it had been her first kiss. Her hesitance had told him. His lips had been the first to touch hers. The thought clasped at his groin even as he walked.

He'd kissed Alethea, yes, but she was not like her sister. She

142

had kissed other men, or probably boys, before him. She had pressed her lips back against his with confidence from the very first time he'd leant forward to lead such an exchange.

Damn it, he'd been awake for all the hours of the night, thinking about Susan.

Yet there was Alethea… But he could not think of Alethea, his mind was too flooded with Susan.

Her bloody sister.

Of all the women to engage his heart—*her damned sister.*

Hell! He'd known Susan all his life, why had this only happened now? Why not when they were younger? Why at the point that he'd been about to commit to Alethea? He'd made things a dozen times worse.

His strides were long and swift as he walked to his rooms, but he did not go to his apartment, he went to the mews and asked them to prepare his curricle while he waited. Then he drove to White's where he hoped to find William, or if not him, one of the others.

Three of his friends were sitting at a table together. "Who wishes to race me, London to Brighton, now?"

They all stood. "I thought you had given up racing." Fred laughed.

"Not today." Today he needed to burn off his energy and explode with recklessness, today he needed to do something wild to help him forgot the even wilder—wrong—thing he had done last night. He needed to feel careless. He needed to not care about Susan.

But *damn it*, he did not wish to forget, he wished to repeat it. If he had last night to live again, he would do the same.

Dusk descended on the world when he neared Brighton. Henry whipped up his horses, encouraging them on, flicking the straps against their rumps. It was a breezy day, and the wind sailed past his ears, ruffling his hair. He'd removed his hat long ago. This was freedom. This was why he had not wished to be married yet,

143

because he would need to tame his appetite for recklessness if he settled.

He was not ready to settle.

~

"More flowers from Henry…" Susan's mother said when Alethea walked into the room, bearing another vase to fill up the occasional table near the window in the drawing room.

"Yes, but his notes are just rhymes, there is nothing personal in them, he does not even sign them. I think he set up an agreement with a florist to send them daily on his behalf. I do not take them at all seriously anymore. They have been arriving from the day we arrived, and they are still arriving even though he has left London without a word."

Heat rose in Susan's skin. He'd gone the day after Sarah's debut ball. The day he had asked to meet Susan in Bond Street and she had not gone. Nothing had been heard from him since. They only knew that he had gone away because Uncle Robert had told Papa that Henry had left town, but even Uncle Robert did not know why, or even where Henry had gone and it had been a week…

Yet still the flowers came.

Alethea was probably right, they had been ordered prior to Sarah's ball. It hurt less to think that at least.

Susan's gaze turned to the window and she disappeared into daydreams, imagining what might have been said if she had gone to Bond Street.

But what could have been said? *Nothing!* She would not hurt her sister.

Yet I kissed Henry!

That thought had twisted around in her head for days and it had sharp, vicious edges. It was more like a dream now than truth. A dream? No. A nightmare. She could not believe it had happened.

But it had and now Henry had disappeared and there was a ball this evening.

Alethea had complained all of yesterday. Henry had promised to escort her and he was letting her down.

Susan was partly glad. Which was a cruel thought, and made guilt flick its whip at her even harder, tearing slashes open within her. She bled with the constant pain of having betrayed her sister.

Was that why he'd gone away? Because he did not want to face Alethea…

Had he run away from the guilt that surely—if he was capable of any emotion beyond recklessness and selfishness—he must feel? She wanted to know.

Not knowing where Henry was, or what he thought, was becoming as unbearable as the guilt.

There had been emotions in his eyes beyond recklessness—she would swear it.

She would know if she had gone to Bond Street…

But even if he declared love for her, it could change nothing, he was Alethea's.

Echoes of the sensations generated by his lips and his tongue, and his hand at her nape played through her body.

Yet he had deserted Alethea. He had been reckless and self-centered… and…

Where was he?

~

When Susan faced the receiving line at the Brookes' ball, her heart pulsed with the quick beat of fear. It would be extremely unlikely for Henry to attend and yet she hoped, and yet she should not hope, and yet she feared. Her heart skimmed skipping stones across her emotions, dotting ripples of excitement into a lake of anxiety. Those sharp sudden moments of longing wished to know what would happen next time she met Henry—because

145

of course she would meet him again, his parents lived beside hers, they were close friends. He was supposed to be courting her sister!

The other part of her was terrified—because she did not know what would happen next.

The Martins' butler introduced her. She accepted Lord Brooke's offered hand and curtsied. When he let her hand go Susan turned to his wife. The couple were still quite young and it was only the two of them welcoming their guests.

When the cordialities were done Alethea slipped her arm through Susan's, and drew Susan on into the ballroom as their parents' followed. It was such a crush it was hard to see from one side of the room to the other, she could not see whether Henry was there.

"I can see Robert and Jane over there," her father lifted a hand in the direction. "Shall we will join them? Perhaps he might have discovered a cause for Henry's silence, although he had still heard nothing when we spoke yesterday."

Henry would not be here then. Susan's heartbeat slowed, but the sense of risk hovered—not a fear of seeing him, but a longing for it. If he came tonight and asked her to talk privately with him again, she would go. The magnetic pull in her stomach made her wish to cleave to him. She would betray her sister again.

When they neared Uncle Robert he lifted a hand to acknowledge them. The group he stood amongst contained Uncle Edward, Aunt Ellen and some of Aunt Ellen's family and John and his wife Katherine, and Mary and Drew.

Uncle Robert took Alethea's hand and kissed her cheek. "I am sorry on behalf of my vagabond of a son," he said as he drew back and released her hand. "I am ashamed of him. I have no idea why he has left. But it is par for the course with Henry."

Alethea smiled, but when she turned away Susan saw a look of doubt cross her sister's face. It was heartless of Henry to leave her…

To leave us both! Yet she had left him alone, waiting for her in Bond Street. This was all her fault.

The Earl of Stourton approached before anyone else had had chance to welcome them. "Miss Forth," he said to Alethea, with a bow. "May I have the honour of this dance?"

Alethea smiled at him. He'd sent her a posy of flowers after Sarah's ball, too. "Of course."

He offered his arm. Alethea lay her fingers upon it and then they walked away.

"Susan."

She turned to face John.

He smiled. She did not know him even a quarter as well as his half-brothers Harry or Rob.

She curtsied, deeply.

He bowed slightly, in acknowledgement of the gesture as she rose. "How are you?"

"Well. I thank you."

"How are you enjoying the London season?"

"It is a little hectic."

He smiled.

"—I have no idea where my son is…" Uncle Robert's pitch expressed annoyance, and his voice carried through the family group.

"Peter the same," Lord Sparks responded, "and so they must be together, wherever they are."

Susan's heart pounded once more.

John looked away from her. "Why do you not know where they've gone?"

Uncle Robert rolled his eyes in a jovial, mocking manner. "Must I say it again? Because that is my son, John. Have we not covered this ground a hundred times?"

A note of humour escaped John's throat before he answered. "We have, but on this occasion I happen to know exactly where he is. I would have thought you—"

"Where?" Uncle Robert and Lord Sparks interrupted and asked together.

John smiled at them, in a wry manner, as though he thought them foolish for not knowing. All the men looked at him expectantly, including Susan's father. "Henry went into White's a week ago and challenged William and Frederick to race him to Brighton, and Peter accompanied them."

"Bloody hell!" Uncle Robert barked, then looked at Susan. "I apologise. I should not have used that language."

"Where are they now?" Uncle Edward asked

"In Brighton still, I believe. I have not seen them in the clubs in London nor heard of them visiting…" He glanced at Susan for an instant before continuing. "…since then. They are probably at this moment drunk and losing money over a hand of cards somewhere there. I am surprised you did not know?"

"How are we to know when no one has told us?" Uncle Robert growled in a low voice.

"Perhaps people are too scared of what you might do to them if they tell you these things when you snap like that, Robert." John turned and looked at Uncle Edward. "Of course Harry's regiment is there."

"I do not need to be reminded, and he would need little temptation to leave his post in the evenings and join them."

"That is probably why they have stayed there." John laughed.

"I do not find it amusing, John, and you do not wish to know what I will do to my damned son—" Uncle Robert stopped and looked at Susan. "Sorry. Forgive me again for my language. Is there no one to dance with you?"

"So he may swear as much as he wishes," her father leant to whisper near her ear.

"Come, Susan." John lifted his arm. "I do not believe you have ever been introduced to my cousins on my father's side."

"What will you do?" Her father asked of Uncle Robert, when Susan accepted John's arm.

Chapter Fourteen

Henry leant back in his chair and tossed his cards on to the table, in anger and frustration. "I am done. I give up. I am having horrible luck, so why play."

Harry laughed and squeezed the waist of the woman who occupied his knee. "And I am having great luck. Show me your cards, Fred, I'm calling you?" Harry's speech had become slurred, but so had Henry's. They were all four, or perhaps five, sheets to the wind, and the sheets were dancing on a strong breeze.

Fred lay down his hand of cards face up. Harry leaned forward, drawing the woman forward too and set down his cards.

"You damned well win again!" Fred declared, in a voice that resounded with annoyance as he picked up his glass. He drained it in one quick swallow, then stood up, swaying a little. "Fuck you," he grumbled, reaching into his pocket, then tossed his promised bets on to the table.

Harry leant over and picked up the money Fred had dropped, and the money left by the others who had bowed out earlier in the game. They'd left a significant sum for the poorest of them to claim. Harry gave Henry a broad smile, then pulled the woman he held more fully on to his lap and pressed a kiss on her lips before saying against her mouth, "Are you ready to celebrate with me, darling?"

Henry looked away and lifted a hand to obtain the attention of a woman on the far side of the room. When she looked at him he pointed at the empty bottle on the table then lifted his glass. She smiled in way that implied she'd give him far more than a new bottle of brandy.

He just wanted the brandy. A bitter disgust turned over in his stomach even at the thought of the offer of anything else.

What the hell was wrong with him?

When the woman brought the bottle she leant forward so the top of her breasts spilled out from the loose bodice of her dress as she set the bottle on the table before him.

Henry leant back as revulsion sailed through his blood. These were new emotions. He had never turned a woman away through lack of interest before. Perhaps when he'd been too drunk and incapable, or too tired, or not in the right mood, but never out of a lack of interest in a woman.

But his ailment was not about a lack of interest in all women.

The woman ran her fingers down his cheek and leant farther forward to whisper in his ear.

Henry caught a hold of her wrist and pulled her hand away before it could descend to his groin. "No thank you."

"Oh come on, my Lord, play with me…"

He turned his head away as she tried to kiss his lips. "I said no."

He was not interested in any of these women.

His ailment was an interest in just one woman. A woman he ought not to be interested by.

When the woman walked away, he leant forward and filled his glass with brandy. He immediately drank it all down. He'd come to Brighton to escape the emotions which kept kicking him in the gut, with the sharp punch of a horse's hoof. But the unbidden feelings and thoughts would not stop. All he could recall was what it had felt like to look Susan in the eyes, those pale grey eyes that he had once ignored as though they had been mundane in colour and yet now he had looked he knew them to be enchanting, glorious eyes… and to kiss her.

He should not have kissed her.

He poured another glass of brandy as Harry laughed when the woman he'd held stood up. Henry slapped her backside in a careless gesture, then held his hand out for her to pull him up and lead him to a room upstairs.

He threw Henry a smile. Henry tossed him a smirk. He was not jealous. He was merely… in pain.

Lord, he longed for that sense of carelessness that Harry still lived within. Nothing had worried him. Nothing had disturbed his thoughts. That was why he'd slept with these women, because there had been no need to consider past or future. That was why he had loved to pierce his silent thoughts with shocks of dramatic recklessness.

Now his thoughts would not bloody-well shut up, and the emotions… To care came at a cost. A burden of bitter tasting feelings that were ripping him apart.

"I am seeking Lord Henry Marlow. I was told he is here. Have you seen him?"

Bloody hell! Henry immediately stood and swayed. He looked across the room towards the door leading into the front hall. The room swayed too.

His father!

"And Harry Marlow, is he here?" Uncle Edward was with his father.

"And Peter Sparks…" And Lord Sparks was keeping them company!

What was wrong with them?

What was wrong? His mother… One of the family…

Henry strode across the room, some of the liquor clearing from his head with a sudden rush of adrenaline although it did not stop him walking a little askew. "What is it? What has happened?"

"As if you care…" His father stated. "I have come to take you back to London, there are people waiting for you there. A respectable woman, the daughter of my friend."

Henry's brow scrunched in confusion. His father had come to drag him out of brothels before, but not since he'd left Oxford.

"Harry!" Edward yelled across the room his eyes looking beyond Henry.

Henry looked back at Harry, the liquor stealing his balance a little as the room swayed again. Harry had heard. He'd been half way up the stairs. He said something to the woman then let go of her, and turned to come back downstairs, leaving her there. He jogged down the stairs in a very Harry like way. Harry was the epitome of uncaring.

Henry looked back around and smiled at his father's small group.

Harry walked past Henry, more steady than Henry was and growled in a low voice at Edward, "Go away."

They were Henry's sentiments exactly. He smiled at his father particularly, probably in a drunken manner.

"I am not a boy to be dragged out of brothels anymore," Harry continued.

"You ought to be in the barracks."

"I shall be, by six, and no one gives a damn where I am until then. Oddly enough I am a man and able to manage my time and my life without your oversight, Papa. Go away."

"Henry."

Henry faced the diatribe awaiting him in his father's expression.

"My sentiments are Harry's, go away." Henry swayed again when he spoke, as the liquor he'd only recently drunk poured into his veins to join the effects of the rest of the liquor he'd drunk tonight.

His father grasped his arm. "You were supposed to spend this time with your family, for Sarah's debut and with Alethea—clearly you have forgotten the promises you made."

"I attended their balls and I have not forgotten, believe me." Of course he had not forgotten. How could he damned-well forget? He'd attended Alethea's and Susan's ball and found his eyes, his awareness and his soul constantly drawn to the wrong sister. Then at his sister's ball he'd ceased arguing with his urges and acted upon them and kissed the wrong sister, who had then expressed her judgement of his error by leaving him standing in a bloody street quite obviously alone in his obsession. And his obsession had not abated! Of course he remembered. He remembered and cared!

His father's glare intensified.

"Please go away, Papa, I have no idea why you thought coming here would benefit anyone." Henry would have turned away but Lord Sparks gripped his arm before he could.

"Where is Peter?"

"In bed, enjoying the sport I should imagine."

"As I will be any moment if you go away, Papa," Harry added looking at Edward.

"Damn you, Harry."

Lord Sparks let Henry go.

"Goodnight, Father. Enjoy your journey home." Harry turned away and walked back across the room, to return to his bird of paradise. Henry turned, his gaze following Harry's retreat. "Good evening to you too Uncle; Lord Sparks!" Harry called without looking back. But then Harry stopped and turned around, holding the attention of every man and woman in the room. "Oh. Shall I tell Peter you were looking for him? I am happy to, if you like, Lord Sparks?"

The judgement of the liquor lifted Henry's lips into a smile. He looked back at his father's group.

Lord Sparks's face had twisted in a bitter expression, and he'd turned a deep pink. He did not look amused by Harry's comment. In fact, he looked as though he was considering going upstairs, thrusting open every door and when he found Peter, dragging him out of whichever bed he was in.

Henry's smile widened, because the thought of Peter's father dragging him from a whore's bed was amusing. Peter was a grown man. They were all men. Yet their fathers seemed to constantly struggle with that fact.

"And you, Henry..." his father said. "You began this from what I have heard, even though you had obligations in town. Is there a woman upstairs?"

His father's image blurred. *Obligations...* He hated that bloody word. And of course the implication his father made was that he was breaking his obligation to Alethea by bedding another woman.

"My obligations..." Henry slurred. Obligations that had been created for him from the day he was born. Obligations that had not been his choice, and were no longer his preference. Obligations that he had been tricked into through his entire bloody child-hood. How could he have known as a child—when he had not refused his father's or Uncle Casper's desire for him to wed Alethea—that there were emotions to be discovered that would defy obligations, sense and morality. He had been a child—how had he been supposed to know that he should say no?

He stepped back, to lean on to a table, only when he leant back he caught the round table at the wrong angle, lost his balance, and fell, like a heavy sack of wheat. He'd become a drunkard, but he did not care. He would rather that liquor claimed him, flowing through his blood, it silenced the fighting going on his head. A fight between obligation and desire.

"Harry!" Henry heard Edward shout. "Tell us which hotel Henry is staying in?"

"The King's! They are all there!" Harry called.

~

Henry woke with a hammer thumping against the inside of his skull. The devil. He rolled on to his side. His stomach spun with nausea. The room charmingly smelt of vomit.

He opened his eyes.

His father sat in a chair facing him. Henry was no longer at the brothel but in his bedchamber in the hotel, and on the floor beside the bed was a soiled chamber pot. He had cast up his accounts since returning here, and he could not remember how he had returned.

It was only his father in the room, his uncle and Lord Sparks were not here.

"Have you any idea what a mess you appear?" his father stated.

Henry did not particularly care, except it did not feel good to think that his father had been taking care of him while he'd puked up the brandy he'd imbibed in his desire to get lost in a world of delirium.

"May we not be rid of that chamber pot, if you do not wish me to be ill again?" Henry groaned.

"I have a mind to leave it there, if only to make you ill again. It may teach you a lesson. You have never learned anything from me, neither from what I have said, nor what I have done."

Henry rolled on to his back, and his arm lifted, so the back of his hand lay on his brow. *Bloody-hell*, he felt like death.

His father stood and went across to pull the cord. "When the maid comes, I will ask her to bring you something to eat. Eating will settle your stomach."

Henry doubted it.

"There is water beside you."

Henry looked across to see a clear glass jug, with an empty glass beside it. He sat up. His brain rolled forward in his skull, crying out against the movement. His stomach lurched. *Damn*. He should not have drunk so much, and yet the oblivion had felt good while it had lasted.

His father came back and poured water from the jug into the

glass. "Here." He handed it to Henry. His father was still angry, his movements were stiff and his voice low and bitter. There was a stern conversation to come. A conversation Henry did not care to have.

Henry sat up a little farther and took a gulp of the water. His stomach lurched again.

"Sip it." his father ordered, before turning away.

Heat flooded Henry's face; embarrassment and guilt slapping him. He was ashamed that his father had needed to look after him it made him feel like a damned child.

A knock struck the door. "Lord Marlow?"

"Come in!" his father called.

"Oh. I'm sorry, sir." The maid stepped back startled. She had obviously not realised Henry had been joined by his father. Until this moment she had been giving Henry the eye his entire stay. He had probably shared his bed with her in the past, he did not remember her face, but that would not have been abnormal if a maid was willing. The thought kicked him sharply in the gut and set the nausea spinning once more. He sipped the water.

"Please take the chamber pot." His father pointed to it. "Then bring up some bread and cheese."

She bobbed a curtsy at his father, then picked up the chamber pot, and threw a smile at Henry, out of sight of his father, before bobbing another curtsy. Then she left with the soiled pot.

His father walked over to the window, with his back to Henry, as Henry sat up straight and turned so he sat on the edge of the bed. His head thumped.

His father leant and rested his hands on the windowsill, with his head down, in an expression of defeat. "You invited Alethea to town," he said without lifting his head. "And then deserted her. Do you know how ill that looks? Do you realise how that impacts upon me?"

His father straightened suddenly and turned to look at Henry. "And damn it, this sounds like a conversation my father had with me when I was younger than you, and in pain because your mother had rejected me. But I do not wish to push you away, I only wish you to see sense. When will you grow out of this recklessness? When will you care what others think and feel?"

Henry cared what Susan thought. He feared what Susan thought. "I care."

"Then you show it poorly. The way you act bears no impression of it."

Henry grimaced. He was not in the right temper for this.

"Do not make a face at me. You are becoming an embarrassment. You must know it. Casper has made some bitter comments to me in these last days. You are destroying my friendship when I am naught to do with your foolish acts and self-centered nature. I have tried, Henry, by God, I have tried to make you see sense. I have failed. I thought this summer, when you invited Alethea to town that your accident had encouraged you to grow up and change your ways; then I hear you have challenged the others to a race again, on a whim. Why?"

Because I needed to escape. "Because I felt like it." He'd never cared to hear his father's opinion when he was in an oppressive mood.

"Reckless; as I said. Uncaring; as I said." His father walked closer, with quick strides.

Henry stood, so his father could not lean over him, and wave a damning finger as he'd done when Henry had been a boy— Henry was not being regressed.

"I am tired of this Henry! Grow up!"

"I am grown. It is just that you do not recognise it, and come and drag me out of brothels as though I am a youth still."

"Because you cannot behave like a grown man," his father growled before Henry's face.

Oh, no. He could. He could behave too much like a grown man; that was his issue. But the charge of recklessness was true.

Why the hell did I kiss Susan? He might have stayed in town

157

and pretended all was right if he had not. He need not have—

"Alethea will not wait forever. I was at a ball which she attended last evening. Do you think she sat out all the dances, awaiting your return? No. Of course she did not. She danced every one."

There was a pause as though his father assumed Henry might express a horrified reaction to the news. None was forthcoming. He knew very well that Alethea would meet other men and he did not care if Alethea found another man to propose to her, it would be simpler if she did. It meant that his guilt would at some point subside.

But whether Susan might ever be persuaded to relinquish her sense of loyalty—

"The Earl of Stourton sends her flowers, did you know that? Casper told me so very proudly last evening."

Henry sighed. He had not known about the flowers. He did now. As Uncle Casper had intended.

"Alethea and Susan are making a grand impression in town, and you… You leave. You will lose her."

Susan was making an impression…

What impression had she made? "Did Susan dance every dance too?"

"Yes. But do not think that it means that Alethea was not particularly popular, only that Susan is also popular."

Henry shut his eyes as the words jabbed at his ribs. *Damn!*

He sipped the water to give him time to compose himself.

His father turned away and paced across the room, then turned back and stood still, his hands clasping behind his back, as he stared at Henry. "Do you care?"

Henry said nothing.

"I mean do you care for her?"

He had known the question his father was asking. "I like her… and you know I asked her to come to London to see if it might become more than like," *and I have discovered a burning hunger for her sister—a thirst that is so fierce I cannot imagine that it will*

158

ever be quenched. But he still liked Alethea, only it was no more than that.

"Casper and I have hoped for a union between you since the moment she was born."

"I know, Papa. It has been forced down my throat since the moment she was born." Henry had no patience for this talk; or his father's cursed dreams.

"You have always been willing…" His father's pitch was deep and serious. "Are you no longer willing?"

"I have not said that." He had not said anything, he could not form the words that would tear the two families apart and destroy his father's hopes. He was not as recklessness nor as selfish as they thought.

Damn it, what might he be saying now, though, if Susan had come to him? What might have happened next?

The words inside him were a constant running waterfall of desire, guilt—fear and hope. That was why he'd come away from town. Not to run, but to deal with this riot of emotion. It was a melee of feelings storming at each other. He had been managing it with a daily substantial dose of liquor since he'd arrived here.

"You have embarrassed me." His father repeated in a blunt low tone, that hinted at the emotion beneath the statement. His father rarely showed his emotion, he hid it behind a habitual mocking expression. "The whole of London will learn that you are here, when you have Alethea there." He paused for an instant and swallowed. "And damn I sound far too much like your grandfather." He looked up at the ceiling, as though asking for Divine help. Then looked back at Henry.

"I have been you. I have drunk myself stupid, gambled and acted irresponsibly, my father sent me abroad so I would not be an embarrassment to him. I have always regretted that I cut myself off. He died before I returned." He sighed, then in a lower softer voice, said, "Perhaps this is justice, that I have such a son in return. But I will not cut you off."

159

Henry said nothing. What was there to be said?

His father sighed again. "I do not wish you to feel forced to take Alethea. That would not work for either of you. I married your mother for love, you ought—"

"I know—"

"If there is no feeling there, then perhaps we should simply make it clear to her and Casper that you are unable to fulfil our hopes. I know he only wishes Alethea happy too, he would rather that than you were forced."

"I do not feel forced, Papa." *Only confused.* But if he was going to back out of their arrangement then Alethea ought to be the first to know; not his father.

"Then when the hell will you accept some responsibility, and cease this behaviour?"

Henry put down the glass, then his hand lifted so his fingers could rub his temple. "When I do not have a thumping bloody headache. Must you shout?"

His father stared at him. "Will you come back to London with me?"

To face the mess he had made of things… "Yes." He had to face it at some point, he could not hide from it forever.

There was a knock on the door, his father walked over and opened it, then held it open. It was a footman with a table for them to eat at and the maid with the meal his father had ordered.

"What am I to do to get through to you?" His father asked as they sat down to eat.

"Nothing, Papa, I must get through to myself. I am certain no one else will achieve it…"

"Am I to give up on you then and wait for Percy to leave university?"

"Have no hope of Percy, he is as bad as me and you know it," Henry said as he spread butter on the fresh deliciously sweet scented bread, that had suddenly made his appetite roar.

"Then perhaps I should wait for your younger brothers, perhaps Stephen will step up to the mark."

Henry looked up. "Except that he looks up to Percy as Percy has always looked up to me."

"Then I shall separate Gerard and William from the three of you, so they cannot be tarnished. I shall move them to a different school where they will not hear of your antics and never let them home when you three are there, and they'll attend Cambridge not Oxford. There, so now the situation is resolved." It was said with his father's usual note of satire. He would not do it.

Henry smiled. "You have good odds, with five sons, that at least one of us will meet your expectations. Perhaps William as the last will be the best of us all."

A note of humour rumbled in the back of his father's throat.

His father may frequently express his anger and annoyance, whenever he and Henry were in a room together, and yet, despite it, they were still very tolerably close. He liked, nay, loved, his father. Love. The emotion stirred inside him, topping all the others. The intensity of his feelings for Susan resembled the clasp of love.

Chapter Fifteen

A swift knock on Susan's door gave her a moment's warning of Alethea thrusting it open.

Susan turned

"Henry has come," she breathed excitedly. "He is in the drawing room, you must come down and give me some solidarity. I cannot stand up to him alone. He must understand that his disappearance was unacceptable, and Mama will not let me be mean to him as I wish to be."

Susan had been tidying her drawers, merely to have something to occupy her mind, it would not be occupied by reading, Henry interrupted her thoughts too regularly. "As he deserves for you to be," Susan answered when she crossed the room. *As I deserve for you to be.*

Yes, she would go down with Alethea to see his expression when they walked into the room—and she would not admit that her heart had leapt at the news that he was here, nor that she wanted to be in the room to know what he said to Alethea.

Susan's heart whipped up into a hearty gallop when she walked along the landing with Alethea. Alethea threaded her arm through Susan's as Susan tried to hide the pace of her breaths.

Susan's hand lifted. She pushed her spectacles up the bridge of her nose. They barely moved; the action was merely a nervous habit.

Alethea let go of Susan's arm and ran down the last few steps of the stairs, hurrying ahead.

Nausea clasped tight in Susan's stomach.

"Henry! So you have finally crawled out from whatever stone you have been hiding under!" Alethea cried as she entered the drawing room.

Susan followed her in. Henry was sitting beside their mother, who had a tea tray in front of her. He stood. His eyes were on Alethea as she walked briskly towards him.

"Alethea." Her mother reprimanded as Henry took Alethea's hands when she offered them.

He'd have kissed her fingers, but she pointedly turned her cheek to him, and so he kissed that.

If they had been in private, if Alethea had offered her lips, would he have kissed them... The thought lanced through Susan with a sharp pain as jealousy whipped out its dagger.

He had kissed *her* only days ago. The knife turned back upon herself and stabbed at her heart. Guilt.

Alethea pulled her hands free from Henry's and turned to collect a cup. Henry looked at Susan. He blushed.

So he was capable of feeling guilt too then, and embarrassment, and so he should.

Her urge was to walk over and rain her fists down upon his head. Hate sliced at her suddenly. She hated him for destroying her happiness. She had been content with her life. She had known who she was, and the woman she would become. Then he had upset everything. It was his fault she could not cease thinking of him. It was his fault she could not sleep. It was his fault she had betrayed her sister.

And what now? What did she do now?

Her skin heated too, with embarrassment and anger, and she turned to her mother, who was in the process of pouring a cup of tea for her.

Susan took it from her mother's hand, very deliberately preventing Henry from making any gesture of welcome.

Where had he been?

Oh she should not care. But she was so muddled. As much as she wished to hit him, she longed to hold and be held by him—for his embrace to take away all of the pain inside her.

Alethea sat on the sofa next to Henry and twisted sideways a little to speak. Her knee touched his. It spoke a whole volume without needing a single word. She still liked Henry, perhaps even loved Henry. He may have deserted her without a word, but she still had feelings for him.

Susan sat down on a chair opposite them and looked at Henry, he was looking at Alethea. Pain tore at her heart with sharp fingernails. She wished to set down her cup and leave now—to escape, not to rebel.

If she could do neither thing she wished, to either scream at him or hold him, then let her just go.

His head turned, as though he knew she was looking at him and he smiled at her, but the smile lacked his usual confidence, and he blushed again.

Susan did not smile, or show any sign that she welcomed his shallow attentions.

He faced Alethea once more. His Adam's apple tried to stretch his neckcloth as he swallowed.

Susan's mother led the conversation from then on, as they drank their tea, avoiding the potentially dangerous topic of, *where were you, Henry?* While Susan stared at her cup to equally avoid looking at him.

But once the teapot was empty, Susan's mother stood. "I shall leave you young people to talk. I have duties to attend to. Susan will you remain with Alethea and Henry, please?"

Lord. As their chaperone? That was cruel beyond belief. This was a modern day torture chamber. How much more was she expected to tolerate?

She wanted to run… Rebelliously or not.

~

Embarrassment heated Henry's skin. Susan had not spoken yet, not one word, and apart from when she'd first come into the room, she had hardly looked at him—and he could barely bring himself to look at her. Shame. He'd suffered many emotions in Brighton, but this was the first moment that Shame had spun into the mixture.

This was insanity. To sit with one sister, when he had kissed the other but days before, and all of his awareness sat beside Susan as he faced Alethea. He'd forced his eyes to remain on Alethea and her mother as they'd talked, while all he wished to do was look at Susan.

He wanted to look into her eyes and see what she thought of him? He wanted to see the awe-struck look that had been in her eyes the night of Sarah's ball, when she had looked up at him expecting him to speak—to say all the things they both knew they ought not to voice.

He wanted to shout the words. He favoured her. His heart felt tied to her, not her sister.

His stomach had turned to aspic from the moment she'd walked into the room, and his heartbeat had doubled its pace, while the pain of need flooding through his chest swelled with the force of a tidal boar.

His mind fell empty of words when Aunt Julie stood and walked out of the room, and his conversation ran dry. He looked from Alethea to Susan. She was sitting still and silent, staring at her cup, holding in whatever she thought. She must be longing to scream at him—or to simply rebel and leave him in this room to suffer the fate he had created.

He'd never lacked confidence in his life, but now he had no idea how to act or what to say. This was the knot that caring had tied about him. Carelessness was such an easier choice—but this was not about choice. He had no choice in this. The emotion within him had seeded and grown of its own accord.

Susan turned red, set her empty cup down on a low table beside her chair, then looked at her hands in her lap as they clasped together, as though running from the room with her eyes as she could not use her feet.

Alethea turned a little more sideways on the sofa, her knee brushing against his thigh. He was about to be held to account, her eyes said so, and yet her body told him his desertion had already been forgiven.

"Where did you go, Henry?" It was the question that had been hanging in the air for the last half hour.

"To Brighton, I thought you knew." He looked at and spoke to Alethea, fighting his desire to look at Susan once more. She sat only three yards from them.

"Well, only the day before yesterday. But I did not mean to which town. I meant to where in Brighton?"

Henry swallowed. "To a gentleman's club, with my friends. We had a curricle race—"

"When you nearly killed yourself doing so before!" Susan had sat forward in her chair, grasping each arm.

Their gazes met and melded. Her feelings towards him had not changed. The knowledge yelled out within his senses. Now he wanted Alethea to go; so he could speak to Susan and dispel the agony within him, and her. Susan was in turmoil too; he could see it in her eyes.

"You should not be so reckless, Henry." Alethea gripped his hand, drawing his attention back to her.

Alethea's eyes shone with a desire to please and amuse him, but there was no fire, no heart, or… who knew what it was between Susan and he, but the same emotions were not engen-

166

dered when he looked at Alethea. "Well, I am back now." he looked at Susan, speaking for her benefit. "And I survived and am healthy as you see, regardless of the risk."

Susan made a face at him, then got up out of her chair. Damn was she going to run and leave him with Alethea. No. His urge was to stand up, to stop her—

"I have not thanked you for the flowers yet," Alethea stated.

"Flowers?"

He glanced at Alethea then back at Susan as Susan stopped on the far side of the room and looked out of the window.

Susan's short flight had obviously been made to avoid the need to look at him.

"The flowers you sent me," Alethea prodded in a voice now full of annoyance.

He looked at Alethea, who widened her eyes in a look that said, *you do not even remember.*

Oh. Damn. The flowers. He had set up an arrangement with a florist for the whole period Alethea was to be in town.

Good Lord, what must Susan have thought.

She was looking out of the window not at them. She did not even appear to be listening to them any longer. But perhaps that was pretend.

Her hand lifted and her fingers pushed her spectacles higher up her nose. He wanted to take off her spectacles and kiss her, with his fingers about her nape and in her hair.

"Why did you go, though?" Alethea asked, her fingers squeezing his hand.

He looked back at her. "To race, I told you."

"But why leave me?"

He'd insulted her. But she would be a hundred times more insulted if she knew the truth. At least Susan had not bowed to the pull of honesty. He was certain that she would have had need to fight it. The guilt within her must be leagues deeper than his. He swallowed back his own battle with the truth.

"It was a lark, Alethea. An amusement. I fancied a distraction. Life can become monotonous in town, *and things do not always go as one wishes.*" He'd raised his voice and used the last words for Susan's benefit, he wanted her to know he'd been hurt too—when she had not come to Bond St.

"So if we are married, would you disappear on a whim like that?"

His mouth dried. He would never marry her.

But... He looked at Susan. "When I marry I will live a very different life, but until then..."

Susan made a scoffing sound as she turned from her observation of the street and looked at him.

What was she thinking? Was she wishing him to Hades? Would she be snarling fire at him if Alethea walked out—or kissing him breathless.

He looked at Alethea, desperate to find a way to speak to Susan. "Where will you be this evening? May I escort you?" If he joined them, then there must come a moment when he might converse with Susan in private. A moment she would not be able to avoid.

Alethea laughed in a teasing way, it echoed with flirtation. She had always flirted with him, but there was an edge to this that had not been there before. Her sculpted pale eyebrows lifted "The Earl of Stourton has already offered to take us there, in his carriage. He is also calling any moment to take me for a drive about Hyde Park."

She had been waiting ever since Henry had arrived to deliver that *coup de grâce*, it was in her eyes as she lunged with the fine tip of her fencing sword pointed at his heart. Her eyes said, *it is your own fault, Henry, you were not here.* She wished him to be jealous. He was not, he was glad.

What he ought to do, though, before seeking privacy with Susan was to find a moment to tell Alethea that his intent had changed.

But then… The opportunity of Alethea's arrangement registered. "I have my curricle. I'd intended to ask you, Alethea, but, Susan?" He looked at her. She had been looking out of the window again. She turned, the colour in her skin increasing. "As Alethea is already engaged, we could make a party of four. What do you say? It is a lovely afternoon…"

Alethea let go of his hand and stood up, physically protesting against his lack of reaction to her endeavour to stir his envy, and yet… "Oh, that is a wonderful idea. I may ride with the Earl and you with Henry. Susan, you must come. We may parade about the park together." Alethea was a master at social engagement. She knew how to turn things to her advantage. In her mind she had her beaux escorting her in the park. But it was her social ease that would have made her a good countess.

Susan looked at her sister and her lips parted a little. Given a choice she would refuse. Why? Through guilt, or anger?

Alethea crossed the room and clasped her sister's hands, holding them together. "You cannot say, no. It would be so unfair on Henry." *And me.* Alethea's unspoken words echoed about the room. He'd never thought Alethea selfish before, but— "Go up and fetch our bonnets…"

Henry stood. "I'll ring for a maid to fetch them." He did not like the way Alethea had manipulated and employed Susan. Had she always done that? Had he carelessly disregarded that too?

Yet he was glad she had persuaded Susan to join him. He walked over to the bell pull.

When the maid came, he said, "The ladies require their bonnets, please."

"And my shawl!" Susan called before the maid could disappear.

Susan had accepted the finality of this then.

He turned about and caught her gaze before she looked towards Alethea. He sighed. She would not be able to avoid talking to him soon; yet his head was empty of words now. What was there to say.

Love…

The word whispered through his thoughts.

He shoved it away—and yet emotion grasped about his heart and held firm as something also clutched in his stomach. Was it love? To feel half alive and desperate with need for a woman. That was not the love he knew for his family, there was no pain in that.

A footman appeared at the door. "The Earl of Stourton has arrived, Miss Forth."

Henry turned and swallowed against a sudden sense of anger in his throat. But why anger?

Jealousy. It was the emotion Alethea had wanted him to feel.

He had no reason to be jealous of Alethea, though, and yet… He had always thought of Alethea as his. Like a damned possession… Who was he?

Who had he been?

An arrogant, careless, reckless fool.

Susan walked past him as a maid entered the room holding two bonnets, in the wake of an older man.

Henry's gaze followed Susan, she had seen his emotion. Her posture had stiffened. He wanted to grasp her arm, to stop her and tell her it was no more than habit, a familiarity. It was not because he cared more for Alethea. But Susan took her bonnet and shawl and walked out into the hall.

"Lord Stourton, this is Lord Henry Marlow," Henry turned as Alethea looked from the man to him. Henry had seen him before but never been introduced. "My Lord," she said to Henry, "have you met the Earl of Stourton?" Her voice dripped with a snide sort of pride as she waved her trophy at him. *Look what I might achieve without you, Henry*—was the message in her eyes.

So what? He was not jealous. He was glad, if she had another choice it would ease the upset when he told her the truth. He looked at Stourton and held out his hand then bent his head a little, as Stourton did the same. "Good-day, sir. It is a pleasure to meet you, and a fair day for a ride out. Myself and Susan are to follow you in my carriage."

Stourton's eyes narrowed ever so slightly, it was barely notable, and the muscle at the edge of his lips twitched on one side in the moment before he spoke. "Lord Marlow. That will make the drive more entertaining." Disdain hissed through the pitch of the man's voice.

"I shall go and ensure Susan is ready." Henry turned and left the room.

What had Alethea said to him? Did he think Henry a rival? Did he know of their supposed engagement? Or had he heard rumours of Henry's reputation?

Whatever the man knew, he did not like Henry, just as Henry was starting to dislike himself.

When Henry walked into the hall Susan was looking at the drawing room door. She had probably listened to their conversation. Her head turned away, hiding her face behind the broad rim of her bonnet, as her body was now hidden beneath a large loose shawl.

Alethea followed him out, on the arm of her new beau, and she smiled as she passed Henry with another look that sought to ignite his jealousy. He hoped she had not seen his first reaction. If she had it must have misled her. His heart hovered across the room, amidst the air another woman breathed.

"Are you ready, Susan?" He asked as Alethea put on her bonnet.

Susan glanced at him, her grey eyes looking very directly into his. "Yes." She was scared of this—scared of speaking to him.

The rhythm of his heart lifted in pace. He was suddenly scared too. Scared of what was happening to him, the emotion that was gathering.

As soon as Alethea had tied the ribbons of her bonnet, the front door was opened by a footman. Susan walked forward, as though she was avoiding the chance that he might offer her his arm.

He wished to yell at her. *You did not refuse my kiss!*

171

She was acting as though this madness was solely his. It was not, she had responded. She had kissed him with passion. Yet that argument could wait until they were in his curricle.

Before he could follow, Alethea walked ahead of Susan, probably to ensure that Henry had a good view of her with Stourton.

Susan let her sister pass.

He would have lifted his arm to Susan in that moment, but out of sight of her sister she made a bitter face at him, before turning to walk outside.

Yet—*she had kissed him.*

Susan walked down the steps ahead of him.

Alethea laughed exuberantly as her earl clasped her hand and held on to it while she climbed up into his carriage.

Susan stood on the pavement beside his curricle. Her back to him.

She had nowhere farther to run. She could no longer avoid him. Now they might talk.

When he reached her side, he lifted his hand, without a word. She gripped it, silent too, without looking at him as her other hand grasped the metal bar beside the seat, then she climbed the steps up. Yet the awareness of the simple contact they shared, the first since the moment of their kiss, clasped within in his stomach. Need. He needed her, with a sense of desperation he'd never felt for another woman.

What to do?

When she let go of his hand, he left her to settle herself in the seat and walked about the curricle in front of his horses. He stroked their heads as he passed in an idle manner, but within he was not calm. His heart raced. He had returned to London to speak with her. Yet, he ought to speak with her sister first. Damn, this was a mess.

He gripped the rail by the seat and climbed the steps on the driver's side, then slid into his seat beside Susan. She was his captive audience now. She could not escape.

Yet what did he say?

He leant down and took the leather straps for the horses from the groom who had held them. Then looked ahead.

The Earl of Stourton flicked his reins and his carriage pulled away.

Henry followed, setting his horses into motion too.

Susan looked at the houses on the edge of the street, presenting him with the back of her bonnet. She could not hide from his voice, though. He looked ahead as he spoke. "I take it you did not come to meet me because you do not wish to talk to me, you have made that very plain today. But that will not change what happened. It cannot be undone nor forgotten simply because we have not spoken of it."

Her head turned and he glanced at her, but she was not looking at him, only straight ahead, at Alethea and Stourton. "It must be forgotten."

"Why?"

"How can you say any different? Alethea is my sister. I am ashamed of myself."

Her colour had heightened. Shame… It was not a word any woman had used to him before. "Do not feel ashamed. Attraction is natural. We like each other and you—"

"And I am angry with you!"

He glanced at her as she looked at him at last, but she looked at him with an accusing glare. He looked ahead once more, to steer his horses, but he felt her stare boring into him.

"You should not have kissed me."

"Then you should have slapped me and not kissed me back."

"You are dreadful, and Alethea does not know it!"

So all the blame was on him. He'd be damned if he would accept it all. She had kissed him back. He wished to pull up his curricle and speak with her properly. Alethea chose the moment to turn to look over her shoulder and wave at her sister.

His head turned and he barked at Susan. "Alethea does not

give a fig for me. Look at her. This is nothing to do with she and I. This is only about us."

"You should care for her!"

He would not. He could not anymore. This, his feelings for Susan, was no meagre partiality, it would not be set aside.

He glanced over at her again, then looked ahead as they were in a busy street. He would have rather had this conversation when he was not also trying to drive. "There is nothing fixed between Alethea and I. I invited her to town to see if we would be compatible and to discover if a greater measure of feelings grew, but it is not Alethea who is inspiring finer feelings in me, it is you." He neared a crossroads in the street, that required all of his attention.

A large black enclosed carriage had turned into the road and so Alethea and Stourton were now a carriage ahead of them.

"But you cannot have feelings for me."

It was as though she begged him not to have any interest in her, but he'd discovered in Brighton—such things would not be ordered away. "I cannot help how I feel. I have not chosen to be attracted to you, it is an emotion that has gathered of its own accord."

"Why?" She sounded as though she could not believe that anyone would be attracted to her.

He looked at her, for a moment only. "Because you are beautiful, strong-willed, more independent of mind than your sister, and intelligent, you spar with me… I like your wit."

"While you are reckless, proud, spoiled and everything I dislike."

That was arguing against herself, not him. She was battling her feelings as strongly as he'd wrestled his in Brighton.

But like him, she had not won.

He glanced at her. "Do you like me as I like you? Perhaps there is no accounting for it but why should we deny it—"

"Because you are meant for Alethea, my sister!"

He looked back at the street. "You would have me make her unhappy then? Because if I offered for her now I would spend every day looking at you and wanting to be with you."

"Then I will move away. Far away."

"To where? You have no income."

"To anywhere, I can find a husband or a position."

He glanced at her again. A husband. Another man. "I know you have kissed no one else. You cannot have felt this for anyone else." He looked ahead at the rear of the black carriage. "It probably scares you. Hell and the devil, Susan, it scares me. But how do we deny it?" He took a breath. Perhaps it was too soon to try tell her the full depth of it on his part. "I raced to Brighton to out run it. I could not. It is like an itch inside me. I have not ceased thinking of you. Please," he looked at her again, as they turned into another street and neared Wellington Arch and the entrance to Hyde Park, "let us explore it at least. It is the same for you, I know." He steered the horses beneath the arch and on towards the gates of Hyde Park, past Apsley House, the Wellington's residence.

He flicked the straps as they turned off the road. They were once more directly behind Alethea and Stourton.

He encouraged the horses to progress from a trot to a canter as they moved on to the green grass, heading towards the ring on the far side of the park.

"You cannot pretend you feel nothing; I saw it in your eyes before we kissed."

She did not answer.

He looked over. Her colour had heightened again, but at least she had ceased denying that what he'd said was true.

Stourton's carriage slowed before them and Alethea turned to beckon him forward, with an intent for him to draw up beside Stourton's carriage.

Henry obeyed the summons. He could hardly not, and besides, he had no idea where his conversation with Susan was leading.

He and Stourton kept their horses to a walk as they rode on, side by side, so the sisters were able to talk. Henry participated intermittently, as did Stourton, when Alethea drew them into the conversation. Stourton contributed with a beguiled smile. He was interested in Alethea whether she was taunting Henry or not.

Good luck to the man then.

Henry glanced at Susan. She had leant a little forward to look around him so she might see Alethea, he straightened his back and sat back against the seat so she need not lean so far. She glanced up at him with a look of surprise before focusing back on her sister.

Of course, she thought him *self-centered and careless*.

He sighed. Perhaps her sentiments had been applied to his behaviour towards her too? Perhaps she believed he'd acted rashly, and only thought of this from a personal view—perhaps he had? Alethea was her sister…

Perhaps he should declare the depth of his emotion, so at least she would know this was not a shallow thing?

But he ought to speak to Alethea first. She should know that he was withdrawing from any interest in matrimony before he told Susan.

His next steps confirmed in his mind, Henry tried to relax and behave as he normally would by joining in the conversation and talking to Stourton. When he became more engaged, though, Alethea focused more of her enthusiastic discussions on him, Stourton looked from one to the other and Susan ceased to speak.

It was the first time that he'd noticed Alethea subtly cut Susan out, but that was what had been done. She had called him forward to drive his curricle closer to speak with him, she had used Susan to draw him into conversation, and that done… Susan was then ignored.

He glanced at Susan after he'd said something, in a moment when Stourton responded to Alethea. Susan was looking ahead, watching others in the park. Hiding in full sight.

He sighed as he thought back. He could not remember how things had been when they were young, but certainly, when he'd been injured at home, on the rare occasions the sisters were together in a room Susan was silent and Alethea talkative. Yet Susan had not been uncommunicative when he'd been with her alone.

Perhaps that was why Susan had learned to hide herself in corners and in libraries—to escape her sister's silent cuts? *Self-centered and careless...* Susan had very good reason to think of him thus. She had endured such cuts in his presence and he'd done nothing certainly, and even possibly played his part.

Damn.

His change of heart towards Alethea was a blessing, then, he may be self-centered but he had never been cruel, he would loathe that in a wife. Although he doubted Alethea realised she was doing it, it seemed a habit rather than an intent, and verbally she had always protected Susan. It was selfishness. The characteristic Susan abhorred in him.

When they left the park to return to the Forths', as they pulled out of the gates of Hyde Park, he looked at Susan in the moment when he flicked his reins to lift the horses pace into a trot. "I will tell Alethea tonight that I have made up my mind and that I have decided against a match between her and I."

Susan's head spun and an expression of horror faced him. "No! You cannot! It would break her heart, Henry!"

"Her heart is not involved any more than mine is."

"But she is set on you. No."

"We are all of us to suffer then? Is that the way you would have it? She and I to marry for the sake of a foolish promise, probably made when our fathers were deep in their cups, and you... You would choose to suffer too, because you would have to stand outside this marriage and watch us learn to hate each other. And besides, Alethea is not set on me, did you not see her flirting with Stourton?"

"She is only flirting with him because you left her and went to Brighton!"

He glanced at Susan as a spike of anger pierced through his side. "What would you have had me do then? Call at your house and act as though nothing had occurred between us."

She looked at him, her grey eyes stark with confused emotion. "Nothing should have happened." He voice broke with the pain that she had spent the last hour and a half hiding. "And… I do not know what to do." Fear. She had been upset, afraid and full of guilt. "I am miserable," she stated in entire honesty when she looked ahead at the busy street.

"I shall be more miserable, Susan, if you do not agree to explore this." He spoke with honesty too.

She did not respond.

He would kiss her again, that would be how he would manage this. She would not be able to deny another kiss. He did not then attempt to talk to her, and so they travelled the rest of the journey in silence, behind Alethea and Stourton, as Alethea continually glanced back, as though to check that he was watching her.

When they reached Uncle Casper's, Susan claimed a headache and ran away to her room, leaving him to act the damned fool in the middle of Alethea's flirting with Stourton. It annoyed him, but not for the reasons she hoped.

Chapter Sixteen

While Alethea was introduced to Baron Stokes and his young wife, Susan looked beyond them into the ballroom.

It was full of people. Alethea had told her she did not think many of Henry's friends were expected as most of them had remained in Brighton. Also her father had said that the Duke of Pembroke was hosting a family dinner and so Uncle Robert, Aunt Jane, and most of John's relatives and Susan's mother's and father's friends, would not be in attendance.

She hoped and prayed, that the family dinner would keep Henry away too.

Her stomach rolled over in trepidation.

But without Henry and his friends, the room was full of people she did not know well.

"And this is my youngest daughter, Susan." Her father introduced her.

Susan curtsied as the Baron said, "Good evening." She curtsied again to his wife.

Her father touched Susan's elbow and turned her away.

She faced the Earl of Stourton greeting Alethea. He bowed deeply as he kissed the back of Alethea's gloved fingers. The invitation to this ball had only been accepted because the Earl of Stourton had encouraged it. The Baron was his friend and the occupants of the ballroom those within his social circle.

Susan's assumption was that the invitation had been sent to her father on the Earl's request. It gave her another reason to hope that Henry would not be here, if he had not received an invitation.

Stourton led Alethea away. He was avidly courting her. There had been three posies from the Earl this morning, in different colours.

And none from Henry.

Stourton had called today too.

Henry had not.

Oh but she had to stop thinking of him, she had been unable to do anything else but think of him since their carriage ride—no, since their kiss. It was only that now the memories of their conversation outweighed the memories of his kisses. She did not wish to think of him. Nothing might become of her thoughts or any feelings she had for him no matter what he'd said. She would not betray Alethea.

Yet you did! The accusation charged through her as it did each time any thoughts of Henry began circulating in her head.

"Lord Henry Marlow, my Lord."

Susan turned and looked back as she heard Henry announced to the Baron.

He was here.

Her heart leapt, skipping into a sharp beat—pleasure. Happiness. It lanced through her, no matter that she knew she should not be happy to see him. The emotions he stirred inside her would not be silenced. It was the reason she had dreaded him coming because she had known she would feel like this, and she was ashamed of it.

He bowed to the Baron and his wife, then turned in the direction of Susan's father and mother with a smile. Her father smiled stiffly back. He was still angry with Henry.

Susan turned her back and watched the couples gathering for the next dance. If Henry spoke to her she would not know what to say.

Alethea's gaze focused upon the Earl, they were not dancing, but standing together on the far side of the room. She had not noticed that Henry had come.

"Uncle." Even his voice, as he acknowledged her father, sent tremors of emotion through Susan. It was a voice that belonged to the man her body craved, and when he spoke it called her to respond. She could not.

"Have you come alone?" Her mother asked.

"I have. Papa, Mama and the others are at John's."

He was alone. Had he come to battle Stourton for Alethea? Or to court her? *I will tell Alethea tonight that I have decided against a match between her and I.* He had not told Alethea, he'd left without speaking and not returned.

Susan had begged him to say nothing. Perhaps he'd listened? Perhaps he'd changed his mind once more?

"Good evening, Susan." The words were very directly spoken to her, so she had to turn and answer.

"Henry." She nodded her head slightly in acknowledgement and gave him a very shallow curtsy her gaze on his polished shoes, then she straightened and looked up into his brown eyes; his eyes asked her a hundred questions, and they made it very clear he had not come to court Alethea. He had come to see her.

Heat flared in her cheeks and she looked at her father, guilt flicking its whip, because her thoughts were not loyal to her sister.

"Will you dance with me?"

No. The word snapped through her mind because she could not trust herself, there was too much longing to dance with him in her heart. "Yes." She could not say no before her mother and father, there was no reason for her to refuse to dance with him.

He lifted his hand and she accepted it. Normally a man would have offered his arm, but they were only a few steps from the

181

dance floor, and the dance was a waltz. Her heart began following the steps.

He held her hand in a way that seemed to say, *I have you now*, and when his arm came about her and his palm rested against her back, his embrace was protective.

The music began in full, flooding the air in the room. They'd not spoken beyond their greeting and his request to dance with her.

But what was there to say?

She looked about the room as he turned her. Her parents left the room, passing through a door which appeared to lead into the refreshment rooms.

Her stomach was all twisted, tangled threads and her arms and legs trembled.

Henry was looking at her, as she did all she could not to look at him.

There was nothing to be done. She was in love and there was nothing to be done. She could not let things continue. There was no place in their situation for any feelings between them. Did love die? Did it come to an end? Would her heart stop feeling as though someone had squeezed it so hard it was bruised and sore?

"Susan…" he said quietly as he continued to spin her about the floor.

She looked at him. She could not help it. The magnetic tug, that had begun forming as a sympathetic pull was now a thick rope of longing coiling around her.

His eyes said everything that should not be said between them. She had called him self-centered and she had thought him shallow in his interests and his enthusiasm reckless and fleeting. The look in his eyes denied every one of those things. It promised forever.

The warmth in his eyes reflected back the sparkling light from the chandeliers above them.

She could not look away.

But soon she must walk away. She would not dance with him

again. But she'd hold on to this memory and when she was old and her heart a dried out, shrivelled thing, she'd look back and remember this moment of happiness.

When the dance came to its conclusion and everyone spun to a halt Henry's hands let her go. She stepped back falling out of a dream.

His hand cupped her elbow. "Shall we walk outside?"

That would be the most foolish thing to do. But Henry was reckless and she was heart-sore. She nodded. It was easier to admit in an action that she would betray Alethea again than to speak the word, *yes*.

They were close to the doors, there was only a few steps to take, perhaps if there had been more she might have come to her wits.

His free hand twisted the handle and opened the door, the cool night air swept in. It was still light; it was not even twilight yet. Later, when the ballroom had been warmed by the exuberance of hours of dancing, all the French doors would be wide open and the terrace area would be full of people seeking fresh air but this early there was no one else.

"I do not know the Baron well and so I know his garden not at all," Henry whispered in a light tone as the pressure of his grip on her elbow urged her on.

She glanced back at the windows behind them as they walked down a few shallow steps and on to the lawn. She had not even looked to see if her parents or Alethea saw them leave.

Henry did not allow her time to think, or change her mind. He kept her walking. "There must be somewhere private here."

Where we might kiss… The thought whispered through her mind

She was numb, she could not believe that she was allowing this to happen a second time. Yet she had dreamed of his kiss, thought about it every night when she had gone to bed—and if this was the last time she would let herself see him… What would one more kiss that she might keep in her memory matter? She'd already stepped across this boundary, the betrayal was complete, repeating it would add nothing to her guilt.

"There's a path here." His touch turned her towards an opening in the high yew hedge, it led on to a path which then turned to the left and ran on between two high hedges, progressing farther away from the house.

The sound of the music grew more distant as their steps crunched on the fine gravel.

"Here." A stone arbour was set back into the hedge. He stepped inside the curved, arched structure. It had a low seat about its edge. He did not sit down but faced her.

No one on the path might see them, in here, yet they would hear someone else coming and could step out as though nothing odd had occurred.

His hand braced her nape and drew her closer.

She lifted her mouth, entirely compliant.

She had no urge to fight this, her heart was full with longing.

I love you. The words whispered through her soul when his lips hovered above hers. He breathed out. She inhaled the air from his mouth. Then his lips pressed on to hers gently, caringly, without any sign of recklessness. Her hands lifted and held his upper arms as she pressed her lips back against his tentatively. She knew nothing of how to do this. Why did he like her?

With one hand still embracing her nape, his other came about her and rested against the curve of her lower back, over the first flare of the skirt of her dress. Her hands slid upwards and gripped his shoulders. His tongue slipped through her lips. She caught it between her teeth softly then engaged in a circling dance, and when his tongue retreated, she chased it into his mouth. He sucked on her tongue in an intimate way.

When she had painted the orchids she'd studied the tiniest detail and now she felt every detail of her body's response. It ran into her blood, with the flow of water, and it made her muscles

184

ache with a sweet pain as her body pressed against him of its own accord. This *was* a physical choice, not a decision, he'd told the truth if it was the same for him.

Her arms wrapped about his neck as the skirt of her dress crushed against his thighs and her breasts brushed against his chest. Her corset and bodice were the only things stopping her heart from leaping from her chest.

His hand slid from the small of back to her bottom and pulled her tighter against him.

She was breathless and thirsty.

His other hand left her nape and fell to clasp her bottom too and then she was leaning back against the cold stone wall of the arbour.

She could feel the pressure of his fingertips through her skirts and petticoats, squeezing her bottom as his kiss left her mouth and touched the skin along her jaw.

Her head fell back against the stone and to one side as he kissed the skin below her ear and then a pathway down her neck.

"Henry."

They should not be here. She should not be allowing this.

He kissed the hollow where her neck turned to her shoulder and his hand came about her and cupped her breast over her gown. He'd taken the speaking of his name as a request for more. It had not been that.

His thumb slid over the material stroking her nipple.

Her nipple swelled and became sensitised and taut—

"I know, my Lord, I was charmed by it too, I cannot believe…" A woman's voice swept along the path.

Henry's hand fell and he straightened instantly, then leant to one side, looking along the path. "They are on the other side of the hedge," he whispered. "Come." He grasped her hand and pulled her out of the arbour but he did not turn towards the house, instead he drew her in the direction that led farther into the garden.

He pulled her through a break in the hedge on the right, their shoes crunching on the gravel. She hoped the couple beyond the hedge could not hear their haste or the stealth in their behaviour.

She was drawn about the end of another hedge and pushed back against the prickly branches. He still held her hand as his other hand gripped her nape, his thumb reaching to press against her throat.

Henry breathed heavily as his gaze met hers. His thumb lifted and brushed along the line of her jaw. "Let me tell Alethea about us?"

"No. There is nothing to tell. She has grown up thinking you will be hers. She believes it. She's waited for you."

"She is happy enough with Stourton…"

"Only to make you jealous. Henry, you cannot like me."

"I have no choice in it, Susan."

She knew.

The pressure from his thumb against her jaw, lifted her chin, angling her lips, and then his covered hers.

Her arms wrapped around his neck. She would never feel like this again—never be happy again—she wished for every drop of these last moments, and they would be moments, her parents would miss her if they stayed here much longer.

His tongue danced with hers and the heel of his hand braced the edge of her breast as his thumb lifted and then stroked her nipple through the cloth. The movement drew all her awareness.

She longed for more. To discover every sensation with him. But there was Alethea to be remembered and tomorrow guilt would set her on a pyre made of hell's fire.

She broke the kiss, breathing hard. "Henry."

His forehead rested against hers, as his thumb continued to stroke across her nipple. "If I could, Susan, I would release the buttons at your back and unlace your corset, and lift your breast to my mouth and suck your nipple. If I could I would lay you down and do far more." His brown eyes burned as they looked at her with a desire for the things he'd described.

186

The ache that had been twisting through all her muscles grasped at those between her legs.

"But we must return to the ballroom, Uncle Casper will be looking for you, and I shall restrain myself until we marry."

Marry…

No. No. There was no hope of that.

He pressed another kiss on her lips, then his tongue slid into her mouth, she sucked it for a moment and then danced hers about it, then pulled away.

Her forehead fell on to his shoulder, and she held him tighter leaning into the crook of his neck. "You were promised to Alethea. You cannot marry me."

She breathed in, lifted her head and let her arms slide from about his neck.

His hands grasped her waist, holding her between his body and the hedge.

She met his gaze. "You have to let me go."

"I will tell Alethea now—"

"It does not matter." Her voice flooded with the pain she did not want him to hear.

"She and I cannot—"

"I know." Her hand lifted and her gloved fingers covered his lips to stop him arguing. His warm breath seeped through the silk. "And I cannot. It would not be fair on her. She is my sister, Henry. Do you not see?"

"And that would be fair on you and I?"

He would have kissed her again, but she turned her head. "Let me go. We are being selfish."

"I wish to be selfish in this!" He was getting angry.

"If I was in Alethea's shoes I would not be able to bear it. To have to watch us together. To know my sister cared so little for me she would do such a disloyal thing… It will hurt her, Henry. I cannot hurt her like that."

"She would not sacrifice herself for you."

187

He was wrong, she knew. "She would." But how could Henry understand when all his life he'd only had need to think of himself.

"And this little *tête-à-tête*?" His fingers tightened on her waist.

"It must be our secret. But I shall remember it, rejoice in it and regret this carelessness forever."

He frowned and shook her, making her body sway, as though the gesture might sway her judgement.

She shook her head. Then gripped his wrists and pushed his hands away. Then she smiled awkwardly and moved out of the space between him and hedge.

"Susan," he said as she began walking back along the path. "Susan," he called.

She did not look back. She would not have been able to see him clearly anyway without her spectacles—and through a haze of tears.

When she reached the open lawn there were couples on the far side, but from what she could see of their movement through her blurred gaze, none of them noticed her walk out from the path.

She hurried up the steps to the terrace, wiping away the tears that had slipped free and blinking others away. One of the French doors had already been left open. She passed through it and looked about the room, squinting, to try and see her parents, it was Alethea's tall hairstyle that identified them, and then the colour of their clothes. She walked about the floor unmindful of those she passed.

As she neared her parents Alethea walked away on the arm of a gentleman.

Susan was glad, she could not face her sister. Now that she'd left Henry her mouth had flooded with a bitter taste of disgust. She did not like herself anymore.

When she reached her mother, she said, quietly, "May I go home, Mama." She did not want to see Henry come back into the ballroom. She could not speak to him again, or Alethea. She'd broken her sister's trust.

"Why?" Her father stepped closer. "What has happened?"

"Nothing. I just… I have a headache. I went outside to try and relieve it but it is worse. Please may I go home?"

"I shall take you," her father answered, then looked at her mother. "Will you remain with Alethea?"

"Of course." She smiled at Susan and embraced her. "Go straight to bed and have a maid bring you some herb tea."

Her father held her arm as he guided her from the room.

Tears ached at the back of her eyes and dammed her throat as they awaited her shawl and her father's hat. She had made a mess of everything. She *was* as rebellious and reckless as Henry in her way.

She wrapped her arms about herself. Her father glanced at her with concern.

She had never been a weak woman she never gave in to ill-health, he must think this odd.

During the carriage ride home she was silent and so her father was silent, yet he watched her.

When they reached the house, he asked, "You are not too ill?"

"No. It is only a headache."

"And nothing has happened to upset you?"

"Nothing."

"You are sure?"

"I promise."

"Susan?" He did not believe her.

"You may re-join Mama and Alethea at the ball. I am fine, Papa. It is probably only that I am tired. I will do very well here on my own. I simply need to sleep, that is all."

"You are sure?"

"Yes, Papa." She held his arms and rose to her toes to kiss his cheek, remembering another kiss that had not been so innocent. "Goodnight."

"Goodnight." He nodded.

He did not turn away but watched as she walked up the stairs.

Once her back had turned the tears within her broke through the dam and flooded over, running down her cheeks in silent misery.

When people fell in love was it not supposed to be something that was happy, not tragic?

~

Henry clasped his head with both hands, his fingers clawing in his hair as his elbows stretched out in a gesture that implied a lack of control. Susan had walked off the path. He could no longer see her. He looked up at the sky which had turned the deeper blue of twilight. His arms fell. How the hell did he manage? What was he to do?

He sucked in a breath.

Damn. He did not want Alethea. If he took a wife it would be Susan. *I still cannot.* She had thrown the idea of marriage back at him. Her loyalty to her sister was commendable, especially when he had now realised that at times that loyalty was not returned. Yet he did not wish Susan to be righteous in this, he needed the rebellious Susan.

He drew in another breath. He would persuade her. Convince her. He would tell Alethea that there was no feeling on his part, and that she was better off pursuing her Earl and he would damned well court Susan. He was not so loyal, or moral or obliging that he would give Susan up and accept misery only so that others might not think ill of him.

Self-centered.

Damn it, he was, and he was glad to be, and proud to be, and he would not walk away from what he wanted. He would fight for what ought to be. He would be self-centered for them both!

He sighed out and began walking back towards the house, his arms swinging with the pace of his strides.

When he entered the ballroom he saw her.

Uncle Casper held her arm in a way that seemed protective as he led her from the room. Henry looked at Aunt Julie. She watched Susan and Uncle Casper leave with an expression of concern.

The current dance drew to its conclusion with a crescendo of music and the space about him became full of heavily breathing, hot and perspiring dancers. He was lost amongst them.

Which way to turn? What to do? He could hardly follow Susan, and yet his heart seemed to have left his chest and walked out of the door beside her.

"Henry where have you been? I was going to save the second dance for you but you were not here?"

He faced Alethea.

She had danced the last, her skin was glowing with warmth and her eyes bright with the fun she was having. Her eyes said, *dance with me,* even if her lips had not been so forward.

He lifted his arm and complied as he'd always done. "May I have this dance then?" He could not continue to carelessly comply. Because now he cared, and he cared for someone else.

The music began, announcing another waltz. Of all the dances. He was in no mood to dance it with anyone but Susan.

Alethea smiled broadly as her hand lifted to his shoulder. She was being her most charming. Perhaps she had realised that her flirting with Stourton was not having the desired effect.

He took her hand and slid his other to her back, aware of every difference between the sisters.

The music swelled and he began to turn. Alethea's bright blond hair caught the candlelight and reflected it back and her very blue eyes looked at him with the smile that sought to allure him.

He longed to look into pale grey eyes that expressed a depth of truer emotion.

191

Yet he and Alethea had been friends for years, it was not difficult to dance with her and make conversation, and here was not the place to tell her the truth. So he danced, and breathed, and his heart continued beating no matter that it felt as though it might shatter. What he talked of though, was Susan. He sought stories of her.

He wished he'd made an effort to know her well when they were young. He had been so self-absorbed he'd never noticed the things that were the same about himself and Susan. They might have been friends then. It *was* unsurprising that she had not liked him before and it was no wonder she had no faith in him now.

~

Susan lay in bed hugging her damp pillow, she had cried more than she had ever cried. But then she had never had a real cause to cry before.

A slight tap struck the bedchamber door, then the door creaked open. "Susan…" Alethea whispered when she entered the room.

Susan let go of her pillow and swiped the cuff of her nightdress beneath her eyes as the candle Alethea carried spread light into the room.

"Do you feel better?" Alethea asked as she walked around Susan's bed.

No. She felt worse now that Alethea was here. Guilt dropped like a heavy stone into her stomach. She had not been crying out of guilt or for her sister's loss, she had been crying for her own loss. She wanted to be with Henry. "A little."

Alethea set the candle down on the far side of the bed and climbed in beside Susan then turned back and blew the candle out. The room descended into darkness as the smell of burnt wax filled the air.

The mattress dipped as Alethea lay down and turned towards Susan.

".I waltzed with Henry after you left."

Susan thanked God for the darkness, otherwise she could not have hidden her pain.

"I have forgiven him, I think. He is too charming for me to be able to remain irritated and of course he waltzes divinely, so how can I stay angry with him."

Tears filled Susan's eyes. One slipped on to her cheek then dripped on to the pillow.

"When he danced with you did he say anything about me?"

"No, we were speaking of silly things," *of things found only in foolish dreams.* "You know how he likes to tease."

"Yes."

Susan's heart cramped, becoming hard and painful at the sound of contentment in Alethea's agreement.

Henry's fist was clenched about her heart.

Yet she could not love him. He belonged to Alethea.

The sense of empathy, that had always pulled her one way and then another, for any wounded thing, tugged at her, pulling hard. She was sorry for her sister. It was guilt and empathy that stood as a wall between her and Henry.

Chapter Seventeen

Susan leaned aside slightly as a footman poured her a third cup of coffee, then took away her barely touched breakfast plate.

"Darling you have hardly eaten a thing, are you still feeling unwell?" Her mother asked from the end of the table to her right.

Susan had endured half an hour of Alethea stating her hopes that Henry would call today, and that he would resume his attentions.

If he did come Susan could not be within the house. She would be called downstairs and she could not claim a headache every day.

Her stomach coiled and twisted with nausea, fear and guilt. She could not eat. She had no sense of hunger only distress.

"Are you unwell, Susan? You're very pale," her father stated.

Alethea had left the table and gone upstairs, to prepare herself to ride out in Hyde Park with the Earl of Stourton, no matter that she hoped Henry would call.

Susan had remained at the table to enable this conversation.

"Did you not sleep?" her mother progressed.

Susan breathed in. She did not like to lie, but she had to. "I could not sleep," She looked at her mother. "I do not feel well. The air here disagrees with me…" That was the only excuse she had been able to think of in the dark in her room as Alethea had slept. "I wish to go home." She looked at her father, he would be the one to arrange it if she was allowed to leave. "Papa…"

"Where has this come from?" His fingers touched the end of his pale moustache and twisted the tip. "You have seemed merry enough, until last night."

"I have been trying to enjoy myself for Alethea's sake, but I shall only ruin things for her if I stay. I can no longer pretend. I have a headache daily, and… I hate it here." She looked at her mother. Her mother would react from emotion; she would be the one to persuade her father. "I feel sick, constantly, Mama. Please may I go home?"

"We are only to be here four more weeks. Can you not bear it for that long?"

"It will look odd, Susan." Her father added.

They sounded annoyed.

If they did not agree she would run away, she would not remain in this house if Henry called. She looked at her mother, then her father. "No one will notice I am not here." Six months ago that would have been true. It was not true now. Henry would notice. But he could not care. What had grown between them, had to die. "I want to leave today. My trunks may follow." She looked at her mother her voice shifting from a plea to desperation. "I want to be at home, Mama. I do not like it here anymore. London has made me unwell."

Her mother stood up and came about the table, then wrapped her arms about Susan, holding her firmly. "What has happened?"

Susan did not reply but nor did she pull away, she had craved comfort last night when she'd lain in bed. Her arms wrapped about her mother's waist as her mother pressed Susan's head against her midriff, and her fingers stroked over Susan's hair. *I love Henry, Mama, I love him, and I cannot even speak of it.*

"Susan." Her father stood and came about the table too. His hand rested on her shoulder.

She could no longer hold back her tears.

"What has happened?" Her mother asked again more quietly.

Her father pulled out the chair beside Susan and set it down so it faced her, then sat with his legs wide as he leant forward. His fingers embraced her chin and turned her head so she would look at him. Her arms fell from her mother, but she caught hold of Susan's hands.

"You worried me last night, Susan, and now you have worried me more. This is not like you. What is wrong?" Her father's face was a shimmering blur through the cloak of her tears.

"Susan, please tell us."

She glanced up at her mother, and her father's hand fell to rest on her shoulder. "It is nothing, Mama, I promise—"

"Something must have occurred. We are not fools, Susan. Something has made you decide to leave in such a hurry," her father said.

"Nothing." She met his gaze which looked all of his fear.

"Last evening, Susan—"

"No." She knew what he thought. "I promise no harm came to me. I am simply not a town person, it has made me melancholy and miserable and I want to go home."

"But you enjoy dancing…" her mother said.

"Not at the expense of fresh air and fields and flowers. Please let me go?" She looked at her father. "Papa?"

He sighed.

She looked at her mother, who squeezed her hands. They did not want to let her go and yet she could see their argument was weakening. "Please?"

Her father sighed once more.

No, her parents were not fools, they knew there was something behind this, but she would never say, and they could not force her to speak.

"I will take you home," her father said in a low pitch. "But I wish you would tell me what this is about. What has really made you choose to leave?"

"Nothing," she said again.

He rose, his hand slipping from her shoulder. "I will tell them to prepare the carriage."

When Susan would have stood, her mother pressed her shoulder to stop her. Her father left the room, and her mother asked, "Will you not tell me?"

"There is nothing to say."

Her mother cupped her chin and lifted her face. "Then if it is nothing you may wait a couple of days—"

Horror shot through her heart. "No." She had won; her father was taking her. She could not stay even until luncheon in case Henry came. She stood, slipping free from her mother's hold. "May I go upstairs and pack my things." She wished to be ready before Alethea heard of this. Alethea would try to make her stay too.

Her mother sighed, as her father had done, a note of doubt, concern and acceptance. "We know something has happened, it is the only reason your father has agreed to your leaving. But now I must fret over you from a distance because it would be unfair of me to come with you and take Alethea away."

"There is no need for you to fret. You may stay with Alethea without worry."

Her mother shook her head, but she held out her hand. "Come along, let us go to your room and pack your trunk together, and if you have a change of heart and wish to tell me what has caused this sudden need to leave then I will be very glad to hear it."

As they walked up to her room Alethea came hurrying down past them. "Lord Stourton is here." Her bonnet was gripped in her hand.

Susan stepped back against the wall out of her sister's way.

"I waved from the window, Mama, and told him to wait in the street, you do not mind if I go straight out?"

"Of course not."

Alethea hurried on past them. She put her bonnet on in the

hall, as the footman opened the door. Then she rushed out without looking back.

Her mother's arm settled about Susan's shoulders as they walked on, offering the comfort Susan appreciated but did not deserve.

She had stolen Henry from her sister. She was a horrible person.

Tears leaked from her eyes, and ran from beneath her spectacles. She pulled away from her mother took off her spectacles and wiped them away.

~

Susan's parents refused to let her leave before Alethea returned from her outing with Lord Stourton. Then they made her wait until after they had eaten luncheon, as though they hoped she would change her mind. She did not.

As the clock ticked away each minute, anxiety danced through her nerves. What if Henry called? He would come today, she knew it.

Of course Alethea had urged Susan to stay, and then become distressed because Susan would not. Then angry because Susan would not tell her why. They had eaten luncheon in silence.

Then the moment finally came, when no more excuses to make her stay were possible. The carriage waited before the house. Her father settled her shawl over her shoulders.

Alethea's eyes glittered, full of tears, and some tracked on to her cheeks.

Their mother wiped away tears too.

Susan embraced her mother. She wiped Susan's tears away with her handkerchief, while Susan's father watched with a bitter stare.

He wrapped her mother up in his arms and kissed her cheek as Susan looked at Alethea.

Alethea had forgotten her anger now. She hugged Susan, then let her go and gripped her hands. "Do not go."

"I must."

"Why?"

"Because I wish to." The whole shabby story hovered behind Susan's lips. But confessing would destroy everything—she would lose Henry and Alethea.

"Susan…" her father stated gruffly to ask if she was ready to leave.

She was more than ready.

She turned away from Alethea, biting her lip to hold back more tears. Her father lifted his hand to encourage her to walk ahead of him, then he looked back and nodded a final goodbye.

"Goodbye!" Alethea called, when Susan neared the door.

Susan looked back. "Goodbye."

Her father offered his hand and Susan held it as he led her out to the carriage. He helped her climb up as her heart beat rapidly, out of fear that Henry might arrive before the carriage drew away.

She sat back in the seat. The tears that had trickled before, flowed. She took off her spectacles so she might wipe her eyes.

Her father sat opposite her. As the carriage rocked into motion he reached into his pocket for a handkerchief and passed it to her. He sighed when he sat back, as he had sighed this morning. "I do not know how to make you speak of what has upset you, but if it is to do with a man… If anyone has harmed you…"

A flush warmed her skin. "No one—"

"I am just saying, Susan. If it were so, then I will do whatever must be done to see this put right."

Susan did not answer. Nothing would put it right.

Chapter Eighteen

Henry stood before the door of the Forths' town house and breathed in, his hands clasping into fists. His fingers flexed as he breathed out.

His heart beat out an erratic pattern.

He had come to resolve the mess he'd created.

He was here to speak, to tell Alethea that he did not wish to marry her. Then tell Susan that he would not take no for an answer. Admittedly he and Susan would need to be mindful of Alethea, there could be no hasty proposal, but he needed time to adjust to this storm of emotions anyway.

He was tired. He'd barely slept through the night, thinking constantly of Susan, of kissing her and the words that might persuade her to accept him. He'd fallen asleep at sunrise, finally, and then remained in bed until after luncheon.

He raised the large circular door knocker and dropped it down once, heavily.

His stomach was a tightening knot.

As the door opened, nausea twisted through him. He'd come here to escape the heavy chains of one obligation and yet to potentially snap another manacle about his leg.

He was still not certain he was ready for marriage, and yet he wanted Susan, and the only way he would ever wholly have Susan would be to marry her…

Dodds, the butler, smiled at Henry. "My Lord." Dodds bowed then stepped back, pulling the door wider. "Come in, sir. Shall I announce you in the drawing room?"

"Yes please, Dodds."

Dodds lifted a hand to take Henry's hat and bowed again before he passed it on to a bowing footman. Henry handed his cane over too.

"My Lord." Dodds encouraged Henry to follow him.

Henry walked across the hall at Dodds's heels, with the eagerness of Samson, his heart thudding in his chest. Susan had made him thus.

Dodds pushed the drawing room door open a little wider and knocked it gently. Henry heard the women's voices.

"Yes!" Aunt Julie called.

Dodds stepped in. "Lord Henry, my Lady."

"Come in, Henry! You have no need to hover outside the door!" Aunt Julie called.

He walked in to see Alethea turning to face him, she was sitting on a sofa with her mother, from the movement it looked as though they'd been holding hands. Something was wrong. Their eyes were red rimmed and watery. They'd been crying.

Heat flushed his cheeks, they watched him walk across the room.

Henry's hand lifted as Aunt Julie stood, although he had no idea what to say. "Aunt…"

"Do not mind me, I am being foolish, Henry." She kissed his cheek, then wrapped her arms about his neck, giving him a brief embrace. When she let him go she looked at Dodds. "Have a maid bring some tea." She looked back at Henry then. "Sit down and make yourself comfortable. Alethea will appreciate your company."

He did sit, only because he did not know what else to do as Aunt Julie gave Dodds more directions.

Henry leant towards Alethea. "What has upset you?"

"Susan has gone."

"What? Where?"

"She went home. She insisted on going today but she would not say why."

She had run. "Was she upset?"

"Yes, but she would not even tell, Mama, why."

He took a deep breath. Damn. She had been upset because of him.

"You were the last person to speak with her at the ball, was she distressed then? Mama thinks something happened."

The air caught in his lungs. No. Yes. Something had happened and then she had run, and kept running. "No she was happy…" The lie left his throat with no strength. "You said she left the ball with a headache…" *I cannot… She is my sister, Henry. Do you not see? If I was in Alethea's shoes I would not be able to bear it. Henry. I cannot hurt her like that.*

"That is what she said. But this morning she said London has made her unwell."

The nausea spun in his stomach. "And she gave no reason beyond that?"

"None," Aunt Julie answered him. He looked at her. She had sat down in a chair near them.

Heat burned beneath Henry's skin. He'd chased Susan away from her home, and her family. No. That was not true. She might have stayed, if she had been stronger. If she had been more self-centered. The word mocked him.

If she had been more like him in that regard they would be sitting here telling her sister together. But then Susan would not be Susan.

She was care full, mindful of others—as he now cared for her. But damn it… The thought of her in tears here… Of her leaving in distress… Leaving the sister she loved… Last night she had talked of standing in her sister's shoes, now he imaged standing in hers. The pain, guilt and regret cut deep inside him. He was no longer a careless man, he could not hurt her any more than she would hurt her sister. She had been the first to accuse him of self absorption, it had been true, but she had also been the one to break him free of it.

And last night…

Last night was going to be all that he had then. His heart broke, cracking as though it was china, pressed under the heel of her shoe.

Remember it, rejoice in it and regret forever… He would not regret his carelessness in that, only that it was all that he would have—forever. The cracks in his heart ran into his veins reaching deeper. He'd thought his emotions love, now he knew it was love, this pain was what his father had spoken of when he'd talked of losing his mother.

"Henry." Alethea's fingers gripped his hand. "Did you see last night…" The conversation was swept off Susan and became focused on Alethea and the occurrences of the ball last evening, and the balls that were still to come this season and how they would be impacted upon from Alethea's perspective by the loss of Susan.

He had been as careless and selfish before.

After the tea had been served and drunk, Aunt Julie looked at him. "Why do you not take Alethea out in your carriage? That will brighten your mood, Alethea."

He looked at his aunt. "I cannot." Then he looked at Alethea. "I'm sorry. I did not bring my curricle, I walked."

He'd needed the activity of walking to fight the noise in his mind, a slow crawl through the streets would have driven him mad.

But he should have brought his curricle, then they might have talked. Yet he was no longer in the mood to speak. His insides had become a vacuum and his heart… It was shattered.

Susan had run. The truth of it settled over him, and if he loved her as much as he claimed, then he should allow it, and not follow.

He stood up, half in a dream. "I ought to leave anyway. I agreed to meet someone at my club."

Aunt Julie and Alethea looked at him in surprise, he'd not been here long.

"Are you going to the Tomlinson's musical evening?" Alethea asked.

"I am not sure, perhaps. Good day." He bowed towards his aunt.

Alethea stood.

He would have bowed to Alethea to take his leave, but she gripped his arm. "I will walk into the hall with you."

She held his arm firmly in a way that reminded him of how Susan held his arm. The memory was agony pinching in his chest. This was the wrong sister.

She talked in a whisper as they left the room. "Mama believes something dreadful has happened to Susan, but Susan denied it."

"Nothing dreadful would have happened to her," he said in a dry tone. "She was at a ball surrounded by people."

"You think it happened at the ball then…"

"I think nothing happened. She is probably just bored of such entertainments." Yet, she had loved them, she had come to life every evening. He'd selfishly taken that from her too. "But you know her better than I do." He knew nothing of her really, he had only begun to discover Susan and now he would know no more.

Alethea looked at him. "It was not boredom. I heard her crying last night."

Henry swallowed against a dry throat.

That was what his love had done to her. He'd hurt her and he had to withdraw if he was going to stop her from hurting any more.

Yet his desire, the feeling of love inside him, wanted to go to her—to comfort her. To just bloody hold her.

He moved, so his arm slipped loose from Alethea's clutch.

"When you write to her, tell her that I passed on my regard." I will be thinking of her. Daily. Constantly. I will let her go, but I will not forget.

~

The door into her father's small library opened wider. Susan looked up. She was painting a picture of a rose which lay on the table before her, trying to recreate it on the paper as the artist had recreated the orchids in Uncle Robert's book.

When she painted she could often manage not to think of Henry for minutes at a time.

"There is a letter for you, miss." The footman held it out as he came in.

"Thank you." She lay down her paintbrush with a sigh as her concentration was once again captured by thoughts of Henry.

She held out her hand to take the letter.

"Do you require anything, Miss Susan?"

"No, thank you." She glanced down at the address. She knew from the structure of the letters who they'd been written by; she had seen several dozen letters written to Alethea in the same hand. Henry's.

She turned away from the desk and broke the seal. There was no need to hide anywhere to read it. There was no one here other than the servants. Her father had stayed with her for two days, until she had managed to convince him that she was truly not injured in anyway, and then he'd returned to London.

She walked to the window. Her heartbeat fluttered in a stuttering rhythm. She should not be pleased to hear from him. She should not want to hear from him. Yet as her fingers held the paper that he'd written upon, warmth and longing filling every artery.

And Alethea? "Hush." She refused to hear the whisper of guilt. To read his letter was not acting upon her desires. They were only words on a page. Yet they were his words.

The paper trembled from the unsteadiness of her hand.

Dearest Susan,

I am trusting that this will reach you unopened as I know your father is here in town so I shall write honestly. I wish you had not run. I miss you.

I miss you too. The words breathed through her soul. But how could she have stayed?

But I understand your reasons. I did not mean to upset you any more than you meant to upset Alethea. Forgive me. And I know I should not write, but I could not help it.

I called the day you left. I had selfishly planned to invite you to view the Egyptian Exhibition Hall only so we could speak. I wanted to persuade you to accept me. But Alethea told me how upset you were, and then I saw what you had asked me to try and see, a view through your eyes. Yes, I see, this is too hard for you, and I expected too much of you to lose your family.

I would rather that you were not a martyr, and yet I love you because you are. It is who you are. And so I must be a martyr too and sacrifice my happiness with yours. But I wish you to know my choice for a wife, is you. If I had a choice.

But as I do not, I will rejoice in the hours we were together too, because I love you. But for that same reason, I will not chase you, I have let you go because I cannot see you hurt.

She took off her spectacles as the tears fell.

Your most sincere admirer,

H

Love…

Alethea had read out many of the letters Henry had written to her. They had been factual accounts of things he'd done with friends. His letters to Alethea had never contained words expressing emotion and he'd never written the words, I love you.

She folded the letter, left her paintbrush un-rinsed on the side, and the painting half complete, and took the letter to her room, where she put it in a drawer out of sight.

She would not write back. It would be utter folly to begin an exchange which could lead them to nothing other than more pain.

Ever since this foolishness had begun, her heart had gone out with a sense of pity to her sister, because she had taken what Alethea wanted—now it reached out to Henry. He sounded as though he hurt as much as she did.

Life was cruel. If only her father and his had not made their stupid agreement!

It was not fair!

When she retired to bed later the letter whispered to her. Before she blew her candle out, she got up, fetched it from its hiding place and re-read it. Then she fell asleep with it in her hand.

In the morning, she watched herself in the mirror as a maid helped her dress. The letter was back in hiding—just like her feelings.

But it had made her realise she could no more stay here than she'd been able to stay in London. Henry would return and their paths would cross again and again. And what then? She would be cut down with embarrassment, longing and guilt for the rest of her life.

She shut her eyes as the maid pulled hard on the lacing of her corset.

The only option she had was to find a teaching position in a school, or to become a governess.

After she'd eaten her breakfast she wrote to her father and proposed the idea that she might find a position, it was better that she did so with his consent.

Then after luncheon another letter arrived from London, from Alethea.

Dearest Susan,

I miss you so, I have no one to share my confidences with and Henry is being his usual distracting self. He dances with me but he never sends me flowers and he has become melancholy. I call him miserable to his face. He merely gives me annoying pretend smiles. I told him I shall choose the Earl of Stourton. He said he did not care.

I think he has changed, but he wrote to me yesterday and asked if I would ride out with him today because we needed to talk. If it is to propose after his behaviour the last few nights I am of a mind to refuse him. It is what he deserves. But in truth I still favour him over Lord Stourton. I shall write more tomorrow before I post this, and tell you what Henry has said.

Susan looked up from the page and glanced out of the window into the distance, to the woodland, on the border of her father's land.

That woodland would one day be Henry's.

A sharp little blade pierced through her heart. She took a breath and looked back down. She had to learn to face her guilt, she would not estrange herself from her sister, or her sister's words, because of her love for Henry. She could not lose her sister as well as him.

It is the next afternoon but I cannot tell you what Henry has said. He cried off. But I will allow him that it was for a good reason, poor William has a fever and Uncle Robert was

busy so Henry drove his mother to Eton. They are to bring
William home to recover. Of course Henry was not at the ball
last night either and so I danced with Lord Stourton, and do
not tell Mama, for she was not counting, we danced thrice. I
may well come to favour him over Henry yet!

My blessings, dearest sister, I hope that you feel better now
you are home.

Alethea

Susan's heart became a dead weight in her chest as she set down
the letter. She had been trying to paint again today but it was
too difficult to concentrate. She looked out of the window. It
was a cool middling day, the sky was grey and the branches and
leaves on the trees were being tossed about on a breeze. Even so,
she wished to be outside—to feel. She needed a distraction from
thought.

She went upstairs, she'd intended to fetch her cloak and walk
outside, but when she reached her room and looked out of the
window the open grass meadows beckoned her. She turned and
pulled the cord to ring for a maid, and when the maid arrived
she asked for help to dress in her riding habit.

She did not send word to the stables, but walked down there,
her legs kicking out the skirt of her habit as she hurried.

"Where is my mare? Where is Copper?" she asked as she
walked into the stable yard.

"In her stall, miss." One of the grooms pointed across the
yard. Copper's chestnut head appeared over the lower gate of a
stall in the far corner. There was one wonderful thing about being
the daughter of a horse breeder, she had a fabulous horse. Papa
had given Copper to her three years ago, and Susan was the only
one who rode her beyond the grooms.

Susan walked up to the stall and petted her. Copper was all
sleek beautiful, muscular lines. She was beautiful.

Like Henry, Susan's heart whispered.

"Shall I ready her for you miss?"

"Yes, please?"

A groom walked about her and opened the stall, then walked in as Copper backed up a couple of steps, the straw on the floor of the stall rustled beneath the mare's hooves.

Susan followed him in. He took Copper's bridle from a hook on the side of the stall, Susan patted the mare's neck, then she took the bridle from the groom and slipped it on. "Hello, girl." She'd ridden since she was four, she was entirely at home around horses. Her father treated them like children, the horses on the stud farm were a part of their family. Perhaps it was why she'd become attached to all animals. She thought of Samson, at Farnborough, and wondered if he was still sitting near the door in the hall.

The groom set Susan's saddle on Copper's back, and leant to buckle the girth strap as Susan patted Copper's neck .

She would always feel as though she was sitting before a door waiting. Perhaps she should ride over to Farnborough and commiserate with Samson.

The scents of the horse, of the straw and leather, had always reassured her before, but even that did not settle the pain or ease her loss.

"There you are, miss." The groom slapped Copper's rump gently.

"Thank you."

He bowed and lifted his cap.

Susan led Copper out into the yard and walked her to a mounting block. The grooms carried on about their business. She usually rode out with Alethea, they were both confident riders, but her mother still preferred them to be accompanied by a groom. Yet they preferred to ride alone, so unless their mother knew, they did.

She hooked her knee over the pommel of the side saddle, then settled the skirt of her habit about her. The sharp beat of her heart was now from the expectation of a gallop over the meadows.

Copper sidestepped, sensing Susan's energy.

She gripped the reins tighter, so they held against the bit in Copper's mouth, then she tapped her heel to urge Copper into a trot.

"Have a good ride, miss!" One of the grooms called out as she rode out of the yard.

As soon as she was away from the house she set Copper into a canter, and then into a gallop as she leaned low against the mare's neck. The wind blew at her face and whipped the loose strands of her hair from beneath her hat. Energy filled her up, capturing her senses. She would conquer her feelings and she would make a life for herself somewhere away from Alethea and Henry.

She'd ride out to where her father's land joined Uncle Robert's, to the abbey ruins. She had an urge to stand amongst them and feel the passage of time, and her own smallness within it.

The walls became visible above a hedge when Copper jumped a narrow stream. The plants before it had been pruned to frame what was left of the abbey like a picture.

She rode on, slowing Copper to a trot, then ducked down and rode beneath a low arch into the ruins.

She looked up. The walls were still as high as the ceiling must have been in this part, but the sky above them had become almost as dark a grey as the stone, and the clouds swirled about in an argument with the wind.

The arches of an old passageway, ran along near the top of the wall.

The haste of the clouds, blown by the wind, the passage to nowhere… Everything spoke of time, just as she'd known it would, of how quickly it passed, of how tiny her own perspective of it was.

She dismounted, sliding off the saddle.

Life did not centre and revolve around her or Henry. The world was much larger than the two of them and their insensitive infatuation. Love… There were a hundred books on love being won and lost, and hearts warmed and broken.

She let go of Copper's reins, leaving the mare to graze on the grass which covered what had once been floors full of ornamental tiles.

The grass was wet from an earlier rain shower. The damp darkened the hem of her habit. She walked towards the abbey's minster, passing beneath a giant arch which had retained some of its ornate decoration and faced the remnants of the stone altar.

She should set her love for Henry there as a sacrifice. She had given up the thing she wanted most in her life.

She missed him. There was a hole within her that ached as though she had been shot through with a bullet. How did such feelings pass? How did anyone survive a broken heart?

She walked on, not really knowing in which direction she was walking. Her fingers clasped the skirt of her dress, lifting it away from the damp grass.

There was a low wall before her.

Many of the stones from the walls in the ruins had been taken to build houses, and so there were some walls as low as her hip, and some she could step over.

When Susan reached the wall she could see over the top; a view of the woodland that would become Henry's as the ruins would become Henry's.

Bitterness, jealousy and… loss, whirled through her. Someone would marry him. He was the heir, he would take someone, if not her or Alethea.

Tears made the valley a shimmering mass of green. She sobbed as the tears ran on to her cheeks, crying noisily with a childlike release of pain. It echoed back from the high walls. But there was no one to hear. "I love him!" She shouted out the words that fate, and their father's plans, had forced her to keep silent, yelling them at the walls. "*I* want him! I want to be cruel and selfish! I want to keep you Henry!"

She breathed steadily. Letting the words echo into silence. "But I can't," she said in a low whisper.

A raindrop fell on to her shoulder. She looked up. Another dropped on to her chin. She opened her lips as the rain fell harder, and let the raindrops fall into her mouth and dampen her face, mingling with her tears.

She kept her face turned up to the sky and her hands on the coarse stone wall, as the rain fell in earnest, and prayed it would wash her pain away.

~

Henry's elbows rested on his thighs. He was sitting on an upturned bucket near his brother's narrow bed. While his mother was sitting in the only chair, close enough that she might hold William's hand. William lay unmoving and silent. The only sound in the room was his breathing.

Henry sighed out a breath and reached out to hold his brother's arm. William was burning up. He'd lain in a stupor ever since they'd arrived, exhausted by his battle with the fever. He'd not even opened his eyes. He shivered, even though his skin bore the heat of a poker in a fire. Henry let him go.

This, was not right.

God, Henry's chest hurt from the lump of pain in his throat that longed to scream out his anger and frustration. It was torture sitting here and watching his little brother suffer when there was nothing he might do.

The doctor had warned them three hours ago that William was not well enough to be moved. He'd said the fever could yet increase and so it was better to let William remain at the school to ride the fever out. But fever was not always a journey that was passed through, sometimes it claimed its rider.

William could not die.

The words of denial breathed through Henry over and over as he saw a hundred images of William in his thoughts. William was thirteen. They were not close but he looked up to Henry as all his younger brothers did.

Responsibility hung like a heavy weight from Henry's shoulders. He had been battling with a need to become responsible, but here there was no battle nor choice; it gripped him about the neck, and its grip was tightening, closing off his throat so he could not breathe.

William had been playing a reckless prank. He'd been climbing up to one of his masters' rooms to fulfil some dare. He'd fallen. Apparently the school had thought him well but two days after the fall, after he'd been shut into a room in isolation for punishment, they'd discovered that he'd collapsed with a fever.

There were cuts on William's feet where the doctor had bled him to release the bad humours in his blood—whatever that meant.

Henry looked at his mother. "Mama, shall I have someone find you a meal? You look pale, you must be hungry."

"No, I could not stomach food, Henry. I just wish you would open your eyes, William, and speak to me, then I shall feel more certain you are recovering."

Henry wished for it too, a part of him wanted to shake William, and yell at him, *wake up!*

His brother's cheeks held red roses, where the fever had bloomed so high, and his skin glistened with sweat, even as he shivered again.

Henry gripped William's hand. He would not let his brother die. He squeezed his fingers to tell William not to be afraid.

The sense of responsibility clung on. Only days ago, he'd made the most painful decision of his life, to let Susan go, he'd praised himself for doing so, for being so damned responsible and caring that he would crack his own heart. The whole thing, the whole

214

sense of his growth from a careless youth to a caring man who knew how to love, paled to a watery bland shade in this room.

This was responsibility. He had his mother and his brother to protect. But how could he make William better?

Henry wanted to speak, to encourage William to fight and yet his mother had returned to silence and so he stayed silent.

William was too young to face this.

It was half past the hour of ten when the doctor next came to the room. It was dark outside.

Henry had lit candles a couple of hours before.

He stood up, moving out of the way, so the physician might feel William's forehead.

"He is no better."

The man was stating the bloody obvious. Henry's teeth gritted against sharing those words, as he stared down at William.

How could William be both pale and flushed? But he was. He was an odd colour. He did not look well at all—and he had still not opened his eyes.

The doctor looked at Henry. "I would suggest you send for The Earl of Barrington."

A frown clasped at Henry's brow. No.

The man would only propose sending for Henry's father if he thought there was little hope.

No. No!

The doctor reached for William's wrist. "His heartbeat is very weak."

No! The denial screamed through Henry as he looked at his mother, who stared at William. She was white.

He went to her and lay his hands on her shoulders offering comfort. She leant back against him slightly, her head resting against his stomach.

Emotion and the weight of responsibility coiled tighter inside him, and around him like a twisting, spiralling snake.

There were no tears in his mother's eyes and yet she must be longing to cry, she was staying silent and holding her emotion in only so that William would neither hear nor see it if he woke.

"I'll write a note now," Henry said in a low voice that ran over gravel in his throat, "and I'll send my groom back to fetch Papa."

His mother held one of his hands and looked up at him. "Thank you, I am glad you're here."

He smiled, but he could not answer, the snake with its weight of emotion, had wrapped about his neck.

She squeezed his hand a little, then let go and looked back at William.

When Henry left the room every muscle in his body stiffened with the desire to fight this.

No. No! He refused the doctor's judgement nothing ill would befall William. It would not. It could not.

He found the Matron who administered the hall William slept in. "Have you a quill, ink and paper, I need to send word home to my father."

"William is not improving?"

The words bit into Henry's chest, he did not answer, he refused to contemplate them. Yet it was right that his father came. His father should be here.

He scribbled the note with a shaky hand. All it said was, *Papa, William is too ill to be moved. Please come immediately.* Henry sealed it quickly and walked downstairs to find his groom.

When he handed the letter over he gripped the groom's shoulder too. "This is extremely urgent, do no delay at all. Deliver it to my father as quickly as you can. He will be at home, in the town house. Hurry please, and have him come back with you at once." The man bowed his head briefly then turned away.

Henry turned back towards the school building. The pain in his throat which longed to shout or cry had become agony.

Chapter Nineteen

"Miss."

Susan looked up at the footman standing in the open doorway of her father's library. She was not trying to paint today, she was reading, she was trying to lose herself in a fictional tale so she need not dwell on her own sorry story. It was proving unsuccessful. "Come in."

She had turned sideways in her restless fidgeting and draped her legs across the arm of the chair. She sat up and turned around as the footman walked across the room, a slight amused smile on his lips. He held a letter.

Her fingers lifted and pushed her spectacles farther up the bridge of her nose.

His smile implied she'd become a topic of conversation among the servants. But then her returning alone had been an odd thing to do, and Dodds was still in town with her parents so there was no one to silence their gossip.

He held out the letter and bowed his head swiftly. "Miss."

"Thank you." She took it, her heart leaping. But then she could see it was not Henry's writing but Alethea's.

When the footman left Susan set down her book and opened the letter.

It is terrible news. The words jumped out from the first line. Had Henry told her?

Susan sat back in the chair as fear gripped in her stomach, and clasped at the breath in her lungs. What had Henry done?

Dearest Susan,

You will not believe what has happened, it is terrible news, poor William has passed away. It was awfully quick, and I am unsure whether that was a blessing or not. The family only had the news yesterday that he had a fever. Henry and his mother went to the school to bring him home but he was too ill to be moved, and at eleven in the evening they sent for Uncle Robert. William died a little after midnight. I am wiping away tears for him as I write. I feel so for Uncle Robert and Aunt Jane. Of course they have gone into mourning.

Sarah wrote to us this morning. They are shutting up their town house and returning home immediately. William is to be buried in Yorkshire. So of course out of respect Papa has said we shall leave town and come home too. We should be with you in three perhaps four days. You must tell the household to expect us, Mama, said.

I cannot write more, we are all in shock.

Your beloved sister,

Alethea

William had died…

Susan stared at the letter, unable to believe it.

He was a boy. How could he have died?

Her heart drained of emotion, all the pain of the last few days fell silent. An acute sense of loneliness struck at her. She wished

218

for someone to hold. Henry… Poor Henry. Poor Uncle Robert and Aunt Jane… How must they feel?

Yesterday she had sulked and moped about the ruins pitying herself and what she'd lost, while Henry had been at William's bedside watching his brother die. She had not once thought about Alethea's letter saying that Henry had gone to his brother. She should have spent the hours praying for William, not lamenting over her selfish longing.

William had no more life to live… The words sliced her in two as all the pain now filling her heart and soul was for Uncle Robert, Aunt Jane, Henry, Sarah, Christine and the others.

~

Nausea twisted through Henry's stomach as he watched William. But it was not William, it was William's lifeless body. The laughing, energetic boy who Henry had spent half his life impatient with was no longer here. Pain swelled and rocked in Henry's chest.

His father had arrived too late to say goodbye. He'd looked tortured when Henry had told him the news. He'd walked into the room, dropped to his knees beside the bed and gripped William's body, his forehead pressing against William's, and he'd kissed William's cheek. It had been minutes before he'd let go, even though Henry's mother had come about the bed and held him.

Henry had stood back and watched, with his hands clasped behind his back, and said nothing, because he'd had no idea what to say, no words would bring William back. Nothing would take away the pain.

Yet what he watched might, a few months ago, have been his parents' grieving for his loss, if he'd broken his neck with his reckless carriage racing—but better him than William. William had barely begun life.

219

When his father had risen from his knees, Henry's mother had wrapped her arms about his waist and his arms had settled on her shoulders as she'd sobbed against his lapel. His father had not arrived in time to say his goodbye to William, but he had, at least, arrived in time to comfort Henry's mother.

His father had not cried, though, his eyes had been dry, but full of torture, of an agony Henry probably only felt one tenth of.

Henry had left the room, then.

Now he focused on William's face. He was glad he'd stayed— glad he was the only one who'd watched the last signs of William's life ebb.

As soon as his parents had left he'd helped dress William in his school uniform. William's colour had darkened as they'd worked, becoming grey and the muscles in his body had stiffened.

Henry wished this was a dream. It had happened so quickly. He could not believe it was real. But it was.

A desire to hold William, to clasp him firmly, shot through Henry.

His mother had not wished to leave, but when Henry had offered to stay with William to allow his parents to return to London, his father had urged his mother to go. They'd taken his other brothers, Stephen and Gerard, with them. It was not William who needed his parents now it was the others. They had been in shock, caught off guard by the speed of this and Christine and Sarah had still been in the town house.

Before William had died, in his last hour of life, Stephen and Gerard had been sent for and had come into the room and stood by William's bed to say their farewell. They had tried to hold back tears, but it was such a bewildering sight Henry was not surprised when they had failed.

Stephen had told Henry that two days ago they'd been playing cricket with William as though he'd expected William to get up and play then. Gerard had turned and gripped Henry's waist seeking comfort that none of Henry's siblings had sought from him before.

His arms had surrounded his brother in a tight embrace. Stephen at sixteen had looked at them, his eyes glittering with moisture, as his expression held hard. The boys had wanted his father, but his father had not been there and so they'd looked to their elder brother because to turn to their mother would have felt weak.

And besides his mother had been crying quietly, she would have been unable to comfort them. Henry had learned a new strength he'd not known was within him in the last few hours, and now he was gripping at it, his fists holding tight. He was being strong for his younger brothers, strong for his mother, and stronger than his father because his father needed to focus on the others—and grieve.

"The coffin is outside, it is ready, my Lord. I am sorry the stairway is too narrow to bring it up."

Henry looked at the man who stood in the door. The school staff had left him alone in the attic room, out of respect probably. He hoped not out of lack of care. Yet he felt as though the world should be wailing with sadness—not enough fuss was being made. This was his youngest brother—and he'd become nothing but cold flesh and bone. The snake clenched hard around Henry's chest and tightened about his throat, trying to strangle him.

"Shall I wrap the body in the sheet, sir?"

The body… *William! My brother!* "No. I will carry him down."

Henry walked to the side of the bed, as the man held the door open. Henry's heart pumped hard, pulsing blood into veins which felt dry.

William had grown much taller in the last year. He'd begun to grow from a boy to a youth.

He would not grow now.

Henry leant down and slipped an arm beneath his brother's knees, and another under William's shoulders, then gripped his

221

stiff body and lifted his weight, to hold William against his chest.

He was taking on his father's task. But he was glad his father had not had to do this.

"When will you grow out of this reckless stage? When will you care what others think and feel?" Those were the words his father had yelled at him. The answer was—now. He had known love for a woman and let her go and he'd thought he'd changed then. But now—now he held his dead brother in his arms. Now he knew he had changed.

If William had not looked up to Henry's reckless ways, perhaps he would not have tried to climb up to his master's room?

If Henry had paid more attention to his younger brothers, certainly he would not need to feel this intense weight of guilt.

He'd always believed they would be friends when his brothers were older, as he was with his cousins… It had never occurred to him that any of his brothers would not reach maturity.

He wanted William to come back. He would trade anything for it.

William's body was heavier than Henry had anticipated, but the weight—the burden—was what Henry deserved. He would carry it his whole life. He wished this was him.

William's forehead rested against Henry's cheek as Henry carried him towards the narrow door of the small room.

"My Lord." The school's master, who had held the door, followed Henry as he walked out and began his descent down the narrow staircase. Henry was careful not to catch William's feet, or bump his head.

William was so cold—so grey.

Henry had never played with his young brothers. The gap in age had always seemed too wide to him. His cousin Harry was tactile with his young siblings and his nephews and nieces. Henry had never been like that.

It cut into his soul to hold his brother in an embrace when it was too late.

The sense of Gerard's body close to Henry's, yesterday, as Gerard's arms had wrapped about Henry seeking comfort, held tight in Henry's emotions. He would rather think of William like that, like Gerard, embracing him back, even though William had never done it.

Henry continued walking down the stairs, his pace steady. He would embrace his brothers and sisters frequently now.

He turned the last corner on the narrow staircase and reached the much smarter hallway which led to the main, grand area of the school.

The hallway, and the stairs, were much wider here but still there was no one else around him bar the one master who'd followed him. It was late for a school for boys and the daylight shining into the hall from a window behind him was fading, but the candles had already been lit; they cast pale shadows about Henry as he walked down the last set of stairs.

Henry had sat with his brother the entire day, after his father and mother had returned to town. He had not wished to leave William for a moment. He had a sense that William might be afraid, which was stupid. William was beyond feeling afraid yet Henry was not beyond being able to see his brother alive.

It was as though Henry was back in that damned curricle when he'd taken the turn and there had been no time to adjust his hold, no time to grasp anything as the thing had lifted off the ground on one side, tilting, and then rolled. He'd just been thrown into the air and landed hard. He'd landed harder now.

Wherever the William who'd gone from his body was, Henry hoped that he was happy and did not feel alone or frightened. They had grandparents on the other side, people they had never met, perhaps William was with their grandparents?

When Henry stepped from the last stair into the school's entrance hall, he expected to see someone. Again there was no one. Perhaps the staff were all busy keeping the other boys out of the way.

Or perhaps now that his father had gone they felt that they'd scraped and commiserated enough. They'd no need to repeat their bowing and scraping to his heir or the dead child. Boys died in this school all the time, diseases spread, accidents happened.

Henry had lost friends when he'd been here. He'd always thought himself invincible, though. That belief had applied to his family too. Never had he thought any of them might be lost.

"Reckless," he sighed out the word quietly on his breath. The word he'd forever been accused of.

Reckless! It barked at him in his head.

He'd carried the word like a badge of honour. He hated it now. It was a cursed word. It had killed his brother.

The master who'd walked downstairs with Henry moved forward to open the front door.

The undertaker who had come for William waited for Henry outside in the cobbled courtyard in the middle of the school's ancient buildings illuminated by the eerie light of dusk.

This was sordid. Wrong. It should not be happening.

The open polished ebony coffin rested on a low cart. From the outside it was worth every penny his father had paid, but inside… it was bare wood. But it had been acquired in a hurry. It looked cold. Harsh. Austere.

He was meant to put William down within it.

He wished he had let the man wrap a sheet about William, or that he'd brought down William's pillow from the bed, or a blanket.

The tears that had been a lump in his throat for hours became pressure at the back of his eyes.

He did not wish to leave William alone, not in a cold wooden box, in the dark.

Yet the boy in his arms was not the living and breathing William who would feel discomfort or terror. He no longer existed.

224

The urge to hold William in his arms all the way home shot through Henry. That was not possible though.

He walked closer to the cart and leant over to set William down inside the damned stark box. The weight and angle jarred Henry's lower back. It was a pain he welcomed; he deserved to feel pain. He should be the one in the coffin.

The urge to protect his brother, to keep him safe and comfortable was such a storm within Henry. He began stripping off his coat.

His gaze did not leave William's face.

He lay his coat down on top of William's chest. The action, the ability to do something for his brother, took a little of the pain from Henry.

He stepped back and two men who Henry had not previously noticed came forward. They moved the lid on to the coffin. Henry's arms crossed over his chest and he rubbed his arms, but it was not because he was cold even though his arms were now only covered by his cotton shirtsleeves.

He sighed.

The men began hammering nails into the wood and the strikes jolted through Henry. What would his family do without William in the world? What would the world be without William?

He sighed out another breath.

"My Lord." His father's groom lifted a hand to direct Henry to the waiting carriage he was to travel in. He did not wish to ride in the carriage, he would prefer to sit in the cart and keep a hand on William's coffin. He could not walk away from it.

A raindrop fell on Henry's head. He looked up. The sky had become dark not only from night drawing nearer but due to a dark cloud. Another raindrop fell and hit his shoulder, then the rain began in earnest. He shut his eyes and let it wet his face and his clothing. It helped ease the pain inside him a little.

"My Lord." Three voices said to him at once, requesting that he climb into the carriage, out of the rain, so that they might be on their way.

He could not stand here forever.

His shirt and his waistcoat now clung to his body they were so damp.

"My Lord." Henry looked at the groom who encouraged him to go to the carriage again.

He nodded, then walked to the carriage in a daze.

Behind him there was the sound of the backboard banging against the cart, and chains moving to secure it.

He and William had a long journey. His father had asked him to take William home, to Farnborough. Henry was to meet the rest of his family there.

Henry gripped the edge of the carriage by the door and climbed the step, then dropped back into the leather seat and looked out of the window. The groom shut the door and knocked up the step. But they did not then begin to move. The groom lit the oil lanterns on the corners of the carriage. Henry had ordered that they travel night and day.

The cart pulled away first and passed the carriage, then the carriage moved forward, following it. Henry's awareness was outside in the rain, on the cart with William.

When he could no longer see it, he tipped his head back and shut his eyes.

He wished to wake up in a brothel in Brighton and for this all to have been nothing more than a liquor induced nightmare.

Emotional pain welled up inside him, overwhelming pain. The hours he'd spent in agony from his shoulder had been nothing. He was drowning in pain. His hand lifted and ran across his face.

He wished his brother alive.

He needed Susan... He wanted her with him. That too was impossible.

Chapter Twenty

Susan looked out of her bedroom window when carriage wheels and horses' hooves stirred the gravel below it. Her father's carriage. The book she had been trying to read slipped from her fingers and fell to the floor as she stood up hurriedly. She ran from the room, catching hold of the door frame as she passed and spinning about it. She gripped the skirt of her dress and petticoats and lifted the hems up to her knees so she might indecorously run along the hall. She longed to hold her mother.

When she reached the stairs she held the bannister and continued hurrying, the wood slipping through her fingers. Her mother and Alethea walked through the front door into the hall as Susan reached it.

"Susan!" Alethea rushed towards Susan, as Susan ran from the bottom step. They embraced firmly. It was wonderful to have Alethea back.

"I have missed you," Alethea said.

"I have missed you too." *Terribly.* But Susan longed to hold her mother most. She turned to her.

Her mother's arms wrapped about her and squeezed her tightly, expressing the concern she'd spoken of before Susan had left town. Susan held her mother tightly too and breathed in the scent of her perfume.

"Are you well, dear?" Her mother stepped back as her palms pressed either side of Susan's face, knocking her spectacles askew in the urgency of the movement. "You look as though you have not slept."

"I have been worried for Uncle Robert and Aunt Jane." And Henry and the others. "How are they? Have you seen them?"

"Your father called on them the first day that we heard—"

"And they were as you would expect," her father continued. "Distraught. Robert was quiet and subdued and Jane in tears. None of the children came to the drawing room, but I believe they were all there. Uncle Robert had brought the boys back from school, and Percy had come up from Oxford."

"They should all be here at Farnborough now," her mother added.

"I have not heard of their return."

"They would have kept it quiet," her father said. "They are in mourning, they will not wish for visitors."

Susan looked at Alethea, she swallowed sharply before speaking the words which had run through her. "How is Henry?"

"We have not seen him, he stayed at the school and was to bring William's body back to Farnborough."

"He should be there by now too," her father stated.

Susan looked from one to the other. She knew what she wished to do, she wished to go to Farnborough, she could do nothing to comfort and help them from here.

"Your mother and I plan to call on Robert and Jane this afternoon. I shall write now to check that we will be welcome. Shall I ask if they are happy for you to join us?"

"Yes, please." Susan had to do something other than sit idly with hours to think and let the emotions of empathy overwhelm her. She needed to help them actively, in some regard.

"Yes, I wish to see Henry," Alethea said.

Oh. Alethea's words sliced through Susan. This was why she must leave her family; she could not live here when he would be spoken of as though he belonged to other people.

She did not want Alethea to speak to him, she wanted a private moment to hold him and ask how he was.

Susan's mother looked at Dodds. "Will you have tea brought to the drawing room?"

He caught Susan's eye and smiled, then bowed. He'd guessed Susan's return had been due to some upset in town, then. He'd probably worried over her. Certainly his expression implied his approval of her parents' return.

"Susan."

She turned to her father and he caught hold of her hand.

"Stay with me a moment I wish to speak with you."

She glanced at her mother, who smiled then turned Alethea to guide her towards the drawing room.

"Come along."

Susan was led by her hand clasped in her father's, to the library. Once there, he let her go. "Do you mind if I write to Robert first? It will only take a moment." When she nodded, he turned away from her and sat down at the desk, then took out a sheet of paper from a drawer, before reaching for a quill. He dipped the quill in ink and wrote only about four lines, then blotted his writing, folded the paper and sealed the letter. The scent of the melted wax hovered in the air as he stood, holding the letter in his hand.

Susan waited by one of the windows, her fingers clasped together at her waist.

Her father smiled at her when he passed her on the way to the door. He leant out into the hall calling, "Dodds! Have a groom deliver this to Farnborough immediately please, and ask him to await a response! Thank you."

"Yes, my Lord."

Her father shut the door, then turned back, and frowned as his lips twisted with a look of concern, making his waxed moustache slant at an odd angle. "Susan," he said on a sigh when he reached her and then he took hold of her hands, lifting them away from her waist. "What happened in town?"

This again. She was in no mood to manage his concerns. "Nothing for you to be worried over, I promise." Tears gathered in her eyes. She swallowed, trying to hold them back, but she was sure her eyes must be sparkling behind her spectacles; she was standing by the window in the sunlight.

"You admit there was something then?"

The news of William's death was too great a sorrow to allow her father any concern over her. "But it does not matter. I was not harmed in anyway, Papa."

"You promise."

"Yes."

"So I may focus my attention on Robert and Jane and need not fear for you?"

"Yes."

"I have been laying awake worrying over you, Susan."

"You need not have been."

He leant forward and kissed her cheek, his moustache tickling her as it had done since she'd been a child.

"I hated leaving you," he said, quietly

"I have been well enough, and happy on my own." She'd spent hours crying. She'd made such a fuss over a broken heart, which seemed so pathetic now.

"And so this nonsense you wrote to me about, about seeking some employment is it in the past then?"

Oh, no. She could not turn back on that. "No, Papa, I still wish for that. Alethea will marry, and what then? I am not the marrying sort. Being in London taught me that—"

"Susan. No one will see you destitute even if you do not marry. I will provide for you, despite the entail, and Alethea will not wish to lose the companionship of her sister."

She would if she knew the truth.

"I know you will provide for me, but I would rather do something more worthwhile than spend my life as Alethea's companion."

"Every breath you take is worthy. You are a much loved daughter and sister, not simply a companion. You know we believed we were unable to have children, and then there was the miracle of Alethea, and we had no expectation that the Lord would be so kind as to bless us again, and then came you…"

Tears gathered in Susan's eyes. It had been the wrong time to speak of worth. Her mother and father had probably spent hours imagining themselves in Uncle Robert's and Aunt Jane's place. Susan blinked away the tears. She must stop crying for herself.

Her father drew her into a firm hug. "Enough of that nonsense. I will not allow you to leave us."

~

When Susan, her parents and Alethea walked into the drawing room at Farnborough, after an introduction from Davis, they were greeted by a scene which Susan had never imagined she would see.

Henry's family were dressed in black, and for a family who always smiled, no one in the room smiled at them as they entered. Uncle Robert did not even stand up. He had been staring out of the window, and merely turned his head to look at them. He looked dazed.

The only thing that appeared normal in the room was the presence of Uncle Robert's dogs, three of which sat about Uncle Robert's chair, but the fourth—of course Samson was beside Henry.

His tail thumped on the rug as Henry stood, then Samson stood too. "Uncle Casper." Henry walked across the room to greet Susan's father, Samson following. He held out his hand so her father might shake it. When her father accepted Henry's hand he also pulled

Henry forward and wrapped his free arm about Henry's shoulders, giving him a brief one armed masculine embrace.

When Henry pulled away he gave her father a stiff, closed lip smile. He had not appreciated the embrace.

Samson came to Susan to be petted.

"Samson, away, lay down," Henry ordered. Then he looked at her mother. "Aunt Julie." She immediately lost all composure and cried.

Susan's heart beat out the pounding rhythm of a gallop.

Henry embraced her mother, offering comfort, not receiving it. He looked sallow, a little thinner, and so very serious—so unlike Henry.

Susan's father walked over to Uncle Robert, who finally stood, but he rose slowly as though he lacked energy. He'd probably not slept for days.

"Casper." Uncle Robert said, but he avoided the embrace her father offered pulling back as her father's arm lifted. The movement, and his expression, was a wince; it implied the thought of comfort was too painful.

"Julie." Aunt Jane stood. Tears shone in her eyes and ran on to her cheeks as Susan's mother turned to her. The two women did embrace and let their grief show with no restraint.

"Henry…" Alethea stepped forward. Her arms lifted and wrapped about his neck, offering comfort, but Henry's body remained stiff and the muscles in his face tight and resolute as his arms loosely held Alethea in return. "I am so sorry." Susan heard Alethea whisper before she let him go.

Henry looked at Susan.

Alethea turned to Sarah and Christine, who were dabbing handkerchiefs to their eyes. She held them both and cried.

Henry stepped towards Susan. His eyes saying so much, all the emotion in his letter hovered there, and she could see the depth of the grief running through him. He needed her to hold him but she could not.

"I am sorry." Her hands clasped behind her back. She would cry if she so much as touched him, and her tears would not all be for William.

"I wish you had not gone," he said in a low voice.

No one was watching them, no one would notice them talking more privately. "I had to."

"I know. But I may still wish it were otherwise."

She bit her lip. She could not discuss it without becoming emotional, because now he was here in front of her again the pull towards him was overwhelming—magnetic and empathetic; it called her a fool for running away. Yet it had become insignificant in the shadow of William's passing. "Where are your brothers?"

He flinched in the way his father had done. The question had lanced him. There was one less of his brothers. The tears Susan fought stung the back of her eyes.

"Percy took Stephen and Gerard out riding. They are not coping well. Boys do not weep out their grief as women do." The answer was spoken in a stiff pitch. He had not wept then either.

Perhaps males ought to cry, Henry and his father appeared to be in agony.

"I am sorry, Henry, it was a careless thing to say."

"What, to mention my brothers? It was not careless. You cannot be careful of every word you speak and I do not want people to tiptoe about us trying to not mention William." His answer was sharp, but then he said more gently. "Nothing you could do or say, Susan, would be without care. If anything your fault is that you care too much about what others think. I know you asked out of concern, and the issue is that we are all torn in two and nothing will bring William back, yet everything reminds us of him."

She longed to reach out and hold him as Alethea had. Her hands unclasped and fell at her side.

He reached out and held one. It was not a formal gesture it

233

was as if he'd needed to hold her too but had not known how.

She held his hand in return, her thumb pressing against the back his. *I love you.* The words whispered through her head as she looked into the unbearable level of sadness in his brown eyes.

"Susan…"

She let his hand go and turned to face his sister. "Sarah. I am so sorry."

Sarah's distress was not disguised with the stiff countenance Henry and his father displayed. Sarah's grief shone in her eyes and trembled in her lips. Susan held her as pain pressed into her heart too. A couple of weeks ago Sarah had been enjoying her first season clothed in bright colours.

Sarah pulled away and withdrew her handkerchief from her sleeve to dab at her eyes.

Susan wiped the tears from her cheeks with the cuff of her sleeve.

"I am sorry," Susan said. "I should not be making you weep but offering you comfort."

"I have been crying for days," Sarah answered, "I think every day my tears will run dry but still they fall. It was just so fast you see. I cannot accept that he will not walk into the room with the others when they come in. I expect to see him every day now we are all home again and he is never here."

Susan looked at her aunt. Alethea stood with her. She was trying to be stoic and smiling slightly as Alethea talked but she had dark shadows beneath her eyes.

"I will ring for tea, Mama," Henry said behind Susan, "You sit." It was a thoughtful thing for him to do, and very un-like Henry.

Susan glanced at him. When he walked past her he gave her a shallow closed lipped smile.

Her awareness of him as he walked away was not like the normal all-consuming pull—instead it became a sharp jerk on her heartstrings when he left the room. He'd looked so solemn. Henry had never been solemn.

Alethea sat on an empty sofa. Susan remained on her feet uncertain where to go.

When Henry came back into the room Aunt Jane said, "Sit down with Alethea, darling."

He glanced at Susan before consenting to the suggestion.

He wished to sit with her, she knew it. He sought her comfort as much her heart longed to give it. But as things were both their families believed his arrangement with Alethea still stood. He could not favour Susan over Alethea.

He is only fulfilling his duty. The sharp words struck through Susan in denial of the flash of jealousy that sparked from a flint. But what point was there in jealousy, they had agreed that nothing might progress.

She turned away and sat near Sarah and Christine, trying to stop herself from straining to listen to Henry and Alethea.

She talked with them of William, of their fondest memories and the things they would miss most about their beloved brother. Henry's voice was low as he spoke with Alethea and she could not hear a word. She heard some of Alethea's words, though, she was speaking of things that had happened in town. Susan doubted Henry cared today.

When the tea arrived Susan stood and offered to pour it, to save Aunt Jane, Sarah or Christine from the task. Susan's mother smiled acknowledging her kindness. Alethea had not even turned her head from her conversation with Henry. Henry glanced over and gave Susan a smile that said, *thank you.*

She poured while Sarah and Christine circulated with the cups. She, Alethea, and their mother and father, were dots of pale colour in a room of blackness. And the blackness hung in the air too, every conversation was so much quieter. Only Alethea's voice carried with lilting emphasis. Henry's father conversed with hers rarely responding and using a succinct, measured, brief tone, while Aunt Jane punctuated the conversation with Susan's mother with dabs of her handkerchief against her eyes. Henry's family were still in shock, as Sarah had said it had happened so fast they had not had time to adjust, they had not even really begun mourning.

But even Susan could not believe that at any moment William might not walk through the door with Henry's other brothers. She could not imagine him gone.

After the tea had been drunk and the cups gathered up Susan continued her quiet conversation with Sarah and Christine. The drawing room door opened. Everyone looked.

"We are back," Percy said walking into the room.

Gerard and Stephen walked in behind their older brother.

The three of them were flushed from a hard ride, and their clothes a little dishevelled, but the sense of a crushed spirit hung about them.

Susan stood, compassion drawing her to her feet. Of course Stephen and Gerard must have been closest to William. She did not know the younger boys well, there had been too great a gap in their ages, they had not played together as she had with Henry and Percy, and yet still her heart went out to them. But once she was on her feet she did not know what to say or do; she could see they would not welcome her embracing them.

"Thank you, Susan, it would be very kind of you to ring for a fresh pot of tea," Henry said.

She looked at him. He knew that was not why she had stood; he was saving her from the awkwardness which had gripped her.

He rose and walked across the room. "And I presume you would welcome shortbread or whatever treat cook can send us up. How was your ride?" His hand settled on Gerard's shoulder.

"Good." Gerard answered as he turned and hugged Henry for a moment.

She had never seen Henry hold his younger brothers. She turned away and walked across the room to call for a maid, heat flushing her cheeks, as though she had just glimpsed something private.

"Do not worry, Susan," Stephen touched her forearm, stopping her. "I will walk down to the kitchens and ask, then I may choose whatever cook has on offer." He smiled at her. It was a natural smile.

"I'll come with you." Gerard joined his brother and then both boys left the room barely moments after they had entered it.

"Susan." Percy bowed his head in greeting. She nodded too, then returned to her seat.

"How were they?" Henry asked Percy as he sat again too when Percy occupied a seat near him.

"They rode hard, mad for constant races."

Henry turned his back on Alethea and faced Percy. "I have no idea what to do to help them."

Alethea talked to Sarah and Christine, no one else was listening to Henry and Percy.

"We are doing what we can."

Henry nodded, but she could see he did not believe it.

"What do you think, Susan?" Sarah asked.

Susan turned to look at her, unable to answer because she had not been listening to what was said. Her thoughts and her heart sat beside Henry and took hold of his hand again.

~

"Henry said the funeral is to be in four days, on the Thursday, in York Minster," Alethea announced in the carriage on the way home, as if their father would not know it.

"I shall be going," Papa stated.

"I wish that I could," Alethea answered.

"It is unseemly for a woman to attend," Mama answered "and it is hardly appropriate for you when William's mother and sisters would not."

"I only said I wish, not that I would," Alethea complained.

But Susan knew where Alethea's complaint came from, she

wished she might be there too. She longed to stand beside Henry.

"We will go to Farnborough to support Jane and the girls instead," Mama answered. "We will be there when the men return."

The house would be full. William's family would come and they would fill the local hotels and inns or stay at his cousin Rob's. There would be no chance for Susan to speak to Henry alone even then.

She sighed and looked out of the window. Her heart so heavy.

She had not changed her mind, she had to leave. Yet... It did not mean that she could bear to watch Henry in pain and not offer comfort. *I love him.*

Chapter Twenty-one

When Henry stripped off his black evening coat his gaze caught on his reflection in the mirror in his bedchamber. He turned and stared at his image in the flickering candlelight. He'd become so used to seeing himself dressed in black his white shirt glowed like a beacon in the shadow filled room.

He untied the black neckcloth from about his throat as Samson watched from his prostrate position on Henry's bed.

Henry had never felt so heavy and tired in his life.

It was as though he'd always lived in mourning, he could not even remember how it was not to grieve. He wished William back with them. He'd spent barely anytime with his youngest brother and yet he could see William smiling and laughing, playing some game with the younger ones. Henry had lorded it about his parents' home ignoring them mostly, acting as though, because he was the heir, he was in some way better than the others. He now savoured every precious hour he had in which he could recall a memory of William. They'd been dropped like gem stones into a haystack, lost in the thick of his life, before. But now he saw them.

He pulled off the neckcloth and threw it on to the back of the chair. Then began unbuttoning his black waistcoat.

Susan had given him a new lens to observe his life through, scarce weeks ago, and he'd seen her accusations of carelessness and self-centered behaviour, but he had seen them far too late. Too late to know his youngest brother well.

Yet he was not the only one who was suffering and he would not be self-centered in this. His father had been virtually silent since Henry had returned home with William's body, and his mother could do little without tears flooding her eyes. And his sisters were as silent as his father and as tearful as his mother.

He took his waistcoat off and threw it on to the chair.

The boys' method of coping with their grief, and the silence and tears of the others, was to avoid the others and therefore the house. They rode, they walked outside, they played chess and cards in their rooms and kept away from the drawing room.

Henry pulled his shirt off over his head and threw that on to the chair beside the mirror too. He was not in a mood to be tidy.

The strength within him crumbled. He turned and sat in the chair containing his discarded clothing and gripped his head in his hands as his elbows rested on his knees.

Damn.

He sighed out then breathed in. "Damn."

He'd been the linchpin holding the family together since he'd returned. He'd taken on all his father's responsibilities and duties because his father ignored them, and his brothers looked to him because their father was withdrawn and their mother too upset.

He'd even been the one to travel into York and arrange the funeral, and he'd had his sisters write to all those who needed to know and might wish to come.

Yet he was in pain too.

He stood again because he could not give in to it. But it was screaming in his head. Samson lifted his head. "No, stay," he ordered as he looked at the dog. "There is no point in both of us losing sleep."

He walked out of the room, then, without bothering to put

his shirt back on, and headed downstairs, towards the family drawing room. He could not sit alone in his room and listen to the screaming inside him, it would overwhelm him. Brandy was what he needed. That would drown out his thoughts and deaden the pain—then perhaps he would sleep.

When he pushed the door open the room was lit, not just by the moonlight stretching through the windows, but by a single candle too. "Percy."

His brother stood in his dressing gown, doing exactly what Henry wished to do, pouring himself a brandy. "Would you fill a glass for me?"

"You cannot sleep either…" Percy looked back, a bitter half smile pulling at his lips.

"No." Henry shook his head as he walked across the room to join Percy by the decanters.

His brother handed him a glass. Henry lifted it a little and tapped the base against the rim of Percy's, then he drank its contents in one swallow and held his glass out for a refill. Percy drank his too then filled the glasses again.

"I am exhausted I should be able to sleep," Percy stated, "Stephen and Gerard never rest, they keep me busy all day, and yet my mind has no inclination to allow me to shut my eyes."

"I feel the same." Henry drained his second glass of brandy, then picked up the decanter by its neck. "Shall we sit?" He nodded towards the chairs as the heat of the liquor burned the back of his throat, in a satisfying way.

Percy followed Henry. Henry sat at one end of a sofa. Percy occupied a chair. Henry refilled his glass then leant and set the decanter down on the floor between them. He leant back and his free hand gripped the arm of the sofa.

"Papa is falling to pieces," Percy said quietly as he leant to pick up the decanter and fill his glass.

Henry sighed, the muscle in his stomach tightening. "I know."

"He ignores Stephen and Gerard."

241

"I know." Henry sipped from his glass. It was why he had begun fulfilling his father's duties, because someone had to stop William's death destroying their family. The family Henry had previously carelessly taken for granted and now could not bear to see fall apart. "When Uncle Edward arrives tomorrow I will ask him to speak with Papa."

"He is going to stay with Rob,"

"And he will come here to see Papa, you know he will."

Percy leant to fill his glass again, then sat back and slung one leg over the arm of the chair facing Henry a little. They had not been confidants in the past, and yet this was just how Henry had imagined it might be in the future when all his brothers were grown. It would have been the five of them talking. Now they were only four.

He sighed out a breath then sipped from his drink.

"Do you miss him?" Percy said.

"Yes, I miss William." Henry would not allow William's name to become a dead word.

"You never really spoke to him, you never spoke much to any of us, but you have talked to me most because we were at school together. You virtually ignored William, though, Henry."

Henry took a large swig of his brandy, then looked at Percy, the void William had left inside him burned with guilt. "That is why I cannot sleep. I wish that I had. I miss him even though I barely knew him. I miss the man he would have become. The man I would have known well, had William had the chance to grow."

"He—"

"Say William's name, Percy, for God sake. Do not let him be unmentionable. *He*—was our brother, William."

Percy coughed and swallowed back a rough sound of emotion in his throat, then sipped some of his brandy before continuing. "*William* was the one who always made me laugh the most, he teased me and played tricks, he was the ringleader of trouble

242

even though he was the youngest..." Percy smiled looking into the liquid in his glass, then he looked up at Henry. "He was the most like you."

The words slashed Henry across his naked stomach, and cut into the new fragility he'd discovered in his heart. His heart had turned from hardened rough flesh to weak, soft tissue in the last few weeks.

He looked down at his drink, then drained the glass again, to wash away the bitter taste in his throat. If William had modelled himself on his eldest, reckless, careless, self-centered brother, then Henry was definitely to blame for the trick he had played which had made William fall and ultimately die.

"I wish I had known him better. I would have talked sense into him and persuaded him not to be like me. I was a reckless idiot." Henry stood, and walked back over to the tray of decanters, to hide the emotion he warred with.

Percy laughed, although it had a heavy sound. "You are no idiot and you would not have said a word to William about being sensible. You *are* reckless, you would never have been William's voice of reason."

The statement was true. No he had been the devil on his brother's shoulder, whispering without even being near him—*do bad things.*

Susan had been far more right than even she had known, and now he had to carry a burden far worse than the trauma his death would have wrought on his family. He had to live and know he'd caused his brother's death and watch his family suffer in response.

"I am going back to my room to try and sleep," Henry answered without looking back. He set his glass down on the silver tray on which the decanters stood.

"I shall come too."

Henry turned and watched Percy drain his glass then pick up the decanter and stand.

243

When Percy came across the room to put the decanter back and his glass down, an urge to embrace Percy ran through Henry. He'd promised to himself that he would show his affection now. He did not obey the urge, though, Percy would think it odd. Yet Henry would seek more close conversations like this, building this closeness with the brothers he had left was the only way he knew how to ease the pain and compensate for William's loss. He had to put things right.

But for now, he simply needed to be alone to manage the pain swelling inside him and threatening to tear him in half.

And Susan…

He was trying not to think of Susan.

But an image of her face as she had held his hand, before Sarah had drawn her attention, hovered in his mind.

His spirit wanted to renege on their agreement. But that would hurt her, and he could not do that.

~

Henry had managed to sleep for a couple of hours, thanks to the brandy, but when that wore off he lay awake looking into the dark seeing William's lifeless body as he'd seen him the day he'd carried his brother downstairs.

He got up as soon as the sun rose, dressed quickly and walked down to the stables. The grooms were busy cleaning out the stalls and so he saddled the stallion he wanted to ride himself, then, purely through the strength in his arms pulled himself up to the height of the saddle, and swung his leg over the horse.

It was a reckless thing to do. He knew it immediately he'd begun the action. The horse could have rejected his movement and made him fall. He should have walked the animal to the mounting block. So many new rules that he ought to start living by if he was going to be the responsible son his father needed.

But he was just as reckless when he had the stallion out in the meadows; he kicked his heels hard and set the beast off into a gallop, jumping hedges and walls. The horse's hooves thundered over the grass, kicking aside the low early morning mist and crushing the heads of the clover. Then he raced on to the paths through the woods, bending low to the saddle to avoid the branches. He was simply riding, he had no aim or direction. But the pace and the physical exertion gave no solace to his battered soul. He did not think anything would.

When the sun rose higher he rode off his father's land and on to the land that his exemplary cousin Rob rented. It was time to see if some practical support might be found to give his emotions a crutch.

Rob's house was close and Henry rode hard, it would not take him long to reach it and Henry did not pull on the reins and slow the stallion to a canter until he reached the gravel drive, and he only then set the animal into a trot for the last few yards.

A groom came about from the side of the house to meet him.

The man held the horse's head steady as Henry dismounted. He'd never called here alone before. He'd never been particularly close to Rob. Rob had not joined the family's male friendship group, although he was of an age with Henry. Even at school and university they had only spoken in passing. But he had not come to speak to Rob, he'd come in the hope that his uncle had arrived. Knowing the timings of the journey, it was most likely Uncle Edward would have arrived last evening.

Henry thanked the groom but he did not ask the man if Lord Marlow had arrived, he would knock on the door now he was here whether his uncle was here or not, and if he was not then he would have to spend a few moments with Rob. Perhaps he should have spoken more to Rob when he was younger; Rob had always been responsible. Henry had taunted him with the word dull then. It was not a nice version of himself that he saw in the recollection of his past anymore.

He sighed as he walked towards the front door. It opened before he reached it. A footman stood there. "My Lord." He bowed.

"Is my uncle, Lord Marlow, here?"

"He is, my Lord."

"Please ask if I might speak with him?" A fist thumped out the pace of his heart against his ribs. He hoped for someone to share his burden, though his uncle could never take the guilt away he might take on a portion of the responsibility.

The footman disappeared through a door as Henry waited in the hall. He took off his hat and gripped the rim in both hands.

It was not the footman who returned but Harry. "Come in you fool!" he shouted as he walked out from the dining room. "What are you doing loitering in the hall?"

Swallowing my pride. "Kicking my heels. I wished to speak with your father about mine."

"Well he is breaking his fast with us. Is that what dragged you out of bed so early? Come in and eat." Harry was wearing his scarlet jacket, and the brightness of it compared to Henry's blacks glared at Henry. Yet the black armband cutting across the scarlet clawed at Henry's chest more.

He breathed in, to keep his breath steady, as he walked towards Harry. It was so strange to see Harry. Harry was a figure from yesterday, part of the Henry he had been considering in his recollections moments ago… He was not the same now. Life was not the same. It would never be the same again.

"I am sorry about the news." Harry gripped Henry's shoulder for a moment, as he turned to walk beside him. "It is a tragedy."

God, it felt so much more than that. It was an irreparable tear ripped open in life. Henry did not answer. There were no words to respond with.

The solemnity which hung over his own family was not in this dining room, they were not in black nor whispering, they were talking busily and yet when they saw him the air filled with pity. The women stood immediately. Rob's wife, Caroline, Henry's aunt Ellen and his female cousins.

Mary, the eldest of his female cousins, who was here with her husband, and Helen, Jennifer, Georgiana and even the youngest Jemima, who was twelve, were all drawn across the room to him, to offer condolences and comfort. Bees coming to his flowering misery. Women were like that. Alethea had been like it yesterday. Revelling in the opportunity to commiserate and show their capacity for compassion.

The reaction was shallow when moments ago they had been speaking as though the world was unchanged.

It had changed entirely for him.

After he'd been relieved of his hat and endured their kisses on his cheek, and their kind words, and accepted a chair at the table and then a dainty china cup filled with tea from Rob's wife, he looked about the room. Edward, Rob, Harry, and Drew, who was Mary's husband, sat together at the table. They all looked at him with eyes that carried the pity the women had shown.

The younger boys must have remained in school, at Eton, where William had died—but they would be like Gerard and Stephen, continuing life and denying that anything had happened to disrupt it. But they had been close to William.

An urge shot through Henry, to stand up and walk out. He could not abide this; the pain of facing others still leading a normal life. He sipped the warm tea to dispel the tight sensation in his throat and let its sweetness take charge of his senses.

"You wished to speak with me…" His uncle said in a compassionate pitch.

"Yes, but alone."

"Very well, we will talk once you have finished your tea."

Henry could see the next question on his uncle's lips. *How are you?* He could not answer it now. He looked at Harry to stop his uncle asking. "I am surprised to see you, I thought you were with your regiment."

"I have a leave of absence to attend the funeral."

Henry looked at Rob, fighting to deflect the conversation from

247

himself. "I am sorry if this has meant you are descended upon by visitors you did not expect."

"I do not mind. I am happy to be descended upon by my family. It is not so good, though, when what has brought us together is such a sad event. We all miss William."

William's name on Rob's lips whispered through Henry's soul. He longed to thank Rob for speaking it. Rob smiled at him.

Henry looked at Drew as he began speaking. "We came straight here when we heard." He smiled with a look of sympathy.

Henry looked away searching his thoughts for another question to ask someone so he did not have to face more consolation.

Harry provided the distraction. "Can you believe a brother and sister of mine have developed such boring streaks, Henry? They both rarely come to town and so it is so easy for them to change plans in the drop of hat."

Drew laughed with a bark of humour before answering, "Your sister is not boring, just carrying another child. And some of us prefer a sedate life Uncle Baba…"

Uncle Baba was the name Drew had bestowed on the black sheep among Henry's cousins and he loved teasing Harry with it.

"Baaaa." Harry made the sound in a way that said the name was as good as a sash of honour. "You were a black sheep once and now you might act as white as snow but I have heard of your past. You lived far more wildly than I may ever achieve."

"Those times are precisely that, *in the past*. Now *I am* as white as snow," Drew answered with a smirk

"And as boring and dull as Rob," Harry retorted.

The teasing and debating continued as Rob took exception to the charges against him.

Henry looked at his uncle. He drank the last of the tea then set his cup down on its saucer. "May we talk, Uncle?" he said over the others' conversation.

Edward smiled and set his cup down too, even though it was half full. He stood up. "Let us go outside."

Henry had always liked his uncle. Henry's father was full of mocking humour and sharp wit—much like Harry, or himself. Edward was more serious and measured.

When they left the table he lifted a hand, directing Henry towards the door into the hall.

As they reached the hall he told the footman who had followed that they did not need him, then looked at Henry. "If we go out the front door the others will assume we have gone to look at horses or something else more business-like. Shall we do that?"

This was how his uncle was, always insightful.

Once they were outside, he did not turn towards the stables, though, but away from them, crossing the gravel frontage. Henry walked beside him.

When they entered the yew lined avenue that led around to the garden at the rear of the house, Uncle Edward's arm wrapped about Henry's shoulders. The comfort gripped at Henry's heart. It was what he had needed his father to do—but then perhaps his father needed to be held too… Yet, he would never accept the gesture from Henry. Would he?

Henry sighed.

Uncle Edward's arm slipped away. "Tell me how I may help?"

"It is Papa." Emotion swelled in Henry's throat blocking it and it pressed at the back of his eyes too. He swallowed as he tried to speak. "I would be grateful if you spoke with him…" His voice had dried, strangled by the grief he battled with.

"Why?"

"He has become withdrawn. He barely speaks, and Stephen and Gerard are not coping, and Mama…" Henry had to swallow. "She cries all the time."

"And you?" his uncle asked.

I need help. I wish to grieve and I cannot because I need to help them and I'm not succeeding. Desperation gripped Henry and shook him.

"I will speak to him." His uncle answered without waiting for

Henry's answer. "Robert has always run from grief." He stopped walking and turned to look at Henry, then clasped his upper arm. "He will recover, Henry, time will pass and then things will go back to a normal life of some description. Never the same, but normal. The loss of someone never heals over completely, yet the rift in life knits back together with time."

Henry did not worry for his father suddenly, but for himself.

Would he recover from William's loss? He could not imagine the slashes of guilt and grief healing. Damn it was a selfish thought, and he had sworn to himself he would not be selfish again.

Chapter Twenty-two

The ebony coffin was far too narrow and light to contain William, no human could be within it. Henry, his father, his uncle Edward and Percy carried it among them, on one shoulder, walking in even, steady strides as they entered York Minster. But Henry had placed William within it, he knew William was inside, alone. But not alone, because they were here with him today—to say a final goodbye.

The giant decoratively carved stone walls swallowed him, suffocating him, as he walked into the Minster. Like Jonah sucked into the belly of a fish. Yet, its height, breadth and grandness, and the beauty of the carvings on the towering columns and the ceiling above them made William's life, that had ended in this narrow coffin, appear insignificant.

It made them all insignificant. Henry wanted William's life to have had some significance, some outstanding moment that would be forever remembered.

William's laughter ran through Henry's head.

He cursed himself again for not giving his brother more time. Perhaps he might remember something of significance if he had.

It was too late now.

He'd contemplated his own legacy months ago, when he'd

fallen from his curricle, or rather the lack of it. William had had no time to create a legacy. Henry had never previously cared enough about anything to leave one. He cared now.

There was no music to distract them as they walked along the broad aisle, only the sound of the people in the full pews either side of them. It was not only the higher and middle class who'd come, those faces he recognised from the assembly he'd attended, but there were those here who were in service with his father and others from the city who supplied his father's estate.

Henry's footsteps rang out on the ancient painted tiles as he continued to process. The people in the pews whispered. A man coughed. People ahead of them looked back, straining to see the coffin and its bearers.

Henry did not look at anyone particular but ahead at the altar, and to the wooden trestles where they were to rest his brother's coffin.

The weight of the snake of grief was tightening about Henry's neck, strangling him, and yet he had to keep going, because his father had crumbled; this morning he'd barely said three words.

Henry swallowed.

A heavy scent of incense hung in the air when they reached the trestles. Once they'd set William down, Henry bowed to the altar before turning to find his seat in the front pew.

Edward nodded at him.

Henry smiled at him and then Percy as he let Percy enter the pew before him. He took the seat beside his brother and let his uncle sit next to his father.

Gerard and Stephen sat on the far side of Percy, they had come into the church with Harry. In the pew behind them were Drew, Rob and John, and behind them were the men who were his father's friends including Uncle Casper and Lord Wiltshire and some of their sons, his own friends with them. The inns and hotels in York had been populated by the privileged for the last couple of days.

Henry leant forward to look at his younger brothers. Gerard was biting his top lip and his eyes glowed with the sheen of tears in the flickering light of a candle which burned on a pedestal near the pulpit.

The muscle in Stephen's jaw flickered as he stared at the coffin, as though he, too, could not believe it contained William.

Henry looked up as the Archbishop began the service.

He knelt with his family when it was time to pray, and his voice rose as he participated in the hymns the fist thumping against his ribs with the pulse of his heartbeat.

At the end of the service Henry allowed himself a selfish prayer; for strength to continue to support his family. He could feel himself weakening, his strength and sanity were slipping through his fingers like rope, and leaving burns. He was not succeeding.

They stood then, with his father and uncle and Percy, to pick up William once more and carry him back outside, to be driven home, for the last time. He was to be entombed in the Marlows', the Earls' of Barringtons', mausoleum.

With the ebony coffin balanced on his shoulder again, Henry walked back along the aisle. Behind him he heard the men who had come to show their respect for his brother leave their seats and follow. The sound of their footsteps as pallbearers were no longer solitary.

When they walked out of the Minster, the hearse which had brought William to York, stood awaiting him.

They were helped to slide the coffin back on to the glass sided carriage by the funeral's director.

Henry's body had never felt so heavy as he turned away from the coffin, from his brother, to follow his father back to their carriage. It was the Earls' of Barrington's state carriage so it was highly polished and gilded, and their brightly painted coat of arms was on either side.

There was one less son in the Barringtons' dynasty now... One less in the Marlow family.

The knowledge screamed at Henry as he gripped the hand rail on the carriage's side and climbed the step then dropped into the seat next to his father, to face his brothers.

His uncle took the seat beside him.

None of them spoke, even when the carriage pulled away.

Henry did not look out through the window. He could not face the stares of the interested ordinary folk of York. They saw this as nothing more than a moment of ceremony. It was the loss of his youngest brother, *William*. His brother who was undeserving of that fate.

Henry would say William's name every day, at least once, for the rest of his life to ensure William had a legacy.

The hearse travelled ahead of them leading them back to his father's property in a slow procession. After an hour of travelling it turned through the gates into Farnborough. The giant lion statues that guarded Henry's home greeted them.

William must have seen the statues as a welcome home just as Henry had. But the carriage did not take them home to the house, the hearse turned left on to the grass and led them away from the house—towards the mausoleum.

Nausea twisted through Henry's stomach and rose to his throat, to think of his brother lying in the dark amongst the entombed bodies of their ancestors, on cold stone. But he would be with their grandfather and grandmother, whom they'd never met. Henry must remember that; William was not alone.

He breathed out, disguising the shiver that gripped his body.

When the carriage stopped, the weight of responsibility, of being the one who stayed in control made him rise and open the carriage door, before the footman had reached it.

Henry jumped out and then knocked down the step with the heel of his shoe. He held the door for Percy, his father and uncle, then Gerard and Stephen.

Edward smiled at him slightly. Henry turned away, pain tightening about his throat; the lump of emotion there pressed with a need to explode. He longed to shout, or growl, or hit or throw something.

Oh, to be young enough to be allowed a rage. He longed to rant at God, and life and fate. William should not have been taken.

The funeral director organised his men to lift William's coffin from the hearse. When they walked forward Henry's father followed. Henry followed him walking between Stephen and Gerard.

He lay his arms on their shoulders. Gerard leaned into him a little. Stephen glanced at him and acknowledged the gesture, but his stiffness said he would rather be left alone to deal with his emotion. Henry's arm fell away from Stephen, but his other remained around Gerard.

The doors to the mausoleum's crypt stood open. His father stopped walking as the coffin was carried in. Henry stopped too. He took a breath then said quietly. "Goodbye, William."

"Goodbye," Stephen repeated.

"Goodbye," Gerard and Percy said together.

"My son…" Henry heard on his father's breath.

Percy coughed, as though his throat was blocked. Henry glanced at him. He stood beside Edward. Edward braced Percy's shoulder as Percy's eyes glittered in the sunlight, but he did not allow the tears to fall.

Gerard sobbed.

Stephen sniffed and then wiped his nose on his sleeve.

Henry's heart banged hard in his chest, as though it wished to be let out. He looked at his father. He wanted to go to him, to hold him, to give and receive comfort, but his father was staring at the open doors the coffin had been carried through and he did not look as though he would welcome Henry approaching him.

When the funeral director's pallbearers came back out, it was without William. They turned and closed the giant doors.

He'd gone. They'd never see his face again, only in the portraits at the house.

Stephen looked at Gerard, and then reached past Henry to grip a handful of Gerard's coat sleeve. "Come on." Gerard consented and turned with Stephen.

Henry breathed out then turned away too, and walked back towards the carriage behind his young brothers. Percy sighed. Henry looked back. Percy walked a few paces behind him. Henry waited for him to catch up.

Beyond Percy his uncle and father still stood looking at the mausoleum.

His uncle said something to his father then turned and walked away. When he met Henry's gaze he made a grim expression.

His father did not move.

Henry turned to head back.

"Leave him!" Uncle Edward called.

Henry looked at his father, he wanted to be able to do something.

"He needs time alone," his uncle said when he reached Henry. "Come along," he caught hold of Henry's arm and drew him back towards the carriage.

Henry glanced over his shoulder before he climbed into the carriage. His father had not moved.

When Henry sat down, he leant against the squabs and looked up at the roof of the carriage while his uncle spoke to the coach man outside. "Wait a moment please."

A sense of helplessness hovered around Henry. He wanted answers, actions… But there was nothing to be said and nothing to be done to heal this.

Henry looked out of the window. His father stood staring at the closed doors of the mausoleum, saying who knew what to William.

Henry remembered the women who awaited them at the house, along with his friends and the rest of the men who had been in the first few pews behind him in the Minster. He would not be able to speak with his friends, he needed to welcome everyone if his father was still so silent. But it did not matter, the life and conversations he'd shared in that friendship group now seemed like they'd occurred years ago. He was no longer the man they knew.

Edward breathed out heavily.

Henry's gaze passed to him.

"If you would rather…" he looked from Henry to Percy, to Stephen and Gerard, "avoid the wake, then show your faces for a short time only, I am happy to ensure people are cared for sufficiently. You have done well and endured enough today."

Gerard and Stephen said nothing, but they would be happy they'd been given permission to abscond. Percy nodded.

"Thank you," Henry breathed out heavily too, as relief washed through him. He'd hoped his uncle would take some of the burden, and he had.

The carriage door opened. They all looked. His father climbed in.

They did not speak again then.

~

Susan rose. She had heard the carriages arriving in Farnborough's central courtyard a few minutes before, and fresh tea had then been sent for, but the women had remained seated. Now the door opened and a footman stepped in to hold it wide, then the men walked into the room.

Some of the other women stood.

The room had the sense of a macabre painting. The mirror above the hearth had been covered in black as the family were in deepest mourning, and all the women of Henry's family wore black, while Susan wore her dove grey and Alethea and her mother were in dull mauves and Aunt Jane's friends were in similar drab colours.

Aunt Jane walked across the room with purposeful strides to greet her guests. Susan's father came in. When Aunt Jane greeted him he pressed a kiss on Aunt Jane's cheek, then moved on as others walked in.

Henry and Uncle Robert were not among the men behind him. Susan looked through the doorway but no one remained in the hall.

Her hands clasped together as she stood near the hearth. She'd never taken part in mourning and so she had no idea what was the right thing to do or say. Since she'd arrived she'd been terrified of saying the wrong thing to Aunt Jane, or any of the women in Henry's family.

If she could have chosen to, without causing offence, she would have remained at home and pretended this had not happened. But that was a selfish, unkind and insensitive thought that was unlike her.

Her teeth nipped nervously at the inside of her lower lip.

She sat down once more, her hands trembling. She clasped them together in her lap. Her mother was in conversation with one of Aunt Jane's guests, trying to ease some of the pressure on Aunt Jane.

It was Aunt Jane's duty to play hostess and yet she must feel as though she were walking in her sleep. She had lost her son. Susan's only sense of comparison was the thought of losing Alethea, or her mother, or father and that would be unbearable. Losing a child must be a far worse loss.

Alethea sat across the room speaking with Sarah, Christine and Uncle Edward's and Aunt Ellen's daughters. There had been no seat near them for Susan to sit amidst them.

Quiet conversation developed around her. The fresh tea arrived. Susan sat silent and watching, awkwardness hovering over her like a hunting kestrel.

The sound of another carriage on the cobble outside filtered through the windows.

Susan wished to stand again, but no one else turned to the door or moved.

Yet when the door opened her emotion drew her to her feet regardless. Henry walked in first. Longing lanced at her, a desire to hold him, to offer comfort, her heart beat only for him. Her feet moved of their own accord. But she stopped herself after two steps as his father, uncle and brothers followed him in, their expressions sullen.

She looked about the room to ensure no one had noticed her unguarded response. They had not.

Susan's heart reached out yet she was too tongue-tied with fear of uttering the wrong words to walk over and speak.

She sat down again and then her fingers lifted and pushed her spectacles a little farther up the bridge of her nose.

Henry circulated about the people in the room and his voice became the loudest and most assured. Uncle Edward stayed beside Uncle Robert and joined a quiet group that contained her father, Lord Sparks, John and Lord Wiltshire. Rob Marlow left that group and walked across the room to join his wife, Caroline. They shared a look expressing intense sadness and sympathy.

Susan stood as the silent communication they'd shared drew tears into her eyes, and she walked across the room to stand beside her mother, no longer able to sit alone. She longed to run. Henry had told her long ago, that was her habit, and now she absolutely recognised it. The desire screamed. She could not cope, not only with the number of people in this room, which was normally her weakness, but the level of emotion and her inability to help.

~

For the rest of the afternoon, Susan stood near her mother, and watched Henry. He spoke to all of his parents' guests, though he did not approach her or her mother. She thought about the other day, when he'd held her hand. She longed to hold his hand again.

She had deliberately sacrificed his love. But as she watched him, that decision felt cruel. He did not look at her, and it was as though it was deliberate, as though he was afraid to look at her.

But then she had told him, no, so what value was there for him in looking at her, it would be no comfort to him.

Her heart felt as though it expanded, inflating with the intensity of her empathy, bursting with feelings that longed to hold and then cling to him.

He escorted Sarah into dinner. Percy walked with Christine.

She walked in beside her mother. She could not see him, or over hear his conversation at the table, he sat at the far end. But when Henry walked into the drawing room to re-join the women later he was amongst his friends, those he associated with in town, those who had danced and flirted with her, the reckless sons of his father's friends, Harry's relations, and Harry was with them. They were not laughing, though, as they would have been in town, they were all subdued today, in their black.

Alethea stood up and walked over to Henry. She had not spoken to Henry all day either.

She spoke hurriedly and tearfully.

An outflow of emotion was not what Henry needed. His jaw stiffened. He'd been more relaxed when he'd walked in with his friends, but before that, he'd been tense all day, fulfilling what must have been a very difficult responsibility. He'd changed since the spring. She had seen the changes shifting by small degrees in town, but today he appeared to have swung about a half circle. He'd become the opposite of the arrogant self-centered man she had disliked so intensely.

A closed, distant, sombre look set a mask across his face, yet he gripped Alethea's arm and turned her, then led her across the room to a corner where they then stood alone together.

Susan's heart whipped up into a race of jealousy. It screamed for him. She wanted to walk over to him and push Alethea away.

Love, came with a sense of possession, even though the love had been cast down. That was so unfair on Henry.

She looked at Christine and Mary, then left her mother and walked over and tried to join their conversation, though all her awareness remained on Henry and Alethea who she could still see.

He faced Alethea, his head slightly bowed as he took her hand and spoke earnestly. He had spoken to Susan in that way in London, with such deep intent in his eyes. Her heart ached at the memory.

What were they talking about?

She looked at Christine and tried very hard to concentrate.

She hoped her parents would not remain late, not when Uncle Robert and Aunt Jane were in mourning. She hoped they would leave soon.

Henry suddenly walked across the room, his strides swift.

Susan looked at Alethea. Her lips were pursed in an annoyed expression as she walked over to their mother. She whispered something in their mother's ear.

Susan looked at Henry.

When he neared the chest close to the door he grasped a decanter by its neck, then walked out of the room, at a pace that implied he would not be coming back.

Susan looked at Alethea. She came towards Susan. *Oh Lord*, whatever Henry had said to her, whatever had transpired between them, Susan did not want to know. She could not be Alethea's confidant when the topic of secrecy was Henry.

"Forgive me, I need the retiring room," Susan said to Christine and Mary then left them before Alethea might reach her, and she deliberately avoided Alethea's path as she left the room.

A footman awaited orders in the hall. "Where is Lord Henry?"

The footman pointed into another room. "Through the French doors, in the garden, Miss Forth."

She walked on. If he'd run, then she could.

Chapter Twenty-three

"Henry! Where are you?"

Susan. He looked over his shoulder. She was not visible. He could say nothing and hope she did not find him. Except he rather wanted to be found by her and he did not have the energy to stand up and get out of her way anyway. His legs were heavy with brandy and grief and he was in no mood to rise and run. "Here, Susan! In the rose garden!"

After a minute or so he heard her footsteps on the gravel path. Then her voice reached across the garden as she entered on the far side. "Henry…"

"Here!" he called again.

It was a round garden, with a central circle of roses surrounded by grass, and all about the edges were rose borders and arches. He was sitting on the ground, on the grass. Life had pushed him to the floor.

"Henry…" Susan said again as she approached him, only now his name was a question that asked, *is anything wrong.*

God, yes, Susan, everything is bloody wrong.

"Can I sit beside you?"

"If you wish." His voice said he did not care, but he did. His heart warmed at her nearness.

She swept the skirt of her dove grey dress and her petticoats beneath her then sat on the grass. The ground was becoming damp as the sky had flooded with the orange, reds and pinks of sunset.

The descending cooler evening air was also intensifying the perfume from the roses around them.

Susan suddenly wrapped her arms about his shoulders and held him, as they sat upright beside each other. "I am sorry."

"Thank you." His response was terse and in a low pitch. He did not hold her in her return. He'd heard those words too much today. He'd been sitting out here and beating himself about the head, wishing he'd done so many things differently. He did not feel inclined to accept pity.

When she let go of him he lifted the decanter and drank from it. He was sitting with his legs bent and his feet wide. He put the decanter back down on the grass between his legs and rested his elbows on his knees. "I suppose you think this is self-centered of me?"

"You have been working hard all day doing everything you can to make your parents' guests feel comfortable, I think you deserve some freedom."

"I have been trying hard to do everything my parents would wish of me since the hour I heard William was not well." No, that was a lie, he'd begun doing that when he'd been here in the spring, and then agreed to court Alethea, and he had only done that in response to Susan's terse assessment of his self-centered nature. That was comical. He did not look at her.

"I know, Henry, I am not arguing the point with you, I've seen what you are doing. It is commendable how you are supporting your family."

Commendable. That was a sickening word. He preferred the word reckless, at least that had been true. He glanced at her.

She bent up her knees and wrapped her arms about them.

"My family should be supporting each other, but William's death is dividing us."

"I am sorry."

God those words were not good enough, no amount of sorrys would change anything. "I am in pain."

She twisted sideways and touched his arm as she met his gaze. "I know. You should let yourself cry."

Cry. A bark of bitter laughter left his throat then he took another long swig from the decanter of brandy to let the liquor seep deeper into his veins. "Crying will not bring him back, will it? I wish to scream. I wish to damn well punch the living daylights out of God for taking my brother if that man would come down from the clouds and face me. Why William? Why not me when I turned over my curricle?"

"Your family would be just as distressed if it had been you."

"But William would be here and I would not be in pain, and I would have deserved it. Remember?"

She ignored his mean challenge. "But then William would be in pain. He idolised you."

He looked at her. "I hate you sometimes, Susan, the times when you are unbearably and annoyingly logical."

She smiled as her hand lifted and slid her spectacles farther up her nose.

His lips pulled up into a smile, and he shook his head at her. She turned around and clutched her knees again. "It is self-centered to want to be the one who is lost."

"Too much logic, Susan, I do not want to hear that. I feel guilty enough. He is dead because of me. Did you know that?"

"You are not—"

"Do not deny it. You have just said he idolised me. He did. That was his error, he mimicked my recklessness, he would not have become ill had he not fallen from a climb to his tutor's window."

"You cannot know that, Henry—"

"I know it."

Her hand settled just above his left knee on his thigh, trying to offer non-verbal comfort as he took another swig from the decanter of brandy. He'd drunk a good measure of it. His brain swam a little, the rose garden blurring.

"I still say you cannot know."

"I am not in the mood for a woman who likes to have the last word. Leave it be, Susan. I know."

She sighed heavily. "You will make yourself ill, Henry, if you hold all the responsibility on your shoulders and do not take time to grieve."

"I have no choice but to hold the responsibility on my shoulders, my father is in no state to accept it, and barely weeks ago you told me I was too selfish, you cannot have it both ways. How would you rather I be?"

She did not answer.

He drank again.

"The way I feel is your fault regardless, it is you who has made me feel. You opened my eyes so I see what others feel and my heart so it would hurt when others hurt."

The liquor became a warm rush of strength and oblivion. He looked at her when he heard her take a breath to speak. "And do not say I am sorry, please."

"I am—"

"Susan!"

"Sor—"

"Susan!"

She took a breath. "How was the service?"

"Awful."

"Everyone was so subdued when you returned. It is so sad."

"Sad… That is just another form of sorry. An inadequate, pitiful word."

"Sorr—"

"Susan!" he growled at her.

"I do not know what to say, Henry. I have stood and listened to conversation after conversation today, saying nothing, I am so scared of offending some one, and now you are... Oh." Her eyes glittered as they filled with tears and she turned to rise from the ground.

He caught hold of her arm. "Do not go. I am sorry. I did not mean to upset you. I am just in an ill-mood and you are in the firing line. Ignore me. I am in a mood to be pig-headed."

She sat back on the grass.

He let her go, took one more drink, then set the decanter aside on his right, at the end of his arm's reach, with an aim to stop himself drinking more.

"Are you going back indoors?" she asked.

"No. Edward has things in hand and everyone will go home as soon as the sun has set."

"I wish there was something I could do to help. I have been longing to have something to do all day..."

Ah, darn, that is a foolish thing to say, Susan. He knew just how she could help.

Without another moment's thought he braced the weight of his body with one hand on the grass as he turned. His other hand reached out and lifted her spectacles off. She squinted at him. Lord, he'd longed to kiss her all day—and all night. "I cannot tell you how much I wish I had not promised to let you go. I want to go back on my offer and be selfish..."

He reached over to put her spectacles down by the decanter, losing his balance a little as he turned back around.

"Henry..."

Her pale eyes showed her confusion. But he'd longed to look into her eyes for days and they were almost the exact colour of her dress.

One hand braced his weight on the grass while the other lifted to her nape and brought her mouth to his. "If you want to help me, kiss me."

She answered by pressing her lips against his.

He opened his mouth and kissed her more earnestly, then his

266

tongue reached for hers with desperation as he leant her back, his hand bracing her neck so she descended gently. Then he was leaning over her, his forearm resting on the damp, cool bed of grass as his tongue delved into and out of her mouth.

After a moment, he broke the kiss. "Susan," he said her name over her lips then kissed her cheek and her jaw, and her temple. There was one thing that would take away all the pain.

His hand left her nape and curved about her side over her ribs.

She arched upwards when he kissed her again, her body crying out for exactly what his wanted.

She could comfort him. She had all he needed to find comfort.

Her tongue reached out and danced with his, in his mouth, while his hand embraced the curve beneath her breast.

Her hand moved and gripped the back of his head, not stopping him, and by not stopping him, agreeing to this.

His hand covered her breast, and squeezed firmly. She sucked in a breath through their kiss. His fingers released and squeezed again. She sighed. His thumb ran over the nipple he could feel hardening through the material of her gown.

He kissed her jaw again and her neck as his thumb continued to stroke across her breast.

"Henry…"

He looked at her. "Susan…"

She had spoken his name with a sound of awe. He'd used her name as a question. He wanted more. He needed all the comfort she could give—everything.

His desire spurred him to open her bodice, free her breast and touch her flesh, but her dress was buttoned all the way up the back and even if he freed those buttons there would then be her chemise and corset to master. Such clothing did not welcome intrusion. But her skirt and petticoats. His hand fell and began drawing them up, his hand opening and then clasping in the material and pulling it up as he kissed her again.

She gripped his hand. "Henry." His name was spoken with a note of caution as they looked each other in the eyes.

Her gaze searched his with a mix of desire, wonder and doubt. She wanted him physically just as much as he wanted her. She might have turned her back on him for the sake of her sister, but her heart had not turned away.

"Susan…" he asked the question again, his hand still clasping a fist full of material that he rubbed against her thigh, so she could not be in doubt about what he was asking, what he wanted—her.

She stared at him for a moment more.

His gaze left hers. Her heartbeat pulsed in the artery in her neck below her ear. He kissed the place, wishing that the neck of her gown was not so high and that he might kiss her shoulder and her clavicle. Women's fashion had her so tightly buttoned up. He wanted to release and kiss her breast. He needed to feel the softness of a woman after so many days of facing the hard realities of life.

He kissed along her jaw, his hand still holding a fistful of her dress and her petticoats, with her hand clasped over his.

"Henry." She let his hand go. It was a final agreement. Her body arched upward as his fist lifted her skirt and undergarments higher. She was as reckless and as foolish as he was. He'd always known it.

His hand left the material bunched above her hip and slipped across her cotton drawers, circling, imaging how it would feel to touch her skin. Her skin would be pale. He imagined his lips on it, kissing her inner thighs, while in reality he touched her there and kissed her deeply.

When his fingers found the slit in her drawers, he intruded gently, pressing through the cloth and into the silky, moist haven of her body. Her muscles jolted and her fingers clawed into his shoulders as she broke the kiss. "Henry…" Uncertainty echoed in her pitch now.

He did not want her to feel uncertain.

He kissed her jaw, then sucked lightly on the curve just beneath it as his fingers stroked in and out of her in the rhythm of a liaison.

She tilted her neck offering it up to his adoration and her breathing changed, it became deeper and ragged as the sensations he must be introducing her to, took hold.

He used his thumb, brushing it over the sensitive part of her skin as his fingers continued invading her, he curved them so that he stroked her more intimately internally.

She was beautiful in every way. Perfect. Her breath kept catching with little sharp pants of sound when he did something different, and she reached Eros's agony of bliss when his fingers were deep inside her, throbbing about his intrusion, as the moisture of her release spread across his palm.

Lord, he hoped, prayed, she would not say no now. His throat was parched, and his desire like a desperate beast.

"Susan…" Her eyes had been shut but they opened as he moved over her. They sparkled with the residue of the ecstasy of release. That was the emotion that he craved.

He knelt on the ground between her legs half on her dress and the petticoats beneath her as he unbuttoned his flap. Then with them both still fully clothed he bent down, leaning over her, his hands either side of her shoulders. Her hands held his upper arms, in that gentle way that was unique to Susan, gripping as gently as if he was walking her out to the dance floor.

"May I?" he whispered.

She did not say yes, she merely nodded. He pressed inside her. Damn. It was heaven. Warm. Tight. Slick. Heaven. He moved gently at first, and then more swiftly, his pace becoming firm as well as quick as he dropped heavily against her.

~

Susan's hands clawed into the material of Henry's black morning coat, her body rocking in a resonance of his movement. What was she doing? This was madness. They were in the garden. Anyone might walk past and see. Her heart raced—ached. This was a thing for a marriage bed. They had not even taken off their clothes. But why would they, when they were so exposed. She tilted her head back, to look at the house, she could see some of the upper windows, which meant if anyone looked out of those they would see them.

Yet he'd needed this. She knew the moment he'd begun kissing her that he was seeking this comfort. No words would have helped him, but this. She had wanted to hold and help him.

She was insane.

Reckless. As he was being reckless. Only this time he was being reckless with her. His upper body lowered, and his cheek pressed against hers, his hair tickling her skin, as his hips continued to lift and fall.

One of her hands lifted and clasped in his hair.

She had not been able to fight the pleasure his fingers had created, the sensations still danced through her nerves and pulsed in her blood. But this was sore.

The scent of the crushed grass beneath her lifted on the air, joining with the perfume from the roses and the smell of brandy on his breath.

He breathed hard near her ear and at last the soreness began to ease. The emotions she'd known before swept up again. Her legs lifted so her thighs could press against the side of his as he moved.

The sensations teased and tormented as he withdrew and pressed back in, in a swift pattern.

His body lifted again. "Open your eyes." His voice was husky and deep. She had not even realised she'd shut her eyes, but she opened them then.

He withdrew a little and played a game of short sharp little pulses of invasion near her entrance where she was more sensitive. Her fingers clawed more firmly into the material of his coat, as her thighs lifted higher and clasped about his hips. "Oh." A ripple of deeper sensation spun in her middle and down to the place where he invaded. Then he thrust in deeply again striking his pelvis against hers.

Her gaze clung to his as she tried not to cry out. She would break apart. "Ah." The breaking came as an even stronger sudden flow of sensations.

"There," he leant near her ear and said, as he pumped even faster into her body.

She swallowed the pleasure down from the back of her throat as after three more pulses, he sighed into the air with an animalistic gravelly note, pressing his hips against hers. She felt him throb inside her.

His head hung down, and he breathed heavily near her ear.

What had they just done?

It had been stupid to do this.

What about Alethea?

He withdrew from her body and tumbled on to his back beside her, his legs still tangled up with hers, and sighed.

She lay there for a moment as he did, looking up at the blue and orange streaked sky.

Yet what about Henry? She'd been so desperate not to hurt her sister, and yet what about him? She did not wish to see Henry upset either. Her longing to protect and not wound had led her into this mess. With either step she would hurt someone.

Birdsong swelled around them, a loud chorus of sound as the birds sang out in the last moments of sunlight. Perhaps it had been building all the time they'd been here. But it meant the sun was about to go down. Her parents would be leaving, and looking for her.

"I suppose we ought to go back in," he said towards the air.

She sat up brushing down her dress, then stood up as he buttoned his flap. She brushed the grass off her skirt.

He leaned over and brushed the back of her skirt, still sitting on the ground.

"Is it stained?"

"No. No one will know."

But she knew and she must ride home in the carriage with Alethea knowing how disloyal she had been.

He stood up then and before she could turn to go back to the house, his hand curved about her nape and then his lips pressed over hers for a long moment. "Thank you," he said when he broke the kiss. Then he lifted his hand. "Your spectacles."

He turned and picked them up.

Her hands shook when she accepted them and put them on. It felt as though she had stepped back into herself. All the nice, enchanting sensations his caresses had engendered had gone, leaving her standing on a barren island. What had she done?

"You should go back in first. I'll follow in a few moments."

She nodded.

He seemed so matter of fact. How many women had he done this with?

Warmth flooded her cheeks when she turned away, she did not even say goodbye to him, her mind was too muddled.

When she walked back into the drawing room she was certain she must be bright pink, and that everyone in the room must know that she'd changed. She looked at the clock. She had been out of the room for less than an hour—her life had changed entirely in less than an hour. No. It had not. She would leave just as she'd planned she had to find employment, only now she must find it quicker.

Henry arrived back in the drawing room just as the carriages began pulling around to take away his family's guests. He shook hands with people, nodding his head in recognition and shared a masculine embrace with Harry and Uncle Edward. He looked as though nothing had happened in the rose garden.

Yet he did not look at her, and if he had, she would have

looked away. If she caught his gaze she would blush the colour of a ripe strawberry.

She hugged Aunt Jane when she said goodbye, and held Uncle Robert's hand for a moment, his eyes looked so empty. Then she turned and hugged Christine and Sarah, and said goodbye to Mary, Aunt Ellen and her daughters, then Harry and the Duchess of Arundel… The number of people to say goodbye to seemed endless. Yet in all her goodbying she managed to avoid Henry entirely.

When she sat down in the carriage beside Alethea, it was with a heavy heart, and her hands still shook. She gripped her shawl and pulled it tighter about her shoulders as she shivered.

What had she done? What had they done? He had never been more reckless, and nor had she.

Her journey home was silent. Probably because it had been an emotional day for all of them—yet for her… Such a day.

As soon as they reached home Susan retired to her room and her bed. When she lay in the dark she smelt the perfume from the numerous roses that had surrounded them and the scent of the crushed grass in her hair.

She would never forget those smells.

Her fingers touched where Henry had invaded her body. She was sore still. Yet her senses seemed to hum the tune of his rhythm.

A slight knock struck the bedchamber door, then Susan heard it open.

"Hello." Alethea became a dark shadow in the unlit room. "May I sleep with you, I feel miserable."

Guilt was no longer a little sharp thrust of pain but a spearhead wedged in Susan's side that twisted about fiercely. "Yes, of course." She moved the covers back and felt the mattress dip when Alethea lay beside her.

"I told Henry after dinner that I understand."

"Understand what?" Had he told her that he did not intend to marry her?

"That he cannot propose to me while he is in mourning, and therefore we will have to wait until next year before our courtship can progress."

Tears gathered in Susan's eyes, and she bit her lip to stop herself from speaking.

"He was so quiet I think he would have liked to speak with me in more depth but we were surrounded by people in the drawing room and so he could not. He is so upset, though."

"Yes." Susan breathed. The image of Henry's eyes and the emotion they'd held displayed in her mind's eye. He had looked lost outside in the rose garden.

Her heart spread a soft ache through her chest, it felt the same as the soft ache in her thighs.

"I wish I could do something for him," Alethea said.

Something. The word struck Susan. That was what she had said to Henry, and then they had done something to comfort him.

Nausea turned over in her stomach. What would Alethea say if she knew?

Alethea carried on whispering, talking about Henry and his family, and the others who had attended today.

Susan whispered acknowledgements in return, but did not really talk, her mind and her body were too full of Henry. What was he thinking? Was he upset still? Did he regret what they'd done?

Chapter Twenty-four

Lord. Henry rolled on to his back. His head had a hammer bloody hitting it. He'd drunk himself into oblivion last evening. Once everyone had left he'd brought a fresh decanter to his room because he wished to drink alone, and not risk Percy or his father joining him and he'd drunk until he was too drunk to lift a glass.

God what had he done? He could feel himself pressing into Susan's body, the warmth of her, the softness of her receipt. He could smell the damned roses mingling with the scent of sex.

He shut his eyes as he felt himself kissing her mouth, and his fingers invading her.

Why had she let him do it for God sake? Because she loved him in return. There was no doubt of it, she would not have allowed if she did not.

Damn.

His hand was on Samson's ear; his fingers began idly stroking the dog as the thoughts span around in his head.

She had been mad.

He had been mad—and intoxicated.

And the foolish woman had allowed it when she had denied their future. He'd forced her hand now.

Damn.

What a bastard. *You utter bastard.*

He opened his eyes, pushed Samson, so the dog jumped off the bed, then threw back the covers and walked across the room to open the shutters and let the daylight in. The sun was high. It was probably already midday. Samson yawned behind him, then began to whimper in a need to be let out.

Damn. What must she be thinking?

She'd be cursing him.

He turned away and walked over to a chest of drawers, then pulled out fresh clothes and found out his riding boots. There was clarity in his mind, certainty.

None of his family were in the halls he walked through, with Samson at his heel, and he did not go in search of them he imagined today they would mostly keep to themselves. Percy would look after the boys, and the girls had each other.

All would be quiet now the funeral was over. They could live here in peace for a week or so, wallowing in their sorrow. Then the boys would go back to school and normal life would begin again, although the family would remain in their blacks.

He lifted a hand to a footman who had passed him and stopped to bow. "Here," he pointed at the dog, "Take Samson outside, and then to the kitchens." The man gripped Samson's collar and held him as Henry walked on, to the tune of Samson's barked complaints.

He should have complained to Susan like that, barking his sorrow and disagreement. *To hell with sacrifice.*

He did not walk out through the front door but made his way to the door that led out to the stables.

"The stallion!" he called to a groom in the courtyard. The man turned around and walked ahead of Henry to fetch the animal Henry had been riding during his stay.

Henry lifted off his hat and tapped it against his leg as he waited in the middle of the busy area. The carriage they'd used yesterday were being cleaned and polished. He could not look at it, he did not want any memory of yesterday.

His gloved fingers ran over his hair as he watched the activity about him, as a couple of the grooms returned riding his sisters' horses that had been taken out for exercise.

The stallion was led out from its stall, saddled and ready for Henry to ride. He walked over to the groom, took the reins, then led the horse to the mounting block, climbed the steps there, then swung his leg over and sat astride the saddle. His feet settled into the stirrups.

"Thank you," he said to the groom, then to the horse he said, "Go on." He struck his heels against its flanks and rocked his hips forward encouraging it to walk until they were out of the stable yard. Then he lifted up setting the horse into a trot with his rise and fall movement as he steered it on to the drive and past the house. He pressed his weight into the stirrups and his knees against the horse, and lifted off the saddle to set the animal into a canter along the avenue of tall horse-chestnut trees.

To reach the Forths' the best way to go was along the road. He did not try to gallop, but cantered the horse all of the way to the Forths', finally turning off the road and along the drive which passed the fields where the stud horses grazed. Some of the mares whinnied as the stallion trotted past but Henry held its head hard to stop any nonsense in reply.

When he reached the house a groom appeared and came to hold the horse as Henry dismounted. "Thank you."

The gravel crunched beneath his boots as he walked to the door and a cuckoo called from somewhere in the trees behind the house.

Apt.

Henry lifted off his hat as he walked the last few paces. His other hand ruffled his hair.

When he reached the door it opened before he could knock.

He looked at the footman, it was not a man he knew, and probably therefore not a servant who knew him. "Is Lord Forth at home. I am Lord Henry Marlow."

"Yes, my Lord," the man bowed. "Would you wait here a moment."

"I wish to speak with him privately," Henry said before the man turned away.

"Yes, my Lord."

He stepped inside. Whenever he'd called at the Forths it had been to a welcome of Alethea running downstairs, or Aunt Julie rushing into the hall to embrace him, but he'd never arrived when he'd not been expected before.

"Henry!"

He looked up to see Susan leaning over the bannister of the landing above him. Then she was hurrying down the stairs. She wore dark blue, a colour which set off the fascinating quality of her eyes. Her beauty gripped tightly about his heart as it had done every time he'd looked at her yesterday. This had become a rushed thing, but he was not going to feel guilt for it, nor regret, it was right for them.

She stopped before him, her gaze questioning and a blush colouring her skin. "What are you doing here?"

He would have held her hands but he still had a hold of his hat and wore his riding gloves. "I have come to speak to your father."

"About wha… Oh no. No, Henry."

"There is no choice now, Susan." He did grip her hand then, before it could lift and lay against her bosom in a gesture of shock, he held it firmly too. "You cannot complain nor disagree I am fixed on this, after yesterday there is no other choice. You think of Alethea, you think of me, you worry over all of us, trying to stop us all from feeling pain, but in that commitment to concern, you forget yourself."

"But Alethea…"

"Damn Alethea. She will manage well enough. It is you I care for. There might be consequences, and if there are no physical consequences then there will be sadness regardless. I will not allow it. I had thought I was hurting you less by letting you walk away but that is hurting you too, and me. Let us have each other. Let us be happy. Alethea will find her happiness too in another way. Please…"

"I do not—"

"My Lord." The footman reappeared and interrupted her outcry.

Henry let go of Susan's hand and turned.

"Lord Forth asked me to bring you to the library."

"Thank you." He looked back at Susan only for an instant, then followed the footman, as though he did not know where the library was. When they reached the open door the man stepped out of his way. Henry walked past then shut the door.

"Uncle Casper," he said in greeting when he turned and looked across the room.

"Henry… What might I do for you? Can I be of some help?"

"I have not come to ask for help, but to ask for something else, Uncle." Henry set his upturned hat down on a side table, then stripped off his gloves and threw them into his hat. His hands were damned well shaking, but whether it was nerves or a hang-over from yesterday's liquor he did not know.

"What is it you need?"

Henry walked across the room, Uncle Casper was still sitting behind his desk. "I wish to ask for the hand—"

"Now, Henry?" Uncle Casper stood up, the surprise twitching his pale moustache and distorting his brow. "I am sure Alethea is willing to wait, if—"

Henry swallowed hard against what felt like cowardice in his throat. "Not Alethea's. I wish to ask you for Susan's hand."

"Susan…" Uncle Casper walked about the desk, his expression now declaring that he was entirely perplexed.

"Yes, sir. Susan." He did not think it necessary to explain, it was just a fact. He loved one sister and not the other. Not the one they had tried to force upon him.

279

"Is she aware of this?" Uncle Casper's eyebrows lifted in punctuation of his shock.

"Yes, sir."

"Good Lord," he leant back against the desk. "And Alethea?"

"She is not aware. I have not had opportunity to discuss my feelings with her."

"Well, this is going to be a to do then is it not?"

"I know, I am sorry for that, but I cannot help what I feel for Susan." Henry's voice was deep and his throat dry, as the emotion stacked so tightly beneath his skin that if he let himself yield to it he might go literally mad. The snake would be back about him soon.

Uncle Casper nodded, his gaze looking into nowhere as though he was thinking about the consequences.

It would mean a lot of upset, both in Susan's family and his, but there was nothing to be done to avoid it, he had been reckless again and they both had to face the consequence of that. But he refused to regret it. He had wanted this, and so had Susan, even though she had not admitted it. She had admitted it on the grass in the rose garden through her silence.

Uncle Casper focused on him. "But why now, Henry? Surely now is not the time. It would be better for us to tell Alethea and then for you to give her a few months to become used to the idea of you courting her sister before you take the step of becoming engaged, and surely it is better to wait until the end of your mourning."

Henry swallowed. He'd known he would be asked to wait. He'd thought of nothing else during his ride over here, and there were no words with which to explain the urgency without telling Susan's father the truth. So he spoke the truth. "We have anticipated the vows, sir. I am sorry. Susan has no choice but to marry me, and we need to be married now."

"You…" Uncle Casper straightened up, his mouth dropping open and his skin colouring up with anger. "Well now that explains much," he barked in an impatient, angry tone. "For instance why Susan has asked me to look for a position for her, and why she ran away from London. Yes, Henry, you had better marry her." He walked past Henry. Henry looked over his shoulder.

Uncle Casper walked to the door. He spoke as he pulled it open. "Would you send for... Ah I see you do not need to. Come in here, Susan."

~

Guilt and shame swept up into Susan's blood in a rush as her father glared at her, holding the library door wider as he beckoned her in. She'd been leaning up against the door, pressing her ear to the wood but she had not been able to hear their conversation. But Henry had clearly done what he'd said and told her father.

"I am sorry," she whispered as she walked past him.

"I should hope you are," he snapped back. After he shut the door he added, "I am disappointed in you," then he looked at Henry. "I am disappointed in you both."

He lifted his hand. "Susan." Her name was a sharp order, telling her to walk across the room to join Henry.

She was going to be scolded for stealing Henry from Alethea.

"You have shamed yourselves and I hope you know it." When her father was unhappy he was like an army officer; his pitch heightened, sharpened and became barked words. His hands gripped behind his back as his eyes looked his annoyance.

He was truly upset. His cheeks were red-veined by temper.

He looked at Henry. "You will have to marry within the month otherwise if there are consequences then it might become obvious."

"I know, sir. I will not have Susan suffer that."

Her father knew everything! Susan coughed on her embarrassment, and her fingers lifted to push her spectacles farther up the bridge of her nose as heat flushed her skin. Why had Henry told him that?

She looked at him with as much accusation as her father.

"We will marry as soon as I can arrange it."

"You will require my consent!" Susan complained as the conversation seemed to ignore her.

Henry looked at her his eyebrows lifting.

"From what Henry has said," her father charged, "you have already given your consent." Her father turned his back on her, and walked about his desk. "You had better see the Archbishop and obtain a special licence, Henry. I will not have my family embarrassed." He sat down then and looked at the papers on his desk. "Now get out, both of you, I am trying to hold on to my rage over your foolish, thoughtless behaviour and I am likely not to succeed."

Susan bit down on her lip as she turned away. Tears pressed at the back of her eyes. Henry's arm came about her and his hand settled at her waist.

"And you must think of the kindest way to tell Alethea!" Her father called.

Susan looked back, heat flushing her skin. Her father had looked up and his gaze speared her with the accusation of her disloyalty.

Henry did not look back, or stop walking, or remove his hand from her waist. He did lean across, though, to pick up his hat from a side table.

He removed his hand from her waist when they reached the door. He needed his hand to be able to open it, unless she opened it, but she had rather that he moved his hand.

"Susan." He pulled the door wider and then stepped back giving her a stiff smile.

"Why did you tell him?" she accused in a quiet voice after they had walked past the footman.

"Because there is only one reason why I would not wait until after we have finished mourning. It is the day after William's funeral there's no other explanation."

"But to tell my father."

"He would have known anyway…" His voice was low and husky. He turned then and held out his hat towards the footman who still stood to one side of the room trying not to listen to their whispering. "Please put that somewhere out of the way." The man came across the room and took it. Then Henry turned and grasped Susan's elbow. "Now where may we go to talk?"

"Not the drawing room, Alethea is there."

"Where then, the garden?"

She nodded.

He walked her, by the pressure of his grip on her elbow, into the dining room and out through the French doors, and shut the door behind them. As soon as the door was shut he began speaking, while a cuckoo called repeatedly in the distance. "We must—"

"Why did you tell my father?" Her fingers curled into fists.

"Why would you think I would not?"

"Because, I… *Alethea…*"

"Damn it, Susan, I told you that I love you, and I know you love me, please stop fighting happiness. You give everything of yourself to everyone else, but do you not think that if Alethea truly loved you she would want to see you happy too?"

"But she loves you, Henry, and she is my sister."

His hands came to each side of her head, his palms pressing against her cheeks. "She does not love me. And I know she is your sister, but that does not mean you must lose everything for her." He looked into her eyes through her spectacles. "You father said you had asked him to look for a position for you, why?"

Her gaze and her head lowered and she stared at his chest, not able to face this, or him. "I needed to get away so I did not have to face you marrying anyone else."

His thumb slipped beneath her chin and lifted her head back

up. "I would not have married. I have found who I wish to marry, she's standing before me, and if she will not have me, I will have no one. Do you hear me?"

"I feel guilty, because I have taken you—"

"You have not taken me, I am yours, and if there is guilt to be faced we share it equally."

"Henry…" Her heart stretched out as his eyes looked at her, focusing through the cloak of grief.

"No. Susan." His hands fell, and instead he stood before her, his hands at his sides. "You must not take me out of pity, or sympathy, you must not accept me for my sake as you did last evening. Accept me because this is what you wish for, for no other reason. Be self-centered."

She swallowed. Her throat was dry. She longed to. Her whole body was engaged with his, humming with feelings of desire, love and… "Yes."

She looked up at the sky rather than at him, as the cuckoo began calling again. "Yes." She smiled, when she should not be smiling.

His arms wrapped about her and he lifted her up and twirled her about once, then his hands were either side of her head again and his lips pressed on hers.

When he pulled away, he said, "We have to act now, Susan. Shall I go into the drawing room and then you might come in with an excuse to take your mother away so that I may speak with Alethea. It is my responsibility to tell her."

Nausea twisted through Susan's stomach, she could quite easily cast up her luncheon. "She will be angry with me."

"Then return to the drawing room after awhile and let her take her anger out in front of me so I may protect you from it. I shall steer it in my direction."

"She will never forgive me."

"She will forgive you, if she loves you, and I think she loves you far more than any feelings she has for me."

Susan swallowed against the fear in her throat.

"Come along let us get this over with." His hands fell and then he gripped one of hers and turned to lead her back indoors. He let her hand go as they walked into the drawing room.

"Henry!" Alethea set aside her sewing and stood up. "I did not know you were coming."

"It was a moment's decision," he said as he walked away from Susan, crossing the room.

"Henry," Susan's mother stood and embraced him, as she always had. "My dearest boy." Then she stood back, her hands sliding down his arms and then gripping his hands. "How are you all faring today? I should imagine it feels very strange."

He nodded and glanced at Alethea.

Susan's mother let his hands go. "Of course, you do not want me fussing over you, I shall not. Sit with Alethea and I will order tea."

He did as he was bid and sat by Alethea.

Susan's hands shook as she turned to her mother. "Mama, I need new curtains in my room I think, would you come and look?"

Her mother frowned. Susan clasped her hand and pulled a little.

"Now?"

"Yes, now. Please?"

She looked at Alethea and Henry, then Susan. Her eyes widened and she smiled, making entirely the wrong assumption; she thought that Susan had planned this with Alethea.

Susan did not correct her even when they walked into the hall and her mother said, "There is nothing wrong with your curtains."

"I know, but please leave Alethea and Henry alone for a moment?"

Her mother sighed then smiled and shook her head. "Very well, I shall walk down to the kitchen and order that tea and choose some cakes to accompany it, but Henry and Alethea shall only have as long as that."

Susan nodded.

She looked back at the drawing room door that had been left ajar as her mother walked away. She heard Alethea talking nonsense, about shopping in York. If Susan stayed here she would hear everything. She could not stay and eavesdrop, it would be cruel, Henry had been Alethea's since birth, the conversation would be embarrassing for Alethea.

But now he is mine. It was a selfish voice that whispered through her.

Susan turned away and followed her mother, if she was in the kitchen she could not even be tempted to come back so she might listen.

When Susan returned, it was with her mother. Her heart had been racing in a ridiculous pace that had made her lightheaded as they'd walked through the hall.

No sound came from the drawing room when they neared it. The only noise was from the china rocking on the tea tray which the maid carried behind them.

Susan swallowed back her anxiety, and her fingers pressed on the bridge of her spectacles, then fell.

Her mother pushed the open door wider. "Alethea... Henry..."

When they walked in Alethea was standing, Henry was still sitting down. He rose and turned to face them. Susan could see from his face the conversation had not gone well.

"You are..." Alethea began to declare... then her words ran dry.

But Alethea's eyes, as she stared at Susan, listed all the words she had not spoken—a traitor, a liar, betrayer, cruel, heartless, sour, thief...

I am sorry.

"I cannot believe you did not tell me! You said nothing!"

Susan's skin flushed with warmth and probably flooded with colour. "I did not know how to."

"Know what?" Her mother asked as she gestured for the maid to set down the tray and leave them.

286

"She has been making-up to Henry, Mama, and now Henry wishes to marry her!"

"Alethea." Henry's voice was a reprimand.

He crossed the room to join Susan and his arm settled about her waist as her mother looked at her. Her eyebrows lifted. "Susan?"

"We are engaged to be married." Henry told her. "I have spoken with Uncle Casper."

Her mother frowned. "But you are in mourning… Oh… Oh good Lord. Susan." She came towards her and gripped Susan's hands. "Why you left London…" Then she looked at Alethea. "Oh my dear…" She left Susan and walked over to Alethea. "Oh my dear." She embraced Alethea.

Alethea glared at Susan and Henry across their mother's shoulder.

"Do not worry," Henry said quietly.

She was not worried—she was embarrassed…

I hate you! Alethea's eyes screamed.

Henry's arm lifted and his hand settled on Susan's shoulder, drawing her gaze to him and then turning her so she faced him. "We should speak to my father and mother too."

His hand slipped from her shoulder, and instead he took her hand. "Come along, we will leave."

She let him lead her out of the room, there was no point in her staying, she would not appease Alethea when she was in this mood, and yet—this was everything she'd feared. She could not simply walk away from her family.

"I foolishly did not think to bring the carriage. What would you have us do? We might both travel in your father's carriage, or I can wait while you change into your habit and we'll ride home together?"

Home. He'd said home, because it was his home, but when they were married it would be hers too. The thought scared her. She did not want to leave her family.

"We will travel together by carriage," he decided for her and

287

looked at the footman. "Please have the carriage made ready."

The footman disappeared.

"Would you like to go upstairs and fetch your bonnet and a shawl?"

She nodded, her gaze saying, thank you, although her mind and her lips no longer seemed to be able to form words.

"Go." He nodded at her.

She turned away and ran up the stairs.

Her heart pumped hard, thumping in her chest as she sought out a bonnet which would match her dress. There was a straw one, with grey ribbons. At least she had dressed in something dark that would be appropriate to his mourning, she would not feel as though she was insulting his parents.

She pulled out her paisley shawl, she did not have a dark shawl, though.

When she reached the landing she looked down. Henry was no longer in the hall.

She ran back downstairs. "Where is Lord Henry, James?"

"He is waiting outside, miss." The footman walked across to open the door for her.

She walked quickly past him, her eyes focusing on the carriage that awaited her.

"Susan." He'd been standing slightly to one side of the portico outside the front door. He stepped forward. "Ready?"

No. She nodded regardless.

"Come along then." He held her hand and walked towards the carriage, then hung on to her hand as she climbed up.

He climbed in behind her.

"Where is your horse?"

The door shut behind him.

"Tied to the back."

When the carriage rolled into motion she sat back, as Henry did beside her. He stripped off his gloves and then reached across to take her hand from her lap.

She wore gloves. Thin lace gloves. She could still feel the heat from his hand.

He squeezed her fingers.

She looked at him. "I am terrified. I cannot breathe. Do you think Alethea will ever speak to me again?"

"Yes. She will, once she has had chance to calm down."

"Was she terribly annoyed with us?"

"Beyond terribly. But we knew that would be the case and we made our choice for other reasons."

She nodded. They had made their choice out of selfish want.

"My father will be upset too. I am sorry. He is not in the best state to hear this news."

"No. I am sorry."

"You are sorry that I pressured you into making a choice when you were not ready. Forgive me, but I do not see what *you* are sorry for…"

His brown eyes still had the lost look of yesterday, he was fighting with grief and she had added to his burdens yesterday instead of freeing him. She turned and wrapped her arms about his neck, offering the comfort she'd longed to since the day he'd held her hand in a gesture of such need. "I am sorry, for making you face this now."

His arms came about her, holding her securely and he rested his cheek against her bonnet. "I am not sorry."

She hung on to him as the carriage rolled on, and when they broke apart his arm clung about her shoulders and pulled her close. She leant against his shoulder. "I feel so awful. Treacherous."

"For falling in love… Are we to change that to make our fathers and Alethea happy, and ourselves miserable. I knew nothing of love before this summer, but now I know that love cannot be ordered or told."

Her head rested against his shoulder again, her straw bonnet denting a little.

He was hers.

Chapter Twenty-five

Henry held Susan's hand securely. His plan was written in his head, he would speak with his father and mother then leave Susan here so she need not face Alethea's anger and disappointment, while he went to York to the Archbishop's office and obtained a licence.

They walked across the cobbled central courtyard while the flow of the fountain echoed about the walls joined by the sound of their footsteps. Henry looked up at the windows of the wings of the house that wrapped around them, he could not see anyone looking.

Davis opened the door before they reached it.

They'd climbed out of the carriage on the gravel outside the front, rather than bring the carriage into the courtyard, because his horse had been strapped to the back, yet still Davis had learned of their arrival within the few minutes it had taken them to walk the distance across the courtyard.

Davis bowed. "Master Henry, Miss Susan." He did not look at their joined hands but looked Henry directly in the eyes.

Henry smiled. "Where is Papa?"

"In the family drawing room, my Lord."

It was unusual for his father to be in the drawing room at this time of day, he was usually working on business, and yet… he'd not considered anything about the estate since William had died.

Henry nodded and let go of Susan's hand. "Here, would you take these?" He took off his hat and thrust his gloves into it then handed it over.

"My Lord." Davis gave him a deferential nod.

Henry took hold of Susan's hand once more and then pulled her along with him, squeezing her hand tightly. His strides were quick. He wanted this done. It should be less uncomfortable than it had been talking to Uncle Casper and yet William had only been buried yesterday…

He breathed out a measured breath when they neared the open door. Then looked at Susan. Her free hand clutched his forearm for a moment. She was terrified.

He walked into the room a little ahead of her, her hand still clasped in his.

His parents were alone and standing together. They'd been embracing. They broke apart. There were tears in his mother's eyes, and he could see the barrier holding back the emotion in his father's eyes. Perhaps his mother had been trying to talk some sense into his father, about how life had to go on. It had to. Time did not stop. And there were his brothers and sisters to be thought of.

His father could do that and not forget William.

William. William. William. Henry repeated his brother's name because he would not forget, even though his life was already moving on.

"Papa. Mama."

They looked down at his hand which held Susan's. He raised it, drawing Susan forward so she stood directly beside him. "I wish to tell you that I am engaged to Susan and we are to be married immediately. I am going to ride over to York to the Archbishop's offices and fetch a licence."

"Henry…" His father's pitch was incredulous and his forehead creased into a heavy frown. "What is this?" He looked at Susan then. "Forgive me, Susan. But…" He looked at Henry. "What of Alethea?"

"My affection is for Susan."

"Your affection…" He stared at Susan for a moment. As though he could simply not understand. Then he looked at Henry again. "Why now? Can this not wait? It is hardly the time for family upsets."

Henry's mother stood next to his father her mouth agape at his revelation.

Henry swallowed against a dry throat, he would have spoken bluntly had he been alone, but not with Susan beside him. "It cannot wait, Papa." Was his answer and his voice was loaded with all that that meant. Yes, he'd acted recklessly again. His father's eyes held the accusation.

"Henry." His father's brows pulled together forming an even deeper frown of judgement as his pitch definitely did judge.

Henry looked at his mother. "Mama, will you not welcome Susan to the family?"

"Oh, goodness." She instantly snapped out of her shock. "Of course. Of course, dear." She walked across the room. Henry let go of Susan's hand as his mother embraced her. "Congratulations. We are all topsy-turvy of late for obvious reasons, but you are most welcome, Susan, dear."

His father shook his head at Henry.

Henry shrugged. There was nothing to say, no one would condone this rush, and nothing could change it.

He looked at his mother. "Might I leave Susan with you, Mama, while I fetch the licence? Things are understandably difficult for her at home. I would rather Susan waited here."

His mother looked at him then Susan. "Is Alethea very upset?"

"Not upset," Henry answered. "Angry."

"And Forth?" His father asked.

"Is accepting what must be the next step."

292

His father sighed out a breath of frustration. A breath that accused Henry of being a worthless, reckless son who had failed him.

"I shall go." He looked at Susan. "I should imagine I will be back in a couple of hours, Mama will look after you until then."

"Susan, come and sit with me." His mother held out her hand.

Henry did not let her go immediately. "I'll have them let Samson up to see you, he will keep you company while I am gone too."

She smiled, it was the first smile he'd seen since the moment of her acceptance. "But Samson will wish to fall out with me too when he realises he has competition for your attention."

"Not when it is you he will compete with, you have always been his second favourite, and that I would guess you thought I did not know." He squeezed her hand, then brushed a finger down her cheek before turning away to leave her with his mother and father.

Chapter Twenty-six

He'd felt clear headed today, not anxious. But that was because he'd had something occupying his mind—Susan. "Susan." He looked up at the canopy of the bed. He'd left a candle burning at the bedside. It had burned down to a stub.

He'd not drunk himself to sleep on brandy for a change, because he'd not wished to wake on his wedding day with a thumping head. But consequently the thoughts that had been a blessed distraction all day had been tormenting him for the last few hours in the dark.

He had no idea if this was the right thing to have done. Doubt had set in with the darkness.

Yesterday he'd taken choice from her and from himself.

Marriage… It was such a step, and life had almost seemed to decide it for him. Only months ago he'd been adamantly against the idea. "Coward." He rolled to his back, and then to his other side.

Samson's breathing shifted in its pace as he disturbed the dog, but Samson did not rise, merely stretched out his hind legs trying to claim more of Henry's bed.

God.

Married.

Would he feel suffocated? Drowned. Tied-down. This fear had come from nowhere and crept up on him.

There would be no more curricle racing or raucous nights in brothels. Yet he'd not slept with a whore since… When?

"Before my curricle accident."

He tumbled back on to his back with a sigh, wishing he was asleep and not thinking.

"Susan."

Lord.

He'd had a sexual encounter with her… Susan…

How had that happened? Through liquor, grief and reckless-ness. It had been a moments error of judgement.

But perhaps not an error? Perhaps a very wise decision, albeit made while he'd been deep in the bottle? Perhaps it had been the best decision he'd ever made? It had forced their hands. Without that, maybe they would never have reneged on their agreement to remain apart.

Tomorrow she would be in his bed…

That thought was the one part of marriage he did not have any trouble imagining.

But he would be a married man, committed. There could be no change of heart.

Love. The emotion had proven like bread before baking, it had risen, multiplying to double its size since their hour in the rose garden. He would not have a change of heart. "Stop fearing stupid spectres. I love her."

The candle flickered scattering shadows across the room, then it guttered and extinguished sending the scent of burning into the air along with the more pungent smell of melted wax.

It would never be the same when he met his friends. He and Harry, and he and the others, would be entirely different. As a married man he would not be able to speak of the things they did, let alone do them.

But. "Love." With love came heartbreak.

Love… The emotion was not only in his heart but in his blood. Damn. He had enough responsibilities, he had no need for this now, for a wife. In a year… In six months… When he was not so bruised and broken. He was not ready.

But it was too late not to be ready. "Ahhhhh." The sigh slipped from deep in his throat. His father's expression of judgement hovered in his thoughts.

From tomorrow onwards, he must not be a coward—or reckless—or selfish. He'd forced this. He must protect her from the consequences, and he would do.

She was here. Within yards. Three rooms away from his.

God, he would feel better if he went to her. If he could hold her. The best hours of the day had been when they'd been in each others company, and the best of all when he'd had her hand to grip. It was her hand that had stopped him feeling like he was drowning in responsibility and grief.

Another sigh escaped into the darkness.

He would not go to her.

If they were caught it would make things more awkward for her and she'd not been herself today. If she could have run off to the library to paint damned flowers she probably would have.

But tomorrow… Tomorrow she would be in his bed. Tomorrow he would have the comfort of her body and her hand to hold as he wished.

Tomorrow he might even sleep without the need to mute the voice in his mind with brandy.

This was just jitters. He'd made his mind up when he was in town that he was willing to marry Susan. It was only that the moment had been hastened.

I am not afraid of it! He shouted his mind into silence. He needed to sleep.

But how will you— "Be quiet!"

~

Sunlight peeked through the cracks in the shutters that covered the windows.

Susan rolled to her back.

She had been awake for ages, laying quietly in the Earl of Barrington's plush guest bedchamber. The light crept about the room revealing the pale greens of the furnishings and the gold braiding.

Her heart skipped through a country dance.

In her mind's eye, there was the note her mother had written, '*It would be best if you stayed with Robert and Jane. Alethea is very upset.*' Susan turned on to her side and dampened the pillow with more tears.

Henry had written back on her behalf. She had not known what to say. They'd cast her aside, and she could not be angry, it was her fault. She had become guilt's permanent companion.

Henry had told her parents about the wedding. She was to be married in York Minster at midday tomorrow. She looked at the window and the daylight seeping through. Today…

Today…

She would be married.

She stared at the closed shutters as outside the sound of birdsong rose in a chorus.

Fear twisted around in her stomach, tangling up with the nausea.

Would her parents forgive her? Would Alethea?

"Oh." What if Alethea never forgave her? More tears wet the cotton cover on her pillow.

She longed to hold Henry.

No. To be held by him. She was becoming selfish. She was discovering what it was like to be cared for with the same intensity that she cared. He had shown her that today. Shown her that there was a reason for selfish wants on occasion.

He made her feel better. When he'd been with her today she had felt better, but when he'd gone to York she had been lonely. Aunt Jane had been kind, wonderfully so, considering William, and yet Uncle Robert had left them without speaking.

She'd offended Henry's family as well as hers.

She'd not known what to say when they'd eaten dinner. They'd been quieter than she'd ever known them. Even Sarah and Christine had hardly spoken.

She'd intruded on their mourning. They had hoped yesterday they would at last be left to grieve, she had ruined that and shattered their peace.

Today they would be asked to attend a wedding—and yet her selfishness was there again, because she wanted to marry him, no matter that it was hurting others, not to marry him would hurt her and Henry.

She was to be a wife. "Today," the word whispered out into the air. "Henry Marlow's wife." He'd been Alethea's since before the day Susan had been born. "Now he is mine."

Now he would be hers. Warmth flooded into her blood. She wished he was here. If he was with her she was certain she would not feel so scared.

She would be happy. And married.

Married…

~

A letter arrived from Susan's father just before they ate breakfast. She broke the seal with shaking fingers.

"What does it say?" Henry asked.

Her gaze raced across the words. "They are coming." She looked up and smiled at him.

"Of course they are coming," his mother said.

Susan did not look at her but stayed focused on Henry. "Papa has ordered a carriage. They will collect me here at ten and drive me into York."

His hand cupped her face, and his eyes showed his pleasure for her. "I am glad, Susan."

"Your parents are not people to miss your marriage."

298

She turned and smiled at his mother, acknowledging her reassurance, but yesterday… She had felt vulnerable, guilty and afraid. She had not been certain.

She looked back at Henry. "Alethea is not coming."

"I think we may forgive her that, though."

"Yes, I suppose." But she would still have liked her there.

"Your mother will be there, and your father, to give you away," Henry reassured.

"Yes."

"Cheer up," he said in a quieter voice. "It is our wedding day."

Our wedding… the words swept over her, and made her feel that it was only then she realised just what that meant, even though she'd lain awake most of the night.

"Come and sit down and eat. I do not want you fainting at the altar before you have spoken your vows."

He sat next to her and served her everything himself, filling her plate as he also encouraged Christine and Sarah to eat, and the boys.

Aunt Jane and Christine and Susan spoke quietly, the boys spoke more raucously but mostly with each other and in slightly hushed tones, with odd glances at their father, who did not speak at all. Henry joined in some of the boys' conversation, but he mainly spoke to her. His attention focused on her as it used to be focused on Alethea. But their conversation was whispered too. It did not feel as though it was her wedding day.

Her wedding day…

When she finished eating, she excused herself for a moment, only to be met in the hall by Davis who told her privately a package had arrived for her.

A package?

Her heartbeat raced again as she walked up the stairs. The package lay on the bed, awaiting her as she walked into the room. She ripped it open. "Oh." Her dress. There was a letter. She pulled the paper open.

Susan dear, I am sure you do not want to be married in the dress you left here in yesterday, so here is your pale grey evening dress and your evening gloves, it should not be too offensive with Henry in mourning, but at least it is pretty. I shall bring you a bonnet to match it too.

Love, Mama.

Tears filled Susan's eyes and blurred her view of the gown decorated with fine white lace on the short sleeves, neckline and hem. The material was a pale shimmering grey, with shots of silver thread through it. It would feel much prettier than her dark blue day dress.

She turned and crossed the room to ring for a maid to help her change and let Henry know she would not be able to see him again before she left. She did not wish him to see her in her wedding dress. She did not care that he might have seen her in it as an evening dress. All of a sudden the success of their marriage came down to the prettiness of her dress, and being able to hold on to one single tradition.

All of Henry's family respected her decision and so no one waited in the hall when her parents' carriage arrived.

She hurried down the stairs and out the door, which Davis held open, acknowledging him with a thank you.

Her father held the carriage door open for her. She accepted his hand and climbed up.

"Mama." She smiled at her.

"Susan." Her mother hugged her when she sat down. "You look very pretty." When Susan pulled away her mother reached over and picked up Susan's bonnet. But it was not Susan's it was one of Alethea's with white ribbon and white roses.

She looked at her mother.

An understanding smile twisted her mother's lips, and tears glittered in her eyes. "Alethea said you must have it. It is a perfect match for your dress. She wished you to feel beautiful on your

300

wedding day even though she did not feel able to come and see you married."

Susan hugged her mother again, tears falling from her eyes.

"That's enough of that nonsense," her father said when he sat down with a wry tone and a wryer smile.

"It is your wedding day I will not have any weeping unless they are happy tears."

Susan nodded at him. At last it felt as though she was to be married.

They drank tea in an inn near York Minster before it was time to walk about the green and go into the Minster for the service.

Aunt Jane awaited them at the door.

"Here she is," Aunt Jane stated as though she had feared Susan would not arrive.

But here she was, standing before the Minster, about to marry Henry…

Her father had acquired her a small posy of pale pink chrysanthemums to carry, Susan clutched the flowers with both hands. Aunt Jane, her mother and the minister disappeared back into the Minster to tell Henry that she'd arrived.

"Well then…" Her father lifted his elbow out towards her. "I did not imagine a week ago for one moment that this week I would be giving one of my daughters away, but I am not sorry for it. Henry is a good man despite all this, Susan. You will be happy I am sure. He will make sure you are, that I am certain of."

She looked at her father before they walked through the door into the Minster. "But Alethea…"

"Will find another candidate for her affections. We are going to return to London tomorrow so she might enjoy the rest of her season and resume her search."

Susan flushed. Fear swept up, fear of being separated from her family.

"Here." He pushed open the door and they walked into the huge space of York Minster.

In the pews at the far end of the aisle people stood up and looked back.

"Oh."

Her father's hand lay over hers as she held his forearm. The flowers trembled in her other hand. It was not only Henry's father and mother with him, but his sisters and brothers, and his Uncle Edward, Aunt Ellen and cousin Rob and his wife Caro, and Harry...

Uncle Edward and Harry must have stayed at Rob's after the funeral.

Henry stepped out of the pew and did not only look back but turned around to watch her, smiling, smiling whole heartedly as if he was not in mourning.

She smiled back.

It was such a long walk up the aisle, with her footsteps ringing on the old tiles, she still had her walking boots on beneath the evening dress, and yet she did feel pretty, and she celebrated the bonnet she wore most, it was a precious gift from Alethea. She was with Susan in spirit.

When she reached her position before the altar she mouthed, *Hello*, to Henry.

Hello, you look beautiful.

"We are here today..." The minister began the service.

Susan's father squeezed her hand gently before he passed it to Henry. When Henry received it he squeezed it gently too. She looked into his brown eyes. His lips mouthed, *I love you...*

Had he said that before, in that manner? She could not remember. So much had happened. But she loved him. *I love you too.*

They spoke the vows that bound them together and committed them for life, looking into each other's eyes as though no one else was there, as they held hands.

Then he had to give her a ring. She had not thought that he would have a ring, yet he must have bought one yesterday when he'd been to York because he turned to Harry and Harry handed one to him. Perhaps he'd called at his cousin's on the way back from York, she could barely remember half the conversations of yesterday.

"Here." He smiled holding the gold band in his fingers so he might slide it on to her finger. "And now you are snared," he whispered when it was in place.

She looked up suddenly and a sound of amusement escaped her throat as the minister gave him more words to repeat.

Today he was the Henry she had always known—or not known, she had never really known him until this spring when he'd come home with his injury.

"With this ring…"

Her heart raced as Henry made his declaration.

Married…

Married? *I thee wed…*

Married… His beautiful, perfect brown eyes, looked into hers.

"I now pronounce you man and wife!" The minister spoke as though the Minster was full of people and the words echoed about the great columns and into the choir stalls.

"Man and wife," Henry repeated, then he ducked slightly as she lifted her head, to sneak beneath the rim of her bonnet and press a kiss on her lips as his hand gripped her nape. When he pulled away, as heat crept into her cheeks, he said over her lips, "I love you, my wife."

It was such a beautifully reassuring thing for him to say she rose on to her toes and wrapped her arms about his neck. Her posy of flowers brushed against the back of his head as the rim of her bonnet struck his cheek.

He squeezed her body for a moment then let her go.

"Congratulations."

"You do make a beautiful couple."

"You are a husband then, Henry…"

They were surrounded by members of his family giving them felicitations.

"Come and sign the register," the minister requested.

When that was done they went outside and climbed into his father's state carriage. His parents then travelled with hers, while his brothers and sisters used a secondary carriage.

Henry's arm lifted encouraging her to come beneath it. She pressed against him, her bonnet resting against his shoulder as his arm settled on her shoulders. His free hand pulled the bow tying her bonnet loose.

"May we take this very pretty ornamentation off?" He did not await her answer but slid it off then threw it on to the far seat. Then his lips pressed against hers. Her arms wrapped about his neck, as they'd done in the Minster, and in that small room at the ball where they'd first kissed.

His mouth opened and his tongue danced with hers.

When he broke the kiss, her head fell and her forehead rested against his shoulder. "The bonnet is Alethea's, she sent it for me to wear. Do you think that means she will forgive me?"

A rumble of amusement sounded in his chest. "Either that or she wished to have an element of control over you and I today."

She looked up and into his eyes.

He smiled. "Yes, I have seen how she manipulates you, and yes I know how she has manipulated me, when I played along because I did not care to think of others. But now I care, I care for you, and I do not care for her manipulation. We will leave the bonnet in the carriage and have a footman take it back to Alethea either way. But, yes, I believe she will forgive us, and most particularly you, because for all her tricks to have you at her beck and call, I know she cares for you as I do."

"Henry, it was a kind gesture…"

"Perhaps. But either way, we will send her bonnet back, and send it today, or it will become an excuse for her to interfere in some way and I wish us to continue being selfish for a little longer."

"She will not interfere, she is going to London with Mama and Papa tomorrow."

"Then that I am glad of, but she is still having her bonnet back." His fingers came up and cupped her cheek, and then he kissed her again, and kissed her endlessly until the carriage turned on to Farnborough's drive.

"Is my hair falling from its pins?"

"A little. It looks adorable."

"Henry."

"I swear you look beautiful and not untidy at all, only loved."

"Henry!"

He laughed, probably at her expression of horror.

"Not in that way, Susan, darling." He laughed again.

The carriage rolled on under the arch and the raised portcullis of the old medieval entrance to Farnborough and into the noisy cobbled courtyard.

The carriage turned about the fountain and drew to a halt before the door, then rocked as the footman jumped down to come around and open the door.

"My Lady," he said when he held the door wide. She had not been called that before.

"No Frank." Henry hurried out before she could rise. "This is my prerogative."

She stood up and moved to step down, holding her hand out to Henry but he did not take it, instead in a moment she was swept up into his arms. She squealed and clasped his shoulders. "Henry!"

"A wife is to be carried over the threshold of her new home, and for now this will be yours."

He proceeded to walk across the cobbles with her in his arms.

Davis held the door wide for them smiling broadly. Henry smiled back. "Good day, Davis."

"Congratulations, my Lord, my Lady."

"There is a bonnet in the carriage, to be sent over to the Forths, but pray save my hat from the carriage." He looked at Susan. Her fingers were pressed into his shoulders. "Now I believe we are to have a small wedding breakfast in the dining room, but first of all champagne in the drawing room and so I shall carry you there."

He did so and then proceeded to drop her on to a sofa. "Ahhh! Henry!"

He laughed once more leaning over her and kissing her lips before rising. "Happy, Lady Marlow?"

Lady Marlow... How odd that sounded. But... "Yes."

"Champagne, my Lord..." A footman stood at the open door.

She shared a look with Henry, a look which said they might have been caught kissing.

He straightened up. "Thank you." Then walked across the room to take two glasses from a tray full of them.

"My Lord..." Davis's voice echoed in the hall as the others began to return.

Susan sat upright and then stood as Henry brought the glass of sparkling wine to her.

"Now swear to me you will not rebel and run off to the library, this is our wedding day..."

She shook her head and made a face at him, but in truth she was glad of his humour. It was holding her together.

Chapter Twenty-seven

If his father and mother were still angry that he'd had to marry Susan so soon after William's funeral there was no sign of it on his wedding day. The day may have been a subdued affair, but everyone had been perfectly pleasant, especially to Susan, and quite probably for her sake. Even Harry had kept his lips closed on the reason for the rush.

Henry hoped her day had lacked nothing bar the company of Alethea.

Edward and Ellen and his cousins had left after everyone had eaten an early dinner. A meal that had yesterday become a quickly planned wedding breakfast.

Then Susan's parents had left and she'd cried, his family had drifted away, leaving her to her goodbye. He'd stayed and watched as she'd held them as though she never wanted to let go.

There had been a fear of change in her eyes. *Lord,* he knew that emotion, he'd become used to it in the days since William's death. She'd had no time to adjust to leaving her home and her family.

She'd glanced at him when she'd let go of her father. Her eyes speaking to him. *Sorry.* Why an apology? But the sadness in her expression, her heightening colour and the turn of her lips had

307

expressed her embarrassment. She'd been comparing her feelings of losing her parents to him losing William, and judged herself. He'd stepped forward then and set his arm about her waist. Susan had taught him what it was to be selfless. But in return he would teach her to allow herself to sometimes think only of herself. She was allowed to feel sad over leaving her parents, no matter what anyone else felt.

He'd touched her waist often today and held her hand and rested his palm at the back of her neck, and he'd quietly revelled in the freedom of it. There were things he already knew were good about marriage and the comfort of having Susan in his bed was going to be one of them.

They'd come upstairs before the sun had even set because his parents had not been talkative, and the girls and Percy had already chosen to retire. She'd suggested they retire too. It was going to be an odd thing, though, to spend the night with Susan in his bed, in his home, with his family in the house.

He sighed. He'd been standing outside the door of his own bedchamber for nearly a half hour listening to a maid help Susan undress, waiting and imagining Susan disrobing from her under-garments. He perhaps should have knocked after he'd heard the maid leave, but he'd not been certain Susan would be ready.

But he could not stand here forever, like a coward. His knuckles tapped the door. "Susan! Are you ready?"

After a moment there was a call back. "Yes." The response sounded with a hesitance of, no, though.

He turned the handle. Samson rose to follow him. "No, you stay, and do not dare whine. If you argue over the bed with Susan, she will always win, and you will be in the kitchens."

He walked in alone as Samson padded off towards the chair he favoured.

Lord. He wanted to laugh. He'd stripped off his evening coat, his black stock neck-cloth and waistcoat and taken off his shoes, and yet in his shirt and trousers he was probably as heavily clothed as she was in her bed attire. His gaze dropped to her naked toes peeping from beneath her nightdress then lifted to her face. "You are all buttoned up still."

The nightdress she wore came to her wrists and the lace even hung over her hands, and also formed a flurry about her neck.

At least with her nightdress, though, unlike the dress she'd been wearing in the rose garden, the buttons were at the front.

He walked across the room. She was smiling at him although her cheeks were pink. "There will be a rule, the first in our marriage, I may set them and you may set them as we go on, but this first rule will be mine. You are never to wear a nightdress in bed."

"And what if I am cold?"

"You will not be cold. I shall warm you."

His smile twisted when he looked down at the row of tiny round pearl-like buttons, then he began releasing them. "I do not wish to fight with a thing like this every night."

She was looking at his face. "Every night?"

He glanced up. "Indeed, every night."

She laughed but when she spoke her voice was serious. "Thank you, you have been making me laugh all day and making me feel better, when you must still feel very sad yourself. I have not told you, Henry; I take it back, you are not self-centered. I have seen everything you are doing for your family."

His fingers continued their work releasing the buttons between her breasts as he looked into her face. "No. You were right, I am. You being here is only more evidence of that. The way I behaved in the rose garden was for my own selfish interest I thought nothing of the impact on you."

"You just needed some comfort, I understood…"

"But you had made up your mind not to marry me and I took that choice away." He moved aside her nightdress and cupped her left breast. She stood straight and unmoving as his thumb brushed over her taut nipple.

"I do not regret what we did. I think I shocked myself… that is all."

He laughed at that. She was still an anomaly, but now she was his wife and he could take as long as he liked discovering all the facets of her nature.

Desire, attraction and affection clasped in his stomach tightening the muscle. He let go of her breast and then lifted off her spectacles, then put them on the dressing table beside her.

"Will you take off your shirt? It feels strange to stand here like this when you are clothed."

A low sound of amusement rumbled in his chest. Her nightdress was gaping open, it was only fair that he stripped too. He gripped his shirt above the waist of his trousers and pulled it up over his head, then discarded it in one of the pale green upholstered chairs in his room.

Her cool fingers spread out over his pectoral muscles, her gaze following the movement. "I wanted to touch you in the spring."

When she had come up here to his rooms…

"When you laid on the sofa in the library. You were so bruised, and so beautiful."

"And so reckless and self-centered." His hands pressed over hers.

She looked up. "No, I was trying to convince myself I had every cause to dislike you, but I did not dislike you that day. You fascinated me."

"Like one of those flowers in that book."

"Yes, like that."

"Well you now have a lifetime to explore your fascination, both for me and for that book of orchids."

He leant and she raised her head, and then he kissed her.

Her soft lips pressed gently back against his. Every time he kissed her he was reminded of her inexperience. He treasured it.

His hand slid inside her open nightdress as hers lifted to his shoulders.

He kissed her for a moment more, then bent and kissed the exquisite skin of her upper breast. Her nightdress fell off her shoulder, hanging down her arm. His tongue played with her nipple as her hands stroked across his back exploring the contours of his body.

He lifted his head. "Let us be rid of this nightdress." He slipped it off her other shoulder and pulled the cuffs over her hands. Then she straightened her arms and let it slide to the floor, in a pool of white cotton.

He wrapped his arms around her and kissed her again, glad that she showed no self-consciousness.

She broke the kiss, looking into his eyes with a gentleness he'd never seen in a woman's eyes until he'd started looking more closely into Susan's. "I love you," she said.

To hear those words… They did very strange things to his stomach. "I love you also, Susan. Now run and get into the warm bed, while I finish undressing."

Before she turned away, she smiled widely.

As she did turn he smacked her bottom with a satisfying crack.

She squealed and then ran for the bed as the orange light of sunset shone through the window on to her skin, highlighting her slender curves.

He would have no complaints in his marriage bed.

He unbuttoned his trousers, and then bent and pushed both his trousers and underwear down, stripping his stockings from his feet too. He left his clothes in a pile on the floor beside her nightdress.

"Are you not going to close the shutters?" She asked as he walked towards the bed.

"No. I want to see you in the last of the daylight, and then I will wish to look at you in the moonlight. Now make some space for me."

She moved over, lifting the sheet and blanket.

He climbed in beside her.

"I am used to sleeping with Alethea, we often share a bed…"

Her innocence made him laugh. "I hope sleeping with me will not be at all comparable."

She giggled with a lightness he'd only heard in her voice when she'd been in a ballroom. If he could make her as happy in their marriage as she was in a ballroom, then he would be happy too.

He leant over her, his hand embracing the back of her neck and kissed her again. Then he threw the covers back and kissed a path down her neck and across her shoulder. This is how he had wanted to make love to her in the rose garden. To have been able to kiss her skin.

His hand moved to her hip as her fingers combed through his hair and he kissed a path across her breast then lower, over her stomach.

When he kissed her inner thigh she squealed as she had when he'd smacked her. He did not stop, but held that one thigh and cherished it with several more kisses.

She laughed.

But she stopped laughing when he kissed the place between her legs. Her in-breath was sharp as she gripped his head through the sheet. But she did not stop him, and her hips rocked upward with a natural instinct.

Her naivety was as beautiful as she was.

As he carried on, one of her legs lifted and lay over his shoulder. He used his fingers as well as his tongue, pushing them into her moist warmth. She sighed into the air of his bedchamber.

He'd never lain with a woman in his bed here. She was the first to make those sounds of satisfaction in this room. At least there was an innocence on his part too, in that.

There would never be another woman here. There would never be any other women now.

He lifted up and crawled up the bed, his hands moving either side of her body.

Her legs pressed against his outer thighs.

"Ready?" he asked as he hovered over her looking into her pale eyes.

"Yes."

Her eyes shone with want, discovery and… affection… Love. He'd not noticed any of those things when he'd been drunk, all he'd felt was the acceptance of her body.

He pressed into her.

"Ah." The sound escaped her lips, as her fingernails clawed in the skin of his upper arms, hanging on to him.

He withdrew, holding his weight on his hands so that his body hovered above hers as he lifted his hips. He looked down when he pressed back in, and watched himself glide inside her.

"Ah."

He looked up into her eyes.

"Ah." It was such a soft breathy sound.

He moved more swiftly.

As his gaze held hers, she bit her lower lip. He wished to see all the slight nuances in her expression as the use of her body spun sensations into his blood.

Her legs lifted higher, gripping above his hips as he moved more firmly, but kept the weight of his upper body away from her. Her fingers slid into his hair. She was coming to her end, her gaze had clouded. She shut her eyes as he pushed into her, striking her hard with each thrust.

"Henry! Ohhhh."

Heat flooded about his intrusion as her inner muscles clasped in a spasm about his invasion.

A sound of utter relief and contentment clawed to escape his throat as his end came and his arms trembled as he fought to hold his weight while the sensation of his climax raced through his blood. The feeling was more intense with her. Perhaps that was because of love.

When it passed, he smiled at her.

She smiled at him and her fingers brushed over his hair.

"I love you," he said it to be the one to say it first, because he'd seen the words in her eyes, and he wanted her to know that he would not only say it to her in reply.

He withdrew and rolled to his back, holding up his arm so that she would come to him. Her head settled on his chest. He wrapped his arm about her, and lay there listening to the birdsong that rose outside the window, announcing to the world that the sun was about to fall beyond the horizon.

~

It was dark in the bedchamber.

When Susan had fallen asleep the shutters had been open and the moon had just become visible, but now the shutters were closed, and she could neither feel nor hear Henry in the bed. She sat up. The sheet slid across her skin.

There was a line of light about the edge of the door to Henry's sitting room. Her nightdress caught the light, it still lay on the floor near the bed.

She got up, picked it up and slipped it on, then went over to the door.

When she opened it, she saw Henry. He was sitting in a high-backed, winged arm chair, clothed in the silk dressing gown he'd worn the day she'd come up here in the spring. One bare foot rested on a low table before him. The table held a decanter, half-full of an amber liquid, and he had a half-full glass of the same liquid in his hand, balanced on the arm of the chair, while he slumped back with his head against the seat, as his free hand stroked Samson's ear.

His head turned so he could look at her, but he did not speak.

"Are you drunk?"

"Fairly." He smiled.

"Why are you not in bed?"

"Because there is little point. Why do you have your nightdress on? You are breaking our first rule."

It was gaping open, though, she had not done up the long row of tiny buttons that he'd opened all the way down to her stomach. "You are covered too, and you cannot expect me to walk into a room naked when I do not know who else might be within it."

"I suppose." He looked at the glass he held, then took a sip from it. The pace of his movement declared him either extremely tired or very foxed.

"What is wrong?" She walked towards him, as Samson rose and came to her.

Henry's hand, containing the glass, settled back on the arm of the chair as he looked at her again. "Nothing for you to worry over."

She petted Samson's head as his tail waved back and forth. "Except that you are my husband now and so whatever worries you is my concern too."

He lifted a hand out to her. "That is very sweet of you, Susan."

She held his hand.

He pulled her closer, encouraging her to sit on his knee as he straightened up and set both feet on the floor.

Samson watched them with an intrigued gaze as she sat sideways on Henry's lap. "Tell me."

He shook his head. "It really is nothing for you to worry over." He looked at the dog. "Samson, lay down over there." He pointed at the hearth rug.

Samson did his bidding, as charmed into submission as Susan was.

Henry drank the rest of his brandy and leant around her to set the glass down on the table. Then his fingers wrapped about her neck, beneath her hair, and he pulled her mouth to his. The taste of brandy on his tongue brought back the smell of roses and crushed grass.

315

His other hand slipped inside her open nightdress and squeezed her breast, released then squeezed it again, the action was repeated and repeated, as they kissed. The sensation only he engendered twisted in her stomach and she kissed him more ardently, her hands in his hair.

"Sit astride me," he said into her mouth.

Like that… She had never imagined it like that.

She stood up and turned around. "Dispose of this." His fingers gripped the fabric of her nightdress by her hips.

She smiled as she slipped it from her shoulders, and pulled it off her hands so it fell on to the floor.

"Come on." He tapped the arms of the chair as he made room for her, moving his legs together.

She knelt astride his thighs entirely naked, her hair falling over her shoulders and brushing across her back.

His hand lifted and stroked her hair away from her face. "You are very beautiful, Susan, far more beautiful than I think you know." He would have pulled her mouth back to his but she held back, looking down and pulling the knot tying his dressing gown loose. Her fingers brushed over his stomach, across his midriff then up to his chest. Then they trailed down again and she touched the tip of his erection. His body jolted slightly.

She looked up and smiled at him, as her fingers wrapped around him and squeezed, in the way he'd squeezed her breast.

A sound of amusement rumbled in his chest as the strength of his hold on her head insisted she bend down to kiss him. "I love you," he said against her lips, before he did kiss her. "You are a blessing, Susan."

She positioned herself so that she hovered over him, and she still held him so she moved him to ensure he'd enter her when she lowered down.

"Mmmmm," he hummed the sound against her mouth when she lowered, the vibration trembling against her lips.

His hands braced her waist then slid down over her skin to

her hips when she rose up. She descended again then rose up, her tongue catching at the tip of his as she pulled her mouth away from him. She lowered once more, and then kissed him again. His hands came up and caught hold of her head, trying to keep her mouth against his as she moved.

"Susan," he said in a breathy desperate tone when she pulled away rising right up.

She descended again. His hands fell on to her thighs, and slid up and down them in the pattern of her movement, and he looked down staring at the juncture between her legs, as though he could see everything but she doubted he could see much.

The way he looked at her made her feel as beautiful as he'd said she was. He loved her. Henry…

She was his wife.

Her hands lay on his chest, on his skin, as his hands returned to her hips, feeling her movement.

"I love you."

He smiled rather than said it back, but it was there in his eyes for her to read.

She moved up and down a little quicker, rising and falling, and his hands encouraged her to rock forward and back.

The sensations their joining spun up inside her, with the slow motion of a spoon stirring sugar into a cup and melting the sweetness into her blood, made it harder to move. Her muscles weakened and trembled.

His hands gripped and moved her, as he pushed upward while he brought her body down, and then she entirely melted around him. She sighed out her emotion, her limbs quivering.

"Yes," Henry said.

Yes, her mind echoed. Yes. She loved him, and it might be selfish but it was wonderful.

In the end he held her still and just pumped up into her, pushing hard. Her fingers clung to his shoulders and her head pressed close to his. Her hair brushing his chest.

He growled in her ear when his release throbbed inside her and his hand opened wide embracing her head, his fingers tangling up in her hair.

They stayed still, pressed against each other, her breasts rising and falling, rubbing against his chest which was damp with sweat. Her head rested on his shoulder. He felt like hers. As though she owned him. She smiled against his neck and then pressed a kiss on to his skin.

After a while he said, in a deep voice, "Come along get up. Let us return to bed."

She climbed off him, turned and blew out the candle.

She couldn't see him when she heard him stand up, and she couldn't see him when he bent and picked her up, catching her beneath the knees and about her shoulders.

She squealed.

"Hush. You will wake the boys; they sleep in the room above mine."

He carried her across the room.

"You can see better than me."

"Obviously. You wear spectacles."

She poked her tongue out at him, but that he did not see in the dark.

Chapter Twenty-eight

Susan rolled over and her hand reached across the bed, but she already knew Henry was not there, it was the same as last night. There was no sound of breathing and no dip in the mattress from his weight laying beside her.

She opened her eyes and sat upright. Daylight peered about the shutters.

There was a piece of folded paper on the far side of the bed. She reached across and grasped it, then unfolded it.

Forgive me, sleeping beauty, I am going riding with my brothers, they need me, you see, at the moment. But the girls will be in the house and Mama. They will keep you company at breakfast and through the morning. But if they become too much feel free to run to the library. I should return by luncheon.

x

Yours,
Henry

So she had the morning to herself.

She tumbled on to her back. She could lay here and sleep in, but the energy inside her was too excited to do that. She ached. Mostly from making love in the chair, but it was a nice ache.

I am a married woman! Her soul screamed it out.

She got up and rang for a maid to bring water to wash with and to help her dress.

When she went downstairs, Aunt Jane, Sarah and Christine were at the breakfast table.

"Susan." Aunt Jane stood. "Come and sit beside me."

They talked of nothing really, of dresses, balls and some of the unusual fashions they had seen in their short season in London. Yet Susan was not fooled, they were not happy, they were suffering over William's loss and talking for her sake. As soon as she had finished eating she excused herself. Not because she wished to avoid them but because she felt as though they would rather avoid her, and so she went to the library.

The door had been left ajar, she pushed it open wider, her fingers shaking. Uncle Robert might be there and she would not want to disturb him. He was not. She found out a book to read, a book about Italy, and settled in a chair, pressing her spectacles a little farther up her nose.

When Henry walked into the room she looked at the clock, it had past midday.

"Hello," she said in greeting.

He smiled as he walked across the room. Then when he reached her he bent down to press a kiss on her lips. "Hello," he said against her lips, then straightened, catching hold of her hand. "Come along book-head, it is time for luncheon. Set the book down and come with me."

She put the book on the table beside her and stood. He'd kept a hold of her hand. "Have you just come back?" She asked as they walked.

"Yes, well apart from allowing myself time to change out of my clothes that smelled of horse."

320

"Where did you ride?"

"Along the perimeter of Papa's land."

She nodded.

He looked sideways at her. "Were you lonely? I would hate for you to be lonely here."

"No, I just sensed Aunt Jane, Sarah and Christine would rather have been alone with their thoughts than feeling they needed to make conversation with me."

"You know you are going to have to stop calling Mama, Aunt Jane, it sounds rather odd for her daughter-in-law." He smiled again

She laughed. "I suppose so."

"Sir." A footman stood in their path.

Henry stopped but he did not let go of her hand. "Yes, Peter."

"Mr Hopkins, the steward is waiting below stairs to see Lord Barrington, my Lord, but Lord Barrington is out riding and no one is sure when he will return."

A sigh slipped from Henry's lips and his free hand ran over his hair. "Have cook give Mr Hopkins some refreshment. I will speak with him after I have eaten."

When the footman turned away, Henry's fingers squeezed her hand a little tighter for a moment before he began walking again.

The boys and Percy were at the table as well as the girls, in fact the only person missing was Uncle Robert. The boys talked loudly, full of energy and tales from their ride, which appeared to give Sarah and Christine an excuse not to talk at all. Susan watched them all, silent herself, but she particular watched Henry, he smiled and laughed with the boys then turned and asked his mother something. She smiled before replying. Then he looked at Sarah and Christine and spoke with them. Then he looked at Susan. Their gazes held for a moment and he smiled. Then he looked at the boys again.

He was keeping guard over them all.

It was endearing.

Once they'd mostly finished eating, although the boys were helping themselves to more cake, Henry stood up. "I am going downstairs to talk with Hopkins, if Papa comes home, Mama, please tell him where we are."

His mother gave him an apologetic and appreciative look. Henry nodded. Then he looked at Susan. "Will you find something to do?"

"Of course." She was among the people he was watching over now. She tried to give him a reassuring smile as he turned away.

She did not see Henry again until she was changing for dinner in his room. He walked into the room when the maid was still there, with Samson in his wake. The maid had been putting up Susan's hair. The maid straightened and stepped away, but she had just finished anyway.

"You look beautiful." Henry crossed the room with long, quick strides then bent and kissed the back of Susan's neck.

Susan saw her colour rise as she looked at her reflection.

She looked at his reflection.

He'd dressed for dinner. He must have used another room. He looked strikingly attractive, incomparable to her, no matter that he called her beautiful. He smiled at her, through the mirror. She smiled too.

"Do you need me for anything else, my Lady."

Susan turned and looked at the maid. The term my lady was still a shock to her. "No, thank you."

"You have done a marvellous job with Susan's hair, Sally," Henry acknowledged as the maid bobbed a curtsy. She smiled before she left them.

Henry bent and kissed the back of Susan's neck again. "Have you been lonely?"

"No." She turned sideways in the chair. "I have begun sewing you a new shirt as your mother and sisters were sewing."

A sound of humour escaped his throat, and his head declined a little in a slight nod. "Very industrious, but it sounds like torture."

She smiled, stood up and wrapped her arms about his neck. "I missed you."

He seemed to smell the perfume dabbed on her neck when he hugged her in return. "I missed you too. We will eat dinner and then come up to bed, as things are, no one will mind."

Samson nudged at her hip, for some attention or to break her apart from Henry.

They separated.

"Are you ready?"

"Yes."

"Are you leaving off your spectacles?"

She smiled. "Yes, my hair looks better without them."

"You know I like you with and without them, just so we are straight on that point."

"I know."

"Come along then." He grasped her hand and began to lead her from the room. "Samson, stay."

When they walked outside the bedroom door, he let go of her hand. "Take my arm." He held his forearm up.

She wrapped her fingers about it.

"You know you are the only woman who has ever gripped my arm and not just lain her hand on it…"

"Oh. Am I doing the wrong thing?"

He smiled at her. "No, you are doing absolutely the right thing. That is why I offered my arm, only because I wished you to hold it just so."

She leant against him a little, before they began walking again.

She was still gripping his arm when they walked into the drawing room.

"Papa." Henry's arm dropped and he walked away from her, crossing the room to speak with his father. Uncle Robert kept shaking his head as Henry talked.

"Dinner is ready to serve!" Davis called.

They all turned.

"Susan." Percy was at her side. He'd been talking to the boys but now they were talking with their mother.

She accepted his arm and lay her hand on it rather than held it. "How are you? Everyone seems to be so quiet, yet you are busy entertaining Stephen and Gerard."

"I do not mind. Henry has enough on his shoulders, he needs someone to help with the boys."

Susan looked back across the room. Henry was walking towards her.

"Percy! That is my wife, of one day, I hope you will be gracious enough to let her grip my arm and not yours to walk to the dinner table."

Percy laughed and let her go.

Henry lifted his arm.

She gripped it, held it, not just lay her hand upon it.

They walked ahead of his father and the others, leading the way into the dining room, and once in the room and at the table, Henry withdrew a chair for her, before a footman could, and then sat down beside her, as everyone else sat down around them.

"Your Uncle Edward is going home in the morning," Uncle Robert, Robert, Henry's father, her father-in-law, said as the footmen began serving. Oh it was going to be a task to call him something other than uncle.

"Why?" Henry looked at his father. His tone was sharp, as though he was shocked.

"Because I told him to go. There is no point in him kicking his heels here. I told him to leave Rob and Caro in peace and go home."

Henry sighed, then looked at his wine. He picked up his glass. It was as if he wanted to say something and did not, for some reason.

As she was served, Susan slipped her hands underneath the table and rested one on Henry's thigh, he glanced at her and they shared a smile. Then he sipped his wine and set the glass back down.

"Has Harry gone too?" Percy asked.

"Yes, he had to go back to his regiment anyway. He left today." Uncle Robert was dished up the vegetables to accompany the salmon that had been served.

The conversation then moved on, but both Uncle Robert and Henry were quiet. Susan spoke more frequently, with a desire to compensate for Henry's silence, and stop the others from noticing that something was wrong. But there was definitely something wrong.

As the crockery for the dessert course was removed Aunt Jane stood. "We will leave you now." Sarah, Christine and then Susan rose too, to leave the men and Stephen and Gerrard alone with the port and their private male conversation. Susan lay her hand on Henry's shoulder before she walked away, and for a moment his hand lay over hers and he looked up. His eyes showed his gratitude.

She did not wish to be another burden to him, she wished to take away some of his burdens.

When she walked into the family drawing room Susan looked at the pianoforte. "Shall I play for you, Aunt Jane?" It would give her something to do, she could not sit here with nothing beyond conversation to occupy her mind.

"That would be pleasant, Susan, but please, nothing boisterous, and please stop calling me *Aunt* Jane." She walked across and hugged Susan for an instant. "Please call me Mama now, or just Jane at least."

Susan held her in return, seeking to offer comfort as much as gratitude; all of Henry's family were subdued with grief.

When Susan turned to the pianoforte Christine walked across the room. "Shall we play together?"

Susan smiled at her. "If you would like."

"Shall I help choose the music and perhaps I might sing with you," Sarah offered.

Perhaps they all needed other things to occupy their mind.

325

"Then I shall sing too," Aunt Jane, Mama… Oh. Jane stated, and came to join them.

There was then an excited debate over which sheet of music to choose.

When the boys walked in with Percy it was to a ballad sung by them all in what was a very reasonable harmony. Percy walked over to join in, as Stephen and Gerrard excused themselves and left. Jane… Mama… Henry's Mama, smiled at them and waved goodnight, but did not stop singing.

Susan sat on one side of the stool playing the part at one end of the pianoforte, while Christine's fingers moved over the keys of the other side.

Susan glanced away from the music, looking over her shoulder at the door. Neither Henry nor his father came in. She continued playing, smiling at Percy, Sarah and Jane, as they began the next verse.

When Henry walked in ahead of his father Susan was playing the last chorus. She looked over. Henry walked straight to the decanters as his father walked over to Aunt Jane. Jane. He whispered something in her ear then turned away and walked out of the room.

Susan looked at Henry. He drank the brandy he'd poured, then poured another.

"What shall we sing now?" Sarah asked immediately after Susan had played the final note.

"Let me look," Percy answered.

Susan stood. "I shall bow out and let you play, Sarah."

While the conversation continued over what to play next, Susan walked across the room to Henry. He did not notice; he was staring into his glass.

"Henry?"

He looked around. "Hello. Sorry I have been a bit of a misery over dinner I suppose."

"You have no need to apologise, you have a good excuse to be miserable. Would you like to retire?"

He smiled. "Oh Lord, yes. I cannot tell you how much I would love to escape this damned house."

He drank his brandy then set down the empty glass.

"Let me say goodnight." Susan walked across to the pianoforte. "Henry and I are going to retire, if you will excuse us. Goodnight."

"Goodnight, Susan, dear." Jane hugged Susan, as she'd done earlier.

The others said, "Goodnight."

Henry did not come close to say goodnight himself. His mother lifted a hand in his direction. He smiled, that was all.

Susan returned to him, and he lifted his arm, not offering it, but encouraging her to walk ahead of him. Yet once they were outside the drawing room, his arm fell on to her shoulders and he sighed. She leaned against him as they walked towards the stairs. "What is it?"

"Nothing for you to be concerned over."

"But I am concerned because if it affects you then it affects me."

"That is very sweet of you to say, Susan, but I do not expect you solve my problems."

But I want to. She said nothing more. She did not think he was in a mood to be persuaded with words—but with her body. She could and would comfort him like that, she had learned in only one night, and during that evening in the rose garden, that Henry was more than willing to open himself up in that way.

Chapter Twenty-nine

"Ahhh," Henry sighed as he breathed in Susan's scent, pressing his forehead against her soft stomach as she stood before him naked while he knelt on the floor in front of her.

He'd not let her call for a maid but disrobed her in the sitting room and now her clothes, and his clothes, were scattered across the floor and he was on his knees before her, holding on to her, just holding on.

He kissed above her hairline, then kissed her hip, then kissed the juncture between her thighs and reached his tongue between her closed legs. She moved and stood with her legs apart allowing him greater access as her fingers played in his hair. His hands gripped the back of her thighs as his tongue reached farther.

She tilted her pelvis towards him.

His forefingers and thumbs pressed into the first curve of her buttocks as he sucked her sensitive spot and licked the silkiest flesh.

He was lost in what he did, lost in her. Utterly absorbed. She was beautiful, and so precious to him. So new, and loved.

He used his fingers, then licked his fingers, then used them again as she sighed and rocked against his invasion.

Love.

He loved her.

He'd thought he'd loved her weeks ago. But now…

Now, he *loved* her.

He stood up and kissed her mouth, his fingers cupping her bottom and holding her against his erection. Then he gripped her hand and led her to stand before the fire. It was not alight, it was a luke-warm summer evening, but there was a rug there.

He brushed her hair out of the way, over her shoulder, and kissed the back of her neck, then moved behind her, and sucked the skin on the back of her neck gently as he held her hips and her bottom against his erection. Her head dropped forward. She was dopey with desire—with desire for him. That was a strong aphrodisiac.

"Kneel," he whispered in her ear.

She obeyed, and he knelt too.

"On all fours," he ordered. Perhaps it was a matter of needing to be in control, but for whatever reason, this was the way he wanted it, and he wanted it this way with Susan.

She leant on to her hands.

He kissed her back and his hands ran over the curves of her bottom and her legs, then up along her back and to her neck—that beautiful curve. His fingers gripped her there as he slid inside her, while his other hand held her hip.

"Oh." It was a sound of surprise that left her lips.

He moved slowly and steadily. She was hot, wet and so welcoming. She was everything he needed.

"Oh." Another breathy sound of pleasure and shock escaped her throat.

He knew how to move to the greatest effect. He knew how to heighten her pleasure. He knew how to make her climax in a moment.

He withdrew and then only half penetrated her, moving quickly, caressing her most sensitive points. Her breath became desperate panting. He plunged in deep and hard, then deep and hard again, and after three times he was rewarded with the success of her release. He began again, he wanted more. He wanted control. He wanted pleasure. To be lost for a long period in a world that became only the joy of pleasing a woman—pleasing Susan. This was his precious wife.

~

The clock in Henry's sitting room chimed once. He sighed into the dark air. His skin had become cold. They'd probably been lying on the floor in the moonlight for half an hour. Susan had fallen asleep, her cheek resting in the crook of his arm and his shoulder.

"Susan." His finger stroked across her cheek. "We need to get into bed."

She nodded against his chest, half asleep.

He sat up drawing her with him. Then stood and took her hand to help her do so, but once they were on their feet, he picked her up. Her fingers stroked across his cheek as she fell against him, her hair brushing his naked chest.

She fell asleep once more as he carried her to the bedchamber. "Samson, off," he ordered the dog, who'd occupied their bed as they had occupied the sitting room. As Samson jumped down, in the deerhound's languid style of movement, Henry roused Susan again to get her beneath the covers. Then he walked around the bed and climbed in beside her, but he did not embrace her, he knew he was unlikely to sleep and so it was fairer to let her lie undisturbed.

He lay on his back looking up at the dark shadow of the canopy. The shutters were closed over the windows in here, but he'd left the sitting room door open so that some of the moonlight shone through.

After dinner, as Percy, Stephen and Gerard had left the room. Henry had caught hold of his father's arm before he could follow

330

them and pressed him to say why he'd thought it wise to tell Edward to go?

Henry had received a barked rebuff, asking him why it was any of his business.

In the last few weeks it was as though their roles had turned, Henry had stepped into the role of father and earl, while his father...

Well he did not know what the hell was wrong with him.

No. That was a lie. Of course he knew what was wrong—grief.

The clock in the sitting room chimed twice.

Henry sat up. He'd had enough of the same thoughts spinning about in his head for an hour. He got out of the bed, careful not to disturb Susan, left the room and shut the door.

His dressing gown lay over the back of a chair in there. He picked it up, slipped his arms into it then wrapped it about his middle and tied the silk sash to secure it.

Their clothes were still strewn across the floor. He picked them up by the moonlight and set them all in the chair he'd retrieved his dressing gown from. Then he walked across to the side table by the chair they had made love in the night before. There was a small drawer underneath it. He pulled out the pack of cards that was in it, then sat down to play patience with himself as Samson watched him as though he thought Henry mad. He was still playing when the clock chimed four times.

"Henry... Do you never sleep?"

He looked at Susan. His hand clasped about the part of the pack of cards still in his hand. Susan had stopped in the doorway from the bedroom, and her arms had clasped over her chest.

She was wearing her ridiculous nightdress again, the one that covered everything bar her hands, toes and head.

She still looked beautiful.

"I do not sleep much these days, no."

She walked across the room, the fabric of her nightdress whispering against her legs as Samson rose and walked over to greet her. "Tell me what is keeping you awake, perhaps it will help. Is it to do with William? Is it something to do with the conversation you had with your father?"

He set down the remainder of the cards on the table, and pushed the table away. "I cannot tell you how grateful I am to hear you use William's name. Papa will not. Come and sit with me." He patted his lap as he sat back.

She sat sideways across his lap, with an arm reaching about his shoulders, as she drew her legs up, so even her toes disappeared within the white cotton. He wrapped his arm about her bent knees and her back, to hold her steady, as Samson sat before the chair and rested his head on Henry's knee and Susan's covered feet.

"Why does Uncle Robert not say William's name?"

"I do not know. I think he is afraid of it... It is as though... Oh, I do not know. He has stopped living. He ignores us all even Gerard and Stephen. He is locked away somewhere with no sight of reality. I am worried and Edward was trying to make him see sense, but now Papa has told him to go away. I was angry with him over that. He told me it was none of my business. But Edward was helping me too. He was helping me manage the estate. When I told Papa that, he said it was a selfish view and that Edward had his own estate to manage..."

Susan's head rested against his shoulder, as her fingers laced together and braced his shoulders, trapping him within her arms. "You are not selfish. It is the last thing you are."

His head fell back on to the chair and he looked up. "Remember you have said so yourself, before, and I do not deny it."

"I know, but I was wrong, and you are wrong, and your father is wrong. Your loyalty and thoughts for others have merely never been tested before. You are not selfish, and Uncle Robert will know it in his heart. He is just hurting, Henry. As you are."

Hurting. Lord. Yes. *I hurt.*

Susan's arms kept a tight hold about him. He kissed the top of her hair. "I love you."

332

"I know. I know it in the way that Samson knows it, even though you order us about sometimes."

He laughed. She was very good for him.

"Why do you not speak to your mother in the morning? She must be worried too."

"Because I do not wish to burden her."

"So you are being entirely unselfish and taking every burden on yourself."

That did not seem a wrong thing to do.

Her head lifted and she looked at him, although she still held him. "Henry, you are grieving too. You need to speak to your parents. If you can never sleep you will make yourself ill."

A dismissing sound left his lips, that said he did not particularly care… That was both a reckless and a selfish thought. He should not wish himself ill, there was Susan to think of, and his family who would not wish to lose another son and brother.

He shut his eyes, and breathed slowly, fighting the pain of the emotion gathering in his throat that threatened to choke him.

Chapter Thirty

Henry carried Susan back to bed, asleep, and tucked her in for the second time at half past five, then dressed and walked down to the kitchens. Samson followed, his tail wagging in anticipation of being let out. Henry rubbed the dog's head then asked a boy in the kitchen to take Samson out to the grooms. Then he asked cook for coffee and toasted his own bread on a fork over the kitchen fire, as he'd done as a boy.

Percy appeared in the kitchen as Henry was eating his warm buttered toast and proceeded to copy Henry and toast some more bread. Then half an hour later Stephen and Gerard appeared and more bread was toasted, over a loud conversation, with cook grumbling at them for getting under the feet of those there to work. They were reminded that the rest of the household would be eating at the table upstairs. Henry laughed along with his brothers, because they all knew that cook had always appreciated their raucous company in the kitchen.

A desire for William to have been there with them clasped in Henry's chest. He and Percy had done this together before, and clearly Gerard and Stephen had, but this was the first time all four brothers had sat and eaten breakfast in the kitchen. He wished that William had had the opportunity to be with them at least once…

After they had eaten Samson was returned in the company of his father's other dogs, their tails wagged as they surrounded his brothers. But Samson, as ever, came straight to him.

Gerard looked at Henry. "Can we ride out somewhere with the dogs?"

"We can, and we shall." Henry rose. "Yet we had best dress appropriately."

Percy stood too. "Hurry up then boys, let us get ready."

All of them still called Gerard and Stephen boys, but really they were not, they were youths, tall, and growing fast and they'd aged half a dozen years in the last couple of weeks. Stephen lay a hand on Gerard's shoulder as they walked away. In the same way that Henry might have.

A warm feeling, the emotion of love, spread like a low mist through Henry's blood. It was far better to see himself role modelled in that way than to think of himself as an inspiration for the folly that had killed William.

"Are you walking upstairs?" Percy asked.

"Yes."

Henry did not talk very much as they walked up the servants' staircase to the hall, and then up the main stairs. He thought of Susan. Of the things she'd said to him last night. *He is just hurting, as you are…*

When he and Percy parted ways, Henry sighed out his breath. He had to resolve things with his father.

Susan was still asleep. He moved quietly finding out his riding clothes, then carried them into the dressing room, shut the door and changed in there. He left via the servants' door rather than risk disturbing Susan in the last moment.

While they rode Stephen declared that he and Gerard had agreed that they would like to return to school. Henry later manoeuvred his horse to ride beside Gerard, so he could ask if Gerard really wanted to go. He wanted to be sure the choice had been Gerard's too.

It had been.

The boys had had enough of the miserable atmosphere in the house. Though they'd not said so in words, Henry knew that to be true. He could not blame them; at their age he would have felt the same. He would have returned to school too, to be with the friends that would make life feel normal.

But he did not wish to put the boys in a carriage and send them off on the long journey back to school alone.

Henry walked into the breakfast room a little after eleven, with Stephen, Gerard and Percy.

"There is ham left, and some eggs," their mother stated as Stephen and Gerard sat down.

Despite having eaten toast earlier the boys' appetites had risen again and they both looked at a footman to encourage the offer of plates and food to put on them.

Percy leant over Gerard and picked up a sweet pastry from a plate on the table.

"Sit down, Percy," Mama ordered, in a voice that held a reassuringly normal sound.

It was only his mother and Susan at the table, sitting opposite one another, and it was only Susan who was eating. His mother sat before a cup of chocolate.

He walked over to Susan, she had been watching him from the moment he walked in. He had not left a note beside the bed, but surely she had assumed the reason for his absence.

She smiled.

She was not upset with him, then.

He leant and pressed a kiss on her lips, then sat in the seat beside her facing his mother. He wanted to speak. The words itched behind his lips and tumbled through his throat. He swallowed them back. He would not ask her anything before his brothers.

"Susan has only just come down I am keeping her company..."
His mother smiled at him.

He held Susan's hand as it lay on the table. While she took a bite from the roll in her other hand.

She held his hand in return.

"Would you like anything to eat, my Lord."

Henry looked at the footman. "No thank you, but I would welcome a cup of coffee, Ron."

He nodded. "Sir."

Another footman poured the coffee. Henry leant back so the man could reach the cup. "Thank you, Simon."

His mother spoke to Percy and the boys. Henry wondered if she knew they wished to return to school.

"Did you all enjoy your ride?" Susan asked.

He sighed out a breath before answering, quietly. "Yes, but I am still thinking about the things you said to me last night. I wish to speak to Mama alone…" Her fingers tightened about his hand. "Gerard and Stephen want to return to school, I think it would be best if Papa accompanied them."

"But you do not think he will."

"No." Henry sighed again.

"Smile, Henry. It would not be so awful if you must take them would it? Or are they beasts?" It was a jest, said to lift his mood and make him laugh.

He made a face at her. But within a moment, his mocking face became a genuine smile and he wished to embrace her. That would shock his brothers, and probably his mother. He'd not spoken of his love for Susan to anyone but her.

"When the others leave," she said more seriously, "I will leave too, so you may stay with Au… Jane."

"Thank you." Fear grasped in his stomach, though, and how foolish to be afraid of speaking with his mother?

He kept hold of Susan's hand as they joined the others' conversation. The boys took twenty minutes to eat their fill, then they finally stood to go and find something else to do. Percy stood at the same time. Then Susan rose. Her hand settled on Henry's shoulder in reassurance. He looked up and smiled. His mother had not risen.

He looked at his mother when Susan's hand slipped away, but waited until Susan had left the room with the others before he spoke. His heart thumped in his chest as hard as it had when he'd sat beside William's still body. He breathed in. These words had to be said for the benefit of them all. "Has Papa spoken with you about how he feels?"

She looked up at the footmen about them. "You may leave us alone, thank you."

Henry waited until they left the room, then said again, "What has he said?"

Her elbows rested on the table and her hands gripped each other as she shook her head.

"What does a shake of the head mean, Mama? Are you telling me not to ask? Or has he said nothing? I cannot believe he's said nothing to you. You must see that he is destroying things. He is shutting us out."

"Henry."

"It is the truth. I have no idea how to speak to him."

"*He* is your father."

"It has not felt so for days. It has not felt so to any of us. He has not cared about any of us since William died."

"He has suffered because he was not there."

"But you were. And I was." *And I need him!* It was the first time he'd admitted those words to himself, yet they were true. "And Stephen and Gerard are alive and they need their father. They want to return to school. It should be Papa who accompanies them. They need him." *I need him.* The words ran through his head once more. Susan had been wrong last night she had been right in the beginning—he *was* selfish.

"Ever since I have known your father he has turned away from things that are emotionally painful. He cannot cope with such things, he would rather fight and burn his emotions off with activity—"

Just as the boys were trying to do. "But William cannot be swept away by riding or walking, or—"

"Henry, do you not think that I know?" Tears glittered in his mother's eyes.

He stood up and walked about the table. She turned so she sat sideways in her chair as he occupied the seat beside her. He held her hand.

"Your father is a complex man. I remember one day, before you were born, when he was upset he walked out into a rainstorm and was gone for hours. He returned. He will return to us, when he has come to terms with this."

"When will that be, though? Stephen and Gerard are young. They are in the years that impact on the rest of their lives. They need Papa."

"Give him time, Henry."

"There is not time. They want to return to school. Where is he?"

Her eyes looked up above his head as she sighed. She was suffering too much to argue with him. "Your father went out riding. He rides out every day."

"I know but to where?"

She sighed again and looked back at him. "I do not know, but my guess would be that one of the places he might be is the Abbey ruins."

"Then I will look for him there." Henry stood up.

She caught hold of his hand. "Robert will not welcome your intrusion. He would rather deal with his feelings alone."

"So would I, but he has not given me the chance." He pulled his hand away from his mother and turned away. He would damned well make his father see some sense.

~

Henry rode the stallion hard, its muscles were still warm from his morning ride and so he was not afraid to encourage the animal to stretch out immediately. The ruins were a long ride from the house—on the border of his father's land.

He was delayed at a row of cottages, when the tenants stopped him to speak, but once he'd managed to excuse himself, he kicked his heels again, raced along the road and jumped the wall. Then galloped across the field and jumped a stream. Finally, as he rode out through the far side of an opening in the hedgerow he saw the ruins, stretching up to the sky. An ancient place of worship and life. A spiritual place.

He could understand why his father would choose to come here to think of William.

He slowed the stallion to a canter, then near the wall he slowed the animal to a trot and pulled the reins to halt him a few feet from the walls. He thrust his leg over the animal's rump and then, feet together, balanced with his hands on the saddle before letting himself drop to the ground. He walked over to a tree and wrapped the reins about a branch, then walked back to a low unadorned entrance into the abbey ruins. The ground on the other side was lush green grass and the walls a mixture of coarse flint inner stone and ornate outer carvings.

The ruins were a clutter of walls and old rooms, but the large, long hall he walked into contained his father. He was here. The height of the walls and the remains of the ornate windows denoted the space as the Abbey's former place of worship. At one time it would have been as grand as the Minster in York. His father was kneeling in the place where the remains of an altar stood.

Henry did not call to him. It seemed disrespectful. Instead he walked steadily towards him. Quietly.

Had his father come here every day and spent every day on his knees?

Henry wished to kneel and pray too, to pray for time to turn backwards and give them back William, and yet if time turned backwards it would take Susan, and all that had passed between them in the last days.

340

"Papa…" he said when he was only a few feet from his father.

His father looked back, then stood up and turned. "Henry…" His voice said, *why are you here?*

Because things have to change, Papa. "I need to speak with you."

"So you have ridden out all this way…"

"Yes. As I said, I need to speak with you. Will you listen?"

His father sighed, then turned and walked towards an exit to the right of the altar. It was clear that years ago there had been steps down, now there was a slope. Perhaps the steps were there, hidden beneath the grass and mud, just like the emotions inside him had been hidden beneath a life that had lacked any need to care for others. As Susan had said, he'd never had need to look for those emotions before.

Henry followed his father into an area of numerous walls set out in squares, all only a few feet in height. "Papa…" His frustration rang back from the bare stone. "Will you listen?"

"As you have followed me here, how can I not."

That was not the answer Henry wished for, he needed his father to want to listen. To care. And he was still walking away, with his back turned.

"I do not mean merely acknowledge me! I need you to listen!" In the past Henry had only raised his voice when he'd been defending himself over some accusation about a prank, or some other act of recklessness. But it was his father who was being reckless now.

His father looked back and their gazes clashed. "I am listening. I said speak."

His father sounded as Henry might when accused of something. Perhaps they were too alike. Perhaps that had always been the issue.

"Gerard and Stephen want to return to Eton."

His father turned around. "Already? Why?"

"Because they need things to feel normal to recover from their grief."

341

His father stared at him. "And their home is not normal? I expected them to stay at least a week or two more."

"Their home is full of memories and people in pain. Mama and the girls are often in tears, and you…"

"I what?"

"You ignore them."

His father's brow furrowed.

"I know it is because you are mourning William. I am too. But they were closest to him and they—"

"They have you and Percy."

"We are not their father. They need their father. They need you." *I need you.*

The last words perhaps showed in his eyes because his father walked forward. "And you?"

Henry drew in a deep breath, as the emotion gathered in the back of his throat, but he forced the words out around the lump that formed there. "I am in pain too. I need you too." Guilt cut through him the moment the words were out. The younger ones, his sisters, his mother needed comfort, asking for it himself was another selfish act.

His father walked closer, looking Henry in the eyes. "I am in pain too. I need you all." His arms lifted. Henry stepped into the embrace and wrapped his arms about his father, as his father's arms came about him. He had not held his father since he'd been William's age. He had out-grown such things, and yet he was giving his father comfort as much as receiving it.

His father let go. "Have I let you all down. Is that how it seems?" Moisture caught the sunlight and made his father's brown eyes glitter.

Henry swallowed back against the lump of tears in his throat. "No. You have not let us down…"

His father sighed and his hand lifted and combed through his hair. "But you are telling me that you wished for support and you did not receive it from me, and so I suppose that is why you turned to Susan because she was there."

"No, it was not that way with Susan. Susan and I had become closer in London. You told me months ago that I would know if it was love, I knew in London. I knew when I went to Brighton but Susan would not be disloyal to Alethea, and when I returned Susan left. But love cannot be deterred, I could not deny it and nor could she in the end. There is nothing for you to regret on my part. It is the others…"

His father stared at him for a moment. "If you know how it feels to be in love then you may imagine how it feels to love a child. A child that love has created. I will never forget the day you were born. I had not thought I would marry until I met your mother again. I had never even thought about children until Edward married Ellen and became John's father, then there was Mary. I treated them like my children I was so convinced I would never become a father.

"So imagine then, when you were born, and I held you in my arms for the first time. It has felt the same when each of your brothers and sisters were born, and William… The last… And as special as you, the first. And he's gone, and I was not there to hold him in his last moments as I should have been."

His father's eyes shone brighter with emotion.

Henry wrapped his arms about him, this time only to offer comfort. "Mama was there. She held his hand. We did not let him feel alone. Not for one moment."

His father's arms came about Henry as he accepted the embrace. "I cannot let him go. He was too young."

Henry's embrace firmed, holding his father tighter. "You will not let him go, you will not forget William, and you should not. I have sworn to myself I shall recall his name every day of my life. I did not spend the time that I should have done with the others, but I always thought that they would be there, now, I…"

His father's body jolted and there was the sound of a choke that was half sob.

"Now I am making the most of the time I have." Henry finished.

A sound like an animal in pain breached the air and then his father's shoulders shook as he wept silently. Henry held on. They were the same in height and build, yet Henry held him with a memory of embracing Gerard at William's bedside.

The emotion in Henry coiled but not like the snake, it was as tight as a copper spring, pushed down, the energy it could exude banking up.

His father pulled away and wiped at the tears with the heels of his palms. His leather gloves absorbed the moisture. He sniffed, then coughed. Then said, "I cannot forgive myself for not being with him."

"William would forgive you. It would upset him to see you like this. It would upset him if he thought you were paying less attention to Stephen and Gerard because he had died. He would not want his death to be the cause."

His father shook his head but more tears leaked from his eyes. He wiped his forearm across his face. "Forgive me. I have not let myself cry. It seemed such a selfish thing because my tears would be for myself not William. But these tears are for you all. For you all as the young children that I remember holding, and playing games with—and for William who is missing."

"He will stay with us. He is in our hearts and memories. We will not allow him to be missing."

"No."

His father wiped his forearm over his face once more, then his hand gripped Henry's shoulder and he looked into Henry's eyes. "I love you, son."

"I know." Henry thought of Susan saying that and smiled. But it was true that it was in the way that Samson knew it. There had never been doubt, or need to challenge it. It was why he'd had the freedom to live carelessly. "I love you too. I have loved you even when you have stared me down for my recklessness."

His father's hand fell and he laughed. "I know. I know because I loved my father too, even when he banished me abroad."

Henry smiled, and then they embraced again. But the tone of *this* embrace was an expression of mutual feeling. Love. Loss… Care…

He let his father go. "Will you return with me?"

His father shook his head. "No. I need a little more time alone with my memories of William. I shall ride to the mausoleum. I still have things I want him to hear."

Henry's mind spun with images from the hours he'd sat beside William's body, and the feel of his brother's cold body in his arms as he'd carried him downstairs. His father had not lain William down yet; he was still holding him in his mind trying to keep William with them in a way he could not. Life had to continue, with William as a part of their memories. He'd gone, and it was kinder to the others to remember it and think mostly of them.

"Will I see you for dinner?"

"You will." His father nodded.

Henry turned away. His heart pounded and there was pressure at the back of his eyes. He ignored it, and strode on across the grass to another exit to reach the place on the far side where his horse grazed.

When he reached the horse he gripped the pommel of the saddle and the rear end of the saddle and used his muscles to raise himself up, then swung his leg across the animal's rump to take his seat.

Damn he was no longer meant to mount recklessly like that and for the first time in his life, he cared about protecting his life. He did not wish to risk death now—not now he had Susan.

He rode the horse forward for a few yards, at a walk, until he reached one of the low walls that he could see over. His father had sat on one of the ruined walls. His arm lifted and he wiped his forearm across his face.

Henry pulled the reins and spun his horse about. Then he kicked his heels and set it into a gallop.

Chapter Thirty-one

Henry walked up to his rooms, hoping Susan would be there and not in the drawing room. He was not in a mood to encounter anyone else but her. But she was not there.

He stripped off his gloves and the coat he wore for riding, but did not take off his boots, he was too eager to speak to Susan.

He jogged down the stairs, his palm running over the polished dark wooden bannister.

The door of the family drawing room was open. He could not hear Susan's voice, and yet as she was so often quiet it did not mean she was not there.

She was not, though. His gaze had scanned the room in a second. His mother sat with his sisters and Percy.

"Where have you been?" Percy asked.

"Nowhere, and everywhere. I am looking for Susan. Where is she?" The desire to see her had become desperate.

His mother looked up. "She went to the library, Henry."

He nodded. "Thank you." Then turned away without another word.

It took him a few minutes to walk to the library, and as he walked he thought about the spring, about walking to the library when he'd been tired and needed somewhere to sleep and discovered Susan leaning over her painting. That day had been the beginning of a change in the direction of his life. It had been the first time he'd really noticed Susan.

The door was shut—to protect her precious retreat and her privacy. He turned the handle, uncaring if he intruded.

She was sitting on the sofa where he'd lain in the summer, reading one of the books.

He shut the door. She'd not heard him open it. She'd not looked up. He walked across the room.

Her hand lifted and her fingers slid her spectacles up the bridge of her nose.

He smiled as he neared her, and then she looked up. His heart leapt only because he was near her, he had not even touched her.

She straightened up. "Hello. Did you speak to your father?"

Damn. The words cut through him. In the moment before she'd spoken he'd intended to kiss her, but that desire died within him. Instead he sat down beside her, on the other end of the sofa, leaning forward and resting his elbows on his knees. "Yes."

She stood up and walked across the room, he presumed to return the book she had been looking at to a shelf. "What did he say?"

"That he cannot cope with the fact he was not there to hold William when he died." Henry's voice rasped. He swallowed. But the emotion welling up would not be swallowed down.

"Did you tell him that was foolish?" She was over at the bookcase behind him. He could not see her.

"Yes." He swallowed three times. "He cried."

"Oh." From the sounds of the rustle of fabric she was coming back to him, quickly. "Did that upset you?"

"Yes." His answer was choked by the ball of emotion blocking his throat.

"Oh, Henry." Her hand fell on his head, and clasped his shoulder, and she drew his head against her stomach.

His arms lifted and clung about her waist as her hand stroked

348

over his hair. Love. This was love. The tears that he had not wept since William's death. The tears he'd longed to weep at William's bedside, the tears that had been choking him ever since he'd carried William's body down the stairs at Eton, the tears he'd swallowed back while his father had cried, escaped in rivers as he clung to Susan.

She did not say, it will become easier, or that time heals the wounds of such losses, or that he should not cry for his brother but celebrate the short life William had lived. All of those things he knew, but had not spoken to his father either, because in this moment what he needed, was what his father had needed—just to cry out his loss, anger and guilt—and have someone care.

After a while he became aware only of her slender fingers resting on his hair and of his arms wrapped about her waist holding her as Gerard had held him at William's bedside, and his breathing against the fabric of her dress next to the warmth of her body.

She still did not speak as his tears dried.

Nor did he. He just held her.

This is what love was. It would never have been like this with Alethea, thank the Lord he had discovered this affection for the right sister.

He let Susan go and looked up. "Will you sit on my lap?"

She smiled and slipped off her shoes, then slid her spectacles a little farther up the bridge of her nose as he leant back, resting one elbow on the arm of the sofa. She sat sideways, as she had done last night with her knees bent up. Her head rested against his chest. His arms surrounded her and held her in place.

"Do you remember when you were painting in here and I came in to sleep?"

"Yes I remember."

"The room seemed a dozen times more peaceful with you quietly painting near me. I think that was when I first began to know that you meant something to me. Something I had over-looked for years."

Her cheek rubbed against his black waistcoat as she snuggled in closer to him. "When I watched you, while you were sleeping. You seemed so different that day from the boy I had known—"

"And disliked." A rumble of amusement rang in his chest at the thought of her accusing words. *Reckless and self-centered.* But she had been right about him. He had behaved wrongly towards her, following Alethea's equally selfish lead, the two spoilt eldest children who thought they were owed everything as their right.

Her head lifted, her hair brushing against his neck above the collar of his shirt. "Very well, the boy I had disliked. I could see so many of your bruises, and you looked so… wounded and not arrogant at all."

"Arrogant was that a charge you threw at me too? I had forgotten if it was. But that was also true, along with reckless and self-centered. Well I am doing my best to be none of them now."

"I know."

His hand lifted and he would have stroked her hair but it was secured in a bun, instead he ran a curled finger down the bridge of her precious nose, below her spectacles. "I love you."

"I love you too, but you should sleep, Henry, I would guess you have hardly slept in nights. Take this moment of peaceful-ness. I shan't leave you. I will sit here and read and make sure no one disturbs you."

She would have risen but he held her down. "No. Stay here. If I am able to sleep it will be with you in my arms."

She sighed, yet her head rested against his chest again. "Shut your eyes."

~

350

The sound of a gong woke Susan. Dinner. Henry's hands lay on her head and her shoulder. His fingers moving, stroking in tiny circular movements.

She sat upright. "Have you slept?"

He smiled. "Yes I woke only a moment ago."

"Oh."

His arms fell away from her. She stood as the gong sounded again.

"We are not dressed for dinner."

"I think we will be forgiven. It is only our family."

Our family. Yes. She would not worry if she had been at home, and Farnborough was home now.

"Do I look dreadful? Is my hair tangled?" Her fingers lifted to press against it looking for strands that might have slipped free from the pins.

"You look beautiful, and only as though you have not dressed for dinner, and no one will care." He stood up and tugged his black waistcoat down to straighten it. He was not wearing his coat, only his waistcoat and white shirt. It made him appear so slender, enhancing the look of his figure.

"Come along and cease your fretting, I feel rested for the first time since William died and I am not going to allow you to feel ashamed for enabling it."

No one looked at either of them oddly in the dining room, it was just a family meal, and Aunt Jane—Jane—smiled at Susan regularly throughout the meal as Henry's father laughed quietly, occasionally, at things Gerard and Stephen said. It changed the tone of the conversation. Percy became more exuberant, speaking of horse races and Susan joined in because she knew about race horses as her father bred them. Then Uncle Robert even joined the conversation. Percy grasped at his responses and turned to him, asking him his view. Uncle Robert spoke more quietly, but he continued to speak.

Susan glanced at Henry and caught his gaze, he smiled.

When she looked away, she saw his mother—Jane—watching his father with a soft smile and moisture in her eyes.

Chapter Thirty-two

"Susan!"

"I am in here!" Henry's father had been working in the library and so she had brought her paints up to their sitting room to work, and was currently trying to capture the light as it fell on what was probably one of the last yellow rose buds of the season. It was already autumn.

He walked into the room from their bedchamber. He'd probably thought she had come up to rest. Samson, who had been sitting beside her, rose, tail wagging, and crossed the room to welcome Henry.

"You are painting." He stated the obvious, but he liked watching her paint as much as Samson did, and the words were spoken with that expression. "I have a letter for you, from London." He lifted it and held it out to her as he walked across the room, while she wiped off her brush then set it down and straightened up, picking up another rag to wipe her hands.

"From, Mama?"

"No. It is Alethea's writing."

Emotion spun through Susan tumbling down from her head to her toes. She had not heard from Alethea since the day Susan had married Henry. She put the rag down and held out her hand to take the envelope, then looked at the address. She had missed her sister so much. Her fingers shook making the letter tremble as she broke the seal and pulled open the envelope then withdrew the folded paper.

She had written once, on the afternoon of the day that Henry had wept for William. She had written and told Alethea how much she loved her. But she had told her how much she loved Henry too, and explained that she could no more have set Henry aside than she could Alethea. She had said that she'd tried, but she loved him too much to watch him fret in pain over her either and that she just could not have lived without him, even if it made her selfish and cruel.

Henry reached out and took the envelope from her, then set it down by her painting as she began to read.

She looked at Henry. "She is to be married. The Earl of Stourton proposed and she has accepted."

"I am glad. She will be happy too, then."

Susan looked back at the letter then read more. "She says she has forgiven us," she spoke as she read on, "and that I may happily have you with her blessing because she is far more in love with Stourton than she ever was with you."

A sound of amusement from Henry lifted Susan's gaze. "She says she is glad now that she let me have you and did not fight."

"Susan." His hand lifted and curved about her cheek. "Sweetheart do not take a single word of that to heart. I was never Alethea's to give, you do not have me because she allowed it. You have me because you are the right woman for me, and my heart knew it. In reality I have always been yours."

Tears filled Susan's eyes, blurring her vision.

Henry's fingers lifted her spectacles off the bridge of her nose, then he kissed away one of her tears, before wrapping his arms about her.

"I am sorry. I am far too emotional these days. I weep over the slightest thing."

"That emotion is good." His chin rested against her hair as she leant into his chest.

"Will we go to London for the wedding? It is to be in St George's"

"Of course. When?"

"At the end of July."

"Then you will be very plump and our secret will be out in the open."

She smiled against his chest. "It will be out in the open long before then."

"I suppose. But I have enjoyed keeping it ours. Shall we go down to the drawing room, Mama just called for tea."

"Yes."

As she turned away to tidy up her paints, his hand fell and caressed her stomach.

He touched the place where their child had begun to grow all the time even though it was scarce weeks and she did not show at all.

They walked downstairs together, with her holding Henry's arm as he held the bannister. He'd become ridiculously over protective, to a silly extent, since they had learned about the child. She was to only walk downstairs either holding his arm or the bannister, and she had been banned from riding. He'd told her very bluntly he would not allow any reckless behaviour when this was their child. Which had made her laugh at him, and she'd swallowed several hundred words of argument he'd probably previously thrown at his father.

She had not fought against his riding ban as yet, though, because her stomach felt so constantly queasy she was not in a mood to ride.

They sat and drank tea with Sarah, Christine and Henry's mother, and shared Alethea's news. His father was still busy in the library. Henry went to join him when the tea was cleared away. He'd continued to help his father with the estate manage-

355

ment, only now it was not like a child thrown into deep water, but he and his father worked together, with his father showing Henry the way of things and handing over certain responsibilities when Henry was ready to accept them.

Susan excused herself and returned to their room to rest, in the company of Samson, who now acted her shadow whenever Henry was elsewhere.

Henry woke her when it was time for dinner, and they changed together, with him lacing her corset because he feared a maid might secure it too tightly and hurt the child. She smiled at his image in the mirror as he stood behind her and lay both hands over her stomach.

He smiled at her.

She turned and clasped his hand. "Come along Monsieur Cat."

"Monsieur Cat..." He frowned at her.

"You smile at me all the time as though I am the freshest cream."

He laughed, then he answered, "But how am I to help feeling so happy when your eyes glitter with pleasure as though whenever I touch you we are about to begin a waltz."

After dinner the family, as it was, without the boys who were at school, or Percy who was at university, gathered about the pianoforte. Henry's mother played, with his father sitting beside her turning her pages, while the rest of them sang. Henry stood behind Susan as he had done upstairs before they'd come down, with his hands gently resting on her stomach.

It was still early when Christine claimed that she was tired and said she would retire, and Sarah then said she would walk upstairs with her and retire too.

"We shall go to bed also," Henry stated, letting Susan go.

"Not for a moment." His father reached out and caught a hold of Henry's sleeve to stop him. "We wish to speak with you." He looked at Sarah who was walking across the room to leave. "Will you close the door."

Henry turned to Susan, and whispered through the side of his mouth. "We are in for some sort of scold I think…"

She smiled.

Henry's father stood. "It is not a scold."

His mother stood. "It is a scold."

His father looked back at her with a humour filled smile then looked at Henry. "We believe we are expecting a grandchild and our son has been neglectful and forgotten to inform us."

"Is it true?" His mother's voice had slipped into pure excitement as she looked at Susan. "There have been all the signs, you have missed breakfast more days than not in the last three weeks, and you yawn and then retire in the afternoons, and Henry," she looked at him, "you are forever touching Susan's stomach."

When Susan looked at Henry his smile matched his father's and mother's. "It was supposed to be our secret." His expression instead said how thrilled he was to have been caught out.

"Oh, Susan! That is so wonderful!" His mother rushed about the piano and grasped Susan in a firm embrace.

"Congratulations." His father embraced Henry.

"Oh I am so happy for you both." His mother let Susan go then turned to hold Henry. "But now I shall be itching to tell all my friends, and Ellen and Edward."

Henry settled an arm about Susan's shoulders. "If anyone is to tell anyone, Mama, it will be us, and Susan's parents should know before your friends or Edward."

"But that is so cruel, my tongue will be bursting to say it."

Henry's father settled a hand about his mother's waist. "Let the boy have his moment of wonder and pride my love, do not be cruel and steal it from him, the announcement is part of the excitement and we have stolen this moment from him."

She looked at Henry, then Susan. "Were we cruel? I could not continue pretending that I had not guessed."

Susan clasped his mother's hands. "You were not cruel at all.

It is wonderful that you know, Mama. It is only that we wished to be certain—"

"But you are certain…"

"Yes, absolutely certain." Susan was held once more.

When his mother let her go, Susan added, "I will write to my mother tomorrow, and then within a week you may tell whoever you wish."

"But I shall write to Edward," Henry stated.

"And then I will not have many others to tell. Ellen and Edward are in London with the girls, Ellen will tell."

Susan looked at Henry. Then Harry would know, and all of Henry's friends. He had not seen them much in their months of mourning. They would see them when they travelled to London for Alethea's wedding, though. He'd changed so much since they'd married, or rather since William's death, she wondered if his friends would even recognise Henry as he was now.

When they retired, after they'd made love, and she lay on her back with her head resting on his arm and he lay on his side beside her, drawing idle circles on her stomach with his finger tips, she asked him, "Do you ever wish that you were not married, and that you were free to live as you used to?"

"You mean to race my carriage hell for leather to Brighton, Bath or York and topple it over on the road. No, I do not, darling. I am more than happy with our life. I need nothing to inspire me other than your company, this is a very pleasant, if perhaps a tamer source of adventure."

Epilogue

There were tears in his eyes, clouding his view. Henry wiped them away with the heel of his palm. Foolish. So foolish to weep and yet the tears would not be held back now they'd begun. Susan lifted her hand and it stroked across his hair, as his fingers stroked over the softest hair on his daughter's head. The baby was so tiny. He could not believe how tiny she was, and yet he'd seen his brothers and sisters as infants, but this was *his* daughter.

His father had told him of this emotion but Henry never could have imagined the feeling. He and Susan had created this little being. She had come from Susan's body, where she had been cradled out of sight for months, felt but not seen, and here she was. A girl. Juliette.

He leant and pressed a kiss on her soft cheek. She smelled of milk. He straightened and kissed Susan's cheek. "May I take her to show everyone?" Susan looked so tired she would probably be glad to be left alone. It had taken a day and a night of pains and labouring for Juliette to come.

"I think your Papa and mine will be very upset if you do not."

Her eyelids drooped; she was so tired. "I shall keep her with me then for a little while and let you sleep."

"Thank you."

She let him lift their daughter from her arms, and then slid down the bed to lay on the mattress. Her eyes closed immediately.

His heart brimmed so full it might burst, Henry walked quietly from the room his eyes focused on his daughter whose gaze focused on him. "Juliette." With her cradled in one arm, his other hand touched her fingers and instantly she grasped hold of his thumb.

He treasured the little embrace.

Pride. Love. Adoration… The emotions within him were ten thousand times greater than he could ever have imagined.

When he reached the stairs he let go of Juliette's hand so he could hold the bannister as he walked down. The excited chatter from the drawing room spilled out into the hall. Of course they all knew his daughter had arrived. His mother and Susan's had been with her through the labour and brought the news down to the drawing room. He'd gone up alone. But now it was for him to introduce Juliette to their families.

He walked across the hall, a smile splitting his lips as Samson came out of the drawing room, tail waving. Susan had refused to leave Samson at Farnborough to pine. "Here she is, Samson, Juliette," Samson sniffed her head. "Now you must watch over her, just as well as you do over Susan."

A smile swelled from Henry's heart as he straightened and walked on.

"Ah, here he is!" Susan's mother cried as Henry entered the room. "Look! Is she not the most beautiful baby?" She rushed across the room and stroked a finger along the side of Juliette's cheek. Juliette's gaze did not leave Henry. He offered her his forefinger and she grasped it. Then he looked up to see everyone coming to surround him; his parents and Susan's, and Alethea and Stourton, and Edward and Ellen, who'd called at a timely moment.

Juliette had arrived three weeks before she was due, and made her appearance only a week after Alethea's wedding.

360

"She is so tiny," Alethea whispered as she leant to see.

"May I hold her?" Susan's father asked.

Henry smiled at him, pride a strong sword lancing through his heart. "Here." He passed Juliette over, but she refused to let go of his finger. His thumb brushed across the tiny fingers that continued to hold his. He lifted them to his mouth and kissed the back of them before peeling them free, feeling the cut of emotion through his chest and the tears in his eyes.

His father's hand settled on his shoulder. Henry turned and embraced him for a moment. Now he understood so much more of the things his father said and felt.

He let his father go, but his father's arm remained about his shoulders as they turned to watch Susan's father and the women cooing over Juliette.

When the first flourish of fuss had passed and a fresh pot of tea had been ordered for Henry's benefit, Henry's father said, "I think it must be my turn." He walked across the room to Susan's mother who was the current keeper of Juliette. "May I?" He held out his hands.

Henry watched him, a little in awe as his father bent and lifted Juliette from Susan's mother's arms.

His father had, only to Henry, admitted that he'd been a little peeved that Susan and Henry had not stayed at his London home, but as it had been Susan's sister who was married it had been right that they stayed with her parents, so that Susan could be with Alethea and help her prepare. But perhaps it had been too many trips to the haberdashery and the dressmakers that had brought Juliette into the world early.

His father encouraged Juliette to hold his finger then walked with her to look out of the window into the street. He was whispering to her. Telling her something that looked of great importance.

Henry stood up and walked over to join them, Samson accompanying him. "What are you telling her, Papa?"

His father looked at him and smiled. "I am telling her about her father and her family."

"What about us."

"My father would have loved to have known you, and he would have loved to have known your daughter. Your grandparents would have been very proud of you."

"Proud…" Henry smiled.

"Yes, and if William is watching us too he would be happy for us. You once said he would have disliked it if I did not continue to give my all to Gerard and Stephen, the same applied to you, and now to your daughter. My first grandchild."

Henry wished to hold his father, as he saw moisture in his eyes, but Juliette was in his arms. They both looked at her, as she looked up at Henry's father. Henry wondered what Stephen and Gerard would make of a niece…

Susan had not woken when he retired immediately after dinner. She lay asleep in the bed as Juliette lay asleep in her cot. He undressed quietly and slipped in between the sheets next to Susan. The world became peace as he lay close to her. The sense of home wrapped about him with Susan's warmth beside him and the smell of her in the air he breathed.

Home was no longer a place he travelled to, or returned to. Home travelled with him. Susan was his home, and now Juliette…

His heart swelled and ached with a sweet sensation as he wrapped his arm about Susan and drew her against his chest.

She whispered, "I love you," her breath stirring the hairs on his chest. Then drifted back into sleep.

He kissed the top of her head. "I love you."

Author Note

This story is a little different from the others in the Marlow Intrigue's series, in that it wasn't inspired by a real life historical story. But having written Henry's father's story in *The Passionate Love of a Rake*, when the series moved on to the characters' descendants, I wanted to give Robert's son a story too. Then of course there were the Forths who paid such an influential part in *The Illicit Love of a Courtesan*. So Robert's and Jane's son and the Forth's daughter were brought together and the idea of the story unfolded. Of course as always the settings are inspired by the real places I visit and you can see all the pictures on my Pinterest and Facebook pages. The other real life inspiration that did influence the characters, if not the story, was that I was reading Jane Austen's letters at the time and her letters to her sister very much influenced Susan's scenes with Alethea. It is quite funny reading Jane Austen's letter's, especially when she writes her early letters to Cassandra about gossip and teasing and flirting with gentleman, and dancing happily or trying to avoid it with unpleasant partners. She writes some very cutting descriptions of some men while describing other's as Beauties, yes, with a capital B. It was amusing too to read her mentioning a gentleman's 'fine eyes.'